MW00831704

THE WEIGHT OF SALT

SANDRA MONTANINO

EDWARDS PUBLISHING

The Weight of Salt

Sandra Montanino

THE WEIGHT OF SALT VOLUME ONE
A GRIPPING STORY OF LOVE AND COURAGE
Published by: Edwards Publishing Provo, UT

Cover design by:
Bryan Heim Photography and Design - Bryan Heim
Interior print design and layout by:
Erika Kuta Marler
ISBN: 978-1-7345090-0-7 (ebook)
ISBN: 978-1-7345090-1-4 (paperback)
ISBN: 978-1-7345090-2-1 (hardback)
Subjects:
FICTION / Romance. | FICTION / Historical. | FICTION / Coming of Age.
Author Sandra Montanino

-Sandra Montanino
AuthorSandraM@gmail.com

IN SUPPORT OF THE AUTHOR

In support of the author of The Weight of Salt, it would be greatly appreciated if you took a moment to leave your honest review.

-Sandra Montanino
AuthorSandraM@gmail.com

Dedication

It's with a warm heart, I dedicate this book to all my family—those that are here, and those in the hereafter—especially my grandmother, Angelina who left us with a rich treasure chest of Sicilian stories. These tales, both real and imagined, captivated and inspired me to write this book and those that follow. I hope you will enjoy them as much as I have.

CHAPTER 1

YBOR CITY, FLORIDA, 1906

The pendulum clock on the bureau bartered its minutes for hours. Still, the baby had not come. Fifteen-year-old Angelina Pirrello clutched her rosary and recited an impassioned Hail Mary as her mother's cries in labor pierced the air and robbed their home of its bloom.

Carolina appeared fragile and angelic amid a cloud of white sheets. She lay saturated in perspiration on the same iron bed where she'd given birth six times before. Her breathing grew more ragged as Angelina kept an anxious watch on her.

Domenico glanced at the clock and then at his wife. He feverishly passed his hand through his hair. "Angelina, when you left a message for the doctor, did you say to come quickly?"

"Yes, Papa, I said to hurry."

Her father persisted in asking the same question again and again.

Moans swelled into screams, and in Carolina's pale-green eyes, Angelina saw the depths of her mother's pain. She sensed it all around her—in the air and on the floor beneath her feet.

Sicilian women believed in the compassion of the Virgin Mary, who'd experienced the agony of childbirth. Angelina didn't question the belief as she summoned the Virgin for help with fierce prayer, a slight tremor tainting her voice.

The tranquility was fleeting as it stretched across the room, and Carolina's pain momentarily subsided.

Domenico sat on the edge of the bed, raised his wife's fingers to his lips, and then closed his hand around hers.

"*Ti amo*," he said.

The tender moment did not dispel Angelina's uneasiness. Her mother's long brown hair lay outstretched and tangled beneath her head while the agony of labor blemished her face. Angelina had no memory of her mother suffering so intensely during the births of her younger siblings.

The lines penetrating Domenico's forehead vanished when a rapid knocking shook the front door. He hurried toward the sound and, with long strides, passed through the parlor and pulled open the door. "Dottor Martino!"

The doctor wasn't there.

"All this screaming every time I pass your house. Did you suppose I was deaf?" said their neighbor Signora Bertelli. She held a flower-filled vase, a cloth bag, and an oblong object wrapped in a dishtowel. "You insult me by not calling for my help. Only the saints can forgive such a sin."

"I sent for the doctor long ago." Domenico's tone offered no apology.

Angelina understood her father's reluctance to call a midwife. The world had left the past behind and arrived at the dawn of the twentieth century. Domenico wanted his wife to have the best of modern care.

Though middle-aged and with graying hair, Signora Bertelli had something ageless about her—not in appearance but in her enthusiasm for life. With a look of scorn, she waved her finger at Domenico. "Who do you think is more useful, a midwife standing right in front of you or a doctor who's nowhere to be found?" She narrowed her eyes. "This is the reason why God, with His divine wisdom, never trusted a man to have a child."

Signora Bertelli raised her chin, brushed past Domenico, and went straight to the bedroom.

Certain her father would counter the remark, Angelina watched, but he remained silent as her mother pulled herself up in bed and managed a thread of a smile. "Thank you for coming, my friend." Carolina's voice held the hoarse residue of her screams, yet a light glistened in her eyes. "You understand, signora. Like me, you believed in our Sicilian ways—the ways of our mothers and grandmothers before us."

Angelina glanced at her father. Between his skepticism of all things superstitious and her mother's belief in them, Angelina grew uncertain about what she should believe. In previous births, her father had remained outside the bedroom until after a child was born. This time, he stayed by her mother's side through this longest of labors, the absence of the doctor, and a midwife's presence. It all added to the strange imbalance of the day.

Signora Bertelli, not the kind of person willing to suppress her opinion, shook her head in apparent disgust. "I want you to know that I delivered many babies back in Santo Stefano Quisquina."

When did she last use her skills? The thought lingered in Angelina's mind as she approached their neighbor. "What can I do to help you, signora?"

"Right now, we have to wait for nature. With my help, the seventh baby will arrive before your doctor." Their neighbor set her vase and its floral offering on the night table before retrieving scissors and a string from her apron pocket.

Domenico wrung his hands. "She has suffered enough." The remark, directed at no one in particular, could only be a desperate petition for God's ears. He shook his head and rushed from the room.

Compelled by his look of distress, Angelina followed.

Her father dashed across the parlor, then burst through the adjoining door connecting their home to their small grocery store. He passed the deli counter displaying cheeses, meats, and shelves stacked with cans, bottles, boxes, and bins—reminders of their old country across the sea.

Domenico gathered his five remaining children around him. He frowned, and his jaw tightened. "Salvatore," Domenico addressed the eldest of his sons. "Take your brothers and your little sister over to the Ferlita's house and stay with them until I send for you."

Vincenzo, next in line among the siblings, spoke up. "We want to be here when the baby comes." His puzzled look did nothing to change his father's mind.

"I'll call for you when it's time." Domenico turned to Angelina. "I may need you to help your mother, but see if the doctor's coming."

Angelina rushed to the window. Her eyes darted from the carriages to the wagons to the individuals moving about along the walkways. "I don't see him."

Domenico shook his head. "Can he have that many patients to detain him?"

A wooden crucifix—long ago sanctified by a priest—hung over the doorway, spilling blessings on those who passed beneath it. Her father reached up, touched the feet of Christ, and lingered as he made the sign of the cross. The gesture surprised Angelina. She'd come to believe her father only associated with God to please her mother. He'd never been religious.

Domenico hurried back to the bedroom, Angelina trailing behind.

"The baby is not down far enough, but babies come in their own time," said Signora Bertelli.

Carolina's eyes moistened. "It's too much. I can't take it. I'm so tired."

Angelina's heart lurched. "How can I help you, Mama? Please tell me what to do."

Carolina reached for her daughter's hand. "Bring me a little water, *bella mia.* My mouth is so dry."

Angelina hurried from the room and quickly reappeared with a glass filled to the brim. She held it to her mother's lips, but in her eagerness, tipped the glass too far and spilled water on her mother's nightdress. "Oh, Mama. I'm so sorry."

"Look at what a fine daughter you have, Carolina, always trying to help. May my tongue fall out of my head if what I'm saying is a lie," Signora Bertelli declared in her unique way of emphasizing a point.

"Angelina is a blessing." Her mother attempted a smile, but her voice faltered, and her breathing grew cumbersome once again.

The middle-aged woman pushed back a lock of Carolina's hair and felt her patient's forehead. "Poor thing, you're so warm—but in so much humidity, who can tell if it's the heat or a fever?"

The sun passed behind the clouds and darkened the room. Signora Bertelli looked up and narrowed her eyes. For a woman who believed in spirits, this might be considered an ominous warning, but the midwife said nothing. Instead, she reached into her cloth bag, faded from years of service, and pulled out a handful of granules. "It's salt," explained Signora Bertelli as she poured some at each corner of the iron bed.

She then rocked forward and backward and chanted in an ancient Sicilian dialect to lure a new life into the world. From her folded dishtowel, she produced a large knife.

Angelina gasped and quickly drew closer to her mother. She'd never been inside the bedroom this close to the baby's birth, and the sudden appearance of the knife frightened her.

Signora Bertelli slid the blade underneath the bed and uttered a string of words from centuries past. "The knife cuts the pain, and the salt clears away evil spirits. The window is already open for their departure." She spoke as though this should be common knowledge.

Carolina nodded. She'd taught her children to believe in the Holy Catholic Church, the angels and saints, the resurrection of the dead, and forgiveness of sins, but with Italians, there was more. Every child came into the world wrapped in ancient beliefs passed down to them like the color of their eyes and hair.

Her mother released a sudden tormented scream, and a stream of blood tinted the white

bedsheets beneath her. Angelina gasped, and her eyes widened. Something was wrong—she saw it in their faces.

"I think it's better if you step outside, Angelina," Signora Bertelli said.

"No, please, I want to help." Surely her mother needed her more than ever.

"Sometimes to do nothing is to do something." Signora Bertelli's voice sounded mechanical, unconvincing.

Angelina rubbed her hands together to rid herself of this useless sensation. To do nothing was just that. How could it be anything else? Her father had said he needed her. She glanced in his direction, but he remained stoic as Signora Bertelli shooed her out and closed the door behind her.

Why couldn't they let her help? Discouraged, Angelina stepped into the parlor. She slumped into her mother's rocking chair and blinked away the tears that threatened. She slid her hands along the worn armrests and gave a push, remembering bits and pieces of her own childhood as if they were layers of varnish clinging to the rocker. Like a splash of frigid water, a sudden shrill cry came from her mother's room. Angelina glanced toward the door, but it remained closed, and no one called her name.

Frustrated, she went to the front door and stepped out, looking in both directions for the absent doctor. Unsure what else to do, she sat on the steps, wrapped her arms around her folded legs, and lowered her head to her knees in defeat. The only sound was the bark from DiLeto's dog across the street.

When she looked up again, she caught a glimpse of a discarded apple crate on the porch. She rushed to grab it and hurried to the back of the house beneath her mother's window, where she set down the wooden box and climbed on top. Respectful of Signora Bertelli and her beliefs, Angelina allowed room for the evil spirits to depart through the open window.

Her mother's moans twisted, swelled, and spilled from the room, but Angelina remained intent on comforting her. She placed her head against the frame and softly sang the Sicilian lullaby her mother always sang.

"Sing, *bella mia,* sing." The agony in her mother's voice seeped through the opening. Angelina's eyes watered at the somber sound, and she swallowed to loosen the tender lyrics trapped in her tightening throat. Before the song ended, her father's voice ripped through the melody.

"Angelina. Come to the porch."

She moved too quickly, toppling off the crate. By the time she had regained her footing and brushed the dirt off, her father came rushing toward her with a pained expression and grabbed her by both arms.

"Listen to me. Run as fast as you can to get Dottore Martino. I can't leave your mother."

"Everything will be fine, won't it, Papa?"

"Do what you're told, Angelina. Don't come home without him."

Angelina searched her father's eyes and saw something she'd never seen before—he was afraid. A rush of panic ran through her. She turned away and dashed up Nineteenth Street, the unfamiliar strain in her father's voice trailing behind her.

"Hurry, Angelina! Hurry!"

She passed rows of street vendors, the bakery, the tailor shop. Everything blended together, indistinguishable—Angelina tightened her hold on her rosary and ran even faster. She arrived at the two-story building out of breath, climbed the wrought-iron stairs, pushed open the door, and stepped inside. The doctor's wife sat at the desk, but Angelina's orders were to get the doctor, not his wife. Still shaken from the alarm in her father's voice, she shouted, "Dottor, Dottor! My mother needs help right away."

Medicines and antiseptics tainted the air, and the smell of pain filled Angelina's nostrils.

"No one comes in here yelling, not even the injured." Maria Martino stood before her desk and smoothed out the wrinkles in her stylish dress.

Her overbearing disposition smothered the room, along with her look of disinterest in Angelina's cry for help.

"We sent for Dottore Martino long ago, and he never came. We're desperate." Domenico's anxious order still echoed in his daughter's ears.

Something brushed past Angelina's leg.

Maria reached down, picked up a cat who had wandered in through the open door, and gently stroked its head.

"My mother has been waiting hours for help," Angelina pleaded.

"My husband's the only Italian doctor in Ybor City. He can't be everywhere."

"It's urgent. Dottore Martino has to come to my house—right away."

"Well," Maria sighed, seemingly more interested in the feline in her arms, "I'll tell him." She stroked the cat. "Did you know that once, my brother, Claudio, wanted to marry your mother? Now she's having one child after another, and my wonderful brother is still alone." The cat purred, and Maria scratched its neck affectionately. "Life plays tricks."

Angelina ignored this ill-timed attempt at conversation. "Signora, my father is frantic for the doctor to come. He sent me here because my mother's having her baby. She's in terrible pain. I'm afraid something is wrong."

"And who can have a baby without pain? Have a seat and wait." The woman expelled another deep sigh. "Like my brother waited for your mother." Her voice took on a harsher tone. Maria gestured toward a row of wooden chairs where an old man sat with his chin against his chest—asleep.

Was this woman now seeking revenge? Angelina squeezed her hands into fists. "Please, signora. You don't understand. It's been hours. My mother is growing weaker. Even my father is afraid. He said not to leave here without the doctor."

"As you can see, he's attending to someone else. Either wait or leave."

A dismal thought filtered through Angelina's mind. Had this woman not delivered their earlier message to the doctor because Angelina's poor mother had rejected Maria's brother? "You could step inside the room and tell him my mother needs him. *Ho bisogno del dottore.*" Angelina repeated this in both English and Italian. Now the woman couldn't claim she didn't understand.

"In a doctor's office, everyone thinks they're the only emergency. I've had two fine sons myself. They are such a blessing." Maria picked up a small picture frame of two small boys and beamed. "They're the light of my life." She glanced back at Angelina. "Your mother had so many more. She'll do fine," she said, clearly disinterested.

"Signora, I have always been respectful to adults, but I can still see the pain on my mother's face and the fear in my father's. If you won't tell your husband of our desperate need for him, I will." Angelina turned away from the woman and rushed toward the doctor's examining room.

Maria Martino dropped the cat and her smile. After only a few steps, Angelina shrieked as her head was jerked backward and a fierce pain shot down her neck. The woman had grabbed her long hair in a tight grip, twisted it, and dragged Angelina toward the front door.

"You Sicilians act like animals, so we treat you like animals."

"Let go of me!" Angelina fiercely swung her arms to fight the woman and stop the pounding in her head but lost her balance, which only gave Maria a stronger hold. She put her arm around Angelina's waist and tried to yank her off her feet.

Amidst the commotion, the doctor suddenly opened his door. Maria let go of Angelina so abruptly she almost fell to the ground. With her head reeling, she dismissed all thoughts of the doctor's wife. All that mattered was her mother's need for help.

"Please, Dottor Martino, come to my house."

"Yes, right away. I must grab my bag."

Angelina noticed the quick glance the doctor gave his

wife and was certain Maria had never delivered the original message.

As the doctor vanished into his office, Angelina spun around to face her assailant, shielding her long locks from the woman's reach. At that moment, all her mother's warnings about the forces of evil crystallized. Perspiration glistened on Maria's forehead. Her eyes grew more intense as she focused on Angelina, who took several steps back until she hit the wall. *Malocchio.* Maria silently mouthed the Italian word for the curse of the evil eye, with its power to bring misfortune and even physical pain.

Carolina had accepted this deeply rooted belief dating back to the first century BC. She wore a protective amulet to ward it off, hung horns above the front doorway to shield her family, and instructed Angelina on how to defend herself against its force.

Angelina had never encountered malocchio. Though frightened, she responded quickly by pointing her index and small finger toward the doctor's wife. This primal hand signal for horns known as *mano di cornuto* would pierce the evil eye.

Only the appearance of Dottore Martino broke the intense exchange. Yet he failed to notice anything in his rush. "I'm on my way, Angelina." He dashed out the door, down the stairs, and leaped into his carriage.

Angelina hurried outside to the railing and called down to him. "Thank you, Dottor. *Grazie.*" He didn't offer her a ride. Still, a sense of relief overtook her as she watched his carriage disappear toward her house.

Maria Martino slammed the door behind her, but the doctor's wife didn't matter. Angelina had done everything her father asked.

She started for home, looked up at the brilliant blue sky, and pulled out her rosary. She thanked the Lord for the doctor in Italian and English, convinced that each language held its own favor with God. The closing bells of the cigar factories tolled, interrupting her prayer. Hefty doors swung open, spewing the cigar makers onto the streets. Angelina hurried to keep ahead of the crowd.

Shopkeepers' doors remained open to serve the workers, and whether real or imagined, the scent of tobacco drifted about like a mist. Angelina's heels clipped against the walkway as she strove to reach her house.

When she turned the corner onto Nineteenth Street, the sight of the doctor's carriage in front of her home brought a sigh of relief. She took the porch steps two at a time, dashing inside in anticipation of a newborn's cry. Instead, something unfamiliar and frightening eclipsed the house. A loud crash ripped through the air, glass shattered, and her father screamed curses in an almost unrecognizable voice.

"Oh, Angelina," Signora Bertelli said as she wiped her tears.

Frantic now, Angelina rushed past her and burst into her parents' bedroom. The midwife's flower vase lay smashed on the floor, and a chair lay on its side next to the bed. Domenico's face flushed red with rage. He raised his arm, holding the crucifix her mother kept by the bed. Dottore Martino grabbed his hand and struggled to stop him from throwing it across the room.

"We mustn't question the will of God. He understands what we cannot. Carolina was too weak, and the baby was breech, with the cord wrapped tightly around his neck."

"No, Mama, no. Wake up, wake up!" Horrified, Angelina wanted to believe she'd entered the wrong house. She rushed to her mother's side and tried shaking her. The abundance of bloodstained sheets startled her. From a place of intense pain, a place she never knew existed, Angelina cried out in a shrill voice, "Mama! It can't be!" The jolt gave her physical pain. She urgently needed her mother's arms around her, the feel of her touch, the sound of her voice—not this crushing yearning.

Domenico pulled his wife into his arms. Angelina had never heard her father cry. In his grief, he became a stranger. He pressed his cheek against Carolina's, professing his love in a desperate plea to lure her back.

Angelina's body shook uncontrollably.

The day's heat and humidity ripened, spoiled, and then turned cold. Angelina shivered. Her grief overcame her. Something vital had locked inside her, and in this corner of her heart, she'd remain fifteen-years-old forever. "Oh, Mama, please, please don't leave us!" she shouted.

"There was nothing I could do, Domenico." Dottore Martino's voice held the practiced compassion of a man familiar with death. He cleared his throat, then packed his instruments. "If only I could have at least saved Carolina. She tried so hard, but her body couldn't take the added strain of a seventh child. I'm so sorry. This terrible heartache that comes to all of us brings suffering beyond words. May God comfort you."

Her father looked distant, lost, without dimension. The doctor continued his eulogy of Carolina's bravery, accompanied by sporadic apologies and condolences, but Domenico was silent. With nothing more he could do, Dottore Martino lowered his head, gripped his black bag, and slipped away.

Anxious for something of her mother's to hold, Angelina reached down for a flower from the shattered vase, but her hand trembled, and she lost her hold, the delicate bloom falling to the floor.

"Carolina, Carolina, *amore mio*. I've loved no one but you." Her father caressed the face of the woman he cherished. He ran his hand across her forehead, down the bridge of her nose, and past her cheeks to her lips. He'd often said, "We carry the image of those we love inside, where no thief can rob us."

The glass of water Angelina had brought her mother remained on the nightstand. She reached for it and pressed her lips against it. God had made a dreadful mistake. Her mother had taught her God was good, but nothing good was happening. Why hadn't He saved her? Where was the goodness? *Never question God,* her mother had said. God was greater than death and greater than malocchio. He had such power. Angelina felt angry because God had let her mother die. The lace curtains fluttered in the breeze of the open window where the evil spirits had departed. The iron bed where all the children had been born still dominated the room. On the wall, two palm fronds, a remembrance of Palm Sunday, twisted around the large crucifix. Everything appeared unaffected—yet nothing remained the same.

Angelina backed up, her foot brushing against her mother's laundry basket. It hadn't been there earlier, and as she touched it, the small blanket that lay over the wicker edge fell off. Angelina remained powerless to move as she looked inside the basket at the lifeless infant brother she'd never know. Blood tinged his hair. It sullied the blanket covering him, and on his beautiful face, his eyes had closed without ever seeing the world.

Angelina could hear the phantom memory of her mother's voice beckoning her. *Come quick, Angelina, and feel the baby*. Carolina had placed Angelina's hand on her enlarged belly. Together they'd stood frozen in anticipation, waiting for the signs of life. Her mother had loved the little one even then. The child had listened to the sound of his mother's voice and every pulse and rhythm of her heart until the final beat.

Angelina's tears streamed down her face. She wanted her mother back. A tremor of anger ignited within her. She turned away from her father, grabbed the basket holding the baby, then dashed out the bedroom door and through the house, ignoring Signora Bertelli's pleas.

The DiLeto's dog raced after her, barking and jumping about, but Angelina tightened her grip on the basket and kept running, even after the animal abandoned his chase. She moved mindlessly past factories, stores, and vendors until the streets fell away. The earth was flat and formless. All that remained were the fields of saw palmetto. Out of breath and amid the tangle of shrubs, she crumpled to the ground, believing her chest would collapse from the weight of her heartbreak.

Angelina had sung her mother's lullaby to her below the window. Her mother had sung it to all her children. Now Angelina gazed once again at the tiny face of her brother. Even in her profound sorrow, and even as her voice faltered, she sang to the infant so he would know he was loved.

"Ninna Nanna, figghiu miu, tu si duci, tu si miu."

Somewhere in the midst of such a tragedy, the melody lost its innocence and became a requiem for the dead.

CHAPTER 2

For the two days following Carolina's death and losing the baby, the home was draped in almost unbearable grief, the mournful sound of weeping echoing throughout the day and late into the night.

"Our memories of your mother are treasures. They belong to us, and no one can take them away," Domenico lamented after gathering his children. However, the depths of his sorrow tore at the edge of his voice and left him unable to say much else.

Angelina picked up her schoolbook and tried to read, but then set it down. Her grief proved too much, too all-consuming, too painful. She grabbed her veil, hurried to the church, and entered the confessional's darkness to unburden her broken heart and soul. Father Cavalli sat waiting. She knelt, and the priest pulled back the curtain of the small screened window dividing them.

"Forgive me, Father, for I have sinned. It's been a month since my last confession," Angelina said in a tone respectful of the church.

"And what is your sin, my child?"

"A woman cursed me with malocchio. How can I ever forgive her?"

Father Cavalli grumbled. "We teach every parishioner from childhood, even before they receive their First Communion, that the only thing to fear is God—not man or malocchio. Still, every week, someone confesses the curse of the evil eye. There's no such thing. For your penance, say—"

"There's something else."

The priest's scolding quickly dissolved. "Yes, my child?"

Angelina didn't care if what she said next exposed her identity to the priest. Her baby brother needed someone to speak up for him. "My mother and infant brother have died. I pray for my mother's glory in heaven, but when I ask my father for my brother's name, he won't answer. I need his name to pray and light a candle for his soul."

"It's unnecessary. The baby died during birth with original sin. He'll go to limbo."

"But he never sinned."

"Everyone is born with the original sin of Adam and Eve, washed away only by baptism. When an infant comes into the world without a sound, dead and with the cord around his neck as Dottore Martino said, the sin remains."

Angelina leaned closer to the screen separating them. "Maybe the baby couldn't make a sound because the cord was wrapped around his neck, and maybe he didn't move because he was unconscious and about to die—but not dead. He could have lived long enough to remove original sin. Why not baptize him now—as a precaution? What would it hurt?"

"The position of the church is clear." The priest's voice grew a little louder and less pliable. "No one goes to heaven with original sin. You learned this in Catechism, Angelina. For your penance, say ten Our Fathers and ten Hail Marys. Now, let me hear you recite a heartfelt Act of Contrition."

It didn't matter if the priest knew her. Nothing had been

resolved. Her unnamed brother remained in limbo—at the hem of heaven—a son without his mother and a mother without her son.

~

THE EVENING OFFERED ONLY the slightest breeze as the constellations illuminated the sky. Friends and family came to the church to pray the five sections of the rosary for Carolina's soul. The open casket sat at the altar, and the priest led the recitation. It was still impossible for Angelina to accept that her mother had died. Why did someone so needed and loved have to slip away? And why, after countless centuries of living and dying, struggle and despair, had no one discovered the remedy for a broken heart?

When the rosary ended, the mourners offered their compassion, condolences, and tearful farewells. Angelina remained beside the coffin. She gazed upon her mother's face and then at the infant son in her embrace. The priest would soon close the casket for the final time, and it would remain closed at the funeral Mass. Angelina bent over and kissed her mother and infant brother. She slipped the rosary she'd layered with so many prayers under the silk pillow. Her mother would have it throughout eternity to remind her that her daughter Angelina truly loved her.

On the morning of the funeral, rays of sunlight beamed through the enormous Rosetta window of Sacred Heart Church. The family solemnly genuflected before the altar, then took their seats in the front pew according to age. Angelina took her mother's former seat between the youngest, two-year-old Giuseppe and five-year-old Lily. Next to them sat her brothers—nine-year-old Filippo, thirteen-year-old Vincenzo, and fourteen-year-old Salvatore. Domenico sat next to the center aisle, closest to the casket.

Candlelight illuminated the altar, the perimeter of the church walls, and the feet of the saints. The enormity of the high ceilings stirred Angelina's belief that angels, with their broad expanse of wings, had come to carry her mother and brother through heaven's gate.

"Mia figlia." The cry tore through the chapel. "My daughter, la mia bambina."

Angelina turned to see her white-haired nonna Cacciatore hurrying up the aisle with the uneven gait of so many of the elderly. At the front of the altar, before the immense crucifix, Angelina's grandmother tightened her hand and hit her chest three times while reciting, "Mea culpa, mea culpa," as if the tragedy had been a penalty for her 'most grievous fault.' Then, in an unexpected move, she dashed toward the coffin and threw the lid open. From every corner of the church, gasps echoed from those reverently awaiting the funeral Mass. They watched as Nonna attempted to lift her daughter from the casket.

"Carolina, it's Mama, Carolina. Mama." Angelina's grandmother raised a hand heavenward, begging God to return her daughter and take her instead. Nonna's youngest daughter Gina rushed to her side, pulled her back, and lowered the coffin lid.

Angelina kept a wary eye on her mother's eldest sister, Violetta, who got to her feet, crossed the aisle, and came to stand before her brother-in-law. Angelina's mother had often said her sister never cared what others thought. Angelina feared the worst, so she stood and spoke up. "Zia, please don't."

Violetta ignored her niece and raised an accusing finger at Domenico. "Two years ago, the doctor warned you my sister was weak and should not have another child, but you didn't listen." She made a sweeping motion and pointed to the casket. "This is your work. My sister is dead. You even killed your son." Violetta stepped closer, making no attempt to lower her voice. "May you burn in hell."

A tremor of shock swept through the church. All eyes were fixed on Domenico and Violetta.

"Stop." Angelina attempted to silence another cruel remark. Only her Aunt Violetta would think to curse a grieving man in the house of the Lord and in front of all in attendance.

Domenico shot to his feet and faced his sister-in-law. "Don't come near me, Violetta." He pursed his lips as if trying to control his anger, but Violetta didn't look as willing to hold back.

Angelina raised her voice. "Please stop. You're hurting all of us." Her mother would never have tolerated the accusation Violetta had leveled at Domenico, and he'd never forgive or forget it.

Violetta caught her niece's pained expression, paused, then walked coolly back to her seat. With no way to reverse the fury that had been unleashedå, Angelina rubbed the chill from her arms, hoping her mother hadn't viewed the scene from heaven.

THE CACCIATORES SAT on one side of the church and the Pirrellos on the other, separated by an invisible yet insurmountable wall down the center aisle. Both sides of the family cried, both wiped at their tears, but neither comforted the other.

The organ music began to play. Its inspirational, spiritual hymns resounded throughout the church. Everyone stood and looked back at the entrance, where an altar boy led the procession with a large crucifix balanced in his hands. Two more carried brass candlesticks. Father Cavalli followed, swaying the traditional brass censer. The incense perfumed the air and, like a prayer, its smoke rose heavenward.

The priest approached the casket, sprinkled it with holy water, and the service began. The Mass went on with quiet sobbing, except for one man's tormented moaning from the back of the church. Angelina turned to see who grieved so hard for her mother, but she'd have to stand to see past those in attendance and draw even further attention to the already excessive drama.

Angelina fidgeted in the wooden pew as she listened to every phrase with no mention of her baby brother in glory. Offended, she refused to look at the priest again. She did not believe a word he had told her in the confessional. He had no right to slam the door of heaven in her brother's face.

Father Cavalli prayed for God's companionship. "Dominus vobiscum."

Throughout the service, responses came from the parishioners and server.

"Deo gratias." The priest's final words of thanks ended the Mass.

Mourners rushed up, offered Domenico their condolences, and hugged the children, but Angelina's mind drifted to her infant brother. She knew her mother wanted him with her throughout eternity. What if heaven had a celestial clock that allowed only so much time to rectify earthly mistakes before they became irreversible?

"We will make our way to the grave," Father Cavalli announced, then signaled the family and parishioners to follow him. Angelina walked alone among the mourners, her thoughts returning to her mother.

"Mama, what will you name the baby?"

"The baby will be born around San Giovanni's name day. Giovanni and Giovanna are good, strong names. Don't you think, Angelina? In Sicily, on the eve of San Giovanni, we'd collect dew off the grass and flowers and rub it on ourselves for good luck."

Angelina could still hear her mother's voice and hoped it would remain forever in her memory.

She stared at the glass-sided carriage holding her mother's casket. Each spoke on its wheels displayed a single vivid color. As the wheels spun, the colors merged, like the spectrum of a rainbow. Or perhaps it was a trick of her tears. Domenico had ordered eight horses to pull the wagon instead of the usual two. The procession appeared regal. Even the weather-beaten coachman who sat round-shouldered and slumped in his seat wore a top hat and a fine suit as he guided the horses to their usual destination.

Deep sobs racked Angelina's body. Signora Bertelli came from behind and put an arm around her. "Your mother's a saint in the heavens, Angelina. I brought you this small vase of fresh flowers to put at your mother's grave, and I promise I will not abandon you."

Angelina took the offering and inhaled the fragrance. "Thank you, signora. The flowers are beautiful. I wish I could have been with her at the end."

The middle-aged woman patted Angelina's arm. "Do you remember the last thing your mother said to me when you brought her the glass of water? She said, 'Angelina is a blessing.' Never forget these words. Save them in your heart and know that the angels took your mother away in a chariot of glory. I felt it in my bones and sensed it in my soul, and I'm never wrong about such things."

Angelina attempted a weak smile as she envisioned what Signora Bertelli described. The scene offered a measure of comfort, and so she took her neighbor's hand.

"Most of us have mothers in the beginning, Angelina. Few of us have mothers in the end. We must appreciate whatever time we have in the middle."

As the procession ambled unhurriedly along, Angelina was again overwhelmed with sadness.

"I miss her so much I think I'll die from it."

Signora Bertelli stopped short. "Absolutely not. Your mother won't hear of it. We'll scrub the sadness from our hearts and polish our wonderful memories of her."

When they reached the grave, Angelina believed she could sense the earth beneath her feet as though it were alive. It would soon cradle her mother and brother.

Father Cavalli blessed the site. "In nomine Patris, et Filii, et Spiritus Sancti. May eternal rest be granted unto you, and may perpetual light shine upon you." After these blessings, the priest nodded at those in attendance. "This concludes our service. Go in peace to love and serve the Lord."

Domenico stepped forward to address the crowd. "Please, do us the honor of coming to our home to enjoy the food we've prepared."

As saddened mourners once again offered their condolences, Aunt Violetta led her mother's family away from those accompanying her father.

Domenico's jaw tightened as he walked home surrounded by friends and neighbors. Angelina trailed behind until the distance between her and those in attendance had grown long. With a quick glance around, she turned and hurried back to the same spot where Father Cavalli had presided. At the open grave, she made the sign of the cross and bowed her head. She did not see how a loving God could permit a newborn to languish in limbo, and she thought that perhaps one day the church would reconsider the idea and eliminate it altogether. Until then, Angelina would do what she felt necessary.

Alone now, she took the flowers from the vase Signora Bertelli had given her and sprinkled the water over the grave to bless her infant brother.

"In nomine Patris, et Filii, et Spiritu Sancti, I baptize you, Pirrello. May God bless you and keep you. May eternal rest be granted unto you, and may perpetual light shine upon you." As Angelina spoke, she visualized angels in a chariot of glory arriving to take the child to his mother in heaven. Like Signora Bertelli, she felt it in her bones and sensed it in her heart. As she glanced across the cemetery, she saw the priest. He hadn't left with the others and must have realized what she'd done. However, with the baptism over, the blessing would remain. This would be her last gift to her mother. Once again, Angelina inhaled the fragrance of her handful of flowers, pressed them to her lips, and tossed her offering into the grave.

Against a cobalt sky, Angelina raised her face heavenward and whispered her farewell. "I love you, Mama, and I will love you forever."

CHAPTER 3

It had been three weeks since the funeral, and since time had a way of eroding memories, Angelina wrote her remembrances on the blank pages of her school notebook each day, unwilling to take a chance on forgetting. It would be like losing her mother all over again.

Domenico kept to his thoughts and brooded about the house. Now, he stood at the window and stared out at the train station across the street. Angelina followed his gaze but saw nothing of interest. She sank into a chair by the lunch counter and resumed committing memories to paper, knowing it would please her mother. Still, her father didn't leave the window.

"Angelina, when did you return the neighbor's plates?"

She stiffened. "I forgot. I'll return them tomorrow."

"Forgot? There's no excuse for that." Domenico gave her a stern glare. He did not tolerate disrespect. "We always show our appreciation to our friends, repaying the compliment by never returning a plate empty. Capisci?"

"Ho capito." Angelina hated it when her father questioned

her ability to understand. She changed the subject. "Why did so many people bring minestrone?"

"It's a tradition in Italy. The soup is meant to replenish our tears."

Before she could respond, Domenico turned away and glanced out the window again.

"Are you expecting someone, Papa?" Moments passed, and if she'd held her breath waiting for him to answer, she'd have fainted. Annoyed, she resumed her writing.

At long last, her father sighed. "Did I ever tell you how I came to open this store?"

"No."

Her father rarely offered anything about his personal life. Angelina quickly closed her schoolbook. "You've never told me."

Domenico sighed and took a moment longer, exhaling as if the past weighed heavily upon him. "In Sicily, life can break a man. We toiled on someone else's land from daybreak to nightfall and received so little of what we earned —not enough to fill our bellies."

Angelina thought of all the stories her father had told her about Sicily. Each story had a lesson between the lines.

"We worked hard—not to live but to exist. One day, I went to see my cousin Fabrizio. His mother had baked bread and tied it with string. She'd climbed on the kitchen table and nailed it to the ceiling."

Angelina's brow furrowed. "The ceiling? Why?"

"I asked my cousin the same question. He said, 'So no one eats the bread before it's time.'" Domenico shook his head. "I sat with my cousin awhile. Now and then, I'd look up at the bread. The more I stared at it, the more I wanted it. I told Fabrizio, 'If we don't leave Santo Stefano Quisquina, we'll spend the rest of our lives waiting for a piece of bread to come down from the ceiling or until one of us buries the other.' The next morning, before the sun rose and before our mothers could cry, we left for America."

Angelina had heard many stories of the moneylenders and how they offered the price of passage at exorbitant interest. "Papa, if you and Fabrizio had little money for food, how did you pay for a trip to America? Did you borrow from a moneylender?"

Her father offered no explanation, and Angelina didn't ask again.

"When I arrived in Florida, I worked in a farmer's field, enough to save for the most basic materials to build a tiny stove with my hands. I took it down to the train station, where I cooked sausages and made sandwiches. I timed it with the train's arrival. The first rule of business: if you want to sell something, sell food. No matter what goes wrong, you'll never go hungry. The second rule of business: when the sun rises, it rises for everyone, so start early."

Angelina considered how her father had rules for everything. These rules made sense—others did not.

"It's no mystery. A full stomach has no interest in an empty one." He reached behind the counter and pulled out the photograph of Carolina he kept near and placed his hand on her face. "I couldn't speak English very well, but when the smell of sausage, onions, and bell peppers filled the air, customers stood in line. It took time, but when I had enough money, I purchased the land where we're standing. Much later, I built the store and then the house."

Domenico glanced at his daughter, then back at the train station. "One day, the most beautiful girl got off the train. She had pale-green eyes and a smile that made me smile. She came to my stove with her sisters. 'My name is Domenico Pirrello,' I said to her. My hands trembled, and I dropped the bread. Still, she smiled at me, and her smile filled my heart. If I said I didn't love her at that moment, I would be lying. I loved her against all reason, against all I was ever led to believe was possible for someone like me, and I left tormented that I would never see her again."

Angelina had never heard her father's version of how her parents met, and she was eager to hear how well it matched her mother's.

"After that, I looked for her every day. I could see by their clothes and jewels they were a family of means. Rich and poor never mix in Sicily, but in America, a poor man can dream." He sighed.

"I waited so long to see her again. When she finally stepped off the train, I thought she might be a vision. Afraid this might be my only chance, I pulled off my cap and rushed over. 'Buon giorno, signorina. Do you remember me? Domenico Pirrello?' She looked at me, and with her beautiful smile, said yes."

Angelina didn't even have to close her eyes to envision the moment.

Her father gazed at the photograph. "Carolina, Carolina." His voice sounded younger, as though he'd lost his way in time. "Life was simple then. When I thought of her, I smiled. Now, when I think of her, I die a little. When the sun shines, we think nothing will change. We refuse to believe the darkness will come, but we have no way to stop it." He wiped away a tear. "Love comes to us in brief moments of happiness, and if there are enough of them, we gather all we can. They become our life." Domenico's chin quivered. "I just never thought I'd lose her."

Angelina rose from her chair, put her arms around her father, and leaned her head on his chest. Neither spoke. It was the closest she and her father had ever been. Domenico didn't pull away. The wonder and tenderness of the moment lingered for a long time.

~

DESPITE ALL THEIR GRIEVING, the family had to eat and needed clean clothes. And so Angelina tied her long hair back, went outside, filled the washtub, and set the scrub board inside it.

Signora Bertelli came through the house, stepped out the back door, and made her way past the goat to where Angelina stood surrounded by laundry.

"There you are. Such a glorious day we have today. Even the chickens have agreed to lay more eggs."

Angelina attempted to sound cheerful while leaning over the washtub. "Hello, signora."

"Your brothers told me you were out here."

Angelina slapped a shirt against the washboard. "And were they laughing?"

"No, why?"

She wrinkled her brow. "They don't have to wash clothes."

"Washing is nothing. I'll show you how to make it go faster."

"Burn them?" Angelina held up her brother's pants as an offering.

"Well, that's one way, but what works best is to keep your mind as busy as your hands."

Angelina sighed. "I used to help my mother with the work while she sang and told me stories. Some of them made me laugh, and some were stories of la miseria. But this laundry is too much for me alone."

"Mannaggia la miseria. It's what we say: damn the misery of life. Perhaps she wanted you to know how bad life could be so you appreciate what you have?" Signora Bertelli nervously rubbed the back of her neck, as if painful memories had reemerged. "You cannot imagine how strange and terrifying the feeling was when we came to America. We were both happy and unhappy to leave Italy. It's like knocking on a door while praying no one answers."

Angelina sank her hands into the soapy water and continued to scrub as she listened.

"From the deck of the ship, we watched those we loved. We all waved white handkerchiefs at them, but then a terrible fear overcame us. It was the last time many of us would ever see our families. Few young women ever saw their mothers again."

Angelina stopped a moment, knowing she would never see her mother again.

"In Santo Stefano Quisquina, we have a saying: 'Go only as far as you can hear the village bell.' Most of us had never seen a city. Now we were crossing an ocean. The day was clear and bright, but for us, there were only dark shadows."

Angelina grew more captivated by the story. "My mother said her strongest memory was when the ship pulled away. Some had changed their minds. They screamed and pleaded to get off, but it was too late."

"Oh, Angelina, you cannot imagine such fear. People gripped their rosaries so tightly the beads made marks in their hands. Everyone prayed to God, and the Virgin, and all the saints. They wore crucifixes and amulets around their necks. They were even fearful that those left behind were angry or jealous and had cursed them with malocchio."

Angelina nodded. "My mother said no matter where she went on the ship, someone was crying." She pulled her hands out of the tub and wrung the water from a shirt. "I can't imagine the fear of leaving what you know to go to where you know nothing."

"I was thirty-five then, but age didn't matter. We feared everyone and everything. The food was strange. We worried about the ship sinking, about disease, and about God punishing us for abandoning the land where our ancestors lay buried."

Angelina pulled out another wet shirt and wondered where the passengers had strung their clotheslines.

"At last, our first glimpse of America—such a wonderful sight." Signora Bertelli paused as if overwhelmed by the memory.

"Frank and I came on the same boat your mother's family did, but we didn't see them on the journey. Then, as fate would have it, she married your father, and we became neighbors."

"That was so lucky for us," said Angelina.

"I've said it before—your mother was a saint. Because your grandfather could afford first-class for his entire family, they went straight through Ellis Island with hardly a blink. The rest of us endured long lines and examinations of our hearts, lungs, and even our sanity. They looked down our throats and in our wallets. The worst came when they used a button hook to pull back our eyelids to check for infection."

"What? They might have put out someone's eye." Imagining the agony gave Angelina a chill. "That's horrible. Aren't there laws to protect people?"

"There are laws, and there are people who use them to make other people miserable." Signora Bertelli shook out the shirt Angelina handed her, hung it on the line, and resumed her sobering story.

"A family from Reggio Calabria had a son with one leg. The officials marked him with an L for 'lame.' The officials said the physically disabled were a burden, and they denied the young man entrance into America. The father argued that his son was healthy and strong and could work as hard as any man. 'My children are not orphans. I take care of my own.' You should have heard the mother pleading." Signora Bertelli's face grew flushed as she continued. "'You condemn the entire family,' the woman said. 'We cannot send one son back alone. If I go back with him, who will care for the other children? If my husband goes back with him, who will care for us?' When the arguing was over, the son said nothing. He walked to the edge of the dock and threw himself into the ocean. By the time they found his body, he was dead."

Angelina gasped. "That's horrible!"

"The mother screamed and screamed. The sound is still inside my head. Then she picked up her son's crutches and forced them against the two officials who had refused him entry. 'The crutches are your cross to bear!' she shouted. 'And the L is yours to wear in this world and the next.'"

"What a terrible thing. That poor family must have been sorry they ever came to America."

"The Italian government had never helped Sicilians, and we didn't expect America to be any different. We had learned long ago to take care of ourselves. We only asked for a chance to live better."

Before she wrung out the last shirt, Angelina paused and reflected on the enormity of this story. Everyone on that ship had taken a big risk. "I never thought of it before, but just one person making a daring trip across the sea could change their family's lives for generations, but years and years later, does anyone remember who took such a daring risk?" Would anyone remember her father or Signora Bertelli?

"I will never forget this story. One day I'll tell it to my children," said Angelina.

Signora Bertelli put her hand on her forehead as though the mere memory of the incident had given her a headache. "They should have let that poor boy pass. In such a big country, what is one more boy?" She glanced at the now-empty clothesbasket. "The clothes will dry quickly. The sun has a temperament, and it's arrogant today. Next week, I'll come early, and we'll do all the washing together."

"Thank you, signora. I'm so grateful for your help."

The woman hugged Angelina and left through the backyard gate.

Angelina picked up the empty basket, entered the kitchen, and cut herself a piece of salami while her brothers chattered in the parlor. A rapid knock at the front door drew her attention. For a moment, she waited for her mother to answer, like always. She'd learned that people didn't die all at once. Those who loved them held on to them for as long as possible, releasing them little by little.

The knock came louder.

"Vincenzo, get the door," Angelina called out.

"What?" her brother said.

Another knock.

Angelina put her hands on her hips. "Salvatore, you get the door."

"What?"

"Oh, never mind." Angelina crossed the short distance to the parlor and reached for the doorknob. As she pulled the door open, a jeweled hand grabbed the edge of the door, forcing it open wide, bending Angelina's hand back, and nearly hitting her in the face.

CHAPTER 4

Tall and sharply dressed, Violetta burst into the house, the ornate black feather on her hat brushing the doorframe as she walked through it. Gina, the youngest of Carolina's sisters and a shorter, rounder version of Angelina's mother, followed behind with a warm smile.

"Hello, my darling," said Gina. She approached her niece with a heartfelt greeting, a hug, and a kiss.

Violetta glanced about the room with agitation. After accusing Angelina's father of killing her mother and declaring that he should to burn in hell, Angelina could not imagine what had possessed the woman to visit her brother-in-law's home.

"How are you, bella?" asked Violetta. She gave Angelina a kiss so quick it missed her cheek altogether.

"How are you managing without your sainted mother?" Gina asked as she blinked away a tear. "It must be so hard."

Angelina didn't want to share what was still so raw and painful. It had been the most devastating loss of her life, and she remained unsure whether she'd ever get over the shock of it. Nothing could replace a mother, absolutely nothing and no one. These were her mother's sisters, yet they still had their mother. How could they understand her loss? How could she describe her sorrow?

Angelina rolled down her sleeves. "I miss her so much every day and in even the little things. I finished the laundry. Mother used to sing and tell stories when we did it together."

"Laundry?" Violetta spat the word as if she'd bitten into something rotten. "She never did that before she married your father. It's unbecoming. My sister should have refused."

Angelina knew why none of the children spoke. After Violetta's outburst in church, it was unlikely any of them had forgotten what their aunt had said about their father. However, the family belonged to a world of traditions. Without smiles and almost mechanical movements, each one gave their aunts the customary kiss.

Gina had her late sister's gentleness and each child received an affectionate embrace, while Violetta offered pats on their heads. It occurred to Angelina that Zia Violetta might have also refused a lame boy entry into America.

"It's so good to see you both. But, Zia Violetta, Papa's still furious over what you said in church. He truly loved my mother. You'd better go. I'll bring the children to visit." Angelina walked to the door and held it open for her aunt.

"It's a terrible thing to lose a mother, but we are here to make necessary arrangements and corrections," said Violetta as she ripped the door from Angelina's hold and shut it. She glanced around the room and viewed the furnishings and other possessions with obvious distaste. "Thank God you have us—the Cacciatore family."

"We only came to help." Gina's voice had an almost musical quality of compassion, like a hymn—a sharp contrast to that of Violetta, who carried a thin blanket of tolerance for those she deemed beneath her.

Unquestionably a beautiful woman, Zia Violetta had an

elegant stateliness and Carolina's pale-green eyes, though they lacked her softness. Zia Gina had Carolina's high cheekbones and delicate hands, and she liked to tell them stories about life in Italy, like her late sister. Still, today wasn't a day for telling stories, not with Violetta striking matches to ignite a fire. Angelina grew increasingly uncomfortable.

"Look how big everyone's getting. Why does time go so quickly?" said Gina with noticeable tenderness. "No one's heart will ever be the same without your mother." Gina spoke as if offering sustenance to her sister's children.

"Yes, that's true," said Violetta, but her abrupt tone eradicated whatever droplets of nourishment were found in Gina's encouragement. If Gina had come alone, Angelina would have relaxed, but Violetta used words to ignite fires, and Domenico was conducting business only a few feet from the parlor's adjoining door to the store.

"Zia Violetta, we love you, but you have to leave now. My father's in the grocery store." Once again, Angelina reached for the door and held it open even wider to stress her point.

"Nonsense." Violetta turned her back to it.

Angelina had long ago observed how her aunt took pleasure in confrontations. She could feel Violetta warming up for a clash of wills. "There's no way to know what my father will do if he sees you."

Memories had consequences, and the younger children stepped away from their Zia Violetta and remained quiet, a contrast to their usual liveliness. They sensed something displeasing and looked to the older ones while Salvatore and Vincenzo sent Angelina silent, rapid gestures indicating for her to throw Violetta out.

"Perhaps your idea wasn't so good, Violetta. Let's visit another time when things calm down a bit," Gina urged.

"Zia Gina is so right." Salvatore spoke up.

"That's true. Why don't we visit you instead?" Vincenzo nodded encouragingly.

Violetta didn't respond well to orders or requests. Angelina could almost feel her digging her heels into the floor. At that moment, the door to the grocery store swung open.

All the children froze.

"I don't know why I can't get the pomegranates to grow. I've tried—" Domenico looked up and stopped. Though the day whirled with stifling heat, a chill settled over the room as he fixed his gaze on his detested sister-in-law. He placed his box of vegetables on the table with a slam. He didn't shout, but there was no mistaking his anger. "Why are you here, Violetta? You are not welcome."

"Buon giorno, Domenico. I'm glad you came in from your little store. I'm here to take my sister's children away and inform you—"

Violetta had committed a crime, but not the usual kind. This crime was executed for the sole purpose of menacing and intimidating Domenico. Angelina could feel her father's anger heat the room. Her aunt had underestimated him.

"Your sister's children are not orphans, and they are not your concern or duty. Go home and stay there!"

Violetta raised her hand. "You are wrong as usual. As Carolina's children, they are entitled to privileges you cannot possibly give them."

"I can give them their father—something you cannot possibly give them." He clenched his hands, and his face flushed red. Convinced nothing good would come of this confrontation, Angelina longed to stop it, but had no idea how.

"My sister made me promise that should anything unforeseen happen to her, I would collect her children and care for them."

Angelina didn't believe it. Violetta hadn't lost her skill at corrupting the truth.

"Carolina would never have asked that." Domenico's voice grew more forceful now.

"Step aside, Domenico. The children need a proper home, not a house with a grocery store stuck to it like a tumor. They need things you can't give them, things we can."

Violetta had a way of verbally demolishing a home, and Angelina visualized theirs crumbling to the ground.

"It was different when we were all young and living in Sicily. There, you can take advantage of the hardworking. The rich make people miserable and destroy families. Without remorse, they throw the poor off the lands they've toiled upon and force them to starve." Domenico stepped closer. "So I left long ago, and you have no rights over me in America." His voice grew louder, his words more distinct. "You'll never get my children. Now get out!"

"They'll live with my mother and sister Gina, raised well, as Cacciatores, with privileges." Violetta continued, still perfumed with her sense of self-importance. "You can come to visit them. I know my sister wanted it this way. May she rest in peace."

For a moment, no one spoke. Gina glanced at the children as if they'd become casualties of Violetta's war. "Please, Violetta, let's go," she urged.

Undaunted, Violetta turned to the children. "Good news, you're all going to live with Nonna. I give you my permission to pick out a few things. We'll buy the rest later."

It amazed Angelina how her aunt expected her father to accept this. Her father's face grew more red as his anger escalated, but Violetta lifted her chin and gave him what appeared to be a look of indifference. In this moment of silence, her aunt made clear to everyone her intention to remain defiant. Even the youngest children understood something terrible was taking place and froze.

Like a wall of bricks, Domenico positioned himself between his sisters-in-law and his children. Then he stepped forward and forced the sisters back toward the door. "You cut your throat with your tongue, Violetta," he bellowed.

Violetta flicked open her fan and waved it delicately, disinterested. "Let's be honest, Domenico. How does a widower whose business is open ten hours a day or more expect to raise six children? It's ridiculous. We're here to protect them from your nonsense."

"We should leave," insisted Gina, but her remark went unnoticed by Violetta or Domenico.

"Nothing in this house belongs to you, and nothing leaves with you."

Violetta shut her fan as quickly as she'd opened it. "Carolina would turn in her grave if we left the man who killed her and her baby to raise her surviving children."

The children stood horrified. Salvatore and Vincenzo held the younger children by their hands, and Angelina picked up a crying Giuseppe.

"Get out of my house!" Domenico bellowed, turning crimson with rage. He pointed to the door. The fierceness in his eyes frightened Angelina, and she grew desperate to stop the exchange.

Undaunted, Violetta continued. "Carolina was lovely. Everyone said it. Claudio Garcia, a prominent man who owned his own cigar factory, wanted to marry her, and her sister-in-law would have been Maria Martino, a well-respected doctor's wife. Carolina could have been wealthy and admired. Instead, all she got was a tiny grocery store, a life of labor, and the grave."

Angelina stiffened at the mention of Maria Martino. She could not imagine her mother being related to the doctor's wife—the same woman who'd cursed Angelina with malocchio as her mother lay dying.

"Get out." Domenico clenched his fists as a vein in his neck pulsed.

Undaunted, Violetta shook her forefinger at her brother-in-law. "You are nobody, Domenico, and you have nothing."

"Then you should fear me. A man who has nothing is capable of anything because he has nothing to lose." He stepped forward again, and the women backed up.

Angelina's heart raced for fear of what might come next.

"I pity you," her father continued. "You will never know the love we had." He gestured toward Angelina and her siblings. "Look upon your sister's children because I swear on my Carolina's grave, you will never enter this house again —capisci?"

"Please, Violetta, let's go." Gina's voice held a tremor.

"You should have died instead." Like a dagger, Violetta's explosive words pierced the room. The children gasped, and Salvatore yelled, "Stop it!"

Angelina wanted to swallow the insult before it reached her father's ears. She knew her father's mind, and she could almost read the meaning of the old proverb—God forgives. Italians do not—in his eyes.

"Papa, please, let them go."

Her father swung open the door, grabbed Violetta by the arm, and forced her out of the house, with Gina in her wake. Their stunned expressions etched themselves in Angelina's mind as the younger children whimpered and clung to the older ones. Domenico unleashed his fury by slamming the door in the faces of the women. In his outburst, he shouted the words meant to sever all ties between the families, "`E finita!" Finished!

CHAPTER 5

It seemed logical to Angelina that if ever wishes came true, they should do so on her birthday. She pleaded with her mother to return, even for a moment. She released her wish into the air to go wherever wishes go. Carolina might appear as an apparition, but Angelina didn't care. Her heart pounded with anticipation. She searched the room for a sign—a shadow, an echo. Again and again, she whispered her plea. "Mama, come back to me." But the soundless minutes gathered and coiled about her—until they carelessly drifted away.

Angelina sat up in bed and wrote in her school notebook. *Today is my sixteenth birthday, and I will become a writer and keep a record of everything important that happens to me.*

She did not expect to see her aunts on her birthday, not since Violetta's explosive argument with her father. However, her father would appear at any moment. He'd kiss her and offer good wishes. He'd tell her how the sun shone early on the day she was born and how surprised they were that she had lots of hair. Her mother had begun this tradition of reminding each child that their birth had been extraordinary.

"Angelina," her father called from the other side of the bedroom door.

"Come in, Papa." She set aside her longing. At least she still had her father.

"No need to come in. Time to get up and come out."

Angelina's heart sank. No good wishes? Had he forgotten her birthday? Convinced he would look at his calendar and realize the date, Angelina readied herself for a wonderful day. She entered the kitchen, pulled out a large pot, and measured olive oil, parsley, garlic, basil, and tomatoes, following her mother's recipe. Today was Saturday. No school. The neighbors would excuse her for the delay in returning their plates during the week.

Angelina reached for the long-handled wooden spoon and stirred the sauce. "Always stir clockwise," her mother had instructed. It seemed everyone had a sharp memory for the old country's superstitions. Since it wasn't possible to unravel pasta sauce, Angelina saw no point in it. Then again, she had never disobeyed her mother, so she began the clockwise motion, and the movement soothed a bit of the ache of not seeing her mother on her birthday morning.

The sauce needed time to gain its full flavor, so she left it simmering. Since Signora Bertelli had offered to help her bake a cake, Angelina walked over to her house. She had just raised her arm to knock when the door swung open.

"If it's too early, signora, or if you're too busy, I—"

The middle-aged woman placed her hand on her heart. "I promised I'd help you bake a cake, and if I refuse, may my teeth fall out of my head."

Angelina smiled, trying to remember if she'd ever heard the woman use a simple yes or no.

An array of utensils and a cake pan lay upon the kitchen

table. Under Signora Bertelli's instruction, butter, eggs, flour, sugar, and milk soon filled the bowl. "My Frank loved lemon cake. A cake is like a good marriage, Angelina—each ingredient depends on the other for perfection."

"My parents had a good marriage too," said Angelina.

"*Two* is right. Two turtle doves, two peas in a pod, two lovebirds in a tree." Signora Bertelli lifted her chin. "If only Adam and Eve had been that happy or smart. I mean, whoever heard of a talking snake?"

Angelina placed the batter-filled pan into the oven, then licked the spoon. This beloved neighbor might be the closest thing to having a mother, and Angelina had grown accustomed to her way of exaggerating things.

"One day, it will be your turn to fall in love, Angelina. I have no doubt you'll have the most romantic experience. Love makes life magical." She sighed. "It will happen all at once, and you won't be able to get him out of your head. You'll get butterflies in your stomach, and you won't be able to eat or sleep. Your heart will beat so fast when you see him, it's like having a heart attack. Nothing will make sense, and your brain won't work anymore." Signora Bertelli looked starry-eyed and released another deep sigh. "It's wonderful."

Angelina saw nothing wonderful about it. "Falling in love sounds unhealthy, painful, and dangerous."

"Ah yes." Signora Bertelli smiled and appeared cheerfully lost in a memory. "That too."

Angelina had nothing to contribute to a conversation about love. "How long will the cake take to bake?" she asked.

Her neighbor took a moment to clear her throat and return to the present. "Forty minutes in Sicily. Thirty minutes in America. Everything here is rush-rush. That's why we use reliable donkeys in Sicily, not Model-Ts. Did you see the Di Letos from across the street holding hands after your mother's funeral? They looked so devoted." Signora

Bertelli sighed. "Such pleasant people. If only they'd get a sensible cat instead of that big dog who barks day and night, I'd visit them more often."

Angelina scooped up the mixing bowl lathered with cake mix and brought it to the sink. "I didn't see them. I went back to the church to light a candle for my mother and brother after the funeral."

Signora Bertelli gasped. "Back to the church? That's the way we walked to bury your mother."

Angelina glanced at the clock to note the time for her cake. "I guess so."

"Oh, Holy Mother." Signora Bertelli jerked her head in surprise and kissed the crucifix on her necklace. "Never go to a funeral and return the same way, or Death might follow you, make you sick, and—" She shuddered and grabbed Angelina's hand. "God forbid."

"I've never heard of that." Angelina patted Signora Bertelli's hand.

"May my hair fall out of my head if what I tell you is a lie."

It didn't seem possible to Angelina that Death followed people around. The world had stepped into the modern times and the twentieth century, yet her mother had said Signora Bertelli was highly esteemed on both sides of the ocean for deflecting evil. Perhaps it was her neighbor's profound sincerity and irresistible radiance that prompted Angelina to trust her. "I'll remember that next time," Angelina reassured her.

"Don't let there be a next time. Powerful forces flow between the earth and sky. I'll teach you as much as I can, but we only divulge the strongest rituals on Christmas Eve."

Wonderful. It's not Christmas Eve, thought Angelina.

"Pay close attention," Signora Bertelli admonished with a forefinger pointed to her eye—a gesture her father often used when he wanted her to be vigilant. The woman's chest heaved as if the power to fight evil lay deep inside her. "The color red fights off evil. It's best to use red coral, but in these times, who has coral? We use what we have, right? Right." She tapped her temple, the sign for being clever. "Say one Our Father, one Hail Mary, and a Glory Be to the Father. God has been fighting evil for centuries and appreciates all the help we can offer."

Angelina listened to the list of warnings with wide eyes, but with less enthusiasm than for the cake recipe. After the *torta alla panna* was baked, she gave her neighbor a hug. "Thank you, signora. I don't remember when I've learned so much in so short a time."

"You'll eat the cake, but my secrets will remain. Knowing them will make all the difference."

"I'm sure you're right." Angelina walked out, entered her kitchen through the back door, and placed the cake in the cupboard, where it would remain until dinner. She then checked her sauce. The tomatoes, garlic, and basil had blended into a familiar aroma that permeated the room.

Angelina's little sister wandered in.

"Are you hungry, Lily?" said Angelina.

"I don't feel good."

"Does anything hurt?"

The child appeared pale. She bent over and expelled the contents of her stomach.

Angelina jumped back, gasping. Her first instinct was to flee the sour smell, but the sight of her sickly little sister stopped her. Who would take care of her now that their mother was gone? With shallow breaths, Angelina comforted her sister and said the words her mother would have. "Now you'll feel so much better." She took a damp rag, wiped the child's face, and cleaned up the mess, fighting her own nausea.

Angelina guided her sister to their bed, where she poured

salt at each of the four corners. She wasted no time placing a string of garlic bulbs around the child's neck as Signora Bertelli had done that fateful day of their mother's passing. She also opened the window so the evil spirits could depart.

Her father would reject the belief that the angel of death followed people around, as he did all superstitions, calling it pure nonsense. Still, if it were true, Angelina could only blame herself. She considered her mother, who believed in such things. And although not convinced herself, Angelina saw no need to take a chance. She'd fight the angel of death on her own. Just in case. *How could it hurt?*

Angelina dashed into her father's room and removed the two treasures her mother had kept in an onyx box.

"Hold on to Mama's silver rosary, Lily." She placed a gold crucifix necklace over the one crudely strung in garlic.

Now, what was it Signora Bertelli had said about protection? Yes. Use red objects to deflect evil. In the absence of red coral and ribbons, Angelina slipped into the grocery store, passed her father, who was distracted with a customer, and bagged some red peppers. She returned to her sister's side and laid a few at Lily's feet.

"My stomach still hurts," said the child.

It was inconceivable to Angelina that she might have to bear the loss of another sibling. More nervous now, she placed a row of red peppers around the entire circumference of Lily's bed. "You'll be fine, I promise." Now the true test remained. Angelina agonized over the details of her conversation with Signora Bertelli. It had seemed like folklore and stories from the old country a few hours before, but could her words have been a prophecy, a warning of more sadness to come to the family?

Angelina wasted no time. She poured water into a bowl, balanced it on Lily's head as Signora Bertelli had instructed, and poured three drops of oil into the water. *If three drops join, something malicious exists.* When two joined, Angelina threw out the water and started over again. The next set swayed and glided. Moments passed. The first droplet pressed against the side of the bowl, then the second. The third wavered far too long but ultimately did the same.

Angelina exhaled, placed the bowl of water on the bureau, and dropped onto the bed, next to her sister. She'd done it. If death had been there—and maybe it had and maybe it hadn't—it was gone now. She handed Lily the rag doll their grandmother had sewn—the one with a muslin head, painted face, and clothes made from an old dress. Angelina put her arm around Lily.

"Tell me a story, Angelina."

"What kind of story?"

Lily cuddled close. "The kind Mama used to tell."

"Did you know that when Mama was a little girl like you, she lived near the Mediterranean Sea? The water is warm there. You can always hear the waves, and there are mountains. And there are children riding donkeys, herding goats, chasing chickens, and rolling down grassy hills, laughing as they see who can reach the bottom first."

Soon they both fell asleep.

Time slipped away, and Angelina opened her eyes to the acrid smell of burning sauce. *The sauce*! She leaped from the bed in a panic, rushed to the kitchen, and pulled the pot from the stove, but it was too late. The smell had conquered the room. She opened the windows. Divine help was always welcome. "Oh, please, Blessed Mother, help me hide this from Papa."

Angelina cringed as she looked into the large, black-bottomed pot. With no time to make more sauce, she squeezed her eyes shut and forced herself to taste it. There was no mistaking the problem, but she could still salvage it. She spooned the sauce onto each plate and added a generous helping of strong, imported cheese—the one her brothers called "dirty socks"—to disguise the smell. If the neighbors noticed the scorched flavor, they'd probably blame Angelina's youth and inexperience.

Salvatore rushed in and made a face. "What d'you do, burn the sauce?"

"No, it's fine. Run out back and throw what's left of the pot into the pig trough."

"You'll poison our only pig," he teased.

"Go." Angelina had no time for an annoying brother. She headed out the door balancing two plates at a time until she had delivered each to those who'd come to the funeral and brought food for the family.

Her father stood at the store's entrance and called out to her. "Angelina, I'd like to see you."

At last, he'd remembered her birthday.

"I'm coming, Papa."

He'd have good wishes for her and a small present. She rushed to meet him, but her excitement quickly evaporated.

"Sweep the floor. A customer's child knocked over a bag of flour. I'll be in the house," he said matter-of-factly, as if she were the only one of his children who knew how to sweep.

Angelina wilted. Feeling forgotten, she grabbed the broom and swung it high, knocking over the wrapped-bread display. "Happy birthday, Angelina," she grumbled to herself, snatching the bread off the floor and sweeping the flour with harsh strokes.

When she finished, she leaned on the broom, closed her eyes, and recalled her mother's voice. "*A first baby takes a long time to come, but you came quickly, with such a sweet face and so much hair. We cried from so much joy that all our sorrows slipped away.*"

Angelina prayed intensely for her mother to appear, but, to her dismay, the room remained still.

The small bell above the grocery door broke the silence. A middle-aged man with graying hair and a mustache entered holding a worn carpetbag of faded colors, a rope tied around it to secure it. *Another recent immigrant*, thought Angelina. However, his dark, bright eyes and winning smile captured her interest. He nodded, removed his cap, and ran splayed fingers through his thinning hair.

"May I help you?" Angelina asked.

He nodded, then bellowed, "Domenico! Domenico!"

Alarmed, Angelina backed away from him.

"Domenico!" he yelled again.

CHAPTER 6

"Domenico!"

Domenico burst through the doorway wearing a wide grin. "Pasquale."

"Domenico, *fratello mio. Non posso credere di essere finalmente qui con voi.*" The man threw his arms around Domenico, and both men beamed with excitement. This was the brother her father had said would arrive from Sicily, but he never came, and her father's words grew old, withered, and blew away.

Angelina studied the two men. They both had wavy hair, but gray speckled Pasquale's. Their eyes were dark and expressive, like they'd seen things they wanted to forget. Pasquale had whiskers, Domenico a mustache. And both had strong, calloused hands from years of toil. More striking, they both had a distinctive upright stature, like descendants of the Roman warriors who later became seamen, and then farmers who were repeatedly invaded and robbed of their crops and land, and, in the end, reduced to peasants.

Her father stood taller and was ready to weather any storm. Pasquale much more gentle and trouble free, with deep laugh lines around his eyes and a sparkle to his demeanor, as if he'd come from a different village than his brother, a village where life had not been as harsh, where hunger didn't exist.

"Come here, Angelina. This is your Zio Pasquale."

Pasquale kissed her and gave her a warm hug, and she knew right away they'd become great friends.

"*Benevenuto.* Welcome. I'm so happy you came, Zio Pasquale."

"I'm so happy I came too."

Domenico pulled out a chair for his brother. "Sit, sit." He then turned to Angelina. "Bring your uncle something to eat and a cup of espresso."

Her uncle hesitated and stood behind the chair. "You excuse to me, Angelina." Pasquale took off his shirt to reveal another shirt underneath and another underneath that one and sat when only one remained.

Domenico belted out a laugh. "Four shirts, Pasquale? I only wore two when I came to America."

"Better to put on than have to hold. Marco Ussi, he look so fat when he get on the boat. He wear five shirts and two pairs of pants."

Domenico broke into an even hardier laugh than before, and it was wonderful, rich, and meaningful. It had been a long time since she'd heard his laughter. Angelina smile widened as she set down a plate of the freshest bread, best meats and cheeses for her uncle.

"Tell me, Pasquale, how's everyone at home?" Domenico asked.

The cheerful moment would certainly shatter. Angelina tensed. News from the old country arrived with sharp edges of melancholy.

Pasquale took a few bites, then closed his eyes a moment as though savoring the food. "I say to everybody, 'Domenico, he go to America. Remember when his belly is empty?' And everybody say yes.

Angelina waited for a story about hunger.

"I say, 'Now, Domenico have so much food, he have to open a store to sell the food he no can eat.' Everybody so happy for you. Mama mia, what a country." Pasquale clasped his hands and raised them to heaven. "You remember all the things the people they say about l'America?"

Domenico nodded. A rare softness seemed to wash over him.

Pasquale turned to Angelina. "In Santo Stefano Quisquina, everybody say they make the streets of l'America with gold and that's for sure. So I come here, but you know what I see when I get off the boat?"

"Gold?" Angelina asked with a grin.

"I see is no true. Some streets dirt, just like in Sicily. So I say, 'Pasquale, you no see no gold. Maybe you better find a job.' And you know what job they give to me, Angelina?" Pasquale raised his hands and sliced through the air with exuberant gestures that emphasized every phrase.

"No, zio, what job did they give you?"

"They fill the wagon and say I gonna pave the streets with bricks." Pasquale slapped his forehead with his palm. "I say maybe somebody make the mistake. What happen to the gold?"

Her father gave another hearty laugh. Pasquale beamed and offered one of those rare smiles that reassured her all was right with the world.

"You lucky, Angelina, you born in America, the land of the milk and the honey. You ask for coffee here, you the get sugar and the cream too. In Santo Stefano Quisquina, if you ask for bread, they say, 'So how come you so hungry you no eat yesterday?' In l'America, you ask for the bread, you get butter, too."

For Angelina, the Sicilian way of life seemed worlds away. "Did you ever have butter?" she asked.

"You gotta have a cow. Nobody have a cow. More people have nothing, but some have too much. Signore Costa, he have a cow, so he make the butter, and he put it on the both sides of the bread, then he walk around the piazza and eat it so we no forget he is a rich man. And he get fat too. Only the rich get fat."

Domenico nodded. "I remember that old man. He wore two different shoes so everyone would know he had two pairs."

"Is true. Only now, he stomp his feet so we no forget to look."

Angelina didn't miss how easily her uncle made her father smile. He made her smile too.

"You know, Pasquale, I have waited a long time for you to come to America and make your home with us. Carolina and I even made sure there was room for you when we built this house. This is your home now."

"You help me, Domenico, and I gonna work hard, and you no have to send money to Mama no more. I send the money. I gonna send Mama so much so she can buy butter and put it on both sides of the bread, like Signore Costa."

The children's voices grew into excited chatter at the adjoining doorway.

"Come, come," Domenico called. "Meet my older brother, your zio Pasquale."

Angelina's siblings all rushed in and introduced themselves. It pleased her to see Lily feeling well enough to join them. Pasquale hugged each one and gave them an affectionate kiss while pretending to steal their noses and ears and put them in his pocket. The children laughed as their uncle's exaggerated hand gestures colored the air and wove stories about his village, donkeys and goats, and a chicken that laid potatoes.

Not since her mother died did Angelina remember everyone laughing so much. If only for a brief time, the heavens had granted a rainbow and placed it over the little grocery store on Nineteenth. Angelina thought back to her prayer. Perhaps her birthday wish had come true in a way she never expected.

The day of excitement wore on. Around dinnertime, Angelina made her way to the kitchen, and Pasquale followed.

"I gonna cook, Angelina. I make you some *pasta e fagioli,* like you *nonna,* she make in Santo Stefano. Is so good, you gonna eat, and you gonna ask for more."

Domenico turned to his daughter. "Angelina, you told me you made pasta sauce today. Is there much left?"

A warm flush washed over her. "Oh, I'm sorry. I made only enough for the neighbors. It's gone."

When Domenico looked away, her brother Salvatore put his hands around his neck and stuck out his tongue as though he were choking. Angelina narrowed her eyes at him and turned back to her uncle. "Thank you, Zio Pasquale. I'm happy to let you cook tonight." With a stern look from her father, she added, "I'll help you."

Pasquale looked at home in the kitchen as he made dinner. Soon, everyone gathered around the table, eating heartily and asking for seconds. With the meal a success, the moment had arrived. Angelina brought out her cake and placed it on the table. She cleared her throat and met her father's eyes. They never had cake except on holidays and birthdays—a monumental clue of her special day.

Zio Pasquale patted Angelina on the back. "You make the best cake in America."

Filippo tried to scoop some frosting with his finger, but

Angelina caught his hand midair and waited for her father to announce her birthday. However, that didn't happen. Instead, Domenico instructed her to cut the cake, then turned to his brother to reminisce some more. The chattering grew louder, bellies filled with cake, and Angelina's heart grew heavy. She cleared the table and entered the kitchen, fighting the tears. Again, she begged her mother to appear. She needed to feel the strongest love. Pasquale returned to the kitchen once again.

"Angelina, is okay I talk to you?"

"Zio Pasquale." She quickly brushed away her tears and nodded. "How can I help you?"

"I wanna to tell you I know you miss you mama. Everybody miss you mama, but she no go away, Angelina. She still see you, and she love you so much and wanna you be happy."

Angelina didn't expect this sudden mention of her mother. She found Pasquale's manner so tender, her eyes again moistened all over again.

"It's gonna be okay, Angelina. You no cry. You Mama no like to see you cry." Pasquale placed his hand in his pocket and brought out its contents. "I have something I wanna give to you. You take this gift?"

She gazed at him, puzzled. How could her uncle know today was her birthday when her own father hadn't remembered? "What do you mean?" she asked.

Pasquale reached for her hand, where he placed a small package wrapped in a muslin cloth and tied with string. "I hope you like. I bring from Santo Stefano Quisquina just for you."

"I don't understand."

"You open, Angelina."

Angelina excitedly pulled on the string until the cloth fell away. In her hand sat a magnificent gold pendant watch with

Roman numerals, intricate carvings of delicate flowers and birds, and small gemstones.

"Oh, Zio Pasquale, it's the most wonderful thing I've ever seen in my entire life." She almost choked on the words.

"It belong to you nonna, who have it a long, long time, and now she say she wanna I should give it to Angelina—the first granddaughter."

Angelina had no jewelry and never imagined anything so beautiful. "How can nonna part with it?"

"You nonna want you should have it to remember how much she love you. Is not so big and not so new, but it gonna work just fine."

"This means so much to me."

"A rich man, he come to see my papa. He give him work. He like my papa. He give him money, corn, tomatoes, and this watch. It belong to his dead wife, and he have no children. The money we spend, the food we eat, and now the watch—she belong to you."

Angelina threw her arms around her uncle. "It's my birthday today. This is the most beautiful gift I've ever received. I'll write to her tomorrow."

"What? I can no believe is you birthday, Angelina. How come nobody tell me? I gonna be right back." He darted through the doorway.

Angelina wanted to embrace her grandmother, gaze upon her face, and look into her eyes. Did she look like her nonna? Since her father's mother was too old to travel so far and Angelina too young, would they ever see each other?

Pasquale reentered the room with widened eyes and a smile bigger than before, one that lit up his face and highlighted his laugh lines. He held out his hand and presented her with a red brick. "I gonna give to you the good luck I get in America."

Angelina stifled her humor at receiving a brick. "I can use good luck. Thank you, zio. I think."

"You remember—I told you I get a job in America? The boss, he say to me, 'Pasquale, you no feel bad about the gold, we make the streets with the bricks.' Bricks is strong, Angelina, better than gold. Bricks gonna last one hundred years. Gold, she's too soft, and everybody wanna steal it. Nobody gonna steal a brick."

Angelina noticed the gleam in his eyes as he spoke.

"This is the first brick he give to me in America. So I say to myself, I gonna be strong like the brick. Maybe I gonna last one hundred years too. Now I give to you, Angelina, so you never forget you strong, just like this brick."

Angelina kissed her uncle and said, "I'll keep this brick close, and I promise to be strong."

Pasquale's eyes lit up.

"Whenever I feel weak," she continued, "I'll hold the brick close to me, like you said. This is the most wonderful birthday I could have ever imagined."

"Non ti preoccupare. You no worry. Pretty soon I gonna get job, and I buy you two pairs of shoes, like Signore Rossi."

Angelina giggled.

Pasquale kissed her forehead. "I go now."

"You should know, Zio Pasquale, I want to be a writer, and when I make lots of money, I'll buy you ten pairs of shoes."

Pasquale laughed. "That's so nice, but what I gonna do with ten pairs of shoes? I only have two feet."

Once again, her uncle made her laugh. Perhaps some of the happiness she'd lost when her mother died had returned. Even after Pasquale left, Angelina continued to admire the pendant watch. She laid it on the counter, a safe distance away, before dipping the dinner plates in soapy water. As soon as she dried the dishes, Domenico burst into the room and raised a challenging voice. "Why did you take my good red peppers and throw them on the floor around your sister's bed?"

It seemed her father was set on crushing any happiness she might unearth, even on her special day. Angelina reached for her newly acquired brick as a surge of anger pulsed through her.

"Angelina, what do you have to say? What are—?"

For the first time in her life, Angelina cut her father off. "Today, I took care of Lily, who was sick and vomiting. Mama believed in curses that can make people sick. Signora Bertelli told me what to do to protect her. I used the red peppers for that. I also baked my birthday cake today, but you said nothing to me. You never even wished me happiness, Papa."

His expression quickly changed one of surprise. He cleared his throat. "It was your mother who remembered birthdays, Angelina." His voice had lost its usual austerity.

"If you don't remember me, then I have no one."

Domenico put his arm around his daughter and kissed her cheek. "I am sorry, Angelina. The day has many hours and doesn't end until midnight. Happy birthday. I promise to do everything in my power to ensure you have the security in your life that I never knew in mine. That's my gift."

Angelina had no illusions. Life with her father wouldn't be the same as before her mother died, and she was unsure if this birthday promise was a blessing or something else.

DOMENICO NOW CONFERRED with Angelina on minor things, like which wholesalers had the best prices on olive oil and imported cheese. She was certain guilt was responsible for the change, though it would have been more meaningful if she'd been allowed to make the orders. As the weeks collected, something else seemed to disturb Domenico. He opened the cash register and pulled out the afternoon's receipts.

"For years, the Scazzari family was in business. Now they've closed their store." He shook his head. "Such good people."

"I wonder why. We can hardly keep up with all our orders," said Angelina.

"And tomorrow, a new day starts. Who knows what it will bring? Some customers can build your business; others can destroy it." Domenico placed his receipts next to the ledger and opened the door to the house. "Your brothers are out back building a chicken coop, but do you hear any hammering? No. It's quiet in the store. Lunch is over, and everyone's belly is full."

"Everyone's but mine."

"And who's tied you to a chair? If you're hungry, eat. I'll be back."

Angelina laughed to herself. In the quiet that followed, she cut open a fresh bread roll from Rizzo's Bakery and rummaged through the bottles of olive oil for one of her father's personal extra virgin, first cold-pressed. It was in a dark bottle, always protected from light. Since he'd pressed olives with stone wheels in Sicily, he'd lectured her how heat spoiled the flavor. He also saved the best for himself and never put it in the same place twice. Angelina suspected he hid his oil because he thought no one else appreciated the difference.

Angelina checked the shelves, moved bottles and boxes, and then . . . "Aha," she said. This time the oil stood next to the aged balsamic vinegar—another favorite. She sprinkled her bread with both oil and vinegar, eager to savor the subtle difference, unlike her brothers, who never paused long enough when eating to notice such a thing.

All things had an order, and so the cold cuts were no exception. Domenico stored them small to large, mild to hot, and moist to dry. Angelina reached for the Genoa—her favorite, along with the premium prosciutto ham, so finely cut that any thinner, she'd see through it—a real delicacy.

The finocchiona came wrapped in memories of her mother. She'd told her the story of a thief who once stole a roll of fresh salami and hid it in a barrel of wild fennel. When he returned, the salami had absorbed the aroma of the fennel with a flavor fit for Roman gods. Angelina cut herself a slice. She suspiciously eyed the mortadella. Her father said the name meant "dead mule." Unsure whether this were true, she'd lost her appetite for it long ago.

After adding mozzarella, provolone, tomatoes, and roasted peppers to the bread, she took her first bite and closed her eyes to savor the flavor. The aroma overtook her senses, and the taste awakened legions of her taste buds. Angelina had grievances about her father, who acted as though he still lived in Europe, but his love of Italian food was not one of them. She was grateful for his knowledge of food and couldn't imagine life without it. She kissed her fingertips like her father did when something was delicious, and then she declared to the four walls, "This is the finest Italian sandwich the world has ever known."

At that moment, the door flew open and bounced against the wall, the windows rattling. Two men burst into the store, knocked over a display, and slammed the door shut. Their abrupt destruction and harsh expressions left no doubt as to who they were and what they wanted.

Sheer terror ignited in Angelina. She had seen them before and knew immediately the evil that drove the Black Hand. Even the police could not stop la Mano Nera. Known for unspeakable viciousness, they had no conscience in committing crimes and no remorse after. Worse, no one in the Italian neighborhood dared report them.

The taller of the two had an overgrowth of dense black hair that appeared to cast a shadow over his eyes. He moved about the store as if taking inventory and chewing on his cigar. The heavier one drew a gun and spun its cylinder. Everything in the room except the gun faded to the edge of Angelina's consciousness. The man tossed his weapon from his right hand to his left and back again, like a set of keys. Then he spied Angelina.

"You're Pirrello's daughter," he said, coming closer. It wasn't a question. The thought of being identified by such men depleted her strength. Her arm dropped, and the finest Italian sandwich the world had ever known fell to the floor.

CHAPTER 7

The tall man glared at Angelina. It was a silent threat, accentuated by the unmistakable evil emanating from his malevolent eyes. "Where's your father?" He tossed his cigar at his feet and ground it into the floor with his shoe.

If fear and danger had a scent, she'd inhaled it. Nothing good would come of this. *Are they here to harm my father?* She bit her tongue to keep from screaming, afraid of inflaming their wrath.

The taller man seemed more in charge and glanced around the store. "What do you think, Matteo? Is it time this man Pirrello learned half a loaf is better than no loaf at all?" He reached for the sign on the door, flipped it to closed, then turned the lock and lowered the window shade.

Angelina stepped back, but the tall man moved closer and grabbed her by the arm. He reeked of liquor, making his closeness more frightening.

"There are other ways to pay a debt," he said as he gazed down at Angelina's figure and, in one blindingly fast movement, forcefully grabbed her breast. She quickly pushed his hand away. "Don't touch me!" she bellowed without considering their violent temperaments. Anger quickly became fear. What was this man capable of doing next? La Mano Nera smothered the air with their threats of evil. Known to have no conscience, no morality, and whispered that they'd forced a baker inside his oven.

The tall man laughed at Angelina, a peal of cruel laughter laced with sharp edges meant to injure.

Matteo, who looked even shorter because of his robust size, made his way around the cans and packages of food, knocking them about and breaking jars of olives and tomatoes. No recent immigrants arriving from the poverty of Southern Italy could achieve Matteo's bulk. He must have been a criminal back in Italy, or he had arrived long ago and began his life of corruption and violence.

He slipped behind the counter, picked up a roll of the costliest prosciutto, and bit off a piece. "*Magnifico.* You know, my grandfather had a little grocery store. I worked for him and ate more than he paid me. When he caught me filling my pockets with his money, he chased me down the street with his belt." Matteo huffed, taking a deep breath between every few words, and pushed up his cap with the point of his gun. "That old man sure could run." He took another bite. "We'll enjoy doing business here, Benedetto."

Benedetto? Blessed? Angelina's eyes widened. Such a name is echoed in church and prayers. Amid the shattered jars and bottles he'd knocked over, the tightness in his glaring eyes, and the grip of the knife he pulled out and was now flashing at her, it seemed inconceivable his mother had named him Blessed.

Benedetto kept his focus on Angelina. "Without protection, a grocery store becomes a dangerous place. When you pay for protection, we're happy, and you're happy. Capisci? It's a suitable arrangement. Ask other shopkeepers."

With a click, the blade shot out from Benedetto's stiletto. He went to the window and with long, harsh strokes, pierced the shade, tearing it in half. "Once, I cut a man in half. Remember, Matteo?"

"Like a butcher with a slab of meat."

Benedetto stepped up to the counter and swung his arm high, knocking over trays of cold cuts and cheese and smashing bottles of olive oil and vinegar.

Angelina's thoughts of what they might do to her father became frantic. She'd already lost her mother. Matteo went behind the counter, pulled out a knife meant for cutting meat, and pierced a fifty-pound bag of salt. He dragged the blade clear across and watched as the salt amassed on the floor. Angelina watched too, nervously smoothing her palms over her skirt.

"Once, salt was precious," Matteo said.

The adjoining door swung open, and Pasquale bounced in, beaming.

"Zio Pasquale," Angelina stammered.

Pasquale stopped short, his brilliant smile evaporating. Angelina grew more frantic for both of them when Benedetto raised his gun and pointed it at her uncle.

"Signor, maybe you make the terrible mistake," Pasquale said.

Matteo narrowed the distance between them. He pulled a paper from his vest pocket and pressed it against Pasquale's chest. "Get her father and give him this."

"Is okay. I gonna get him for sure." Pasquale stepped to the side and, with a firm grip, grabbed Angelina by the arm, pulling her behind him and shielding her with his body. Angelina expected the men to grab her other arm, but they didn't.

"You have four minutes. After that, your inventory becomes garbage."

Pasquale backed out of the store, through the door to the house, and rushed to the backyard without releasing his grip on Angelina's arm.

Once outside, he shouted, *"Domenico, vieni qui, fa presto! Domenico!"*

Pasquale didn't need to use words. He handed Domenico Matteo's cryptic message—a hand imprint pressed in coal, a crudely drawn dagger, and a hangman's noose.

Domenico held only the edge of the paper, as though it could scorch him. He crumpled it and, in a flash of rage, threw it across the yard. "See that, Pasquale? We came to America, and the devil came too."

Pasquale mopped his forehead with a handkerchief. "The devil, he bring a gun and a knife."

Domenico placed his hand on Angelina's shoulder. "Hurry and tell Signore Trezza to come quickly. If he asks why, say la Mano Nera."

"Maybe I should run to the police," Angelina offered.

"That would be far too dangerous."

"Papa, please don't go into the grocery store. One of them said he cut a man in half like he was a slab of meat, and you have no weapon." Angelina's heart beat like a stampeding horse.

"We have one weapon. Do as you're told. Get Signore Trezza."

"Papa—"

"Go!"

Angelina turned on her heels and rushed through the backyard until she reached her neighbor's home, where she pounded on the door, crying, "Signor Trezza, Signor Trezza!"

The front door opened slowly to reveal their aging neighbor, who took a moment to put on his glasses.

"Angelina, why are you trying to break down my door?"

"My father needs you right away. La Mano Nera is in the store."

The old man's kindly expression dissolved. He stepped outside and pulled his keys from his pocket, fumbling with them as though trying to remember which one locked his house. "Forget the door," he said. "There's no time to waste."

This had to be some kind of mistake. "What will you do?" Angelina asked.

"Take care of it," he muttered.

None of this made sense. Angelina reached for his hand and led him over the rows of vegetables, up the back steps, and into the house.

"You stay here," he said. "Anyone can frighten a lion from a window, but it's another thing to enter its den." The old man went through the home's adjoining door into the grocery store and closed it behind him.

If only her father hadn't installed such a thick door, she'd be able to hear more than faint, indistinguishable voices.

"Angelina." Her brothers came in. "Papa told Vinny to clean out the chicken coop," said Filippo.

"No, it's your turn," Vincenzo hollered back.

"Shh! Be quiet," Angelina whispered. "Clean the chicken coop together, and I'll give you each an extra pastry tonight."

The offer accepted, the two brothers bumped into each other leaving. Angelina turned and pressed her ear against the coolness of the adjoining door. Though louder, the voices were still undecipherable until the small bell's high-pitched timbre signaled a departure.

Angelina cautiously opened the door and saw her uncle sweeping away the salt and thanking Signor Trezza. Her father's troubled expression remained as he picked up the displaced cans and boxes. Angelina walked inside and glanced about the room. With nothing new out of place, no signs of a struggle, and no one hurt, quite puzzled, she looked in her father's direction. She never imagined such a peaceful outcome. *Still, they couldn't have just walked away—not those two,* she thought.

Domenico rolled up the slashed window shade, and sunlight filled the store again. Angelina grabbed some rags to soak up the spilled olive oil and vinegar and began removing the shattered glass. She waited for her father to say something, but he remained silent until he'd washed away all traces of these men. Domenico turned the sign on the door to open and signaled for Angelina to come to the back.

"What happened, Papa?"

"Several years ago," Domenico explained, "Signore Trezza's son, Nico, went to New Orleans to work on the docks and met the Lioni brothers. They were worse than La Mano Nera. They robbed everyone, Italian or not. The two had been extorting money longer than anyone. They taught Nico an easy way to make money—carry a gun and shoot whoever's in your way. So Nico returned to his old neighborhood and became the devil to his countrymen."

Angelina trembled.

"However, there is honor among the dishonorable. For years, we have done many favors for Nico's father. As you know, he is kind and old. Those men today work for Nico. When they saw his father walk in—they left out of respect and fear of Nico."

"They left?" Angelina remained incredulous. "They were so intent on . . ." she searched for the right word, "extortion."

"Look at all the damage they did because they didn't know Nico's father is our friend and neighbor. What happens when the next criminals come? What happens when the old man dies?" Domenico spoke uncommonly low.

"These men will not leave us in peace." The faraway look in his eyes made Angelina wonder if these men had revived something terrible in his memory from long ago. "There is a reason I tell you this, Angelina. We all fear different things, but you can't ignore violence." Domenico narrowed his eyes and put a hand on her shoulder. "Fathers protect daughters. I want you to tell me everything that happened when you were alone with them."

Angelina stiffened at the question, her mind reliving the uncomfortable confrontation. She hesitated a moment, then gave a carefully worded account. "They burst through the door, knocked things over, and asked where you were, Papa. I didn't tell them. I'm so glad they're gone."

"Angelina, I want to know if they harmed you or touched you. These men were born no good. They would only have been altar boys to steal the church's offerings."

She bit her tongue.

"Well?"

She cleared her throat and again chose her words cautiously, avoiding her father's eyes. "The tall man reached for me and grabbed me here." She put her hand on her chest and spoke quickly and clearly so she didn't have to repeat it.

Her father's face turned red with rage as his fury erupted. *"Figlio di puttana.* Let them burn in hell. They're garbage. Dirt. Pigs. *Stronzi*!" He waved his fists. "What else happened, Angelina?"

"Nothing." She hated his questions, hated the fact she had been alone in the store, hated that these men had no conscience.

"Are you telling me the truth?"

"Why would I lie?" She clenched her jaw.

"I don't want you in the store alone. Tomorrow you'll go with Zio Pasquale."

Angelina recognized the resolve in her father's voice. "Go where?" she asked.

"I've spent the last year talking to Marco about the threats to his dry-goods store only one block away, and the threats to himself and his family. These men destroyed him. What I'm doing is protecting you. The only safe solution is for you to go."

Angelina frowned and wrung her hands. The look on her father's face made her uneasy. "Go where, Papa?"

"Pasquale will look for work in the cigar factories tomorrow. You'll go too. He'll accompany you every day, and at work, a hundred employees will surround you. There's safety in numbers. These men can't touch you." He glanced across the store at the deli. "Get something to eat, Angelina." As quick as a magician's trick, the life she knew was vanishing. "You think I can eat?" she shouted. "I *have* to go to school tomorrow. I have to turn in my essay on the Civil War. I have a big test."

"It's time you went to work. How old are you?"

Everything her father said offended her. "If you can't remember how old I am, how do you know it's time I went to work?" As usual, Domenico didn't answer her questions, and his expression remained unaltered. "I'm sixteen, Papa. Remember the birthday you forgot? You see how hard I study—and you want me to stop? I go to school, stay in the house and study, do household chores, and come in and help you, but I can stay away. I'm not even here most of the day."

"And when summer comes, you'll be here all day. You'll go to work and be there all day. You live in the cigar capital of the world. People come from every country to find work here, and all you have to do is walk down the street."

"Please don't do this. My teacher told Mama I'm the best student she's ever had. She said I could be anything I want—anything," she pleaded.

Domenico's hands fell to his sides. "Those men walked into my store today, took one look at my school-aged daughter, and saw a blossoming woman. The more they see you, the more they'll think of you, and they're already watching you."

"How do you know that?" Angelina stuttered.

"They told you to get your father. Two or three customers told me they've seen them at the train station, watching people entering the store. I just told you what happened to the Scazzari family. After years of building a business, they had to close their doors. The pressure of being robbed every week was too much."

Angelina felt a wave of emotion, like a train going too fast with no way to stop it.

"The Scazzaris don't have a daughter. I do. The best way to gain control of me is by terrorizing my daughter. They prey on Italians, not on the Cubans or Spaniards who run the cigar factories. You'll be safe at a factory, and should they return to the store, you won't be here. Violent men stop at nothing to get what they want. In that alone, they're predictable."

As quickly as the salt had poured from the ripped bag, all hope spilled from Angelina's heart. She clung desperately to every grain she could. "It's not my fault. You shouldn't punish me. I want to stay in school, learn, and become a writer, a teacher—become something."

Her father looked around the store as though weighing the events of the day. "A furious storm passes quickly, but if this one returns, I don't want you here."

"There has to be another way. I won't come into the store. I'll stay in the house." Perhaps he confused her with her brothers, who would delight in quitting school. Her mother would have found another way.

Domenico frowned. "Do you think men who kick and

break everything in their path can't open the door to a house? Inside a factory, you're protected, surrounded by people. Cigar factories have guards. La Mano Nera is a gang of thieves and worse. Some use the name and operate alone, some in groups of two and four. And every day they grow more violent."

Domenico glanced at Pasquale as he swept and talked to the old man. "You see how much I love my brother? I know that *stronzo* Benedetto. He killed his own brother, and for what? Money. Those men will never enter a cigar factory or bother anyone who works there. Cigar barons are powerful; they pay big money to politicians and the police."

Angelina's shoulders slumped in desperation. "There must be some other way," she said again.

"Who am I, Angelina? A simple grocer. I sell food and make sandwiches, but if those men hurt you, I'll strike back whatever the cost. It's dangerous for both of us and the family. I didn't look for danger—it burst through my door." The muscles in his face tightened. "Long ago, I learned a harsh lesson. When force and reason collide, reason is never enough. Force will always win."

In less than an hour, through no fault of her own, strangers shattered all her dreams. "It's not fair, Papa. Two men destroyed my life."

Her father didn't respond. He never repeated what he knew he'd made clear. She turned away, pushed the screen door open with more force than necessary, and let it slam behind her. She stood on the porch, shaking in anger, ready to lash out, but instead, the tears fell.

A flapping noise drew her attention to a small bird nesting under the eaves. Again and again, the bird tried its wings to no avail. And then it abruptly gained momentum and soared into the sky. Angelina kept her eyes on it until she could no longer follow its flight.

Her heartbeat quickened, her breathing grew more intense, and she squeezed her eyes shut as she vicariously imagined the depth and breadth of soaring through the sky and observing all the wonders and possibilities of the earth below. She made a vow to fly away too.

CHAPTER 8

The sun rose, but Angelina remained in bed, her arm over her eyes to shield herself against this day of dread.

"Angelina, I want to talk to you." Her father's voice burrowed its way through the door.

Already dejected, she wanted to hide beneath her covers. Even better, climb out the window.

"All right. I'm coming." She saw no reason to rush as she glanced at her reflection in the oak mirror that once hung in the parlor but now lived in her bedroom. It still bore the cracks where Giuseppe had thrown a toy at it. If her mother had lived, her father would have repaired it that day, but he'd lost his drive.

The mantel clock chimed like a warning of unpleasantness to come. With trepidation, Angelina opened the adjoining door into the grocery store. The aroma of pasta sauce permeated the air. The longer it simmered, the better it tasted, so Domenico had started his preparations early for the lunch crowd. He sat at the table, puffing on his cigar and making notes in the *libretto,* where customers confirmed their charges signed with the letter *X*. Angelina never understood the concept when every *X* looked like every other *X*.

"I thought I'd walk to see my friend Sophia Esposito and drop off my essay so she can turn it in and I won't fall behind. Education is important, Papa. The world is changing."

"Not our world."

Pasquale burst into the room. Both father and daughter looked up.

"Buon giorno, famiglia. Today, I start my new life in America, and I gonna make you proud. People gonna say, 'Angelina, is that you Zio Pasquale?' He work so hard. And to you, Domenico, they gonna say, 'Such a fine brother you have.'" Pasquale appeared oblivious to the tension in the room. "Angelina, I have good news for you. Last night I go outside to take the garbage, and you can no believe what happened to me."

Angelina wanted to press her argument with her father, but Pasquale's look of enthusiasm dampened the fire in her belly. "What happened, zio?"

"Signora Bertelli's cat, she look at me and sneeze." Pasquale grinned as though awaiting congratulations.

Angelina glanced in her father's direction. He smiled but didn't look up from his libretto.

"What does that mean?" asked Angelina.

"When a cat, she sneeze, you have the good luck. We go see Signora Bertelli's gray cat again. She look pretty sick to me, and when she sneeze, the good luck is gonna be just for you."

"That's all right, zio."

"Angelina, you *non* capisci? How *two* people gonna find work with only *one* good luck?"

Angelina smiled at her uncle. "I'm not sure sneezing cats bring good luck." She put up a hand to stop her uncle from arguing and glanced in her father's direction. "But if I come home unemployed, I'll reconsider."

Pasquale shook his head. "We still get the cat to sneeze for you." He looked at his niece, then glanced up at the ceiling. "And the birds. They fly inside the house?"

"No. A bird didn't fly in the house. Are they good luck too?"

"*Mama mia,* birds in the house is bad luck. So we have the one good luck and no bad luck. We go now, Angelina."

Angelina let the door slam behind her as she followed her uncle to the feline in question on their neighbor's porch. There she waited while her uncle paced. Nothing happened. Pasquale patted her on the back. "You no worry. We gonna share one good luck."

THEY WALKED several blocks and came to the first of the almost two hundred cigar factories in the city, the Garcia-Marcos Cigar Company. It stood draped in whitewashed frame construction, as though angelic amid a battalion of warring red brick buildings.

"*Che fortuna.* Angelina, we come to the right place." Pasquale held the door for her. Inside, the aroma of tobacco seemed to ooze from everywhere, even the walls. It burned Angelina's eyes and invaded her nostrils. She considered running, but her uncle's trusting expression and overwhelming optimism overpowered her.

"Non ti preoccupare. Don't worry. Everybody gonna be so happy to see us."

Inside, another door appeared with the word *Office* in gold lettering on its glass. Again, her uncle held it open and quickly greeted the gray-haired man bent over his desk. "We come to work for you in this very nice *fabbrica di sigaro.*"

Angelina glanced at the man seated behind the desk. She objected to his graying hair and crumpled suit. She made no effort to smile in the hope he didn't like her either.

"We call this place *la tabaquería,*" said the man.

Determined not to impress him or look him in the eye, Angelina stared at the man's teeth. One front tooth attempted to grow over the one next to it. She wondered if he had considered extracting it, but it might leave too wide a gap. Perhaps he should extract the tooth beneath the wayward one, though it seemed unfair to remove a straight tooth to leave a distorted one. After much deliberation, Angelina left the man's teeth as she found them.

"This is my niece Angelina. Do you want we should work today, or tomorrow is better?" Pasquale seemed overjoyed.

The man leaned back in his chair. "We have no room for your niece, and who said we wanted you?"

Angelina breathed easy.

"Signor, we are the best." Pasquale flashed a charming smile.

"Have either of you ever rolled a cigar?"

"No," said Pasquale, undaunted and enthusiastic.

"Have either of you ever stripped a tobacco leaf, humidified leaves, or even set foot in a tabaquería?"

Angelina had never been to a job interview, but it pleased her to think this one might be going rather badly.

"Si, signor, today we set foot in la tabaquería. And you no can find nobody more better."

The man sat upright in his chair and shook his head. "I'll give you a chance, but you'll start at the bottom as a *mojador,* humidifying leaves. Then we'll see how 'more better' you are. Pablo Fernandez will make room for your niece."

What? What happened to 'we have no room for your niece'?

Ordered to another office, Angelina encountered a big man with large, matching circles of perspiration under his armpits and a feast of paperwork before him. He hadn't noticed her, so she turned to slip out, but Pasquale's voice shook the air. "Angelina, non ti preoccupare. Don't forget, you tell Signore Fernandez you are the very best."

Angelina blinked the vision away.

"Te vamos a cuidar y darte trabajo, chica," the perspiring man said to his pile of papers.

"I don't speak Spanish," Angelina replied.

He looked in her direction. "This is a tabaquería. Everybody speaks Spanish. What's your name?"

"Angelina Pirrello." Angelina glanced at the clock on the wall. She should be in class, not trying to get a job she didn't want, to work in a place she didn't like, and make cigars she didn't smoke.

"Italiana?"

"Sicilian."

"So your family is from Santo Stefano Quisquina, Province of Agrigento, Sicily."

Angelina gasped. Her eyes snapped back to sweaty Pablo Fernandez's face.

"I read minds." The big man gave a hearty belly laugh that made his cheeks jiggle. "Would you like to learn how I know so much about you?"

Angelina closed her eyes for a moment and prepared herself for the invasion of her mind. *Yes, I would,* she thought.

He reached into a drawer, withdrew a rather thick book, and turned it toward her. "Tell me what it says."

She glanced at the column "Place of Origin" and saw the Sicilian vernacular Girgenti for Agrigento province. "I guess everyone followed someone else here," she said.

"These are the names of the smart ones who left," he said.

In case he meant to be humorous, she forced a feeble smile.

"You're fourteen, right?"

Angelina stiffened at his remark. "I'm sixteen." She understood the fullness of his question. Children as young as seven worked in factories all over the country, as long as they *said* they were fourteen.

"You'll be an *espalilladora*. Do you know what that is?"

"No."

"You'll remove the stems from tobacco leaves, careful not to tear them. It requires nimble fingers. Do you think you can do that?"

Angelina nodded. It sounded boring, like plucking chickens. Too bad Fernandez couldn't read her mind after all.

"Start learning Spanish today. Tobacco leaves are humidified by a mojador. You'll receive them when they're moist, and you'll strip off their stems. After that, we send them to men we call *los selectores.* They separate the leaves according to color and quality and send them to the cigar makers, who roll the best cigars in the world." He paused and gave Angelina a quizzical stare. "Do you want to work here?"

Such an outrageous question. Angelina met his eyes and gritted her teeth before answering. "Yes, I'd like to work here." This was the greatest lie she had ever spoken, a sin worthy of the confessional and a harsh penance. It pained her to have said it, but the words marched obediently out of her mouth, like a unit of tin soldiers under her father's command.

Fernandez sifted through his papers while humming something annoying. He handed her a slip of paper. "Make your mark."

Infuriated by the assumption that she couldn't write her name, Angelina reached for the paper and read it aloud to show him she was neither illiterate nor gullible. She also suggested a comma where needed, grabbed the pen, and—contrary to her well-practiced penmanship—scribbled out her frustration should she need to deny the authenticity of her signature in case it proved necessary to do so.

"Perfect." Señor Fernandez rose from his desk, stepped into the doorway, and motioned to a young man in the hall who had his thumbs tucked under his suspenders. "Jorge, this is Angelina Pirrello. Take her to the third floor."

The third floor—it sounded disagreeable, bleak, and a lot of steps to climb.

Jorge gestured for Angelina to follow him. When they reached the top floor, he swung open a double door to reveal a great room with high ceilings, legions of long tables in parallel formation, and women peering over anthills of tobacco leaves.

The smell assaulted Angelina's senses, and she screwed up her features in revolt. Her eyes burned, her nose itched, and she could almost taste the odor. This would have been the time to run, but it was too late. Her uncle knew they had hired her.

"You'll get used to it, chica," said Jorge.

She stepped back, hoping she'd faint and they'd have to carry her out, but nothing happened. Women pulled tobacco leaves off their stems. Their arms moved up and down, over and over. Though she'd never been on a boat, Angelina felt what must be seasickness.

"This is where you'll work." Jorge led Angelina to an empty chair at the first table, but she didn't take her seat. Instead, she dashed to an open window, gulped in several deep breaths, and gazed down at the street. Too far to jump.

"Sit down. It'll all pass in a few weeks," said Jorge with a yawn.

In a few weeks, she'd have failed in school, but she'd be able to breathe in the overpowering scent of tobacco without feeling nauseated. It seemed an absurd exchange.

Angelina took her seat before a table clinging to the last

remnants of its varnish. An older man, bent and expressionless, walked past and threw a pile of tobacco leaves down where she sat. They appeared a half a foot long and could not imagine what to do with them.

"Carmen," Jorge said to the young woman seated next to Angelina. The woman held a brilliant smile and had her hair pinned in a bun. "This is Angelina Pirrello." He turned to Angelina. "And this is Carmen. She'll tell you what to do." He walked away.

"Don't mind Jorge. He hasn't smiled since he was six, and even then they had to pay him a penny." Carmen had one of those rare infectious laughs and a voice that rose as it gained momentum.

Angelina giggled. "What does he do here? Does he work on this floor?" Angelina asked.

"All I ever see him do is go up and down the stairs. Some job, huh?" Carmen picked up a tobacco leaf. "Don't worry, you'll learn fast, Angelina. All you have to do is pull the leaves from the stems. It's as easy as fishing in a barrel."

Carmen had a flawless complexion and the unmistakable radiance of youth. She appeared about Angelina's age, maybe a year or two older, but her enthusiasm made Angelina hope something more intriguing had yet to reveal itself. So far, she noticed the dark tobacco leaves had stained Carmen's hands. Angelina wondered how long it took for that to happen.

"Will my fingertips turn brown right away?"

Carmen giggled. "With soap and water, they'll turn pink again. Just do as I do," said Carmen, "and you'll catch on quickly."

Angelina rubbed her hands together as if consoling them for what was forthcoming, then cautiously picked up a leaf with two fingers. She pulled at it slowly, analytically, noting its texture and its resistance to separate from its stem.

"No, not like that. Like this. See the spine in the middle?

Rip off the right side of the leaf and make a pile. Then rip off the left side and make another pile. Two sides. Think of a Cuban sandwich." Carmen giggled again.

Angelina had no trouble understanding it when put like that.

"Cigar makers roll the right side tightly with the left. The darkest leaves have the richest flavors. They wrap the finest leaves around inferior filler leaves, just like the wealthy wrap their arms around the poor." Then she laughed.

Angelina sat with her back to the windows, the sun spilling over her shoulders as she tried to adjust to the powerful odor and follow instructions. She glanced around at the other women. "Carmen, have these women worked here long?" said Angelina. It seemed improbable that anyone could spend years stripping leaves.

"It's not so bad here. Cigar workers belong to social clubs. We have meetings, dances, picnics, and if you get sick, we have the hospital. Pirrello is Italian, right?"

"Yes." Angelina coughed, resisting the urge to hold her nose or race back to the window.

"L'Unione Italiana is for you Italians. We Cubans have El Círculo Cubano. The Spaniards formed El Centro Español. But every privilege has its price. For only 5 percent of what you earn, you can join." Carmen's grin widened. "It's your big chance to go to all the dances and fall in love. Now that's worth double the membership. Only last month I fell in love with handsome Manuel. He had lots of dark curly hair and big brown eyes, but I had to break up with him—too much wear and tear on my heart."

Angelina liked Carmen. The young woman was full of life and an entertaining distraction from what threatened to become a dreary existence. The young, fair-haired woman seated on the other side of Carmen tipped her head forward and smiled at Angelina. "I'm Rosa Caprici."

Angelina strained herself to return the smile. "It's nice to meet . . ." She couldn't finish. The odor overtook her. She jumped from her seat, dashed down the staircase, and out of the building into the street. Like a diver emerging from the sea, she took a deep, refreshing breath, cleansing her lungs with fresh air.

How did anyone get used to the smell? She debated running home when an elegant carriage pulled up and a well-dressed man stepped out. He walked in her direction, his cane held like a scepter. He tipped his hat to her as he passed, and then he entered the factory. Angelina took another deep breath of fresh air and followed ten steps behind as he climbed the staircase to the second floor. Every movement appeared practiced, fluid, and confident as he stepped inside the great room called *la galería*.

Whispers ran down the tables of cigar makers. "Don Carlos Madrid is here." The man's name alone sounded regal. "The best *lector* we've ever had," someone said in a hushed voice. Then the well-dressed man raised his regal cane, and all chattering stopped, the Garcia-Marcos cigar factory coming alive with silence. Even those walking across the plank floor now softened their steps. Angelina stood spellbound in the doorway, momentarily forgetting she was an employee hired to strip leaves and not observe this man.

Angelina remained transfixed. He had an aristocratic nose, a well-trimmed mustache, and a confident presence that implied he was a rung above the ordinary.

Halfway down the great room, between rows of male cigar makers in ties and white shirts and two lonely female cigar makers lacking any sense of formal attire, there sat a rostrum awaiting an occupant. At its base was a carving depicting the union of Castile and León—the shield of Spain. Angelina had seen the image on her father's cigar bands and wondered if this lector had descended from a royal lineage.

This man, Don Carlos Madrid, stepped up to the rostrum, placed his jacket on the railing, and gazed at the sea of eager faces. Intrigued, Angelina fell into the waiting vat of excitement.

"*Saludos, damas y caballeros.*" He raised his right hand as though giving a benediction. Those rolling cigars sat up and tapped their square *chaveta* knives against their worktables, replicating applause.

Don Carlos Madrid picked up a newspaper, and with the right measure of enthusiasm in his voice, events, conquests, and catastrophes came alive. "President Teddy Roosevelt announced yesterday that he would not seek a third term." The reader's voice captivated Angelina. She listened to an entire news article on presidential politics before realizing she had stood at the doorway longer than intended. What would her father say if she were hired and fired in the same thirty minutes? She quickly hurried up the stairs and took her place at the long table.

"Are you feeling better? We thought you died," said Carmen.

"You'll get used to it," Rosa said. "It happened to all of us in the beginning."

"I saw a man down on the second floor. Someone said he was el lector?" She said it like a question, although she wasn't sure what she intended to ask. "No one reads news like that, with such passion."

"Yes. The reader. He reads newspapers in the morning. In the afternoon, it's great poetry and classic literature. Ever hear of Shakespeare, Tolstoy, Dickens, Cervantes, or Hugo?"

Angelina raised both eyebrows, stunned to hear the list of authors. "Why, that's incredible." *How wonderful,* she thought. She might forgive this objectionable omission in her education for el lector's spellbinding tutelage.

Eager now for the big moment and almost giddy, Angelina asked, "When does he come to us?" said Angelina.

Carmen put another leaf on her pile. "He doesn't come to us."

Her stomach sank. "What? Why not?"

"He only reads to those rolling cigars."

Rosa leaned over once again. "You should look out the window this afternoon. Women who don't even work here gather near the open windows. They sit on blankets with picnic baskets, eager to hear a new installment of *Anna Karenina*. At dinner, they share the story with their families and, if their husbands roll cigars, even better."

"We have two choices," said Carmen. "We can join them outside and never get paid, or we can learn to roll cigars and work on the second floor. Everyone dreams of working on the second floor, which is why Rosa and I are learning to roll cigars."

WITH TIME, Angelina made fewer frantic dashes to the window or outside. She became accustomed to the potent scent of the tobacco leaves. Perhaps more precisely, she became less unaccustomed to it. The one enjoyment was her growing friendship with Carmen, who kept everyone laughing, and Rosa, with her sweet disposition. Rosa occasionally spoke to her in their Sicilian dialect, warning her about Dolores, the terror of the factory. Dolores never said anything nice and wasn't above tripping and knocking over other girls' piles of stripped leaves and then accusing them of clumsiness.

Angelina sighed. The days at the factory had collected into weeks and crept their way into nearly two months. Worse, the work remained monotonous and unfulfilling.

Angelina hoped something unexpected would occur to correct this tremendous error of her employment. Time was not her friend. It kept moving forward without preparing her for a successful future. To and from work posters of the suffragette movement appeared, demanding women's rights. Frustrated with the inability to control her life, Angelina stopped to read the passionate, bold-lettered outcries.

ANGELINA PICKED UP HER PACE, crossing streets and turning corners until she saw her old school friend Sophia Esposito waiting for her with a book in her hand.

She rushed over, and the girls embraced. "I can't tell you how much it means to me to borrow your textbooks," said Angelina.

"Well, here it is," said Sophia somewhat indifferently as she handed Angelina the book. "You've been gone a long time. The school year will be over soon." Sophia smoothed her soft, dark hair behind one ear. "You're my best friend, or at least you were until you became invisible and disappeared from our classroom, but I haven't replaced you—not yet."

Angelina gratefully accepted the book. "We'll always be best friends, even when school ends, and when we die, they'll bury us next to each other because we'll still be best friends," said Angelina with a giggle.

Sophia grinned. "Is that supposed to make me feel better?"

"I'll keep studying. I'll read all I can tonight and return the book tomorrow."

Sophia dropped her eyes and gazed at the book. "I don't need it. Keep it another day. If my father ordered me to quit school, I'd never look at another schoolbook. Most of what's in them will never affect our lives. I don't understand the point. Why does it matter if Columbus landed in 1492 or 1493 or 1592?"

Angelina opened the book and glanced through the pages. "Sophia, you give up too easily. You've been like this since we were children. If an egg doesn't break when you crack it, you don't go hungry. You crack it again. So read again."

Sophia let out a little laugh. "You sound like someone's old grandmother. Anyway, school isn't as much fun without you, but the boys are getting much better looking." She sighed. "No one explains lessons the way you do."

Angelina closed the book and gazed at her friend. "Make sure you keep up, Sophia, and we'll go to college together." Angelina hugged her again. "You're still my oldest friend. I miss seeing you every day."

Sophia had the most expressive, large eyes, but looked almost lost. "I know. When I walk past the school, I can almost see us there playing, like ghosts from a lifetime ago," said Sophia.

"Everything's changed. I work all day, and even though a neighbor's daughter comes to help with chores and attends to the children, there's always something left for me to do. I get an hour here and there to go to the park or walk along the beach, and I read until I fall asleep. I know it won't always be like this, Sophia. We'll make something of ourselves." Angelina's mind was crowded with dreams.

"Your father controls you way too much, and it's not for the best. My mother's sister lives in Colorado, but she used to work for the Suffragettes here in Tampa. Know why she moved there?" Sophia forged ahead without waiting for Angelina's answer. "Because she could hang up her sash. They civilized Colorado and a couple other states. Women can make their own decisions there. They have the right to vote in that state. You are too smart to be working in a factory." Sophia fidgeted with the lace on her dress. "Honestly,

Angelina, your life sounds miserable, like you're a slave. I intend to find a rich husband and never have to work."

"I wonder if you're related to my Zia Violetta. You sound like you could be her daughter."

"That's the rich relative, right?" Sophia's face lit up. "Then, yes, I think I'm her daughter."

"Nothing lasts forever, Sophia. Better get our education, just in case," Angelina warned. "Then we'll both move to Colorado."

Sophia wrapped her arm around Angelina's elbow. "I know a better way to change your life. You should plan to attend a small college in New York with me. It's near the larger universities, where we'll find rich husbands and get away from this immigrant world and overprotective Italian rule. It costs nothing to be poor, but it costs a lot of money to be rich. It's easier to marry into it. This is our chance, Angelina. Let's escape."

Angelina could not imagine her father paying for her to move a thousand miles away from his watchful eye. "My father isn't as trusting as yours, Sophia. There isn't the smallest chance mine would let me go."

"Well, don't give up."

Angelina hugged her friend goodbye, went home, and found her father reading the Italian newspaper. She dropped into a chair near him and opened Sophia's book on the American Revolution so he could observe how much she studied. In the room's quiet, with only the ticking of the mantel clock, Angelina sensed something troubling and glanced at her father. Not one to accept the news reported in the papers without voicing his opinion, he seemed too stoic. Still, his agitation seemed real, and he began turning the pages too quickly to read. Something was on his mind.

CHAPTER 9

Domenico glanced up from his newspaper. Angelina could feel him watching her as she read. For a while, he said nothing, but then he shook his paper. "In time, you won't be working at the cigar factory."

It had been months now. Had he changed his mind? Angelina's heart soared. Giuseppe came in, and she gave him a quick hug and a toy. She then directed all her attention to her father. "Is the threat of the Black Hand over, or did you change your mind about school?" It didn't matter which.

"The Black Hand is not a tempest that leaves a rainbow behind. It instills terror and leaves behind its wreckage." Domenico set down his newspaper. "You're becoming a woman, but you know little of the world." He paused for a moment, as though he were getting ahead of himself. "I'll find a nice Sicilian from a good family to keep you safe—you'll marry him, stay home, and have children."

"Wh-what?" Angelina's voice cracked, and a hard knot formed inside of her. "How can you say that? You have no idea who I might become if given the chance. I studied hard in school. Mama and I talked about my going to college, my future, and my dream to become a writer. I can go to college in New York and stay with Mama's cousins. I'd work so hard, Papa." Hadn't she done everything her father asked of her? He should reward her, not discard her to a stranger in a loveless marriage.

"Women are meant to care for their homes and families."

That's ridiculous. A hard, angry lump tightened in Angelina's stomach. "I refuse to settle for that."

Domenico walked toward the kitchen as though he'd made a simple request, like making a bed or peeling potatoes, not eradicating his daughter's free will and destroying her future.

Angelina tried to control the tremor in her voice and followed him. "You're surprising me with someone to marry? Incredible. The arrangement is absurd. The choice should be mine."

"I won't bring just anyone home. He'll be someone honorable who can take care of you and provide for you. Life isn't easy. I intend to protect you." Domenico calmly poured himself a glass of water.

"Papa, once I'm married, I'm married for life. If my husband thinks like you, I'll have no chance at an education. That's like having no life of my own, no dreams. Life is miserable without a dream. I want to marry someday, but not now, not today. You can't find someone for me and bring him home like a puppy. A husband has to be my choice, someone I love."

"Love. Love has many layers. Over time, you'll learn to love a man who provides well for you. It's always the way. A powerful love like the one your mother and I had can also become a curse because the pain I still suffer is almost unbearable and never leaves. I see my Carolina in everything. She haunts my dreams. I don't regret a moment of our lives together, but I don't want that for you. The risk is too great.

No one will replace her. I can never love like that again, and I'll spend the rest of my life alone." He sipped his glass of water and turned toward the parlor. "When you reach the right age, if you meet a *paisano* from a good family who has enough to give you a secure life, I'll consider him." He had little emotion in his voice and walked away as though that ended the conversation.

It seemed unbelievable that a man who loved so intensely believed she would accept such an arrangement. He'd misjudged her. She followed him into the parlor. "You say you'll consider him?" Angelina huffed. "Then you say he must be a paisano from a good family and have enough money for a comfortable life. So you're still picking him out."

"Young girls know nothing of men."

"If I'm a young girl, I'm not ready for marriage. If I'm a woman, I should choose my husband. It's only logical and realistic for women to rule themselves. All women deserve the right to lead the lives they choose. That's exactly why the Suffragettes are challenging the Constitution."

Domenico grunted. "A foolish notion and a waste of time. That law will never pass."

"Why do you still think the world is flat? Everything changes."

"Only the young think like that," said Domenico. "We may live in a new country, but hard work and an unfair world remain as always. It was the same world for my father and grandfather. Our job is to survive. Why should I think it's any different now?"

Angelina stomped her foot in frustration. "You traveled to America so your life would be different. No one arranged your marriage. Fathers don't arrange marriages in America, and America has nothing to do with Italy."

"Nothing? America has everything to do with Italy. America was discovered by one Italian and named after another." Domenico pulled out his libretto, took a seat, and began his daily entries.

Angelina marched past him but dropped one last word at his feet. "Never."

~

THE NEXT DAY might have been a pleasant one, except Angelina remained reticent as she walked to work with her uncle, scarcely listening to his high-spirited banter.

"Why you so quiet on such a nice morning. You no feel good?" Pasquale questioned sympathetically.

"I can't stop thinking about something Papa said yesterday. He thinks he's supposed to find me a husband, a Sicilian from a good family who can support me." Angelina's shoulders slumped as she walked along the wooden walkway.

"*Mama mia*, maybe a *masciata* come and see you papa."

"*Masciata*? Do you mean matchmaker? Are there such things in Florida?"

"*Si*. Everywhere. If somebody wanna marry you, and you papa say maybe, everybody come for dinner, and we eat mezzo-ziti. Mezzo mean 'half.' So, half a pasta, you half engaged."

"How can anyone be half engaged?"

"Is happen all the time in Santo Stefano. And if you papa say yes, you are for sure engaged and we eat pasta ziti." Pasquale gestured broadly with his hands.

"If I find either of those pastas in the house, I'll throw them out," Angelina said. "Papa's unreasonable."

"Did I no tell you what happen to Bruno Stettecassi?" Pasquale opened his eyes wide, the way he always did when a story was brewing. He nearly ran into an open shop door, his attention was so fixed on Angelina.

Angelina had too much on her mind. "No, Zio. Maybe. I don't remember."

Undeterred, Pasquale began. "Bruno, he have a beautiful daughter, Teresa. One morning a young man, Emilio, come to Bruno. He say 'I love Teresa so much. I wanna marry her.' So Bruno say Teresa is his treasure. If Emilio wanna marry her, he have to prove he is brave.

"Bruno say, 'I wanna you go to the graveyard next to the church, put flour all over you, lie down in a casket, and pretend you dead. If you spend the whole night, you can marry Teresa, but if you afraid—then no Teresa.' Teresa, she only have to smile, and Emilio feel so happy. So, he say okay."

Angelina was under no illusions. This story would not make her feel any better, but she let her uncle go on.

"The same day, Giovanni come to see Bruno. Giovanni say, 'I wanna marry Teresa.' Bruno, he tell Giovanni to go to the graveyard and find the casket with the dead man and pray all night for the man's soul, so the devil no take it. At first, Giovanni no wanna go, but Teresa smile, and Giovanni fall in love all over again."

The parallel between Bruno and her father did not escape Angelina. What was the matter with Bruno letting Teresa pick her own husband?

"In a little while, you no believe it, Angelina, but Sergio knock on the door: 'I can no stand it, Bruno, I love Teresa too much. I wanna marry her.' Bruno say, 'If Sergio wanna marry Teresa, he have to carry chains and pretend he is the devil. If he scare away the man praying over the dead man in the casket, Sergio gonna marry Teresa."

Angelina tightened her fists and nodded. She could well imagine her father also giving tests, but more practical ones, like serving the lunch crowd, taking inventory, and balancing the libretto.

"That night, Sergio come back in chains with red pasta

sauce all over him. You no gonna believe what happened next, Angelina."

She smiled at her uncle. "I'm listening to every word, Zio, and I hope this story has a happy ending because I'm feeling very sorry for Teresa right now." Her uncle had a flair for telling stories, and he was trying to lighten her mood, but she doubted this story had anything to do with her dilemma.

"Emilio is in the casket, like a dead man, but that no mean he is deaf. He hear Giovanni praying. Giovanni, he no deaf either, but he stop praying when he hear Sergio's chains, and when he see Sergio full of blood, Giovanni get so scared, he scream and run so fast."

Angelina was visualizing the scene and wasn't sure what entertained her more—the story or Pasquale's enjoyment in telling it.

"You remember Emilio is in the casket, and he hear Giovanni scream because he no deaf. So he open his eyes, and when he see Sergio holding the chains, he jump out the casket, cry for his Mama, and run so fast he almost catch Giovanni."

Angelina tightened her lips to hold back a giggle.

"Poor Giovanni, he look back and see the dead man chasing him. He run faster. Maybe Sergio look like the devil, but when he see a dead man jump out of his coffin, he call God to save him and run to the piazza. 'Wake up, everybody!' he say, but he still look like the devil. Nobody in Santo Stefano like the devil. So everybody chase him with the sticks; even the dogs wanna bite him."

Pasquale shook his head. "Poor Teresa. She no marry nobody."

Angelina burst into laughter, Pasquale laughing with her. However, her thoughts soon returned to her father. He'd said, 'in time,' which also allowed time for a plan. When they arrived at Garcia-Marcos, Pasquale walked down to the basement to moisten leaves, while Angelina made her way up to the third floor to strip the moistened leaves from their stems.

Suitors, devils, and ghosts vanished as she took her seat.

"Stay away from Dolores today," whispered Carmen.

"Why?" Angelina glanced back at the woman.

"It's called the black plague of the mouth. She told Esmeralda congratulations, and for what? For her husband running around last Saturday night with another woman."

"Is that true?" said Angelina.

"No. The man broke his leg in a work accident and can hardly move. Dolores enjoys making people miserable."

"She's too late. My father has already made me miserable." Angelina picked up a leaf and began working, hoping to distract herself from her father's foolish revelation.

Jorge appeared and glanced up and down the rows of tables, then headed in her direction with his usual vacant expression. "Señor Claudio Garcia wants to see you in his office . . . right now." Without further explanation, he turned and walked away.

A bit of a chill ran through Angelina at the sound of the name. She hadn't realized the Garcia of the Garcia-Marcos Cigar Company was Claudio. His name unearthed memories of Maria Martino and her resentment toward Angelina's mother for spurning her brother Claudio.

Zia Violetta had also hurled Claudio Garcia's name at her father like a weapon, shouting how her sister should have married this man who owned a factory and could provide her sister with a secure life. Angelina immediately saw the irony. These were the same qualities her father insisted she marry for. Garcia must have discovered Angelina's identity and decided to fire her himself. Angelina set down the tobacco leaf she held.

"What have you done?" Carmen raised her brows and

opened wide her expressive eyes but kept her voice low. "No one in this room has ever been called into Garcia's office. He deals with the men rolling cigars. I don't think he even knows who we are."

"If I don't come back, Carmen, I want you to know I consider you my friend. I appreciate all you've done to make me feel comfortable here," said Angelina.

Carmen shook her head. "*Ay, chica,* I don't like how that sounds."

Angelina stepped away from her workplace and envisioned the scene with Claudio Garcia. He probably wouldn't say he was firing her because her mother had picked her father over him. What would he say, and how would he word it?

Angelina walked down a flight of stairs as el lector entered la galería. The room grew still, and she stood at the doorway for a moment to watch the pageantry for the last time. Don Carlos Madrid greeted his audience and opened his book. On such a sultry day, he fanned the room with the breezes of Leo Tolstoy's tale. She walked down another flight of stairs to the largest office on the main floor. Termination did not upset her, but if Claudio Garcia was anything like his sister Maria, he'd begin with a verbal onslaught, then drag her out by her hair.

Angelina knocked on the office door and stepped inside. Mahogany dominated the walls, floor, and furniture, and she saw no purpose to the massive mirror framed in gold tobacco leaves. It made her feel small, unimportant, and out of place. She had not imagined Claudio Garcia as bald or overweight. When he looked up, his dark eyes held a glint of warmth, and he wore a pleasing smile, which made Angelina wonder if he was truly related to Maria Martino. He had a rounder face and much thicker bone structure than his sister, and though he remained seated, she suspected he was shorter than Maria.

"Angelina Pirrello." Claudio announced her name as though it were part of a roll call for frightened immigrants at Ellis Island.

Angelina nodded.

"I wondered if you were enjoying your job here?"

The radical question surprised her. Was this the method he used to fire people? Make them admit they liked their job, then throw them out? How could anyone enjoy a job so tedious, a chair so hard, and so many people working so close together day after day in the sweltering heat? She hedged a moment before answering. There was one positive. "Time goes fast when el lector's stories are passed down to the rest of us."

"Ah yes, el lector. If factory owners had their way, there would be no readers at all. The workers hold auditions for new readers, choosing from anarchists, troublemakers, and carnival acts who read the news to incite unrest. Ignore Don Carlos Madrid."

Ignore him? The stories were talked about everywhere. Work would be intolerable without a reader. Discouraged, Angelina gritted her teeth. "Señor Garcia, you sent for me. Is there something you'd like to tell me?"

Claudio cleared his throat and paused. "Although we have never met, I knew your mother and recognized your strong resemblance to her the first time I saw you. You even have her mannerisms, like the way you tilt your head right now."

Angelina straightened her head.

"I'd like you to know I'll watch over you as though you were my dau—I mean, the way your mother would have wanted me to look after you, of course."

Why is he saying this? She was immediately uncomfortable.

He sighed. "I want you to know you can come to see me anytime. We can just talk if you like."

She could not imagine leaving her work to come to his office just to talk. This entire conversation felt awkward enough.

"Thank you for your offer, Señor Garcia. That's so kind of you." Angelina intended to never enter his office again. "If it's all right, I'll return to work now." She surrendered a token grin that narrowly curled the corners of her lips.

He returned a brilliant one.

Angelina returned to her seat at her usual table, and Carmen scooted her chair closer. "So, what's the mystery? Did he give you a big raise, or is today your last day?"

"He mistook me for someone else." True enough. Claudio Garcia had confused her with her mother. If she hadn't looked like Carolina, he wouldn't even have noticed her.

"Too bad." Carmen sighed. "I thought you could put in a good word for me."

"Too bad for both of us." Angelina dismissed all thoughts of the man and readjusted to the muggy afternoon.

CLAUDIO GARCIA APPEARED at the door.

It had been two months since he'd called her into his office for that one simple conversation. "Have a good evening, Angelina. We'll see you tomorrow," he said.

Her cheeks flushed from embarrassment. He'd addressed her in front of the workers. To make matters worse, he didn't speak to anyone else.

"Yes. Thank you. You have a good evening also," she mumbled, moving quickly out of the building and into the street, though the crowd prevented her from slipping away as fast as she wanted. She glanced over her shoulder, hoping no one she knew had noticed this. It was a mistake.

Claudio Garcia looked straight at her and waved. She had no choice but to wave back.

"Wait up," Carmen called and hurried toward her. "How did you get so far ahead of us? You move like someone's chasing you."

Angelina slowed down, exhaled in relief, and forced a smile. If Carmen had seen the exchange, she would have said so.

"Consider yourself invited to our social club. Come to El Círculo Cubano Saturday night. We're having a dance." Carmen beamed. "The band's wonderful. You can meet my family, and you'll learn to dance *el ritmo* Cubano. We're the best dancers." Carmen gave her a wink and began dancing and singing as they walked. Not since her mother was alive had anyone happily danced around Angelina. It brought old memories to life, and she laughed.

"You never know who'll be there." Carmen spoke in a singsong voice that matched her dance moves. "There could be a handsome boy dying to meet you, and if you don't come, you'll break his heart."

Once again, Carmen made her laugh, and the awkward exchange with the factory owner slipped from her mind. "And if I go, my father will break a blood vessel."

"Then bring him along, and we'll teach him a few steps."

The thought of her father dancing to Cuban music made Angelina laugh even harder. Carmen continued her animated conversation, and by the time Angelina left her friend, she'd promised to ask permission to go. Carmen, with her lively spirit, had a gift for making others laugh, but all the playfulness evaporated when Angelina reached her front door. She sobered to the fact that El Círculo Cubano would have their dance without her.

As soon as she stepped inside, the house pulsed with the sound of children's voices. It hadn't been so long ago when one of those voices was hers. She waited until the noise quieted down to ask the hopeless question of her father.

"My friend Carmen has invited me to go to a dance on Friday. It's at El Círculo Cubano. Her family will be there."

"And you'll be here."

"She's invited you too."

"And I'll be here too."

CHAPTER 10

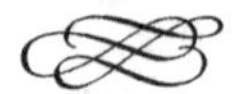

Angelina glided past the rows of benches in the park, headed for the one she favored. It sat under a tree with abundant branches where the leaves offered a soothing sound as they swayed in the soft breeze. When she reached it, someone else was there—a man with one book in his hand and one at his side. Surprised to see el lector, of all people, she hesitated. He appeared less regal seated on a bench rather than behind a podium, but he was just as well dressed, with a handkerchief in his breast pocket, and just as scholarly. He turned a page and looked up. Angelina felt a warm flush.

"You must be busy, Don Carlos Madrid. I won't bother you," she said.

"You know my name—and who are you?" he asked.

"I'm Angelina Pirrello, but I'm on the third floor. I've heard the cigar makers say the factory walls vanished when you read *Les Misérables*, and for two hours, they traveled back in time to France."

Don Carlos Madrid marked his page with a thin ribbon and closed his book. "I'm glad they feel that way. We learn many things when we read, and we travel to many places.

Victor Hugo writes, 'He never went out without a book under his arm, and he often came back with two.' Do you agree with that dedication to literature, Señorita Angelina?"

"Yes, I read as many books as I can."

"Hugo tells us of Jean Valjean's fondness for books—they were his friends."

Angelina paused reflectively. "I hope to write a book someday. I've been pulling apart leaves for many months now. I wish you could read to the rest of us."

El lector offered a vague smile and gestured for her to sit. "I can't be on two floors when I read in the factory, but I see you have a thirst for learning." He picked up his book, then glanced at Angelina. "I'll tell you a secret. No trip will be more meaningful, more magical, or more exciting than the trip you take all alone with a book and your imagination."

"I read all the time and would be eternally grateful for anything you can share." It thrilled Angelina to find herself in the presence of such a man. She sat nervously folding and unfolding her hands and trying not to fidget in her seat. "Why did you choose *Les Misérables* to read at the factory?" she asked to help distract him from her obvious nervousness.

"There are themes within these pages that resonate with those rolling the cigars—hard work, sacrifice, and fighting for a greater good for themselves and the generations to come. Hugo kept his hand on the pulse of the poor. Did you know he even ordered himself a pauper's coffin for his burial?"

"That's incredible." His knowledge extended to the authors. That intrigued her.

Don Carlos appeared to take a moment to study Angelina. "I used to teach literature. I miss it. They say that when the student is ready, the teacher will appear. I would enjoy hearing a young reader's view of the story." He paused and looked down at the book in his hands. "You remind me of myself at your age. Perhaps you can help me recapture those long-ago days of wonder." He handed Angelina Victor Hugo's book. "You may borrow it since Ybor City still doesn't have a library. I have a better copy I take to the factory. Return to this bench next Saturday morning at eleven o'clock, and we'll discuss what you read for a little while."

"Oh, thank you so much." Angelina could hardly believe her good fortune. This was her chance to learn literature from a master. "Thank you," she said again. "I'll start reading it today."

"Each author has a secret in how they season their novel, add multiple layers, and stir the plot."

Angelina giggled. "It sounds like a recipe."

"Precisely. Authors cook up a banquet of stories, then invite us to the feast." Don Carlos lifted his chin and sounded as though he still sat atop the factory podium.

"I love learning and appreciate it even more now that I haven't been able to attend school."

"Well, we must catch up and not live life envious of the past."

The humidity rose. El lector reached into his back pocket, pulled out a handkerchief. The one in his breast pocket remained undisturbed as he wiped the perspiration from his forehead. It's a shame so few at the factory read. Hugo said, 'To read is to light a fire.'" He got up and turned to Angelina. "Every teacher needs a student," he said. "Next week, Angelina." He turned and strolled away.

~

READING EXHILARATED ANGELINA. It propelled her through centuries, countries, and other worlds. By Monday, she'd passed the point of Don Carlos Madrid's bookmark.

"Hey, chica, what happened to you Saturday night?" Carmen waved a scolding finger as she took her seat.

Excited over literature, Angelina had forgotten about the dance. "I asked my father. He wouldn't let me go alone or come with me," she replied.

"What does he think will happen if he's with you?" Carmen eviscerated a tobacco stem with one precise, quick movement.

Angelina followed suit. "I don't know. My mother understood him. Now she's taken that secret with her."

"Well, keep asking until he gives his permission. He'll wear down. El Círculo Cubano is the best social club with the best dances."

Angelina's voice softened. "It's hopeless, Carmen."

"He can't be that bad."

"Yes, he can." Angelina imagined her father's rage if she kept asking the same question after he'd said no. Ever since he'd forced her out of school, they were like two lost ships—always adrift, floating in different directions.

As the day wore on, Angelina stripped leaf after leaf. With each new ripped stem, she thought less about her father and more about Victor Hugo. She was happily reliving the pages she'd read the night before when a stray glance brought her sharply back to reality. Claudio Garcia stood at the entrance looking at her. *Oh no.* Angelina grew warm.

"Hey, didn't you say the big boss thinks you're somebody else? Well, it looks like you didn't convince him," Carmen whispered.

Why is he doing this? "Maybe I should write my name on my dress."

"Better do it on your forehead, so he'll see it from a distance."

Angelina avoided looking up. Claudio might approach

her and start a conversation with others watching. The hair on her arms stood up.

"I'm not imagining it, Angelina—that man is staring straight at you." Carmen kept her voice low. "Why?"

"He knew my mother and wanted to talk about her. I'm not sure why."

"Well, talking can't hurt. Maybe he'll feel some compassion and increase your wages."

"You're a dreamer, Carmen."

Luckily, Claudio walked away. With only an hour left to work, Angelina willed the clock to move faster.

"Oh no, here comes his messenger." Carmen nodded. Jorge approached, stopping before Angelina.

"You're wanted again," he said.

Perhaps she should consider quitting before she gets fired, or ask Carmen to go with her, or refuse to go? Best to get it over with and be grateful Jorge didn't elaborate. Angelina hurried out before anyone asked questions. Once in front of the large office, feeling frustrated, she knocked twice and entered without an invitation. "Señor Garcia, is there something you need?" She kept her tone even.

Claudio looked up. "Please, Angelina, sit down."

She remained standing, saw the disappointment in his eyes, then took a seat.

He smiled and adjusted his position in his chair.

"I wanted to give you something. I thought you might like it." Claudio reached into a drawer in his desk, stared for a moment at what he held, and then handed Angelina a photograph of her mother. "I have another at home."

The unexpected image of her mother jarred Angelina, and a rush of gentle memories gripped her heart. Why did this man have a photograph of her mother? Perhaps she didn't want to know the answer. "It's beautiful. The way she was," Angelina forced herself to speak, although her throat had tightened.

Her mother couldn't have been much older than she was now, and her reflection in the photograph only enhanced the magnitude of Angelina's loss. Her mother wanted her to attend college and perhaps become a teacher or writer as she'd dreamed. Seeing her mother's photograph in the factory where she stripped tobacco leaves, the lowest of jobs, left Angelina feeling deflated. She sat up straight and stiffened her back. The picture gave her an unexpected surge of determination—one day she'd prove to herself to her mother.

"My cousin is a popular photographer. He took pictures of each of the Cacciatore sisters, so I asked him to make me a few copies of Carolina. Once, your mother and I were close, then I went to Cuba for several months. I should never have gone. I should have held her tight and not let go." Claudio Garcia lowered his head, perhaps embarrassed—or perhaps not.

I should have held her tight and not let go. The strange remark spun around inside Angelina and made her uncomfortable. "Thank you. I'm so grateful to have the picture. I'll keep it safe."

Claudio's eyes grew glassy, as though he'd been holding back a powerful emotion. Angelina rose and stood before his oversized desk. When he said nothing, she went to the door apprehensively. It seemed clear the man felt they had something in common, but it made Angelina uneasy to think it might be her mother's love. She reached for the doorknob, but before leaving, she glanced back at this man who suddenly looked smaller behind such a large desk. Angelina sensed there was something inside him lying dormant, and it made her uneasy.

CHAPTER 11

Every morning, before the opening bell, the streets filled with cigar workers making their way to factories. However, today Angelina lost time helping Filippo find his schoolbag before dashing out. She hurried around the corner and bumped into a young man.

Startled by the collision, Angelina quickly stepped back. "Oh, I'm so sorry," she said.

He didn't seem affected and removed his brown cap in greeting. "It's nice to meet you too," he said, but he didn't smile, at least not outwardly, and she couldn't decide if his remark was an attempt at humor or sarcasm.

"It seems you're the one that nearly fell. Are you all right?" He had a deep baritone voice.

"Yes, thank you, but isn't that a question I should ask you?"

"There's no need."

Angelina avoided staring at him, but he had the kind of looks women swooned over. His eyes were dark and expressive, and she was sure that, somewhere, Michelangelo must have chiseled his likeness out of marble. Angelina collected herself and glanced ahead at the factory workers entering the building. She pointed to the Garcia-Marcos factory. "I have to hurry or I'll be late. Again, I apologize."

"No es nada." He tipped his brown cap.

"Disculpeme. Tenga un buen día," she answered in Spanish as she rushed past him. What else could she say after she'd nearly knocked him off his feet, other than she was sorry and have a nice day?

She made her way into the factory and took her seat moments before the opening bell. To distract herself, she reviewed her morning. Did Filippo truly misplace his schoolbag? How did it end up near the chicken coop? It intrigued her that as soon as she'd pointed to where she worked, the striking young man in the brown cap had switched from English to Spanish. No matter where people were from, the Spanish language was the pulse of las tabaquerías.

Everyone spoke Spanish in the cigar factories. Angelina had listened to it over one Easter, a Christmas, and one Gasparilla Pirate Parade until she'd learned to speak this rich dialect from the Iberian Peninsula with all its grace and swirls. She like using holidays as time markers. It allowed her to count the many months of working without being precise because mastering the art of stripping leaves was not the education she had in mind for herself. Still, her imagination soared with dreams far beyond the factory walls, and she believed destiny corrected its errors.

Guilt assailed Angelina for keeping her Saturday lessons with Don Carlos Madrid from Carmen, but if her friend slipped and said something around Black Plague of the Mouth, no telling what she would do to break up their meetings.

"Hey, look at you. You're as fast as I am." Carmen pushed her leaves next to Angelina's. The two piles were equal in height. "Rosa would be impressed if she were here today. She's taken the day off."

A young girl walked by just then, balancing a large stack of leaves she could hardly see over. Dolores walked down the same aisle, wavering back and forth and taking up both sides of the narrow path between the tables. She bumped into the girl, knocking all the leaves to the floor.

"Hey, watch where you're going, *estupida*," Dolores barked, smiling.

The girl's chin quivered as she dropped to her knees to collect the leaves. Angelina bent down to help her.

Carmen sneered and shouted, "Why don't you help her pick them up, Dolores? You're the one who knocked them out of her hand."

Dolores shot Carmen a look of indifference. "What for? That's Mercedes's responsibility, not mine." She lifted her chin and turned away.

"You're spawned from the devil himself!" Carmen yelled after her.

The young girl wiped away a tear with her sleeve. Angelina smiled at her as they gathered the last of the leaves. "Don't listen to Dolores. Is your name Mercedes? How old are you?"

"Mercedes Ramos. I'm . . ." She didn't finish. "Thank you for helping me." She stood and walked away with her arms full of tobacco leaves.

Angelina returned to Carmen and whispered, "Do you know how old Mercedes is?"

"Inside the factory, she's supposed to be fourteen. When she leaves the building, she's nine and goes home to her doll."

Angelina's body tightened in anger. "How is this possible? She's a child. She should be in school," she said. "Also, I should get an education."

"Once, el lector read to us that 5,200 children work in cigar factories. Is there no shame in this world?"

"That's more than terrible. I wish I could help her. Tomorrow, I'll bring some food from my father's store for her family—and a bag of Italian candy." Angelina glanced back at the child. "Two bags."

"Give it to her on our lunch break and make sure Mercedes eats it in front of Dolores," said Carmen.

Angelina pulled apart another leaf and examined it. Each leaf had distinctive characteristics. While stripping them, why not sort the leaves by color, texture, and size? By now, she could quickly tell the difference between the filler leaves and the outer ones. What a waste to pay the *selectores* and give them such prestige for separating the leaves when one person could do both jobs. And with the leaves already right in her hands, why not keep going and roll them into cigars? She could do all three jobs, receive a larger salary, save money, and pay her way through college. Someone should have thought of this.

Something tickled Angelina's nose. She rubbed it and glanced at the clock above the doorway, hoping the day would move along a little faster. She rubbed her nose again.

The faint odor gathered and rose above the pungent smell of tobacco dominating the factory. Startled, Angelina jumped to her feet. "Something's on fire!"

"Ay, Dios mio!"

"Fuego, fuego!" someone yelled. The words sparked panic. Screams engulfed the factory.

Those who'd sat side by side now pushed tables, chairs, and each other to reach the only staircase on the floor, where they collided, shoved, and hindered their own escape. Women mirrored each other's hysteria as they rushed past Angelina, bumped into Carmen, and knocked her off her feet. Angelina grabbed Carmen's arm and pulled her up before the crowd could trample her.

"*Santa Maria*!" Carmen quickly looked in both directions. "Is the fire in our building?"

The smell of smoke grew stronger and darkened the air. If the fire wasn't in the building, it had to be quickly approaching. Angelina searched feverishly for another means of escape, but she didn't know in which direction the fire raged.

Carmen grabbed Angelina's arm. "What if we can't get out before it's too late?"

"What if the fire is already out?" Angelina countered.

"Ay, Dios, ayudanos." Carmen's voice quivered.

Garcia-Marcos employed over a hundred workers on each floor, and nearly everyone was heading for the stairs.

"We'll use the fire escape. It's faster," Angelina suggested.

"I can't. I'm afraid of heights," Carmen cried.

"No, you're not. Not today." As Angelina tried to calm her friend, frantic thoughts of Zio Pasquale raced through her mind. Were the windows in the basement too small for the men to climb through? Could they open them? Did they have to break the glass and risk cuts and gashes? Were the windows blocked?

"I'll take the staircase," said Carmen.

No matter which way they went, women crowded everywhere—some crying, some screaming, some swinging their arms at others.

"Look at the line of people trying to squeeze through the staircase!" Angelina locked her arm around Carmen's and pulled her toward the fire escape.

Black Plague of the Mouth appeared from nowhere, pushing and shoving her way toward the fire escape. "Out of my way, chicas, or I'll knock you over!" she shouted. Angelina kept the woman in her sights.

"I've had enough from that *desvergonzada.* She'd knock her own mother over to get out," said Carmen.

"It's better if she's ahead of us, where we can see her."

Dolores shouted curses at everyone.

Angelina reached the fire escape and glanced down. The third floor seemed higher than before, the descent more dangerous. Years of grueling heat had left the window ledge chipped and splintered. The wood scraped Angelina's hands as she crawled out, but the fire scared her too much to care. She gazed down at the long line of women between her and the ground. The steel of the fire escape vibrated under their gathering weight, the women pushing and elbowing each other while Angelina kept her hold on Carmen and the railing. They only had to hang on to make their way down.

"Stop pushing, *cabronas.*" Dolores's shrill voice spiraled up to their ears.

Angelina wiped at her perspiration. She didn't know how to calculate the risk between fleeing down the fire escape or the staircase. She took a chance, made a swift decision, and prayed it was the right one. "Carmen, don't look over the railing. Pretend it's just a staircase inside the building."

Carmen nodded uncertainly.

Still worried about her uncle, Angelina feared the fire might move toward her father's store. She'd never known anything so ominous or seen so many in such horror. If only she had an unobstructed view of which course the flames had taken. Angelina tried to keep as much of her distress to herself. To react would only hasten the panic. Worse, wherever there was smoke, there had to be fire, and why was there no sound of the clanging bells of fire wagons? Had no one considered the weight of so many people on the fire escape? It quivered as the bolts at the top dislodged and tore loose from the building. The metal contrivance wavered back and forth like a terrifying carnival ride. The heat came in every form: the anguish of fear, the humidity, and the approaching fire. Angelina focused on making her way down and keeping Carmen calm when screaming erupted.

Angelina looked up to see a young girl fall over the railing. "Mercedes!"

"*Ay, Madre Santísima*!" shouted Carmen. Angelina froze in horror.

Arms reached out, but only fingertips grazed the girl. In a horrifying thread of time that went both too quickly and too slowly, Mercedes hit the brick-paved street with a heavy thud, nearly obliterated by the piercing cries filling the air.

Startled faces on the street and fire escape stared at the child's broken body. Mercedes appeared like a rag doll dropped by a child, her body twisted in an unnatural pose, a halo of blood growing larger around her head. Whether from fear, grief, or pity, women wept and pleaded for God's mercy. Cries of disbelief echoed from every direction. Mercedes's terror was made all the more real by her widened eyes and the open mouth of her final scream. Several men who already escaped the factory rushed over, and one knelt to check for any signs of life. He shook his head, passed his hand over the child's face, and closed her eyes. Together, the men lifted Mercedes away from onlookers while factory women filled the heavens with pleadings for the soul of little Mercedes Ramos.

There was no time to mourn, and it caused an ache in Angelina's heart. Carmen grabbed her arm, held it tight, and seemed too terrified to speak. Women grew more hysterical and those at the top of the fire escape screamed flames had reached their floor. Several began jumping as men below tried to break their falls by catching them. With Mercedes body still visible, others cried, too traumatized to attempt it.

A cloud of thick, noxious smoke spewed through the air,

and the women shielded their faces with handkerchiefs and trembling hands.

Catholics and non-Catholics alike called out to God for His deliverance, their prayers tangling around each other, pleading His Divine forgiveness and offering promises to make amends. Even Dolores sought God's help. With the sky tainted gray, the scent of the fire, and the smoke billowing through the air, Angelina's father could not mistake what was happening, even from his store. Workers pressed close together, all surging down the fire escape. They coughed and tried to wipe away the smoke burning their eyes. A woman came from behind and pushed her way down through the line. "I can't stand this anymore. Let me off!" she yelled until she saw Dolores.

Dolores grabbed the woman by the hair. "If you want to get down fast, I'll throw you off myself, and they can bury you with Mercedes." The woman backed away and wedged herself behind Carmen.

On both sides of the fire escape, women leaped to the ground. As soon as Angelina and Carmen got close enough, they too jumped. Carmen got to her feet, hurriedly brushed off her dress, and pushed her hair away from her face. "I've never been so scared. We have to get out of here."

Desperate to find her uncle, Angelina frantically searched the faces of those in the street and asked several men if they'd seen Pasquale. No one had.

"He can find you at home, Angelina. It's too dangerous out here," Carmen said with a start and pointed to the factory. "Look."

Angelina turned to see yellow flames roaring and leaping from the adjacent building to their factory. "Oh, my God. What if my uncle's trapped in the basement?" she exclaimed.

"If he loves you, he won't want you here. I can't stand it. Let's get out of here. I'll walk you home."

"No, I can't. I have to look for my uncle."

Carmen threw her arms around Angelina, her friend's tears brushing against her cheek. "I'll never forget how you helped me today."

"We'll see each other soon, I promise."

Carmen pushed past the crowd and disappeared.

Now alone, Angelina fought to make her way through the crush of people shouting orders at each other as she continued searching for her uncle. In the street, panicked horses with wild eyes reared up, neighing and snorting as they tried to break away.

A group of men passed Angelina.

"Zio Pasquale! Zio Pasquale!" she shouted, but no one answered. Black ashes floated about like unholy snowflakes.

Immigrants, white-faced with fear, reverted to their native languages as they ran through the street. Like the Tower of Babel, foreign words and worlds collided. Some who'd escaped carried their belongings, others had lost the humble possessions they'd brought with them to America, the land of dreams. Their eyes had lost their light reflecting feelings of hopelessness.

The crowd grew thicker.

Our memories are all we can ever keep. They're all we have that really belongs to us. This was the moment Angelina understood the depth of her father's words.

The angry and scared shouted and shoved until a brawl erupted. Angelina kept searching for her uncle among the faces of men surging through the streets, but given the labyrinth of debris and the crowd, her quest grew almost impossible.

Cigar makers wearing soot-covered shirts lined up to pass water-filled buckets to those closest to the fire. In the distance, fire wagon bells clanged. At last, the firefighters had arrived to battle the blaze. Angelina searched the crowd and shouted Pasquale's name, but her voice dissolved in the surrounding clamor.

The fire spread quickly. Down the block, buildings, tenements, and homes became engulfed in flame. Some dragged their belongings outside, while others abandoned everything to get away. Women rushed about with their possessions in their arms and baskets balanced on their heads while several men, like pallbearers, carried an elderly man through the streets in his bed.

From where Angelina stood, the flames grew higher, the smoke thicker. There seemed no end to the inferno's fury. Mixed with the day's humidity, the heat of the blaze became unbearable. Suddenly, the sound of gunshots tore through the commotion. People were pushing through the crowd to get away when a sudden opening cleared to reveal a man standing there, covered in blood, a bullet wound in his chest. He took three steps, stumbled, and fell near Angelina's feet.

Angelina's hands flew to her mouth as the sound of the gun still echoed in her head. Some tried to flee through the dense crowd, while others turned away, pretending not to see, but Angelina recognized the man writhing in pain. She froze at the sight of Benedetto. Her mind sped back to that day in her father's grocery store when this man had knocked over cans, brandished a gun, and reached for her breast—a man his mother named Blessed. He'd stood tall then—callous and menacing. Now he lay like rubbish amid the filth, ash, and discarded belongings. His eyes were wild with disbelief as the blood spread throughout his clothing.

"Blood washes blood." The strained phrase slipped from Benedetto's lips like the confession of a mortal sin, but he offered no plea or prayer, nor did he ask forgiveness. Instead, he gazed toward the sky as though something loomed above him. Crimson spilled from the corner of his mouth. His stomach rose, pressed against the buttons of his shirt, and he took his last breath.

Signora Bertelli had warned of the presence of evil spirits. Angelina wondered if the devil himself might come to claim a soul such as his. A chill passed through her. She made the sign of the cross, choking out a frantic Our Father for protection. Uncertain how the spirit left the body, Angelina stepped back so the dark entity might not brush against her.

Two men ran toward Benedetto's body. The first, a short and bulky man, pointed his weapon at those in the street. The other man reached for Benedetto's gun and ripped a thick, blood-soaked envelope from the dead man's pants pocket. He'd slicked back his hair and had a pencil-thin mustache. He sported spats on his shoes and had contradicted the look with a stained shirt and suspenders.

The unmistakable Nico Trezza, the most notorious criminal of the Black Hand, had terrorized the neighborhood. Angelina would not likely forget his men were responsible for her quitting school, working in a cigar factory, and forced to delay her dreams. Old man Trezza's son stood in front of Angelina with sweat rolling down his face and a deceptive resemblance to the sweet elderly man who lived next door.

Nico glowered over the frightened crowd and then approached Angelina.

"The grocer's daughter," he said. "To forget a face is a dangerous thing in my business." He pointed his gun at the sky and fired.

Angelina jumped at the sound. She quickly reminded herself she hadn't seen who'd shot Benedetto. However, it was only what Nico believed that was relevant. For one terrible moment, time stood still. Nico stared at her, narrowed his eyes, and after a long, nervous pause for Angelina, he turned away.

"Omerta!" the other man shouted at those in the street. Not everyone would have understood the warning—"You talk, you die"—but it had its intended effect on the Sicilians.

"Andiamo," the other man yelled. "Let's go!"

Angelina had no illusions. Still, nothing had prepared her to see a man take his last breath. Men of violence littered the streets, and one of them had shot the bullet that ended Benedetto's life. It didn't matter which one. She stood still until the sensation returned to her legs, and then she lost herself in the crowd.

Smoke from the fire diluted the day's brightness, painting Ybor City with the warm, brownish tones of a photograph. Random fire barricades blocked the streets as the blaze continued to rage. Still desperate to find her uncle, Angelina turned back toward the factory, where the crowds had thinned and buildings had already tasted fire. She reached the once-imposing three-story structure. All that remained of the building were the wrought-iron posts that held the sign—Garcia-Marcos Cigar Company. The rubble around it whimpered, smoked, and sputtered soft crackling sounds.

Angelina stared in astonishment at the metal fire escape that now lay across the walkway with nothing around it to indicate a cigar factory had once stood there. It horrified her to think this was the metal bannister she and Carmen had gripped tightly as they made their way to safety—the bannister that had threatened to dislodge from the outside wall of the building and collapse under the weight of so many frightened women. It now lay as a heartbreaking reminder of Mercedes's fatal fall.

The faint whimpering of a small child pulled Angelina from her thoughts. She followed the sound to the edge of the walkway, where a toddler sat alone. He couldn't have been two yet and looked like Giuseppe, with the same dark eyes, curls, and quivering lower lip when about to cry.

Angelina picked him up, patted his back, and kissed his forehead. She sang to him and spoke in gentle tones as she questioned him, but the child answered her in the muddled language of the very young. He was too small to leave alone, so Angelina walked along a narrow clearing between the rubble and asked every passerby she encountered, "Do you know who this child is?" Heads shook in the tired manner of men who'd fought a war and lost. She tightened her hold on the boy, hummed her mother's lullaby, and wondered what to do with the unclaimed child.

"Angelina Pirrello." The shrill voice startled her and raised the hairs on her arms. She immediately recognized the sound of Maria Martino and turned to see the woman standing behind her. She prepared for an assault. As the doctor's wife drew closer, Angelina rubbed the child's back to calm him and positioned her feet for better balance. She would not be caught by surprise this time.

The woman waved frantically. When she reached Angelina, she ripped the child from her arms.

"Vito, my baby. It's Mama." She kissed and caressed the boy. It rendered Angelina motionless. Out of the hundreds of babies in Ybor City, she had loved and cared for the child of Maria, the woman who did nothing when Angelina's mother and brother had stood at the crossroads between heaven and Earth.

"What are you doing with my son? And where's my Rocco?"

Angelina's head spun.

"Angelina Pirrello, answer me," Maria demanded. "Where's Rocco?"

Torment filled the woman's eyes, and Angelina recognized it as what she'd felt on that terrible day her mother died.

"Where is my son?" Maria shouted once more while Vito cried.

"I don't know. I saw no one. If I hadn't picked up this little boy, he might have been hurt."

The woman turned to her child. "It's all right, my precious. Mama's here."

Doctor Martino caught up with them. "Oh, thank God. You've found Vito."

"Yes, Angelina had him." The remark sat on a figurative fence and could be interpreted as either affirmation or accusation.

"Mille grazie," said Doctor Martino. "Excuse my wife. She's not herself."

"I'm glad I could help. There is nothing more frightening to a child than to lose its mother. Don't you agree, Maria?"

Maria's eyes were moist. She loved her children. Yet she'd been so indifferent to Carolina's ordeal. Angelina considered the irony. The roles were reversed. Now, providence offered Angelina a cup of reprisal for what Maria had done. It would be a measure of justice, but in her heart, Angelina knew she was not like Maria Martino.

"I discovered your son alone over there." Angelina pointed to the walkway. "He was crying. I sang to him and tried to comfort him. I asked everyone I saw if they knew him, but no one did."

Doctor Martino put his arm around her. "You've done a wonderful thing. Our family will always be indebted."

"Grazie, Angelina." Maria muttered her gratitude with an expression Angelina wanted to believe was shame but was more likely meant to impress her husband.

Maria took a step back. It was a small step, but a significant declaration. Angelina realized the woman was maintaining her distance, but to test it, she took a small step forward, and once again, Maria stepped back. Perhaps she didn't want to mingle with the passing working-class provincials.

People were still rushing about in the streets and crying out. Yet, amid all the chaos, Maria managed a moment to smooth out a crease in her dress.

CHAPTER 12

The day had proven too great a burden for Angelina. She pushed her way through the now-thinning crowd and ran toward home, hoping her uncle would be there. Before she reached the next street, she heard someone call her name.

"Angelina."

Her heart jumped, and the tears she'd held inside all day spilled down her cheeks. She rushed toward her zio Pasquale and threw her arms around him.

"Why you cry? I no tell you, Non ti preoccupare."

"Zio, where have you been? I've been looking all over for you." Just seeing him, the tension that had gripped her so fiercely released its hold.

"I get out of the tabaquería, and I say, 'Angelina, Angelina.' You no answer. I look for you, ask everybody. You friend from school, Sophia Esposito, she see you run, and she call to you, but you no hear her." His gentle manner, unlike her father's, was meant to reassure her. Pasquale patted her back the same way she'd comforted Maria's baby.

"Oh, Zio, I've never been so happy to see anyone."

"Something happen to you?"

Angelina trembled as she recounted the panic in the factory and streets, little Mercedes who fell to her death, the murdered man, Nico Trezza's silent threat, and the encounter with Maria Martino. As she spoke, Pasquale looked at the ground as though analyzing what she was saying. When she finished, his voice was calm.

"So nothing happen to you?"

"Nothing happened to me? Weren't you listening?"

"Yes, I listen. You no hurt, is true?"

"Well, no, but . . ." The devastation was more significant than the fire. Did her uncle not understand?

"Such a terrible thing for poor Mercedes. It make me feel so sad." He shook his head. "In Sicily, everybody wear the amulet around the neck. Is protection from the evil eye, so you no worry no more about Maria Martino or malocchio. I get you protection. Trezza is bad man, Angelina, a *criminale*. I no like this man. He is good for nothing and nobody." Pasquale spat on the ground to emphasize his point. "Maybe he kill somebody, and maybe somebody wanna kill him. Is good you run away. You no see nothing, and nobody no see you. You capisci, Angelina?"

Angelina nodded. She had no intention of ever going near Nico Trezza again.

"I know this is bad thing, but nothing happen to you. You still smart." Pasquale tapped his temple. "You still pretty, and you good. That no change, and now you more strong." He flexed his arm. "Bad things make us strong, like the brick I give to you."

Angelina wasn't certain if she had become stronger, but her uncle's kind heart and encouragement reassured her. "Life is uncomplicated for people like Maria Martino. She has someone to cook for her, clean for her, and care for her children. Why did she put a curse on me? Why does she make life hard for others?"

"You think Maria Martino is rich because she have lots of money, but that's no for sure. Maybe Maria Martino is poor. She just have lots of money. Lots of poor people are rich, Angelina, and lots of rich people are poor. It happen all the time. Maybe you think Signora Martino have no problems and you have too much. Is that right?"

Angelina recalled their confrontation in Dr. Martino's office. "If a problem dared to come to that woman, she'd pull its hair and drag it out the door."

"I gonna ask you a question. If you were a donkey, and Signora Martino was a donkey too . . ."

Angelina released a heavy sigh. "Please, Zio Pasquale, I know you're trying, but this story won't make me feel any better."

Pasquale continued. " . . . who carry on her back a big sack of salt, and who carry a big sack of sponges?"

Angelina sighed. "That's too easy. If I were a donkey, I'd carry the heavy salt, and Maria Martino would have the light sponges. It's like I said, zio. Life is easy for her."

"Maybe that depend on which way you go."

"What's that supposed to mean?"

"One day you gonna have to cross the river, and what happen to the salt when is all wet?"

Angelina stared at her uncle as she imagined the scene. "It disappears."

"You see how smart you are, Angelina. Nobody more better than you. Now, what happen when all the sponges get wet?"

"Sponges get heavy."

"So, one day Maria Martino will have to carry the wet sponges on her back, and you no have carry nothing."

It amazed Angelina how her uncle had a humorous story

for every one of life's challenges, but she saw nothing humorous about Maria and shook her head. "I don't know, zio. She'd only avoid the river."

"Angelina, Angelina, everybody gonna cross the river sometime; some cross the ocean, like me and you papa and mama. Non ti preoccupare. Life gonna be so easy for you. Just you wait. One day, the heavy salt gonna be gone." Pasquale beamed and raised both hands in the air as though he had solved all her problems. "And you don't forget, I give you the brick, so now you strong too."

Angelina threw her arms around her uncle. "You're the best, Zio Pasquale."

He kissed her forehead.

"Pasquale!" shouted a young redheaded man from across the street.

Pasquale waved him over, then turned to Angelina. "Please, you go home now, before you papa say I no take care of you."

Home sounded like a refuge from the dread and destruction and from so many reasons to weep.

"Pasquale!" The young man rushed over to them and glanced at Angelina for a moment. He'd been close to the fire. Perspiration beaded on his forehead, his sleeves were rolled up, and traces of soot sullied his shirt. He was taller than Pasquale, maybe six feet, maybe not quite, and he had brown eyes and a vibrant mane of red hair that was unmistakable even at a distance. It wasn't possible to tell a person's character so quickly, but she had the distinct impression he was trustworthy and unpretentious.

He turned to her uncle. "Pasquale, can you help us pass the water buckets on the other side of the building?"

"I gonna help you now," said Pasquale.

"Angelina, this is Rolando Aguirre. We work together to

put out the fire before I find you. He make the cigars and work for us in the union to make everything more better."

Her uncle made everyone sound important. She suspected there was something else worthy in this young man.

"I'm glad to meet you, Angelina." He had a quiet, unassertive voice. He reached to shake her hand and held it a moment longer than necessary, as though he were trying to remind her of something. Angelina combed through her memory, but nothing surfaced. Perhaps her imagination had taken flight because this was a day like no other—a day people would remember for years and recount to their children and grandchildren.

Rolando turned to her uncle. "The men will show you what to do, Pasquale. We have to hurry. The fire is moving fast."

He glanced back at Angelina, their eyes meeting once again.

"We go now," Pasquale said. Both men hurried toward the water brigade.

Mesmerized, Angelina watched them go. There was something warm and comforting about Rolando, like sweet butter melting on freshly baked bread.

WHEN ANGELINA REACHED NINETEENTH STREET, her spirits rose. She felt safe for the first time all day. She stepped onto the porch where the old swing creaked if pushed too high and where everyone she loved lived inside. Then she opened the front door and breathed in the scent of home and well-being.

"Angelina. Where have you been? Papa's out looking for you," said Salvatore.

"Were you in the fire?" Filippo asked.

"She's covered in ashes. Where do you think she was?" Salvatore retorted.

Lily squeezed her doll against her chest. "Did you get burned?"

Angelina stroked her sister's head. "No, I'm not burned."

Everyone followed Angelina to the kitchen, where she grabbed an apple, poured a glass of water, and for the next hour, told them about the fire, the men fighting it, and how she found the Martino baby. The genuine horrors of the day, the tragic fall of Mercedes, and the murder of Benedetto she kept to herself.

Angelina looked outside. The day faded into a strange, lingering yellow, then finally darkened into dusk. Soot clung to her hair and clothes. She'd received a baptism of ashes along with frightful memories that would likely return as nightmares. Angelina made up a bath and tried to wash it all away.

For hours, firemen's bells had clanged warnings, and when the little bell above the grocery door rang, it seemed almost an echo.

"Vinny, if the grocery is still open, why aren't you in there?" Angelina narrowed her eyes.

The boy shrugged. "Hey, why stand over there when I can hear the bell from over here?"

Her brothers had an answer for everything they did badly. "I'll attend to this customer, Vinny, but after that, it's your job."

She stepped into the store and closed the connecting door behind her. "May I help you?" she said to a man who stood by the counter with his back to her. As she waited for an answer, the smell of liquor began to slowly inoculate the room.

He said nothing.

"Parla Italiano?" No response. *"Habla usted español?"* Most immigrants spoke one language or the other—but then there were the Germans, French, Irish, and so on. Angelina approached the counter with some hesitation. "Are you looking for something special?"

He turned and faced her.

"Señor Garcia?" She had never seen the cigar factory owner in their store and wondered if he knew who owned it.

He seemed confused, and disheveled in his appearance, like he'd fallen asleep wearing his suit, awoken, and wandered into their store by accident. Soot and ashes clung to the fibers of his once-white suit. Perhaps he'd tried to make it through the smoke to save some important papers? A button suddenly popped off his shirt from the strain of his midsection. It bounced on the floor of the otherwise quiet room. He passed his hand over the top of his thinning hair and turned toward Angelina.

"May I help you?" she asked again.

Claudio Garcia remained still.

Her discomfort grew. "We're closed," Angelina said with finality. He did not react. With an exaggerated gesture, she took her father's store key off its hook. "If you need to purchase something quickly, I'll ring it up." She raised her voice the way she did when the train clamored as it passed through. "My father will open again at eight thirty. Perhaps you've seen him? A big man—tall, strong."

Garcia fumbled for a cigar, inhaled its aroma, and struck a match. His cheeks became deep caverns as he inhaled. The smell of tobacco rivaled the odor of the liquor.

She tapped her foot. "Señor Garcia, I'm closing the store." Another uneasy moment passed.

"If things had gone my way, you'd be calling me Papa, not Señor Garcia."

In one swift move, he dropped his cigar, lunged forward,

and grabbed Angelina's wrist. Blue, rope-like veins bulged from his hand. She tightened her muscles, struggling to pull away, but his hand was a steel clamp around her wrist. Garcia's eyes bulged. She pulled and twisted, but her efforts only caused her fingers to grow numb. Desperate thoughts raced through her as Claudio's breathing became audibly heavy and his eyes grew wide and wild.

"Carolina Cacciatore. You look like her," he said. "Everyone said she was beautiful, but she was so much more. She touched my heart. I remember . . ." His voice grew thin, as if he were trying to grasp a fleeting memory.

"My father has a gun. Let go of me before he shoots you."

Claudio seemed removed from the world around him. "Sometimes I'd walk past this store and watch Carolina through the large front window. I only wanted to see her one more time. Your mother would have married me if your father hadn't come along. She loved me."

Angelina didn't believe it, but his words reminded her of Aunt Violetta taunting her father with Claudio's proposal of marriage. Angelina had never known the sensation of being in love, but one thing was sure—this man should have forgotten her mother long ago.

"She's dead," Angelina growled.

"She's dead." He parroted the words and held Angelina's wrist with the same fierceness he held on to the past. Without releasing her, he reached into his coat pocket, pulled out a cigar, and raised it like a trophy. "This is one of the finest cigars ever rolled. God Himself nurtures these tobacco leaves at a special plantation in Cuba, and after they've aged for ten years, I let only Pepe Ramirez roll them. He knows the perfect blend." Garcia lowered the cigar closer to Angelina's face. "You see this gold band with the silver bird? It's the mark of my private collection. I may give out a few, but they're not for sale."

His chest heaved, and his breathing grew loud. Still, he focused on Angelina. "I'd have done anything for her." His voice softened. With the splendid cigar in his hand, he placed his forefinger under Angelina's chin and tilted her head back. "Your eyes are dark almonds, not like hers at all, but still, the resemblance is striking. I should have held her tight and not let her go."

He seemed confused and wounded, but he had no visible injury, and his grip around her wrist had not weakened.

"I'm not my mother," said Angelina.

"She should have been mine, and you should have been my daughter." He tinged the words with sorrow.

Nothing about that statement sat well with Angelina. He'd clawed at reality and reshaped it into an apparition. If Claudio's love for her mother had boiled into madness, none of that was her fault or even her mother's. Still, Angelina now understood what fueled Maria Martino's anger toward her. The woman had to know of her brother's delusions and realized his obsession.

Basta. Enough, thought Angelina. When Claudio glanced out the window, she bent down and drove her teeth hard into his hand. When he cried out and released her, Angelina darted behind the counter, grabbed the large butcher knife, and pointed it at him. She expected retaliation, but Claudio slumped against the wall, moaned, and said nothing more.

She'd held this knife many times, but now its weight and size seemed uncomfortable. "My mother married my father because she loved him."

Claudio Garcia made no gesture, nor did he indicate what ran through his mind. He didn't sigh, gasp, or utter a word, and just as when he entered the store, the small bell rang as he walked out.

Still clutching the knife, Angelina dashed to the entrance,

turned the lock, and flipped the sign to closed. Only after she pulled down the shades did she set down the knife.

"Hey, what's going on?" Vincenzo appeared out of nowhere.

Angelina took a moment to decide if she should tell her brother what had happened, but he would tell Salvatore, and the rest of the children would hear, become frightened, and start crying. "Nothing's going on," she lied.

"Then why did you lock up the store?"

Angelina dropped the key into her pocket. "I want it closed," Angelina said. "If you want to watch something, Vinny, watch Lily and the boys."

"I'm telling Papa closing the store was your idea."

It was dark, and exhaustion overcame Angelina. She served fruit and cheese to everyone, and in time, they all drifted to their beds.

Angelina fell into the bliss of suspended time and dreamed of many things. She saw the face of her mother and heard her call her name. *Angelina, Angelina.*

"Angelina, Angelina, wake up."

Dragged from her dream by her father's voice, she opened her eyes and met her father's. "Papa, I'm so tired."

As usual, he ignored her. "Sometimes my brother talks in riddles. He said you saw a man murdered and then someone fall to her death, and that it was a good you didn't come home on account of helping save a baby." Domenico's tone didn't imply admiration. "What's the matter with you? You saw the danger. Why didn't you rush home? Grown men rescue babies in fires, not young girls. How could you be so foolish?"

Angelina didn't get out of bed. "I'm fine, Papa, and I've been home for hours."

"Vincenzo said you closed the store early. There are

people without food and supplies tonight. What were you thinking?"

She shut her eyes, but she was no longer sleepy.

"Answer me."

"Well, a man came to the store . . . I mean . . . there was a problem. Don't worry . . . I took care of it," said Angelina in badly formed sentences.

"What problem?"

Angelina opened her eyes only to catch her father's firm stare. After another tense moment, she blurted it out. "It was Claudio Garcia. He talked about Mama, said he should have been my father. He grabbed my wrist tight and wouldn't let go, and—"

"He did what?"

The moment the words left her mouth, Angelina wanted to retract them. A string of Sicilian curses blazed through the air, and her father's face flushed as red as the tomatoes he grew. He was an uncomplicated man with rules etched in stone. She should have known he'd never overlook such an insult.

"Papa, he didn't hurt me. I think he was just confused."

"Don't lie to me, Angelina."

"As soon as he left, I locked the door and closed the store. He didn't return."

"Smart of you and smarter of him. He's made a big mistake."

Domenico headed for the door but turned back before opening it. "Under no circumstances are you to leave this house. Capisci?"

"He didn't hurt me, Papa." She spun around to prove she was fine.

"Before Garcia set foot in my store and grabbed my daughter, he should have thought of me." Her father walked out, slammed the door, and left his ambiguous intention behind.

Fully awake now, Angelina visualized the confrontation between two men who loved the same woman—one enraged and one, perhaps, deranged. Nothing good would come of it. All factory owners had guns. Angelina pictured every scenario and asked God to protect her father, but the night stirred more fears. Every few minutes, she glanced at the clock or leaned against the window, looking for her father's silhouette amid the streetlamps. Domenico paced when he worried, a habit Angelina had adopted.

The family's statue of the Virgin Mary sat resplendent next to the clock. It compelled Angelina to make the sign of the cross whenever she checked the time. It seemed highly doubtful that her mother had placed them together unintentionally. After much thought, she asked God to protect Claudio Garcia too.

A book of poems sat on the coffee table, the last thing her mother had read before she died. Her father had left it where she'd set it. Angelina picked it up and read a poem by Edgar Allan Poe.

Take this kiss upon the brow
And, in parting from you now,
Thus much let me avow
You are not wrong, who deem
That my days have been a dream

The poem was a metaphor—something profound, enlightening, meant to provoke thought, and titled "A Dream within a Dream." Poets were so cryptic. What did Poe mean? Angelina read the words twice but couldn't focus. She closed the book and resumed pacing until nothing seemed to distract her.

At last, she heard a key fumbling in the lock. She quickly got to her feet, dashed to the door, and pulled it open. "Thank you, God." She exhaled.

"Why are you still awake?" Her father spoke with his usual frustration.

She threw her arms around him to reassure herself he was there in the flesh. "Oh, Papa, it's been hours, and I've been sick with worry. I'm so glad you're safe." Domenico did not appear relieved. He walked into the kitchen and poured a glass of water. Angelina followed.

"Did you talk to Claudio Garcia? Everything's fine, right?" Silence followed her questions, molding a strange disquiet. It loitered between them and rekindled the uneasiness that had haunted her throughout the night.

Domenico met her stare. "Claudio Garcia is dead."

Angelina gasped. It was as if she had returned to the fire and it was ablaze all around her. The man could not have come to a natural end. He'd been distraught, not dying. A shrill cry gushed from deep inside her and erupted over and over again while visions of violence stormed through her mind.

"Stop it at once. What's wrong with you?" Domenico spoke sharply as two of her brothers rushed into the room.

"Get back to bed!" Domenico shouted at the boys. He then grabbed Angelina by the shoulders. "Stop screaming. Do you hear me?"

She covered her mouth, but nothing muffled the sound.

Nearing hysteria, Angelina asked the most sinful of all questions. "How could you kill Signore Garcia?"

CHAPTER 13

Domenico's eyes grew wide. He took a step back and knocked over a chair, but he didn't bother to set it straight. Angelina cried for her father's soul and for her own. She should never have mentioned Claudio's name. Surely God would hold her accountable for her part in such an offense.

"Claudio Garcia came into my store and grabbed my daughter. It's a reason for anger, not murder." Domenico ran his hand through his hair as if the mere concept of such a thought had startled him.

Angelina caught her breath and searched her father's face for evidence of guilt. "Then how did he die?"

"Calm yourself, and I'll tell you." Her father preferred to give orders, not explanations. Still, he continued. "The man lost everything. He expanded his factory, built himself a grand house, and accepted delivery of a large shipment of tobacco leaves before heavy competition between growers drove prices down. Success can make a man reckless and feel invincible. He didn't have fire insurance, and without it, he had no funds to rebuild."

Angelina needed to know how it had happened. She rubbed her arms. "Papa, how did he die?"

"He fell apart, lost reason. He wasn't strong."

"Papa, how did Claudio Garcia die?" Her voice grew thinner with every repetition.

Domenico put his hand on his daughter's shoulder. "Some people can't remember that no matter what happens today, the sun will rise again tomorrow."

"What does that mean?"

"Claudio shot himself."

Angelina's hands flew up to cover her gasp. Her ragged breathing grew worse. She visualized a gun going off and Claudio falling dead when, hours before, he'd stood right in front of her. She rubbed her wrist where he'd held it, and though she didn't know him well enough, a sense of loss came over her.

"Oh, Papa, that's horrible—more than horrible. If only he'd waited. El lector reads how factories merge all the time. Signore Garcia had so many orders from all over the world. Banks would probably have loaned him money to start production again. He even knew a secret blend with the richest leaves, 'the finest cigar ever made,' he told me. Rich men, kings, and presidents pay a lot of money for good cigars."

Domenico gave his daughter a slight smile. "I'm glad you search for solutions, Angelina. One day, you may need that talent to survive." Her father lit a cigar, took a deep puff, and watched the smoke dance through the air. "It's easier to get up when you're not afraid to fall. Some accept failure as final and never try again."

Angelina imagined Claudio's torment. "I can't believe he'd rather kill himself than try to get a loan and rebuild the factory. He could have found partners. Only this morning I thought of a way to save on labor, and I planned to tell him."

"Claudio's father started the cigar business. Claudio only had to show up and sit behind a desk with orders piled on top. He never knew the struggle of building something out of nothing or the satisfaction of the accomplishment. It's easier to lean against a fence someone else built than to sweat, nailing the lumber yourself."

Domenico glanced at the book of poetry. "When your mother died, we'd been married almost seventeen years. That's a long time to think about someone else's wife."

Angelina had not told her father Claudio loved her mother, but Domenico took pride in being observant, especially with his family. "Why do you think he still thought about Mama?"

"They found his body over your mother's grave."

Angelina gripped the wooden arms of her chair as she tried to imagine such a scene. "Oh, Papa, I can't believe it."

"Perhaps, with so much of a loss, he went back to a time he wanted so badly. I'm only telling you this because you visit your mother's grave and may hear of it from someone at the cemetery. I don't want you to mention it to anyone else. Do you hear me? It serves no purpose. His family doesn't want anyone to know either. Capisci?"

Angelina nodded. "Yes, I understand."

"I'm serious. Your mother had nothing to do with the man and never once mentioned him in our years together. I don't want people thinking there was something unholy going on between them. The Italian community in Ybor City is close. His mother's family is Italian, and they come into my store often. After your mother's death, I saw no harm in you and my brother working at his factory. I won't stand for anyone smearing your mother's good name."

Angelina jumped as the front door swung open and a man covered in soot entered.

"*Buona sera, famiglia.*" He threw his hands into the air. "I come home."

"Zio Pasquale?"

"How you know is me?" he said with a wide grin and blackened face.

Domenico pointed to the back door. "Go wash by the pump."

"I think I go now to wash by the pump."

Domenico shook his head. "I'm going to bed. It's late, and the streets are nearly empty. Tomorrow, everything will fly off the shelves. I'll wake your brothers early to help."

Angelina quickly made up a plate of food for her uncle. When he returned from washing, she set it on the kitchen table and sat across from him. He ate while she told him that Claudio Garcia had died, leaving out what her father had told her not to discuss.

"Poor Signore Garcia. Is terrible thing. If only a rich man think more like a poor man. We no have nothing, so we no worry so much, and when we die, we have big smile. No more hungry and no more work hard. When I die, everybody gonna say Pasquale have such nice teeth." Pasquale widened his grin. "The man who have nothing is buried just like the rich man. Soon nobody remember who have too much and who have nothing."

Her uncle's many philosophies made her smile. "Do we have many relatives left in Sicily?"

"In Santo Stefano, you only say, 'My name is Angelina Pirrello. My father is Domenico, and my zio is Pasquale.' The family in Sicily gonna fight over who gonna walk you around the piazza, and they gonna say, "Angelina is *la mia cugina dall'America.* You have so many cousins, you can no believe. We even have cousins that no belong to our family, but why make them feel bad? So I no tell them. Everybody so happy we family. We sing, tell stories, and eat the pasta."

Her uncle could lighten any mood. He always had a reason to smile and make others smile. "I'm happy we're family, too," Angelina told him.

~

IT HAD BEEN two days since the fire, and Angelina spent the early morning chasing Signora Bertelli's chickens. "How did they get out of their cage?" asked Angelina.

Her neighbor sighed. "With such a destructive fire, evil spirits have to find new homes. When they couldn't get into my house, they must have settled on the chicken coop and thrown out the chickens. Who else would let them out?"

"Yes, who else?" Angelina had a good idea, although her brothers would never admit it, and she'd never be able to prove it. "Well, your chickens are back, and I guess no real harm's done."

"We say, 'No trace left, no harm done.' You're a wonderful girl, Angelina. If what I say is a lie, may my chickens lay rocks."

Angelina had never known anyone with such an imagination. She enjoyed these few days at home to visit neighbors, read, and fight off the nightmarish memories of Mercedes and Benedetto still haunting her dreams. Domenico hadn't mentioned her going back to work yet, and she hoped that after some time at home, he'd reconsider her desire to return to school.

Angelina hugged her neighbor and turned toward her house. A newsboy appeared with his bag slung over his back and held up the day's paper. Angelina glanced at the headlines, gave him his coin, and went into her house. With so much devastation to report, every newspaper sported photographs of flames and firefighters to lure readers in. However, one image caught Angelina by surprise. She sat down at the kitchen table and spread out the newspaper. Though younger than the other men fighting the fire, Rolando Aguirre stood taller in the large photograph on the front page. That warm sensation returned. Again, she wondered if she'd met him before the fire and forgotten.

When Domenico entered the kitchen, she wasted no time in relaying the headlines. "Papa, did you know the governor has declared Ybor City's fire a 'tragic loss of homes, life, and factories'? The paper says the blaze started in a rooming house, and the police are searching for the person responsible."

Domenico sat at the kitchen table, poured a cup of coffee, and appeared deep in thought as he stirred in a teaspoon of sugar. "They will bury Claudio Garcia today."

At the mention of Claudio Garcia, Angelina's stomach sank. "May God grant him peace," she said. Who more than Claudio Garcia needed peace?

The somber moment evaporated when Pasquale entered the kitchen. "Good morning, famiglia. Today is gonna be such a nice day."

"Good morning, Zio." Angelina turned the page to distract herself with another article.

Domenico sipped his coffee, then settled his cup on the saucer. "Claudio's mother is Italian, and his father's a Spaniard. Cultures may clash in life, but when the game is over, the pawn and the king go back into the same box."

Pasquale nodded. "Everybody say this in Santo Stefano Quisquina."

"The funeral is at ten o'clock. Be sure you're both ready by 9:15."

The order felt like a frigid draft after Claudio had grabbed her, after she'd bit him, and with the guilt she now felt. Why would her father expect her to attend his funeral?

"Papa, I'm not going."

"Be ready at 9:15."

"Why not take Sal or Vinny?" said Angelina.

"You worked in his cigar factory and knew him. They didn't."

"I don't want to go. I don't want to see Maria Martino." She still believed the doctor's wife had never told her husband her mother was in labor, but she couldn't prove it.

"Forget Maria. She's a fool, like her brother. We'll attend because it shows respect to the family, and in this world, we may lack many things, but never respect. When your mother died, all the adults in their family came to the funeral. Would you have us do less?"

Angelina didn't know the entire Garcia family. "Did Signore Garcia come to Mama's funeral?"

"You have eyes, but you see nothing. Who do you think was crying so loud at the back of the church at your mother's funeral Mass? Learn to observe what's around you."

Angelina grew silent. A man had been sobbing loudly, but she couldn't see him past so many mourners. "I remember that."

"Then there is hope for you because that was Garcia. And as for his funeral, the man is dead—he has nothing more to say to anyone. We go for the family's sake."

Her father didn't specify which family he meant.

At 9:15 sharp, her father held open the front door. Pasquale smiled. Angelina did not. Domenico led them down the street.

"Why are we rushing, Papa? We have plenty of time to get to the church. It's only two blocks away."

"Claudio Garcia's body will not be at the church."

Angelina tossed her hands into the air. "And why is Father Cavalli having a funeral Mass without a body?"

"Claudio Garcia's body is unworthy to enter the church."

Memories of the day the priest attempted to misdirect

her infant brother to limbo returned. The dead truly had no voice—no way to plead their case, present their special circumstances, say they were sorry, or ask for reconsideration.

"He will be at the cemetery, where we'll have the service."

The temperature rose as they continued to walk. Angelina's mind raced. "Papa, how does Father Cavalli know that Signore Garcia didn't change his mind at the last moment? They should offer a high Mass and bury him on sacred ground—just in case. Who would it hurt? If God doesn't think it's a good idea, He can tell Claudio when He sees him."

"We'll never know what went through the man's mind. In the meantime, God will do His job, Father Cavalli will do his job, and you will keep quiet. The funeral will be hard enough on the family—the church believes he's committed a mortal sin," Domenico snapped.

His words were impossible to digest. Angelina didn't believe this, not for one minute, and no one else should either. If Claudio Garcia had been a decent man all his life, would God condemn him to hell for all eternity for one mistake, one moment of desperation, confusion, and weakness? All throughout the scripture it says God is a merciful God. There was nothing written otherwise.

Angelina bowed her head and whispered to God that she forgave Claudio for grabbing her wrist and scaring her. The thought lingered until a shiver passed through her. What if she'd contributed to his decision to kill himself? He'd had a faraway look in his eyes and spoke of her resemblance to her mother. What if he'd held on to her wrist because she remained the only link to someone he loved? Compounded by the cataclysmic loss of his factory, the poor man deserved her pity. Angelina bit her nails in despair, something she'd outgrown long ago.

"We're here," Domenico said.

Amid statues of angels, inscriptions of everlasting peace, and references to the dearly beloved, Angelina stepped onto the soft grass of the cemetery and trudged toward the sea of mourners.

Pasquale bent down and whispered, "You remember you find Dottore Martino's baby in the fire? I have good news. They find his brother too. Everybody okay."

Had her uncle said this because he sensed her anguish or because he didn't?

"Come," Domenico said.

He grabbed her wrist to hurry her along—the same wrist Claudio Garcia had grabbed. The sensation startled her.

"Papa, I can't go."

With total disregard for her remark, Domenico proceeded toward the line of mourners to offer his condolences. A sudden breeze tossed Angelina's hair across her face. She pushed it back and wondered if it was the departed trying to make his presence known. Tiny bumps appeared on her arms, and she tried rubbing them away. "Papa, I can't go through with this. I need to go home."

"I forbid it." Domenico spoke in a whisper, but his words erupted like a shout.

Trapped between her father and her uncle, Angelina drifted toward the coffin of Claudio Garcia like someone condemned. She had not prepared herself for the open casket. Aghast at the sight of his dead body, she squeezed her eyes tightly before looking.

On Claudio Garcia's chest lay dish of salt to ward off evil. To attract angels, they had hung a large gold crucifix around his neck. Several cigars peered from his breast pocket, and between his forefinger and middle finger, he held the 'finest cigar ever made.' The unmistakable gold band with the silver bird was as visible as the bite mark on his hand. He'd entered the afterlife carrying the imprint of Angelina's teeth. At that moment, her stomach sank, and she vowed to never tell a soul what she'd done, not in the confessional, not during her lifetime, and not on her deathbed.

"I'm so sorry for your loss," her father said as he shook hands with Dottore Martino.

"Thank you for coming," the doctor replied with his weeping family at his side.

Domenico placed his free hand on top of their handshake to show support. Pasquale took off his hat. Angelina nodded her condolences. She kept her mouth tightly closed to conceal the teeth responsible for the dead man's injury, fearful they'd be recognized as the ones that left the imprint on him for all eternity.

Father Cavalli approached the grave with the majesty of His Holiness the Pope. He looked around as though taking a visual roll call of the mourners. A group of expressionless women on the other side of Pasquale—silent at first—startled Angelina as they began weeping and wailing in unison until their lamenting built to a crescendo.

Pasquale whispered in Angelina's ear. "Sometime, la famiglia wanna people to cry, so they pay."

Angelina's eyes widened. "They paid for this?"

"Shh." Pasquale put his forefinger to his lips. "Everybody say to me, the Garcias wanna the people should see how much everybody gonna miss Claudio, so they pay people to cry. It make them feel real good. This happen all the time in Sicily."

How did such a vocation come into existence? She stared in amazement at these women who sold their tears. They came dressed in black, wore matching veils, and dabbed at their eyes with white hankies. To think this was a work uniform!

Father Cavalli approached the casket, closed it, cleared his throat, and placed his palms together—fingertips heavenward. All vocal expressions of grief halted, and the paid mourners stopped as abruptly as they'd begun.

"Let us pray for our brother, son, and friend Claudio Garcia," said Father Cavalli.

After his blessing, Father Cavalli called upon Doctor Martino to speak. The doctor began his eulogy in a soothing and melodic voice he'd undoubtedly perfected for the sick. He shared fond memories and good deeds. "Our family is grateful to all of you for coming and for your prayers." Angelina vowed to pray harder than anyone else.

Claudio's uncle Roberto Garcia, short and heavily bearded, spoke next. His voice quivered, and he broke into tears. "What happened to my good nephew Claudio?" he asked. "What could have driven him to such an act?" Angelina feared he addressed her, although she didn't know him, and he didn't look her way.

"Claudio never said an unkind word to anyone. The irony is—he helped a family come to America when they lost their home in a fire, and now another fire drove him to destruction." Story after story recounted Claudio's friendly nature and brought the speech to a feverish pitch. Angelina feared she might faint.

"We've lost a wonderful man. Irreplaceable. And we'll not see him again," Roberto ended. Not see him again? This was the single thread of comfort. All families planned to reunite in the kingdom of heaven.

Claudio's mother seemed near collapse, a relative at each side supporting her. The sobs of her daughter Maria Martino rose above the others. Angelina well understood the pain and heartbreak of losing someone you love.

Suddenly, like a paid mourner, Maria switched off her

display of grief, stepped away from her mother's side, and faced Angelina.

"It seems you were the last one to see him alive. What did you say to him?" Maria spoke in a quiet, almost sweet tone, as though it were a common question asked at funerals—one without repercussions. Her posture straightened. She put her hands on her waist so her elbows stuck out like tree limbs. In contrast, Angelina folded her arms across her middle so they wouldn't shake.

"The streets were crowded. Señor Garcia could have seen lots of people," Angelina replied. "I imagined he'd been near the fire by the condition of his clothes, but he never mentioned the fire or his factory, except to talk of his special blend of cigars."

"And what else was said?" Maria asked quickly, as if trying to cast doubt without lighting the match.

Her elderly mother rearranged the question. *"Per piacere.* Tell me, please, what did my son say to you?" Signora Garcia's white hair peeked out from beneath her black veil, and her eyes glistened with tears. "If you can remember, what were his last words, my child?"

Angelina saw the depths of her suffering. Domenico stood to Angelina's right with a look of warning. Pasquale stood to her left and patted her shoulder. Clothed in the traditional ebony of bereavement, Claudio's mother appeared almost childlike.

"Signora Garcia, your son loved you very much." Sighs graced the air.

Most everyone loved their mother, and God had to consider it a kindness to ease a mother's pain. It might even redeem Angelina and make up for biting Claudio.

The old woman's face became illuminated. *"Mio figlio,* I love him too."

Angelina stood tall. Inspired, she added, "I believe your

son felt confused and killed himself—by accident. With so many desperate people in the streets that day, maybe he had the gun for protection, and it went off—by accident." There, she'd said it. The words took flight and escaped unrestrained into the universe.

The older woman came forward, embraced Angelina, and kissed her on both cheeks. "You see." Claudio's mother turned to those attending. "That's what I've been saying. It was an accident."

Domenico pulled his daughter back, interrupting Angelina's moment of triumph.

"I told you this is all a mistake," Señora Garcia continued. "We should bury my son in consecrated ground. His body should be in the church, with a High Mass offered for his soul."

Angelina wholeheartedly agreed, but remained silent.

With eyes as black as coal, Father Cavalli's peered at Angelina. Once again their swords had crossed. He was without doubt of the same mind as her father.

"Angelina Pirrello, you wanted to send your brother to heaven without the sacrament of holy baptism, and now you send Claudio Garcia to heaven. Who do you think you are, Saint Peter, throwing open the gates of paradise?" Father Cavalli's posture stiffened as he spoke.

Even draped in his flowing priestly vestments, Angelina could tell he'd grown as inflexible as his attitude. His defiance at anyone challenging him did not surprise her. However, she'd shared her desire to baptize her brother in a confessional meant only for God's ears. He should not be announcing it.

She struck back. "I saw Señor Garcia. He was confused, living in the past, and talking to himself."

"A man does not write a letter of farewell to his family by accident or pull out a loaded gun by accident," said the priest.

"Maybe he changed his mind, but in that last second, it was too late."

Father Cavalli's wrinkled brow and intense stare proved he was unwilling to accept her theory that God forgave sinners, loved everyone, and understood profound moments of desperation.

The priest raised a hand to heaven and with a thundering voice, declared, "Claudio Garcia has violated the sacred rite of Almighty God, who is supreme. He has committed a grave offense against divine law, and for this he stands before the gates of hell."

Angelina's mouth dropped open. The sheer horror of such a declaration had the impact of a cannon exploding, piercing ears and aimed straight at the family and mourners —paid and unpaid. These were the bleakest words ever spoken. Was the priest condemning Claudio Garcia to hell at his own funeral? Convinced that nothing like this had ever happened in Ybor City, Florida, and possibly in the entire universe. Angelina made a hasty sign of the cross for protection. Yet she did not believe it for a moment. God was loving, forgiving, and stories of His mercy filled the Bible.

Claudio's mother fainted. Dottore Martino rushed to her side while others, wide-eyed, nervously pulled out their rosaries and blessed themselves. The priest patted his head with a handkerchief. "Our friend Claudio is now in the hands of God, who is omnipotent and can look into his heart and will see a good man. Salvation is God's gift to everyone. May He have mercy on the soul of His faithful servant, Claudio Ruben Garcia." Father Cavalli spoke with audible nervousness and an obvious attempt to redeem himself. He quickly bowed his head and shut his eyes to everyone. "Let us pray for our good brother."

When the service was over, Domenico pulled Angelina

away from Pasquale and lowered his voice. "Go straight home. I'll talk to you later."

Pasquale caught her hand, and in front of her father, said, "You no worry, Angelina. Non ti preoccupare." Angelina closed her eyes and willed that a great gust of wind pass through and blow her far away.

CHAPTER 14

Angelina expected a long lecture, so she sat on the sofa where she'd be the most comfortable while enduring her father's anger. The tension rose the moment Domenico walked into the house.

"In families, we do nothing to shame each other. Why is that so hard to remember?"

"Papa, you never understand me. Claudio Garcia's mother was so sad. I was only trying to help."

Domenico's expression remained unchanged. "Do you know the saying, '*Sangue del mio sangue*'?"

"Blood of my blood." Again, her father had docked his boat at the pier of old Sicilian quotations.

"It means loyalty, Angelina. Think of your family before you speak."

"Claudio's mother looked so sad."

"We go to funerals to show respect and support the family in their grief, not raise emotions and enrage the priest."

It wasn't even her idea to go to the funeral. "I wasn't trying to draw attention."

"Neither does a horse standing among goats, but there it

is. Everything you do affects all of us. That's why we don't act without thinking. Sicilians live by the old ways and the old values. When you talk, you talk for all of us. We're like fingers of the same hand, limbs of the same body. Remember this, or one day you might find yourself without a family."

How could such a thing even cross his mind? "Never say that, Papa."

"Everything we do, we do for the family. Capisci?"

What could be the harm in making Claudio's mother feel better? A lengthy silence lingered between father and daughter.

"You know, Papa, I don't think Claudio Garcia wanted to kill himself. Maybe he was hurting for a long time. The fire made it worse, and he wanted to stop hurting."

Domenico shook his head, and another moment of silence lingered. He glanced at the photograph of her mother, himself, and the children.

"The family is all we have. We stick together to survive. When I left Sicily, your zio Pasquale begged me not to go. I promised him one day I'd send him money enough to travel." Domenico's voice softened.

"And I hope he never goes back. I can't think of a better uncle."

"I told you, I left with my cousin Fabrizio. We traveled in steerage, down in the ship's belly, the only way we could afford to journey to America. We never guessed at the unbearable conditions. We ate only once a day. With so many of us, someone's elbow was always in our side. No fresh air. Vomit rolling across the floor."

Angelina's stomach grew queasy.

"They gave us only one hour on deck. We took deep breaths of the fresh sea air as if we could store it in our lungs and use it later. The hour ended, and we went below again. The captain didn't want to offend the rich with our poverty.

"Sometimes the crew bumped into us so hard they knocked us off our feet—a game for them. Women and children cried." Domenico narrowed his eyes and gave his daughter a hard look. "To come to America, we voyaged through hell. Our torment didn't end on the ship.

"After the terrible journey, not everyone set foot in America. For such immigrants, Ellis Island became known as the Island of Tears. The last insult came when the clerk wrote "Frank Price" instead of "Fabrizio Pirrello" when my cousin came through." Domenico ran his fingers through his hair. "The same man tried to give me a new name. I refused, but my cousin was sick of everything and wanted to get out."

"What happened?"

"Fabrizio said, 'They see us as animals, as cattle.'" Domenico released a painful sigh. "I told my cousin it's better to sit in their cage for a day than to change our names for a lifetime. Otherwise, you dishonor your father and grandfather, who are proud of their name."

"Did Fabrizio agree?"

"'They'll never know,' he said."

Angelina thought back to all the times her father's resolve remained unbending, and she could easily see this argument escalating.

"We were both young, angry, tired of it all. Fabrizio gave up his name, and I refused to leave without mine. 'May they put Frank on your gravestone so no one knows who you are.' I regret my words, but what's said is said. The next day, a Sicilian was on duty and wrote my name correctly." Domenico smoothed his mustache.

Angelina could see her father was as strong-willed then as now.

"Three years later, Fabrizio's father came to America. He was furious and made him change his name back to Pirrello, but he left the name Frank. When I went to visit my uncle,

Fabrizio was there. I asked him why he'd kept that first name. 'It's easier in America,' he answered."

Domenico looked into Angelina's eyes. "Do what is easy, and you have nothing of which to be proud. Do what is right, and you reveal your strong character."

Old wounds leave deep scars, thought Angelina. "It all happened a long time ago, Papa."

He nodded. "He's still blood of my blood—*sangue del mio sangue.*"

"Maybe after such a long, miserable journey, he couldn't stand it anymore and wanted to get off the island at any cost and become an American," Angelina offered.

"A nationality isn't a piece of paper stamped by the government. It's what's inside you, and what's inside *you,* Angelina, are the echoes of Sicilian voices. It's what you inherited, and when you're buried, it's the legacy you'll leave behind. We know who we are."

CHAPTER 15

God and the Catholic Church had rules for Sunday, while the cigar factory and Domenico made rules for the rest of the week. Still, for one hour every Saturday, Angelina ruled herself and basked in the glory of learning. The park, with its mature trees and wide branches, its expanse of grass, and its benches welcoming visitors, became her schoolroom and el lector her *maestro.*

"We'll study *Don Quixote de la Mancha* next week, Angelina." The grey-haired man sat on the same bench where they had first met.

"I already started," she said eagerly. "Quixote tries to revive chivalry. He's old and doesn't see things as they are."

The seeds of a grin nearly took root on Don Carlos Madrid's face, but that would have diluted the seriousness that defined him. "Wisdom ripens with time, like cigars in a humidor." He paused as though he wanted Angelina to agree, but she said nothing. As far as she'd read in the story, Quixote appeared more confused than wise, and she suspected this wasn't the answer her maestro wanted.

"*Don Quixote* is the greatest literary work to come out of

Spain in the last three hundred years. It will be around for hundreds more. Books can become worn and faded but never grow old. Miguel de Cervantes teaches that everyone, regardless of nobility or peasantry, is important. It's a message of hope, and what is life without hope? Do you agree, Angelina?"

Angelina thought of all she wanted to accomplish in life. "Hope is everything," she said.

"We say in Spanish, 'The devil knows more because he's old, not because he's the devil.' Don Quixote is an old man and teaching us something."

Their time had slipped by. Don Carlos Madrid got to his feet. "We'll meet next Saturday afternoon, and if you listen carefully to what I read, we can have a fruitful discussion."

Angelina didn't believe it possible to listen more intently, especially when el lector read with such fervor, as though the pages dripped with gold. "Thank you for your time, Señor Madrid."

He tipped his hat to her and walked away with his shoulders raised. Perhaps after so many years of adulation from the cigar makers, he heard applause when there wasn't any.

On the way home, Angelina analyzed the spectacular popularity of books and the masterpieces Shakespeare and Cervantes had created centuries ago. The lesson was obvious. Great stories far outlived their authors. Angelina's imagination soared. She'd investigate when and where to take the entrance exam and tell no one. Excited by her decision, she went home envisioning an aura of brilliant colors surrounding her as she stepped through her front door. Did those dead authors know the impact their writing had left on the world?

"Angelina, run and deliver my order to Rizzo's Bakery. I've left the list on the table."

Her father's voice pricked her reverie. "Papa, I just walked in, and that's the boys' job." How could she write a masterpiece with so many interruptions?

"I need fresh rolls in the morning. Both Vincenzo and Salvatore are too dirty from working in the vegetable garden."

"A few buckets of ice water should clean them up," Angelina offered.

"What did you say?"

Her father never accepted her opinion. "Nothing." Those two knew more ways to get out of work than anyone. Angelina grabbed her father's list and let the door slam behind her. Exasperated with her family and their interference with her dreams, she hurried along the streets until the bakery sign with an oversized wedding cake came into view. She stepped through the door, intent on completing her task with haste.

"*Benvenuta,* Angelina." Umberto Rizzo took off his baker's hat, laid it on the counter, and shook her hand as if she'd arrived for a social visit.

"Hello, Signor Rizzo." She handed over her father's list.

He nodded as he read it. It was hard not to notice Rizzo's coal-black hair and how the strands appeared dull and stuck together.

"My father increased tomorrow's order. Also, I'm to bring home a dozen rolls," said Angelina.

"Business is profitable, then. May he have continued good luck."

Surrounded by freshly baked everything, it seemed odd that Rizzo stayed thin, although his oversized apron gave him a formless appearance, like wearing bedsheets. "Papa says we make our luck. A good harvest and good luck come after hard work."

"Good Italian wisdom. Pick out a few pastries for your family, Angelina."

"That's kind but unnecessary."

"No, I insist. If not, I'll deliver whatever I pick out myself."

Angelina leaned over the counter and gazed through the glass. "You make it hard to refuse. I guess everyone likes Saint Joseph pastries."

"I'll go get them now, straight from the oven." Umberto vanished behind the swinging doors.

Alone, Angelina focused once more on the display case and its array of pastries. As she pushed aside the baker's hat to look more closely through the glass counter, her fingers became smeared with something black, something tacky, something familiar. She smelled it. Shoe polish! The thought almost caused her to laugh out loud as she pictured the baker dabbing it on his graying hair.

Umberto reappeared with the box of promised pastries. "Tell your father I send these with my compliments." He handed her the bag of rolls and a box of pastries.

Angelina tried not to stare at his hair and again wondered if he'd remained slim because he disliked pastries or had great willpower.

"Thank you, Signor Rizzo. My brothers and Lily will be excited." She had to admit Rizzo's Bakery made the finest pastries. Regardless of which one she ate, that one would be her favorite. It was better than the nuns at a saint's day celebration, even with God favoring the convent.

"Goodbye, signore."

The baker rushed from behind the counter to the entrance. He held open the door for her and grinned. "You're a young woman now, Angelina. You can call me Umberto."

She stepped outside and glanced over her shoulder. What an odd thing to say.

~

MONDAY MORNING STARTED UNUSUALLY TRANQUIL, which should have been a warning. As Angelina entered the kitchen, she saw her father sipping his coffee and looking at the door as if waiting for her.

"Angelina, you'll leave right now with your uncle for Cuesta Rey Cigar Factory. They're hiring." Domenico stood.

Her throat tightened. She hadn't expected to have an argument instead of breakfast. "Papa, I've been at the factory for over a year. It's hard to keep track of time there. I do the same thing every day, all day, all the yesterdays, and all the tomorrows." Angelina exhaled a frustrated breath. "I've been visiting my friend Sophia Esposito, and I've read all her schoolbooks. I want to go to college with her. I excelled in school, and I haven't stopped. I'm still studying. I'm sure I'll pass the entrance exam."

Domenico's shoulders slumped slightly as his voice rose. "You'll pass through that door. My brother waits on the other side."

"I strip away tobacco leaves while you strip away my dreams," Angelina argued. "I want a better life."

"Time to be practical, not to dream."

"What's more practical than to follow my dreams? It brings me happiness and makes me want to succeed."

"I have no time for this argument. You will do as I say." With that, he waved his hand and dismissed her like a general discharging his army.

Don Carlos Madrid had further nourished her dream, made her want it even more. The seed of independence had taken root inside her, and she intended to nourish it until it bloomed. She walked out the door with her uncle, dreading every step she took. Any other day, the fresh air would have invigorated her, but not this time. She had little enthusiasm for what lay in store.

"Zio Pasquale, why is it you never worry or get discouraged?"

"I worry last week."

"About what?"

"I worry I no find work, then I say, 'Pasquale, sure you gonna find the work. You are the best.' So I no worry no more."

"That's it?"

"Like I say, non ti preoccupare."

They turned the corner, and there it was. Though Angelina had never been inside the Cuesta Rey Cigar Factory, she recognized the architecture with its three-story design and rows of large vertical windows precisely placed for cross ventilation. Pasquale stepped ahead and held open the door. They entered the first office, where a man with an unnecessarily long mustache sat behind an oak desk. He quickly hired Pasquale, and then it was Angelina's turn. Pasquale winked and whispered, "Remember, you the best."

In a far more somber mood than her uncle, she introduced herself, answered questions, and listened to her job description from the man with only the surname Cuesta on his nameplate.

"You're hired," Cuesta said. The words almost hurt, like chalk scraping a blackboard. "You'll like it here at our factory. We've already hired many of your old coworkers from Garcia-Marcos."

The mention of Garcia-Marcos prompted Angelina to think of Claudio Garcia. She resisted the custom of making the sign of the cross out of respect for the dead. Cuesta might view it as a display of gratitude for hiring her.

"Take these papers to the office down the corridor. Eduardo will show you where you'll be working." He pushed a small twisted wire against the edge of the papers to hold them together.

Angelina reached for the pages and found she couldn't resist sliding the strange metal configuration off and on again.

Cuesta gave a faint grin from behind his long mustache. "It's called a paperclip. The Wrights make big news with their flying machine, but some little Norwegian called Vaaler bends a worthless piece of wire and patents it. He'll make more money than the Wright Brothers will ever see, and they probably discarded barrels of twisted wire building their machine." The man's laughter filled the room. "Sounds like there's a proverb in this, doesn't it?"

Angelina nodded. "Don't overlook the trash barrel?"

"One man's trash is another man's treasure."

ANGELINA SIFTED through the endless tobacco leaves at her new factory. Unlike the wooden structure of Garcia Marcos, they'd built Cuesta Rey of bricks, and the floors didn't squeak. There were also paintings on the walls to help distract the workers from the overabundance of brick and mortar. The only bright spot was the discovery of her friend Carmen, but then Dolores walked through the door, and all hope of a peaceful workplace lay trampled. Even worse, Dolores sat much closer this time.

Nothing had changed. The days were as long, the worktable as worn, and Angelina did the same repetitious job. She came prepared to stimulate her mind with memorized poetry. *Tell me not in mournful numbers life is but an empty dream.* She solved math problems: *If a train left Tampa and traveled at fifty miles per hour, how long would it take to arrive in Key West?* She incorporated Florida's topography and wildlife. *If the Everglades were seven hundred square miles, with three thousand alligators, how many alligators per square mile?*

Poems, puzzles, and problems distracted her. When her arms grew tired, she counted the tobacco leaves she'd stripped, multiplied the hours she'd worked, and tallied the total in a year. They reached into the thousands while working at a job that was pointless and dissatisfying. *Interesting that* basta *is the same word for "enough" in both Italian and Spanish, and I've had enough.* Her anger flared. In a burst of frustration, Angelina jumped to her feet to leave. She looked across the room and saw the familiar face of a young man staring back at her. He smiled and walked toward her. Her resolve deflated.

"Angelina, do you remember me? Rolando Aguirre?" His calm, masculine voice spread warm, soothing honey upon Angelina's anger. "I ran into your uncle at the barber. He said he was looking for work."

"You're the one who fought the fire with my uncle," said Angelina.

"That's right. We worked together for hours that night until we were as charred-looking as the buildings." Rolando's voice reminded her of a soft breeze combing through tree branches. "I told Pasquale to come here, and then he recommended you, said you were good. So I told Cuesta about you."

"That doesn't sound like my uncle. Are you sure he didn't say I was the best—the very best?"

Rolando grinned. "That's right. I guess you know him pretty well. He reminded me I met you the day of the fire." Angelina glanced around and noticed many women staring at the redhead and whispering to each other.

She lowered herself into her seat again. "In such confusion, you can't expect to remember anyone."

"I hope you like it here. Cuesta's a good man. I also work for the union leaders, and the tension between the union and factory owners is a growing challenge, but when I mentioned I knew some good workers, Cuesta asked for their names."

Angelina pulled on a leaf. "I should thank you."

Dolores gave a loud, raspy, hacking sound, no doubt the only woman who could offend with a cough.

"I have to take these cigar bands downstairs. I'm glad I saw you again," Rolando said.

"I'm glad too." Her words slid out.

Rolando took a few steps and then turned back. "I didn't need Pasquale's reminder. I never forgot you."

Angelina's heart raced, and it revitalized her world. She pulled too hard on a leaf and hit her hand on the table with a bang. However, she wasn't the only one following Rolando's departure. Giggles trickled across the room. Angelina quickly grabbed a fresh leaf without looking up.

"Hey, chicas, I think our little Angelina has fallen in love." Dolores's voice grated on Angelina's ears. "Tell us all about your man."

"I hardly know him," she said calmly.

Dolores's mouth crooked into a wicked smile. "Did you hear that, chicas? She hardly knows him."

"One day, Dolores, your poison tongue will swell up and choke you to death," Carmen said.

"You heard him. He never forgot her." Dolores appeared eager for Angelina's reaction.

Angelina recognized the trap and yawned.

Another woman shouted from the back. "Don't listen to Dolores. Enjoy it while you can. Remember, they all look good at first, but some are full of tricks. It's a big job to tell the good ones from the bad."

The conversation had drawn the attention of the large roomful of women. Silvia from the back row was the first to call out. "That's right. Mine went out with those dogs of women drinking at the cantina. Then he came home, jumped in bed, and I woke up with their fleas. Now he cries at my door, begging to come back."

"To love is to suffer. No one cries louder than cheating husbands. I thought I could make my husband lose his bad habits." Another woman sighed. "But all he lost was his hair and some teeth. He left and took my money and my parrot." She paused. "I really miss that parrot."

The women giggled, and the mood lightened.

"You see that, Angelina? Just because I got married, it doesn't mean I have a husband. It means he got a wife. The man I married likes to spend our money on gambling and saves his voice for talking to the dog." Eva reached inside her pocket and showed everyone her coins. "Before I met him, I was an heiress. Now, this is all that's left."

"Some men are good. I hit the *loteria* with mine. He thinks I'm a princess," came another voice from the back.

"Your husband *is* wonderful, Alicia," shouted Carmen with an eyebrow raised at Dolores. "*Atención señoritas y señoras,* we have the heiress of Havana among us, a princess, and I'm the Queen of Spain," said Carmen.

"Pleased to meet you," said Eva as she jumped out of her seat and curtsied. "Who wants to tell Cuesta he has a princess, an heiress, and the Queen of Spain working in his factory and that they're all on the third floor, stripping tobacco leaves?"

Waves of laughter flooded the room.

Relieved the conversation had drifted away from Rolando, Angelina intended to relive their conversation all day. Had she said anything that sounded foolish? Perhaps it would have been better to ask about his family when he brought up her uncle. Why hadn't it occurred to her? Perhaps she shouldn't have kept her head down so much. She analyzed every word and gesture. She wasn't sure why, but she wanted to impress him.

She stripped a leaf from its stem, tossed it onto the pile, and returned to her mathematical problems. *If Rolando is six feet tall, how much taller is he than Angelina? If Rolando works downstairs, and Angelina works upstairs, how many steps does it take to visit her?* Somehow the factory that employed them both didn't seem so oppressive anymore.

Angelina glanced out the window and saw Cuesta Rey's reader approach the building. Don Carlos Madrid never missed the stroke of the hour, while Gilberto Sanchez typically arrived a few minutes late. He didn't have the same regalia and made no grand gestures as he read. Great literature suffered without a reader's flair. Cigar makers expected magnificence and nobility for their twenty-five cents a week. Don Carlos Madrid had taught her that civilized people needed someone to applaud. He had wrapped himself in the classics of brilliant authors and poets, and there was no releasing him. Soon he would replace Sanchez.

The factory's workday was over, and as Angelina walked out with Carmen, Rosa Caprici rushed up and put her arms around both girls. "You'll never guess. Luca and I are getting married. Tell me you'll come to my wedding."

"Congratulations! Not even the worst Florida hurricane could keep me away." Angelina hugged her friend. "That's wonderful, Rosa."

"Well, it's about time. I'm tired of watching you both smile at each other," Carmen said. "See that, Angelina? A good man and an upcoming happy marriage right before your eyes."

All around, women returned to chatting about men, as though the conversation was left on the clothesline and when they returned it still damp. They complained more about disagreeable men than praised the good ones, but that was because bad men left deep wounds. Angelina sensed there was something sincere and honest about Rolando. She suspected he was a good one.

Dolores picked up some tobacco leaves and walked past Angelina and the girls. She wrinkled her nose and threw them an unpleasant look, as if something smelled bad.

"I think Dolores used to be a pillar of salt," Carmen said.

"What?" Rosa and Angelina said in unison.

"I think people are reincarnated to get another chance when they mess up. Dolores is Lot's wife reincarnated." Carmen narrowed her eyebrows. "It's like this. It was forbidden for the people in Sodom to have guests. So Dolores—I mean Lot's wife—not only breaks the law, she spreads the word of her husband's dinner guests and asks around to borrow salt. Everyone comes running to attack. Lot escapes with his family, but his wife, who enjoys trouble, looks back at the destruction, so God buries her in salt." Carmen gave them a knowing look. "She'll be reincarnated again." Carmen smiled. "And again and again."

Angelina and Rosa giggled.

"Maybe that's why people say someone's not worth their salt," said Rosa.

"No," said Angelina, "I've read the Romans bought slaves with salt. They were worth their salt or not. Salt was money. The word *salary* comes from salt."

"Well, what do you know?" said Carmen.

CHAPTER 16

"Come, Angelina, today we gonna learn how to make the cigars." Just the sight of Pasquale lightened her mood. A large bag sat on the floor.

"Zio, you know how skilled the cigar makers are, and factories expect perfection."

"They make maybe 150 cigars a day," Pasquale said.

"Oh, 150—that many?" Angelina stepped back in disbelief.

Pasquale threw up his hands. "That's what I say too. We can make more."

"El lector says people do magnificent things because they think they can."

"You're right. We can learn anything."

"Angelina, you no worry. I gonna show you." And with that last remark, Pasquale reached into the large bag by his side with such enthusiasm it reminded Angelina of Father Christmas reaching into his bag of toys. Pasquale pulled out a handful of broken tobacco leaves. The grand gesture didn't match the result, although he looked pleased.

"Where did you get all that?"

"I sweep the floors, and I see the broken leaves all over. I say to myself, 'Pasquale you better to save this.' So I put them inside the bag. The bag, she get bigger and bigger. Now, we gonna make the cigars."

Angelina glanced at the bag full of broken leaves and tried to visualize them rehabilitated into cigars. The image eluded her, like imagining her brothers as sweet babies.

"The first thing I gonna do is take apart this cigar our good friend Rolando give to me. Then we gonna put it together like before."

Angelina examined the perfect cigar Rolando had made.

"Maybe you'll create a new cigar, Zio."

"That's for sure. I show you." Her uncle lifted his arms in the air and made large circles, as if he were clearing away an unseen disturbance that might affect his ability to create. He reached for Rolando's cigar and tried to unravel it, but the tightly wound leaves resisted his efforts.

"I think maybe is better we use the leaves in the bag." Pasquale spread out the broken leaves. He rolled them together until he managed only one rather unusual-looking cigar. "I say, no worry. And now I make the very first cigar in *la mia famiglia*." He placed it in his mouth, but before he could light it, his creation fell apart, leaving only a few limp tobacco leaves dangling from his lips. Angelina burst out laughing. The world had to wait a little longer for her uncle to become the great cigar maker he envisioned.

"I'm sorry, Zio. I'm sure your next one will be much better."

"That's for sure. Next time is gonna be the best."

~

THE WEEK FINALLY ENDED. Angelina waited for Pasquale outside the factory. They didn't always walk home together, and when he didn't appear, she considered how he stopped to talk to everyone. The air grew chilly, so she turned toward home but stopped to read a new Suffragette poster. The Suffragettes had grown more intolerant of the unfairness toward women and more dedicated to right the wrong.

"Angelina, wait a moment."

She turned, and Rolando walked toward her in the white dress shirt and black tie of the cigar makers considered artisans and not workers.

"I wanted to give your uncle something, but I haven't been able to find him."

"I couldn't find him either. I'm sure he's talking to one of the Sicilians about cigar making or telling stories about the old country." Angelina tucked a stray hair behind her ear.

"Here, take these two boxes of cigars. Pasquale wanted twelve—all distinct, unique qualities and blends. Do you know why?" Rolando raised his eyebrows.

Angelina had a good idea what was on her uncle's mind. "He probably wants to take them apart and study the differences. He's teaching himself to make cigars."

Rolando chuckled. "That's probably a good way to prepare a chicken for cooking, but it doesn't work when rolling cigars. Tell your uncle Pasquale my friend Belarmino and I will teach him everything he needs to know to get a job. Belarmino sells new and used furniture now, but he's a master at rolling cigars."

Angelina knew the value of the gift and how happy her uncle would be to receive the cigars. "Your friend Belarmino is my mother's cousin, but I don't think my Uncle Pasquale even knows that. These cigars will mean a lot. He's determined to learn." She glanced at the remaining box. "What's in this one?"

"Ah, the other twelve cigars are for your father, with my

compliments. Pasquale told me your father likes good cigars. He'll enjoy these. I made them myself."

Angelina lifted the lid of the box and glanced inside. "These carry gold and red bands." She'd long since learned to recognize the markings of a good cigar. A gold band was reserved for the best of the best, the tobacco leaves aged longest, with a smoother flavor than lesser-made cigars. Her father knew the difference. "He'll be so pleased. They both will. You're very kind and . . ." Her cheeks flushed. "And generous, Rolando."

"Anytime." Rolando offered a warm smile, tipped an imaginary hat at Angelina, and winked. Angelina watched as he walked away.

~

AFTER DINNER THAT EVENING, Angelina left the table and went to her room to retrieve the cigar box. She opened it and inhaled the finest cigars. Without a doubt, it would thrill her father to receive them.

"Papa, I have something for you." Domenico liked a good cigar after his evening meal, so she held out the cigar box.

"What is this?"

"A gift. Twelve of the finest cigars Cuesta Rey makes—Havana's best."

Domenico reached for the box, held a cigar under his nose, and took in its fine aroma. "Where did you get these?"

"They're from Rolando Aguirre, a talented cigar maker. He made them himself. There's a box of mixed varieties for Zio Pasquale, and these twelve he asked me to give to you, with his compliments."

"Why is he sending me cigars?" Domenico raised a suspicious eyebrow.

Angelina should have known. Her father questioned

everything, even gifts. "Rolando helped Zio Pasquale get a job, and because of him, they hired me."

"Why are you using his first name?"

Angelina sensed a trap. "What do you mean?"

"You call him Rolando, not Señor Aguirre. I've taught you how to address strangers."

Sometimes her father was exhausting to listen to. What harm could there be to call him by his first name? She saw no reason for the formality when he couldn't be over three or four years older, not decades, or her superior overseeing her at work, or the governor of Florida.

"Aguirre . . . Aguirre—what nationality is that?" Domenico asked.

"I never asked, and he never said." Perhaps she shouldn't let him draw his conclusions. "Carmen says his people are from Europe, the north of Spain, Basque country."

"There can only be one reason a man sends twelve of the finest Cuban cigars to a man he doesn't know with his compliments." He paused. "He wants something in return."

"Or he's a kind man with a good heart." Her father could be so frustrating.

"Perhaps he wants my foolish daughter."

"Papa, if you met Rolando, you'd know he's nice." She'd called him Rolando out of spite. Was the sky going to fall? Was the earth going to tremble because she had used his first name?

"I do not need to meet him. He can't buy his way into my family with twelve cigars. When the time comes, you'll marry a Sicilian, not a Spaniard."

Angelina's face grew feverish. "He didn't ask to marry me. I'm not even the one receiving the gift." As usual, her father traveled a road that made no sense.

"All gifts have a purpose, like the Trojan horse. If this man had good intentions, he'd have given the gift to my brother, not my young daughter." Sicilians viewed all strangers with suspicion. Angelina considered her uncle and Signora Bertelli and decided not all Sicilians were that way.

"He was trying to find Zio Pasquale to give him the cigars. When he couldn't find him, he gave them to me instead. You contradict yourself, Papa. I'm your 'young daughter' when it's convenient, like when a man talks to me or when I'm invited to a dance, but then I'm too old to be sitting in a classroom, so you send me to work. Which is it? Am I too old or too young? I can't be both."

"No one should question their father."

Angelina picked up Sophia Esposito's schoolbook from the table, opened it, and slammed it shut in the presence of her father. "I am capable of much more, Papa. If you give me a chance, I can take care of myself." Who could reason with a lion that only roared and showed its teeth?

Angelina reached across the table, collected her father's dinner plate with quick, angry movements, and took it to the sink. She considered how she'd left school for her father, had gone to work for her father, did the housework, attended to the children to please her father, yet he still complained.

ANGELINA ROUNDED the corner and caught sight of Rolando in conversation with someone at the carriage house. This wasn't altogether surprising since it was on the same block as Belarmino's furniture store. However, after her unpleasant talk with her father, it was better to avoid him. Then again, Angelina considered the determination of the Suffragettes. They never backed down.

As for her, she'd never had trouble thinking for herself either. However, she didn't want to give Rolando the wrong idea. To approach him might seem forward. She crossed to the other side of the street. She'd see Rolando at work—tell him then that her father enjoyed the cigars. It had to be true. If not, why had he smoked them all?

"Wait, Angelina." Unlike her father, Rolando's voice had an undeniable tranquility to it, even when he yelled from across the street. A vision of her father's angry face appeared before her. She blinked it away.

"I'm so glad I noticed you. I wondered when I could see you without the women at the factory staring at me."

"I'm sure my father has hired them as chaperones. Better talk fast, before they show up."

Rolando's grin lit up his face. "How much time do I have?"

His mild manner put her at ease, but men were a tricky bunch, or women wouldn't be so repressed. Like her father, did he believe men should control everything?

"That's hard to say," she replied. They walked past another Suffragettes poster. "Are you in favor of the Suffragettes or against them, and why?"

Rolando chuckled. "Do you need to know this answer right now?"

"I like to know who I'm talking to and on what side of the fence they're standing." They strolled farther down the road.

"I'll answer your question if you'll answer mine. What do you think of King Alfonso XIII of Spain?" He never lost his smile.

Angelina studied his expression. She saw no relationship between his question and hers. "Why do you ask?"

"It's how I get answers. I also like to know who I'm talking to and what they're thinking."

Suspicious, he might try to outsmart her, she tossed him an answer. "The king of Spain is particular about his cigars. He likes to smoke Perfectos and Havana's best." How could this be wrong? Nearly all men liked a good cigar, and a king could afford the finest. It made perfect sense.

Rolando put his hand on her arm and guided her away from a carriage. "That's an excellent answer. Where did you look it up?"

"That's two questions, and you haven't answered mine. Do you think men should give women the right to vote, acknowledge they are capable of powerful thoughts, and that women should not have to take orders from men—ever?" Angelina prepared herself to strike back if he gave her an unfavorable answer.

"Yours sounds like three questions."

"No, it's one but a long question."

"A long question, huh?" Rolando had a gleam in his eye. "It's my sincere hope that when women get the vote, they won't be too busy."

"Busy?"

"Well, there's no question in my mind that they can run a business. They can also a country, and a family, and do it all at the same time. Is there something left for men to do?"

Angelina caught the humor. He was teasing her.

"What makes you an authority on the king of Spain?" she asked.

Rolando leaned closer. "What makes you an authority on which cigars the king likes?"

Angelina had no way to prove her answer, and Rolando had no way to disprove it. A moment passed before they broke into laughter.

Two men strolled past, one shorter than the other. Angelina lowered her voice.

"Rolando, isn't that the man who makes those intricate labels for cigar boxes? He's talented."

"Are you asking about the Cuban or the Spaniard?" Rolando's grin broadened.

Angelina looked at both men. "The one on the right."

"Ah, the *Spaniard*." He emphasized the word.

"How can you tell the difference? He only said a few words."

"We Spaniards lisp, and we're good-looking." He raised his eyebrows in obvious amusement.

Angelina ignored the latter part of the remark. "Lisp? That's a speech impediment. You can't mean the whole country lisps. That's impossible."

"Everything's impossible until someone does it."

She crossed her arms. "And how did an entire nation start lisping?"

"Our good King Ferdinand of Spain had a lisp."

"You realize lisps are not contagious."

"This one was." He seemed comfortable, as though he'd told this story many times. "Everyone in Spain loved the king, but he couldn't pronounce certain sounds. He even went down to the ocean and tried to cure himself with a mouthful of shells, but nothing worked."

"And?" she said.

"And the entire country started lisping so he wouldn't feel so bad."

Angelina raised an eyebrow. "So people went from village to village telling everyone to start lisping?"

Rolando shrugged. "We excused those who were already lisping on their own."

"You're making this up." She glanced back at the two men. "And how do you know the man on the left is Cuban? He only said three words."

"It's not what he said. It's the order in which he said it. That's too much information all at once."

"I think I can handle it."

"No, I think we'll discuss a different country each time we meet. There are at least twenty Spanish-speaking countries and regions with different dialects." Rolando sighed as though the upcoming task would be a great one. "Next time, we'll discuss the Cubans and why they speak the way they do. You won't want to miss it. Then we'll move on to the Puerto Ricans."

Angelina giggled.

"So, tell me, Rolando, how did you get such red hair?"

"I'm so glad you asked that. It's my inheritance." Rolando reached for a lock of Angelina's hair, held it up, and pretended to examine its color. "I inherited red rubies, but through some mix-up, I got the red hair, and my cousin got the rubies."

"Rolando!" Pasquale's unmistakable voice broke through.

Her uncle hurried toward them with an outstretched hand. "I'm here for my cigar lesson." He excitedly turned to his niece. "Angelina, I gonna learn, and then I gonna teach you. So we both make the cigars, and we gonna be the best."

"The very best, Zio."

Rolando leaned closer to Pasquale. "I'll tell you a secret. There's no such thing as a bad cigar. Whatever you roll, Pasquale, someone will be happy to offer you money to smoke it."

CHAPTER 17

Angelina had no intention of letting the wonderful work of the Suffragettes go unnoticed. She collected newspaper clippings proving they lobbied, paraded, and held elaborate activities to implement their cause. Their strength reinforced her journey toward equality. Inspired, she wanted to see them at least once, but the next meeting was across Tampa, on the more elite side of town.

Angelina rushed into work and took her seat next to Carmen. "Carmen, why don't you go with me to the Suffragette meeting on Saturday? It's on the far end of Tampa, and it should be exciting."

Carmen rolled her eyes. "Exciting? Aye, you *pobrecita*. You don't even know exciting. You are leading a sad life. Dances at the social clubs are exciting. The rumba is exciting. Have you ever met a Cuban who didn't want to go to a dance? No? And you never will. I've seen those Suffragette posters all over town. So let me see, do I want to go to a meeting across Tampa and listen to a bunch of rich old ladies complain about politics, or do I want to dance the rumba with Miguel, Ignacio, and Santiago? This is a hard question."

"Carmen, you are not taking this seriously, and you're missing the point. These are important meetings."

"I agree. You go to the meeting and tell me about it on Monday. I'll go to the dance and tell you all about that."

Angelina suppressed a smile. "All right, then. I'll go alone."

"I will be with you in spirit, and you can come to the dance with me in spirit. And let me tell you, your spirit is going to have a lot more fun than you are."

THE NEXT SATURDAY, Angelina sorted her coins and calculated the round-trip cost for the three trolleys she'd have to take. Satisfied she had enough for the fare, she slipped an apple and a piece of bread into her pocket and left. She jumped on the first trolley, then the second, and sat tall in her seat. As she traveled farther into Tampa, the apparel in the windows became increasingly stylish, the accessories more elaborate, and the window displays took on a distinct, almost artistic flair. The upper class had panache, and Model-Ts dominated the streets, replacing older carriage rides.

Angelina had no reservations. *Nothing can be as exciting as women challenging the United States Constitution and battling the most powerful men in the nation.* To see the women of the Suffragettes and history in the making was worth the trip. Angelina stepped off the last trolley, smoothed her dress, and checked the pins in her hair. A large sign indicated the entrance to the Suffragette meeting. With her best posture, Angelina made her way past the chattering crowd and walked inside the brick building with beveled, diamond-shaped windows.

A smartly dressed young woman handed her a brochure

at the door. "Hello, I'm Isabelle Hastings. I'm glad you came. Please have a seat."

"I'm Angelina Pirrello, and—"

Isabelle was not there to inspire conversation. She hurried on to the woman behind Angelina. "Hello, I'm Isabelle Hastings—"

It didn't matter. There was something momentous here. A vibrancy filled the air. Thrilled she had come, Angelina walked to where women were taking their seats amid rows of comfortable-looking upholstered dining chairs. Angelina pulled out a chair for herself and sat close enough to see well but far back enough not to draw attention. The room buzzed with excitement.

Everyone wore large, extravagant hats. If only she owned at least a simple one, but there wasn't a milliner anywhere near Ybor City. She couldn't even look in a window and dream about hats like these. These weren't the women who worked for a living, or used a scrub board to wash clothes, or could recognize the feel of a tobacco leaf.

Angelina imagined they lived in sizable houses, had hired help, and had their gardeners plant an abundance of flowers to beautify instead of fruit trees and vegetables to nourish. She had never seen such beautiful jewelry and elegant clothing and accessories up close. Angelina realized at once that wealth meant power. *These women have a voice, and they have the ears of the elite,* she thought. *They will succeed.*

She was glad she'd worn her best blue dress and Nonna's pendant watch. She checked the time often to draw attention to the watch's beauty, should anyone be looking.

Even though the day wasn't chilly, a woman taller than most approached the podium in a fur adorned with the head of an ill-fated fox draped over one arm. Angelina didn't know much about the rich, but carrying around a dead animal seemed a peculiar way to exhibit wealth.

"Dearest sisters, please take your seats," the woman at the podium said. "As many of you know, I am Gladys Parker, and we gather today as sisters dealt a terrible discrimination because we are women." Gladys raised her arm and tightened her hand into a fist. "No more, I say."

A sudden round of applause broke out.

"Ours is a nation born of rebellion against injustice. As far back as 1765, James Otis sounded the cry, 'Taxation without representation is tyranny.' Now, nearly 150 years later, we shout the same cry. They tax us yet disallow us equal representation. We, the women of these United States of America, have no voice in our government."

Every word resonated with Angelina. *Women have no voice in government, and I have no voice in my life.* The thought of things changing excited her.

"We, the daughters of this nation, born and raised here, will no longer stand aside while newly arrived male immigrants become citizens with the right to vote. We stand together to break down this brick wall erected by a government that enforces inequality."

The women rose to their feet and gave Gladys Parker a rousing round of applause. She raised her arms as if saluting her troops. "We march on, suffragettes," she said with the passion of a musical crescendo. Her words boiled the pot, and with all critical points made, the ebb and flow calmed. Gladys Parker dramatically picked up a man's hat and held it high. "Sisters, before you leave your chairs, support our conviction. Donate whatever you will and place it in this hat to aid our cry for justice. I will make the first donation." Gladys Parker reached into her ample bosom, pulled out a twenty-dollar bill, held it up for all to see, and placed it in the hat.

Angelina gasped. Never had she seen such generosity, and suddenly she felt trapped. If she put nothing into the hat, she'd embarrass herself, appear disloyal, and perhaps insult them. If she put all her coins into the hat, she'd likewise embarrass herself, appear disloyal, and perhaps insult them. Even worse, she'd have no money for transportation home. If it had taken fifty-five minutes to arrive by trolley, how long would it take to walk home? She'd arrive long after dark and probably lose her way in this unfamiliar part of town.

Several women got up and said a few words, but Angelina kept her eye on the hat as it steadily moved closer. It would soon reach her row. Women around her opened their pocketbooks. Each appeared to be trying to outdo the others. Anxiety was a harsh emotion, and for Angelina, it grew unbearable, akin to having the heel of her tightly laced-up shoe caught on a railroad track with a train racing toward her.

Angelina had read Sophia's schoolbook on American history from cover to cover, she knew the plight of immigrant women, and she'd excelled at oral reports in school. She saw only one way to avoid the offering, but did she have the nerve to do it? Should she or could she address this gathering of society women? With a burst of nervous energy, she shot to her feet, stepped out of her row and, amid wide eyes, went before the podium and faced the audience.

"Sisters, my name is Angelina Pirrello. I am from Ybor City, where there are over two hundred cigar factories and thousands of women working long hours. After this, they go home to wash, iron, clean, cook, and care for their children. These women are not the male immigrants spoken of who enjoy the right to vote. They have no rights but understand that if you succeed, they will succeed, as will their daughters and granddaughters. I want you to know they are counting on you. They are silent and not seated here, but don't underestimate their numbers. There are millions like them across the country, and more arrive every day." Angelina raised her voice to emulate Gladys Parker's passion. "They took a chance and left behind everyone and everything they knew to come to America, where they had to learn a new culture and a foreign language. They believe in our cause and in the words etched on the Statue of Liberty: 'Send these, the homeless, tempest-tossed to me, I lift my lamp beside the golden door.'

"That isn't so, is it? There is no golden door for women. And if nothing is done, the past remains our present. Men will rule us in every avenue of our lives, like the fathers who believe they may choose our husbands. You, sisters, carry the torch for us all. Let's not allow our dreams to remain dreams. United, we can make them come true."

For a tense moment, the room remained painfully silent. Angelina felt her stomach sink and her face grow warm. Suddenly, a resounding burst of applause broke out, and she sighed in relief. Gladys Parker hurried toward her and enthusiastically shook her hand. "Our young suffragette has given us a new avenue of thought and another reason we cannot give up the fight."

Angelina offered a gracious nod to Gladys Parker and the audience. *Thank goodness for all those clippings I collected on the movement. They saved me.* Even more comforting to her, the contribution hat had reached the last row.

This had been a big moment for Angelina, but none of her family or friends had seen it, and she suspected no one would believe her if she told them. Still, a seed had taken root. She could feel it.

CHAPTER 18

Angelina and Carmen took a seat at a picnic table to eat lunch, where Carmen intended to discuss her latest love interest, but when Carmen spotted Rolando and waved him over, the plan changed.

"Why did you do that? He'll think we're forward," Angelina whispered.

"I'll accept your remark as a thank-you."

Carmen gave Rolando a brilliant smile as he drew near. Angelina offered a more timid one.

"Hello, ladies."

"Sit down. Eat with us," Carmen said. "Tell us how things are going with the union negotiations and the factory owners with heads bigger than their hats and money bags bigger than their heads." She took a bite of her Cuban sandwich.

"Are you sure you want to hear it as you eat?" Rolando said, smiling.

Angelina wondered what he would say. "My stomach is stronger than you think."

"Well, we have one rule: *A mal tiempo, buena cara,*" Rolando said.

Angelina set down her sandwich. "So what you're saying is keep a straight face when negotiating."

Rolando nodded. "It's useful. Never let the factory owners know you intend to chip away at their proposal until you've fooled them into thinking it's their idea."

Carmen chuckled. "And, Rolando, that is why we voted you our union representative at the cigar factory."

"It's a strategy as old as the pyramids and rather popular in Spain."

Angelina gave him a penetrating gaze. "What possessed you to leave such a fascinating country?"

With a spark of reignited humor, he said, "I wanted to claim America for the Spanish crown—but I was too late."

He has a wonderful sense of humor, thought Angelina, *unlike my father.*

"That's a real shame," Carmen said with a giggle. "If only one of those explorers had known how to read a compass, this entire country would be speaking Spanish."

"Oh, look, there's my cousin Ricardo. I'll go say hello," Carmen said. She turned her back to Rolando and winked at Angelina.

Rolando's smile broadened. Though he remained quiet, Angelina sensed he wanted to say something serious. With Carmen only a few feet away, it seemed he hesitated to share his thoughts. Still, in that lush silence, without a word spoken, Rolando reached for her hand and met her eyes with unmistakable tenderness.

Angelina blushed and looked away.

~

ROLANDO STOOD near the factory entrance as the workers filed in, and lit up when he saw Angelina. "Angelina, meet me at lunch in the park near the factory."

"The park?" Angelina studied his wide grin and wondered what he had in mind. The only spot masquerading as a park near the factory was a small patch of grass with an old bench jokingly called 'the park' because two old men liked to sit there and smoke their cigars.

"All right, I will see you at lunch at *the park,*" Angelina said, half amused.

"Don't be late." Rolando raised his eyebrows in a good-humored warning. He turned toward Cuesta's office while Angelina reached for the railing and began her climb up the stairs, already eager for the hours to fall away and the lunch bell to sound.

She kept her eyes on the clock. The moment it threatened to strike the lunch hour, Angelina left her worktable ahead of the others and made her way across the room to the large door. As the bell rang, she hurried down the stairs, walked a short block, and saw Rolando waving.

He had a cloth napkin spread out in the middle of the bench and some flowers arranged in a cup as a centerpiece. He'd set out silverware, two wine glasses filled with water, and two plates laden with a Spanish dish of rice, seafood, and vegetables.

"I hope you like paella," said Rolando.

Angelina took a bite. "Oh, my goodness, Rolando, it's wonderful. How did you manage all this?"

"Anything is possible when you're inspired, and you inspire me, Angelina." Rolando met her eyes, and a warm sensation rushed through her.

"This must have taken some time. Thank you for thinking of me." The sweet gesture touched Angelina.

"El placer es todo mío, as we say in Spanish. The pleasure is

all mine." Rolando reached for her hand. "One day, when the world is less complicated and when the union and factory owners untie the knot they've tightened between them, we will have many wonderful meals in elegant restaurants. I will raise my glass and toast you with a special wine from my native Spain."

"How did you happen to come to America, Rolando?"

"It's in my blood. I come from a long line of explorers, and I landed here. You've heard of Christopher Columbus sent out by King Ferdinand and Queen Isabella."

Angelina met his eyes. "Is this the same King Ferdinand with the lisp?"

"A busy man. He sent out Pizarro and Cortes too," said Rolando.

"Which explorer was in your line?" Angelina remained unsure where he was going with such a tale.

"All of them," said Rolando with his usual grin.

Angelina laughed. "That's quite a family."

"Well, I see it this way. As my family has been in Spain for centuries, I figure somewhere in their past, these explorers must have run into the women of my family and couldn't resist their charms." He paused a moment and met her eyes. "I suspect they were almost as fascinating as you, Angelina."

She glanced over the display of food he'd placed before her and once again gratefully looked up at Rolando. "Everything is perfect, Rolando. I can think of nothing more lovely than the surprise on this bench."

"The only lovely thing on this bench is you, Angelina."

Angelina could not imagine ever forgetting this day, or this gift, or how Rolando filled her heart.

CHAPTER 19

Angelina listened as el lector read the same news report in four different papers and from four different viewpoints. Since el lector never came to Angelina's floor, a worker brought the newspapers up to the third floor and read something disturbing.

"A cigar union representative, Diego Montoya, was found shot three times on the front steps of his home. The murder is still under investigation. The powerful cigar syndicates with a strong financial stranglehold on the industry, have denied any involvement in carrying out the assassination. One million cigars are made a day in Ybor City with over ten thousand employees, which is nearly half the population of the city and good reason to prevent any outside interference."

Angelina listened intently to any news about the union.

"The CMIU cigar workers' union vowed that someone would pay for this. There are many issues, but one is the recent dismissal of selectors in Ybor City and the hiring of Cubans to do the same job at lower wages," said el lector as he closed the newspaper.

The story had hit the front pages. It cast a shadow on industry and unlikely to be swept away or forgotten.

"There is a silent war going on," said Carmen. "Factories huge profits, and the owners are not letting anyone empty their pockets."

"A murder? I can't believe it's gone this far," said Angelina.

~

ANGELINA'S EDUCATION was even more important than before and perhaps something else she hadn't considered—her life would be more tranquil and less dangerous. She walked home, carrying another one of Sophia's schoolbooks, and let her mind drift.

Rolando took the time to teach my zio cigar making. He passed my worktable and looked delighted when he saw me. He waves at me, but I can't risk waving back. As these thoughts about Rolando flowed through Angelina, it surprised her how much she enjoyed this little game.

She found a bench, took a seat, and opened Sophia's schoolbook. She had to shake away thoughts of Rolando and study as the day to take her college exam grew closer. She assigned herself the preamble to the Constitution in case its memorization might be a college requirement. Over and over, she read, "We, the people of the United States, in order to form a more perfect union."

She quickly realized a capital mistake. Why hadn't the Founding Fathers noticed? If something was already perfect, how could it be more perfect? It contradicted its own definition of the word. With all those signatures, someone should have corrected this. Angelina sighed, committed the preamble to memory, and continued down the page, saddened that she had no teacher with whom to discuss her discovery.

She walked past the shoe repair shop, the barbershop, and could have turned left at the corner to avoid Belarmino's furniture store, where Rolando helped out. Either way, the distance to reach home was the same, but ever since their delightful lunch in the 'park,' she thought of him all the time and did something brazen for her. She walked past the furniture store and waved at him from outside the picture window.

The moment Rolando saw her, he hurried outside to greet her.

"Were you waiting for me?" she asked sheepishly.

Rolando shrugged. "I'm always waiting for you, but today I offered to help Belarmino lift some furniture. Lucky for my tired arms, you came at the right time." He pointed to the other side of the street. "Shall we walk a bit?"

"I'd like that." Angelina grew pleasantly uneasy in his company. A cool breeze drifted past them, and she pulled her shawl tightly around her.

"Winter's coming," he said. "I was in New York last winter. Have you ever seen snow?"

"No, I've never left Florida."

"It doesn't make a sound. You catch a flake, it melts away, and all you're left with is the memory, like the vanishing puff from a cigar." Rolando's expression became penetrating. She sensed that something other than the weather might be on his mind as he glanced back at the little furniture shop. She followed his gaze to where Belarmino lifted a rocking chair into a customer's wagon.

Rolando took Angelina's hand and led her into a building's alcove, out of Belarmino's sight and the sight of those in the street.

"Is something wrong?"

"Yes, I think so. I'm going away to Key West, Angelina. The alliance of factory owners is forcing a situation affecting the cigar union. I'm not sure what's happened, but it's serious."

"Does this have to do with the Montoya murder?" she said, almost afraid of the answer.

"They keep things secretive to protect everyone and never brief us. All over the country, powerful companies and factories are taking advantage of their workers and sometimes resorting to violence. The unions are the only force that can push back. It's a dangerous fight with threats of dismissals for men who cannot lose their jobs." His look of concern was unmistakable. "I'll be gone for about two weeks."

Angelina was keenly aware that Rolando had not answered her question about the murder. Union men held undisclosed meetings to protect themselves and their strategies, but two weeks sounded unbearably long. Angelina's stomach sank at the threat of working at such a monotonous job with no hope of seeing Rolando, yet she was determined to conceal her disappointment.

"Be careful. The storms are worse when you're between the Atlantic Ocean and the Gulf of Mexico, and then there are the alligators." She wanted to bite her tongue as soon as the words escaped. *What a ridiculous thing to say, honestly —alligators.*

"Assuming I survive the alligators, I want to see you as soon as I return."

Angelina felt a warm flush and ignored his little joke. "We'll see each other at the factory, like always."

He searched her eyes, and she sensed a change in him. "I'm not talking about the factory. I'm talking about meeting with you when the workday is over and on the days we don't work. I want to be with you as much as possible."

Rolando's words ignited a thrilling and unexpected emotion inside Angelina. Still, just as quickly, the blossoming thrill wilted when she remembered that her father would never approve of such a man.

"I'll see you when you return, Rolando," she said. Her answer did not indicate the sentiment churning inside her.

Rolando put his hand on her shoulder and then lifted her chin. "I've never forgotten the day I met you. Amid the confusion, fear, and destruction of a fire, a beautiful flower appeared."

His words dazzled her, and the tight grip she had on emotions loosened.

"Will you think of me while I'm gone, Angelina?"

No one had ever spoken to her in such a compelling tone. She wanted to say she'd be thinking of him often, every day, and with fondness, but she hesitated as her father's voice lingered in her mind.

"Both my uncle and I will miss you while you're gone." She put her hand out to shake his. Rolando took it and gently lifted it to his lips.

"One day you'll know how much you mean to me," He pushed back a tendril of her hair. "It's been a torment having you so near yet unable to reach you."

At that instant, time stopped. Rolando pulled her into his arms and kissed her. The sudden sensation of his lips against hers both startled and wrapped her in silken threads. She didn't think of right or wrong or her father's words of warning. She sought only the luxury of the moment. As Rolando's kiss deepened, Angelina closed her eyes to block out the world and spilled into this splendid place of wonder where time had lost all meaning.

"Where are you, Rolando?" Belarmino's voice bellowed from the street.

Angelina didn't move, and Rolando didn't release her. Instead, he held her even closer and, with a light touch, brushed his lips against her cheek, then whispered, "I have to leave tomorrow afternoon at two, but I'm coming back for you, Angelina Pirrello. Promise you won't fall in love with anyone while I'm gone."

Angelina trembled. She'd never been this close to a man, and inhaling the wonder of the moment, she raised her hand to touch his hair. When Rolando released her, she leaned closer and saw no reason to fight the impulse to kiss him back.

Why hide my feelings when they're so obvious? Rolando's words embraced her. The warmth in his arms made her feel safe, and, to her surprise, the sensation that she recognized him from somewhere long ago returned.

Rolando again raised her hand to his lips. "Something powerful happens when I'm with you, Angelina. Everything around us fades away, but time is too short. It's like all we have is the moment of silence that lingers between the lightning and a burst of thunder." He put his arms around her, and his kiss was light—a fragile, gossamer key unlocking her heart and letting Rolando inside to remain forever.

"Rolando!" Belarmino's voice thundered.

Again, neither Rolando nor Angelina moved. She desperately wanted them to stay right where they were.

"Let's keep this kiss safe, so it will last until I return." He removed a medal that hung on a gold chain around his neck. "It's all I have to give you right now. Keep it with you. It's my promise we'll be together again and something to help you think of me often. I didn't know I'd be going away, and even though it's for a brief time, I'm almost afraid to leave you. It feels as if I'm being warned not to go or something bad will happen, but I can't imagine that's true."

"We can endure it, Rolando."

He reached for her hand, slipped her the medal from its gold chain, and closed his hand around hers. "Saint Jude is the saint of lost causes and miracles. I wore it when it led me to you. Meeting you is my miracle."

"I will never forget this moment, Rolando." An explosion of emotions ran through Angelina. He'd ignited her heart. She never knew such feelings existed.

Rolando embraced Angelina and tenderly kissed her once more. Nestled in his warmth, she had an overwhelming sense that nothing could harm her.

"Adios por el momento, Angelina." Goodbye for the moment, she repeated to herself. She'd think of their separation as a moment. Another shout from Belarmino and their magical encounter ended.

She wanted to say something unforgettable, but the words never came—neither foolish nor wise. Again he kissed her, long and lovingly, before leading her to the front of the building. He squeezed her hand. "I'll be thinking of you every day, Angelina. Will you think of me too?" He appeared almost fearful of her answer.

"Yes. Yes. Come back to me, Rolando." Despite her youth and inexperience, the words spilled out of her as if from some untapped well. Angelina recognized the immensity of what had taken place and believed that nothing could ever tear him from her heart.

He hurried off but then turned back and blew her a kiss. Another moment passed, and he'd vanished.

A gust of wind tossed her hair off her shoulders, but the air no longer chilled her. She opened her hand and looked at Rolando's gold medal. The name St. Jude of Thaddeus appeared above the image of a bearded man holding a large staff. The words *Pray for Us* were etched below the image. It seemed all their prayers had been answered.

~

THAT NIGHT, Angelina fell asleep gazing at the starlight out the window. She thought of Rolando. She'd encased every word he'd said and every sensation in that special velvet place in her heart where she intended to safeguard such memories forever.

The next morning, she awoke with newfound enthusiasm to face her Saturday chores. Today, everything reminded her of Rolando. She gazed at the dress she'd worn when he kissed her and at the beautiful medal, and she thought about how he'd looked at her. It was magical, and she could think of nothing else. Nothing presented itself as tiresome now, not even the mountains of laundry to wash and hang to dry. She imagined Rolando preparing for his journey, packing his valise. As the day wore on, she thought of almost nothing else.

"Angelina." Domenico walked into the kitchen. "I'm leaving to deliver some olive oil to Florencio's restaurant. I told him I'd be there at two, and I'm never late. The train passengers will come in hungry. Your brothers will serve them, but don't be too far away if they need you."

Angelina nearly gasped. How could such an important hour have slipped her? She glanced up at the clock approaching 2:00. Nothing stopped time. Her eyes darted from her father loading a case of olive oil on his wagon to the clock and then back again.

At last, her father pulled away. Rolando had never said by what means he intended to leave, and she'd never told him where she lived. It had to be the train station only a few feet away. Could he be right outside?

She rushed through her front door, crossed the street, and pushed her way through the storm of passengers stepping off the train and boarding. She made her way to the ticket office and glanced up at the train schedule posted above the window. It startled her to see the train to Key West left at two o'clock.

"Angelina!"

She turned around, and Rolando rushed toward her.

Exhilarated and entangled in feelings both thrilling and daunting, Angelina reached for Rolando's hand. Her brothers were only as far away as the width of the street. They'd see her with one glance out the window. But all she had was this one moment to make her feelings known.

Rolando pulled her into his arms. He held her tightly and kissed her with such emotion the world around them slipped away. They'd have drawn stares anywhere else, but not in a train terminal, where people hugged and kissed those they loved arriving and departing.

Rolando released her only slightly. "I can't believe it's you. How did you know where to find me?"

Angelina pointed to the grocery store. "I live right there. My father built the grocery store and then the house, and I realized that if you were catching a two-o'clock train, you'd have to be across the street."

He gazed at the number on the house and repeated it as though he had no intention of forgetting it. He then pulled her close and whispered, "Saint Jude wastes no time working his miracles."

Angelina reached around her neck and pulled out his medal to show him she wore it. "I wish I had something to give you in return."

"Oh, but I already have something. I have your smile, and I hope your heart. I'm taking them with me to remind me that I intend to spend a lifetime with this smile. I have so much I want to tell you, so much I should have told you. I have dreams, Angelina. I have worked two, sometimes three jobs. I have a plan and money saved to make them come true. We have so much to discover together," he said. Time was slipping away with no way to recapture it. "When I see you, Angelina, when I'm standing near you, when I hold you, it feels like we fell in love long ago, long before I met you, in another time and place."

"Sarasota. All aboard!"

The words came too soon. Angelina wanted more time with him. She'd taken such a chance and glanced at those entering her father's grocery store. Reassured now that her brothers had no time to look out the window, she turned back to Rolando. "I'll miss you so much. I don't think I can stop thinking of you."

"That's because I belong in your heart, now and always." His words were gentle and softly spoken.

They gazed into each other's eyes. Neither spoke, but in that moment, much was said that didn't need words. Angelina discovered silence was not silent. It had a rhythm, a pulse, a heartbeat. The strongest feelings didn't need words. Rolando gathered her closer in his arms and kissed her again. "They'll keep me two weeks, Angelina. Two unbearable weeks."

The train blew its departing whistle. Rolando tenderly kissed her forehead, her cheeks, and her lips before he released her. Angelina felt the warmest sensation run through her. Rolando glanced back once more as he hurried to jump onto the train. He made his way to a seat and lifted the window. The moment she saw him, she rushed to where he waved at her. She held out her hand, and Rolando extended his, and for one impulsive moment, they held on to each other. And then the train's steel wheels began their deep grinding against the tracks, forcing them to let go.

"Don't forget me, Angelina. I love you and promise I will return to you." Rolando's voice rose above the sound of the train wheels as they gained momentum.

"And I promise I will wait for you." Angelina could still

feel the impression of Rolando's hand in hers, and it left her with an overpowering sense of loss. "I love you too, Rolando." The train moved too fast and too loudly. Unsure if he'd heard her, she remained on the platform, following the train's departure in case he could still see her. As it grew smaller in the distance and then vanished, an inexplicable sense of danger struck her. She had no way to reach Rolando and no way to rid herself of the crushing impulse to chase after him. Amid all the complexities of conflicting emotions, one sensation surpassed the rest. She'd fallen hopelessly in love.

CHAPTER 20

The trolley jolted to a stop at the platform to let passengers on and off.

Angelina remained inside and gazed at the large advertisement from their seats. "*A Beast at Bay* with Mary Pickford," said Angelina.

Rosa sighed in obvious wonder. "Soon you and your uncle will be watching pictures move before your eyes," said Rosa.

"I've been so excited since my uncle said he'd take me."

Rosa leaned forward to get a better look at the poster. "If you mention moving pictures to my grandmother, she'll pull out her rosary. When *The Great Train Robbery* came to town, my cousin Tony went to see it. My mother, his mother, and my grandmother rushed to the church to light candles for his protection."

"Horseless carriages, flying machines, moving pictures—the more wonderful the invention, the angrier people get." Angelina wondered what Signora Bertelli thought about progress and the industrial revolution.

"Last stop. The terminal!" shouted the conductor.

Angelina stepped off the trolley and looked in every direction among the rush of people for Pasquale.

"That's strange. My uncle said he'd be here when I arrived."

"Lucia!" Rosa waved to her sister and then turned to Angelina. "Maybe your uncle forgot. Come with us. My sister is a magnificent cook."

Angelina gave Rosa a gentle squeeze on her arm in gratitude. "Of course she is, but I'm sure Pasquale will be here any minute."

"Are you really going to miss out on a delicious Italian meal and homemade pastries?"

"He's expecting me." Angelina hugged both sisters goodbye and watched them disappear into the crowd.

She looked around and marveled at the diversity of people coming and going. It reminded her of the train station and Rolando's last kiss. Angelina had said nothing about him to anyone. She feared they'd lose the delicate memory trying to unravel their moment into words. As the days turned into weeks, she decided something unforeseen had delayed him.

An empty bench offered a moment's rest. After twenty minutes with still no hint of Pasquale, her eagerness turned to worry. He'd planned on buying some white shirts in expectation of getting a job rolling cigars, so she focused on men with packages.

The sun grew fierce, and so did her anxiety. She couldn't recall him being late for anything, only early. She became too restless to sit any longer and went to where she had a better view of the walkways along the street.

Another twenty minutes had passed when a man stepped out of the crowd.

"Are you Angelina, Pasquale's niece?" He appeared stressed, uneasy, and rubbed his hands together. With an oversized mustache, a thin, angular face, and a somewhat apologetic tilt to his head, he took off his hat and rotated the brim as he held it. "I'm Antonio Nobili. I saw you once in your father's grocery store. Perhaps you didn't notice me." He lowered his head as if apologizing.

Angelina had no memory of this man, and his expression made her fearful. "Where's my uncle?" she asked.

"I ran into Pasquale earlier today. He planned to meet you here after he bought some shirts. It occurred to me you might be waiting."

"I don't understand. What's happened?"

"Some men in front of Williams Brothers Dry Goods beat Pasquale badly. We put him in Gaetano's wagon, and he took him to Dottore Martino's."

Angelina gasped. "It can't be true. He's so good. Why would anyone attack him?"

"He didn't read the sign in the window."

"What sign?"

"No Dagos Allowed."

"Oh, my God." Angelina knew Pasquale hadn't heard that term. "Why take him to Ybor City? Why not rush him to a doctor here in Tampa?"

"The men who attacked your uncle have great power in this neighborhood. We worried that a local doctor's loyalties might lie with Pasquale's attackers. We've heard terrible stories and didn't want to take a chance."

Angelina's mouth went dry. She caught sight of a trolley. It came to a halt, and its sign said Ybor City. Angelina frantically thanked the man for his information and rushed to catch it. Onboard, she wandered past numerous empty seats, but she was too anxious, too nervous, too frightened to sit down. This trolley went too slow for her pounding heart. The stores along the avenue held no interest now, and when the trolley passed the theater starring Mary Pickford, Angelina lost her resolve. *Please, oh, please, God, have mercy on my zio Pasquale.*

At last, the conductor called her street. Angelina hurried off and ran to the doctor's office. Her previous visit had been the worst day of her life, and now she willingly stepped into the same nightmare. Like before, she hurried up the stairs and entered the office, shaking. "Where's my uncle Pasquale?" Angelina stood straight, meeting Maria's eyes as if daring her to intimidate her again.

Maria Martino tightened her lips when she saw Angelina but remained civil—a result of her husband's warning, no doubt. "The dottore's attending to him." She looked away as she spoke.

Angelina also turned away from Maria. A middle-aged man with a look of concern approached her and took off his cap.

"You're Pasquale's niece?" he asked. "He's proud of you and how smart you are. I'm Gaetano Castellano."

Angelina stepped closer. "Please, tell me what's happened."

"Three men, crackers from Tampa, beat him. Poor Pasquale didn't have a chance. He was lying in the street covered in blood and not moving when my brothers and I picked him up and put him in our wagon. In that part of Tampa, they made my Sicilian neighbor wait so long in the waiting room that he died. This is still the South, and some people discriminate against immigrants, so I brought him here and thought I'd stay until his family arrived."

"My uncle is so sweet. Tell me, Signor Castellano, where's the honor in beating a sparrow?"

The man nodded. "Only God can stop prejudice." He glanced toward the examining room. "Martino's been in there with your uncle for a long time. I'm sure it won't be much longer." He sighed. "Pasquale walked into the wrong store."

"My family will forever be grateful to you. Please come to our home. We want to repay you."

"That's kind but unnecessary, though I'll come by to visit my friend Pasquale."

"We all look forward to it." Angelina turned from Gaetano to Maria Martino. "I have to see my uncle, signora."

Maria raised an eyebrow. "If you rush in there and break my husband's concentration, no one can blame him for whatever happens." Someone else might have interpreted Maria's statement as protective, but Angelina equated it to Pontius Pilate washing his hands of responsibility.

Gaetano leaned forward. "The doctor will help him, you'll see." Gaetano's quiet manner offered a measure of comfort.

Angelina rubbed her hands together. "I know, but it's hard to forget the good doctor could not save my mother."

"Every patient is different. Every illness and injury is different. Pasquale is strong." Gaetano glanced at Pasquale's room. "Did you know he never passed our street without stepping inside our store? He always had a story to make us laugh. We enjoyed his visits so much," Gaetano said. "I'll come this weekend to see how he's doing."

"I'll never forget your kindness, Signor Castellano."

Angelina shook Gaetano's hand and watched him leave. Alone now in the doctor's office with Maria Martino, the memory of her mother's death increased her growing fear that Pasquale might suffer the same fate. When good things happened, time flew by, when bad things happened, time slowed. Angelina felt trapped with only the creaking sound of floorboards as she paced, and Maria's attempt at the exhumation of an old Italian song she'd forgotten the lyrics.

The only distraction was a portrait of George Washington crossing the Delaware. It sat between a picture of the

Vatican on an Italian calendar and a thermometer posting the obviously stifling heat. The three incompatible items appeared more as a disturbance on the stark wall than an adornment, and today, nothing could distract Angelina. She closed her eyes and furiously prayed for her uncle. Her heart could not endure another tragic loss.

At last, the doctor stepped out of the examining room. Angelina jumped to her feet, rushed over, and searched his face for a sign of encouragement. "How is he?"

The doctor placed his hand on her shoulder. "I've stopped the bleeding and attended to his wounds. He has some broken ribs, multiple cuts, and lost a tooth. And he lost consciousness when he first arrived, but he'll recover."

Angelina's eyes moistened at the list of injuries, but she hung on the most critical thing she needed to hear: "He'll recover."

"I must see my uncle."

"I understand, but only for a moment. I've given Pasquale some medication to quiet him."

She suspected the doctor might try to spare her the truth. "Are you sure he'll be all right?"

"Pasquale's worked hard all his life. His body is strong and healthy."

Angelina struggled to draw confidence as she turned the doorknob to her uncle's room, where the white walls appeared indifferent to the suffering. Her fragile confidence dissolved at the sight of Pasquale's beaten body. How had Gaetano and his brothers even recognized him?

Pasquale turned his head with a moan. With his eyes blackened, his face swollen, lips distended, and bandages and bruises covering his body, Angelina's gave out a cry as eyes filled with tears.

"He will heal, Angelina," Martino repeated.

She took her uncle's hand. "Who did this to you, Zio?"

"Let him rest. You'll have plenty of time to talk to him later."

She kissed her uncle's hand. "I love you, Zio Pasquale. I love you so much."

A drop of blood fell from the corner of his mouth, and a tear spilled from his eye. He squeezed her hand.

"I gave him quite a bit of medication. Sleep will do him good. Where's your father, Angelina? I was sure he'd be here by now."

The question struck her like a thunderbolt. In her fear for Pasquale, she'd forgotten about her father. He'd be furious and either scream at her or refuse to talk to her. "Oh, my goodness. He'll never forgive me. I must tell him right away."

She rushed out of the room, through the reception area, out the office door—and right into her father. "Papa," she said, startled by his sudden appearance. "I was coming to see you."

"Where's my brother?" Her father only glanced in her direction, but the look registered his anger and made it clear he'd deal with her later. He brushed past her and burst into the office, much like Angelina had done the day her mother died. He faced Maria Martino and raised his voice. "Where is he? What did they do to him?"

The woman pointed to Pasquale's room without comment. Angelina watched her calm behavior, which contradicted her outrageous curse of the evil eye. It was more likely the woman would never attempt such an outburst with a man as strong-minded as Domenico.

"Papa, Dottore Martino says Zio Pasquale will heal," said Angelina in a low, apologetic tone.

Her father grabbed Angelina's arm. "How is it my daughter is here and I have to wait for a stranger to run to the store to tell me about my brother? You should have told me right away."

Angelina had no answer, and Maria Martino didn't tell him to lower his voice or say Sicilians acted like animals.

The doctor appeared in the doorway. Domenico rushed into Pasquale's room. "Pasquale?" he called, voice cracking.

Angelina's fear for Pasquale, her father's anger, and the cruel memory of Maria Martino's curse of malocchio seemed all too suffocating. She went to the open window, where a slight breeze consoled her. Across the street, a man stepped off his wagon and unrolled an oversized poster. His arm moved with broad, even strokes as he pasted the colorful advertisement to the brick building. *Now Showing—A Beast at Bay—starring Mary Pickford, America's Sweetheart.*

PASQUALE'S long recovery was agonizing to watch. Angelina faithfully nursed his wounds, cooked special meals, and read to him. She kept Rolando's medal of Saint Jude in her pocket. As he remained the saint of miracles, she held it as she said prayers for her uncle's recovery and Rolando's return.

Angelina kept her eye on the calendar. Four weeks had come and gone with no word from Rolando. He held an important place in matters of the union, and if something terrible had occurred, they'd have to release the news. There must have been something unforeseen.

In the meantime, it was only logical for Angelina to stay out of her father's way. He walked about, agitated, and periodically scolded her for not having come straight home to tell him of Pasquale's attack. This went on until one day, as Angelina prepared a meal and Pasquale could sit at the table, Domenico got straight to the point.

"Give me the names of the men who attacked you. I've heard the story from others. Now I want to hear it from you."

Pasquale withdrew from the question. "I think is better we forget."

Domenico pulled out a chair and faced him. "It's not a question."

Angelina wanted to hear Pasquale's story too. Afraid her father might order her to leave, she remained quiet.

Her uncle cleared his throat. "Is better we forget, no?"

"No." Domenico's eyes darkened. "You haven't recovered, but you're well enough to tell the story. Before I rest my head on my pillow again, I'll know what happened to my only brother."

Domenico didn't take his eyes off Pasquale. Angelina took care not to make a sound.

Pasquale cleared his throat and hesitated as if he needed first to untie the knot around his pain. "Everybody wear the white shirt and the tie. So I say, 'Pasquale, you better buy some,' then Signore Cuesta, he gonna say, 'Pasquale sure look nice when he make the cigars.'" Pasquale looked at his brother as if hoping he'd changed his mind about hearing the story. Domenico remained stoic. "Every time I go see my good friends at the Castellano Shoe Repair, I pass the store that sell the white shirts. So I say, first I gonna buy the shirts, then I gonna to see the pictures move with Angelina. It was a nice day, not so hot and not so cold." Pasquale paused as if waiting for his brother to agree, but again, Domenico remained still.

"I go to the store called Wiliason Brothers."

Angelina leaned forward. "You mean Williams Brothers?"

"That's right. I say, 'Hello, Signor Wiliason, how you are this fine day?'"

"What happened, Pasquale?" Domenico never wandered through the bushes to get where he wanted to go.

Angelina stiffened for what was sure to come.

Pasquale wiped his forehead. "I say, 'Signor Wiliason, I

wanna buy two of you very nice white shirts.' Then he say to me, 'You dago?' I say, no, signor, I'm Pasquale.' Then he say, 'You look like you dago. You talk like you dago. Why you no see the sign in the window, No Dagos?'

"I say, 'I no dago. I'm Pasquale Pirrello. My brother, he sell the best food at Domenico's. Maybe you know him?'" Pasquale paused.

It seemed clear to Angelina her uncle wanted to stop.

"That's not the end," Domenico said.

"I show him the money I have, but I think it make him more mad. He say, why a dago like me wanna look so nice? He hit me like this." Pasquale made a fist, reenacting the punch to his jaw. "Two more come. Maybe they brothers because the sign, she say Wiliason Brothers. They hit me too and throw me outside. I fall. They pick me up. Everybody hit me, and they kick me some more. Then a very good thing happen to me, Domenico."

Angelina swallowed hard. Certainly nothing good had happened. The doctor said they could have killed him.

"The big man, he hit me in the head. Then I no remember nothing. I was so lucky."

Her father slammed his fist on the table. The vein in his neck bulged.

"You no worry, Domenico. Non ti preoccupare. Everything is good in America."

Domenico's face flushed red. His molten anger draped the room, but after a few deep breaths, he withheld his emotions and put his arm around his brother. "I promise, Pasquale. This is the last time we will ever speak of it."

Her father suddenly appeared calmer, but Angelina had lived with him for too many years. This was just the beginning of his interrogation.

"What it mean, 'dago'?"

Domenico lowered his head as if the weight of the question burdened him. "Outside Ybor City, people forget their families came here as immigrants. Once, only Indians lived here."

"Non capisco."

"When I came to America with our cousin Fabrizio," Domenico explained, "I was only seventeen. He was eighteen. We were young. We argued and went our separate ways back then. I rented a room with two young men I met on the ship. Men offered us work for a dollar a day. We walked four miles to their farm, broke our backs from sunlight to darkness, and walked home again." Domenico poured himself a small glass of wine. Neither Angelina nor Pasquale spoke. "They told us one dollar a day, but after a week of work, they gave us fifty cents a day. The other men cursed but took the money. I stayed and, in my poor English, demanded seven dollars."

Angelina could easily visualize her father unwilling to accept injustice. Still, it surprised her how young he was and already so defiant in an unfamiliar country where he didn't know the language. She was now the same age as he was then, and she also nourished the drive to stand up for what was right.

"The men, they pay you?" said Pasquale.

Domenico took a sip of wine before he answered. "I was paid, but not in money." He stood and pulled out his shirt-tails. "Angelina, look away."

She turned her head and heard Pasquale say, "No, Domenico, no."

Angelina had never seen her uncle startled. It frightened her enough to ignore her father's order and turn around again. She and her uncle both gasped at the deep crisscross scars that disfigured the flesh all over her father's back.

"They tied me to a tree and lashed me with a horsewhip until I fainted. This was my welcome to America."

Angelina forgot her determination to remain quiet. She

wept openly at the marks that mutilated her father's back and rushed to hug him. "Oh, Papa, that's horrible. I never knew. You said nothing."

He let Angelina hug him. "I was your age, Angelina, when this happened. That's why I always tell you to stay with your own people. Don't trust anyone. Today you learned something. You learn when you listen, not when you speak."

Pasquale looked stricken. "Domenico, why you never tell me what happen to you?"

"And what could you do to help me from across the ocean in Europe? Worry?" Domenico put his shirt back on. "We do not forget hard lessons. The day comes at sunrise, and the day goes at sunset. We worked hard, but we never made the same mistake. At the end of every day, we asked for our money. They called us dagos because we said, 'No *day goes* by with no pay.'"

Her father finished his wine, went to the window, and looked out at the immigrants in the street. Some carried bundles in their arms, a few balanced them on their heads, and still others sold wares from pushcarts. They shouted about their goods in broken English and foreign languages.

Pasquale joined him at the window. Domenico put his hand on his brother's shoulder. "It took courage to leave our country for a better life. We went hungry there, and we're beaten here."

"Maybe that's why they call l'America the home of the brave."

CHAPTER 21

Since the attack on Pasquale, Angelina had only worked half days so she could care for him. In a week, she would return to working full time with her uncle. With so much worry and attending to her uncle, the day of her college entrance exam came and went, but Angelina had another chance. Her studying had never ceased, and she was ready for whatever test was assigned her.

It was a Saturday, and the breeze refreshed her in contrast to the raging humidity and heat of the week before. Angelina arrived early for the exam, passed through the massive double doors of a college, signed in on the roster, and took a seat at a row of desks. The grand moment had arrived.

A man in a three-piece suit stood before them. He passed his hand over his balding head as if smoothing out his hair and an old habit from long ago.

"Attention, please. I am about to pass out the entrance exams. No one will open the booklet until I blow the whistle. You will have exactly two hours to complete the test. All eyes and minds are to focus on the exam and nowhere else. I will blow a whistle when the test is over. Any deviation from this will result in immediate disqualification."

Angelina grew restless in her seat. The man was like a mechanical windup toy soldier—hostile and indifferent.

"If you complete the test ahead of the scheduled time, bring it to me, place it on my desk, and I'll excuse you. Within three weeks, all who pass will receive notification by mail. In addition, we will not allow you to retake the exam until the next school year. We have a long waiting list of applicants and must give all prospective students the same opportunity. Are there questions?"

Tension stifled the air. No one spoke. When the whistle blew, the sound of pages turning filled the room. Angelina could not have been more invigorated. She had studied excessively and filled several notebooks with study entries she'd reviewed. After one hour and twenty minutes, she turned it in and left elated. She could almost touch her dream and had only to wait to be given her wings.

ANGELINA SENSED a void inside the grocery store. "Where's Papa, Vincenzo?" she asked her brother.

"Across the street with Spadaro, Misurace, Viola, Lumia, and some other spaghetti benders." Her brother slid the back of his hand up his neck and off his chin—the Italian hand gesture for "Who cares?" Then he continued. "He's outside talking. That leaves Sal and me to fill the barrels, stock the shelves, and sweep the floor. Hey, Angelina, you can show us how to do a good job." Vincenzo tossed her a can.

Angelina tossed the can back. "Work more, talk less," she warned.

"Hey, Vinny, our sister sounds like she just got off the boat with a fresh bundle of Italian sayings."

Angelina pushed a case of wine vinegar toward her brothers. "It's interesting how you two get older and taller but not any faster or wiser. So here's another pearl of wisdom: 'The faster you work, the faster you finish.'"

Though the maintenance of the store had never been her responsibility, she rubbed a smudge on the front window with the cuff of her sleeve as a gathering across the street came into view. Her father had warned her often enough to be observant. From her vantage point, Angelina saw men with somber faces and angry hand gestures that bruised the air around them. Domenico never left the store without looking "presentable," but now he stood outside draped in his long white apron.

The sound of a cowbell broke her concentration. Old Francesco Giglio and his chestnut mare, Fabiola, rounded the corner. The horse pulled the older man seated in his ice wagon at a sluggish pace that suited them both. The old man announced his arrival by ringing a bell. "Ice. *Ghiaccio,*" he called, in a voice long since lacking vitality.

Angelina surmised the poor man must be in perpetual mourning. "Vincenzo, help poor Signore Giglio. It looks like Papa's too busy."

"And what do I look like, a servant?"

"Helping an old man carry ice doesn't make you a servant. It's a kindness. Don't you want to go to heaven?"

Vincenzo stepped back. "Don't you listen to the warnings in church? You have to *die* to get there."

"Well then, you'll both have no problem. It's only the good who die young—not the lazy or annoying."

"Did you hear that, Sal? If we're good, we die young."

Salvatore set down a case of olives. "This is important information. What luck we found this out now, so we don't take any chances."

Angelina pointed to the door. "Go help that poor old man

and try not to think so much. The pressure is doing damage to your brains."

Her brothers headed toward the door, but they moved as slowly as Fabiola the horse. The moment the door closed behind them, Angelina rifled through the mail, but nothing had the name of the college.

She glanced at the curious gathering outside. Her father always stopped whatever his task was to greet Signor Giglio in the ice wagon, but today he didn't notice.

Angelina jumped when her brothers returned and let the door slam.

"Here we are, Angie, we're back from doing our good deed, and so far you have done none, so you can help us stock the shelves." Salvatore flipped a can from one hand to the other. "It's like playing ball."

Angelina brushed her palms together, then turned them downward, the gesture for *basta,* enough of her brothers' nonsense.

The door's small bell rang, and Signora Zoleo entered.

Salvatore got to his feet. "Our sister has done nothing today, signora. She'll take care of you."

Angelina quickly pulled her attention away from the window. "Please, pay no attention to my brother, signora. He suffers from delusions."

"What's outside, Angelina? A boy you like?" said the older woman with a knowing grin.

"Oh no, signora, I was looking at . . . I just wanted to . . ." Her face warmed. After six weeks, if only the boy she liked stood outside the window with his winning smile and rushing to hold and kiss her. She reached inside her pocket and felt Rolando's medal. Hopefully, whatever detained him had resolved.

Signora Zoleo chuckled. "I was young once too." She sighed, then pointed to the cold cuts in the deli case. "I'll take a half pound of this one, a pound of that one, and then you can go back to your window."

Still thinking about Rolando, Angelina grabbed the large rolls of provolone and salami, sliced and wrapped them in butcher paper, and handed them to her customer. "Here you are, signora. It's so good to see you again. Thank you for coming in." She nodded a farewell.

Signora Zoleo glanced at the package and put her money on the counter. "Does your father know you hand out food without charging?"

A rush of embarrassment raced through Angelina. "No. That would never please him." The rolling thunder of her father's voice rang inside her head, and she quickly opened the cash register.

"Your mind is somewhere else today." The woman nodded again.

Angelina counted out her change while Salvatore coughed and Vincenzo laughed.

"You must excuse them, signora. They tried to impress God today, but it's the devil who's pleased."

"Boys. What do you expect?" The woman sighed again. "It's no wonder you're confused. You work at the factory, work in your father's store, and help with the children. God bless you, Angelina, but you're killing yourself. Hear my words. You're killing yourself."

Angelina nodded, said goodbye, and waited until Signora Zoleo closed the door behind her. She glanced outside again and saw her father pull burlap bags from the trash barrel and handed them to Spadaro. Whether it had been the stoic expressions on the men's faces or the suspicious way they acted, the scene left Angelina with an uncomfortable sense of foreboding. Something wasn't right.

The men shook hands, patted each other on the back, and

walked away. Her father headed for the store, wearing a determined expression.

Angelina grabbed a small container of black olives out of Salvatore's hand. "Let me show you how to go faster."

"Hey, Vinny, look at Angelina. She's trying to get to heaven."

Her father entered the store and brushed past them. His expression did not invite questions.

ANGELINA KISSED THE MEDAL. Memories of Rolando returned every night when she went to bed and every morning when she looked at the calendar. So much reminded her of Rolando—like every time she saw a couple arm in arm or whenever she heard someone speak the king's Spanish with that famous lisp. From time to time, she'd look up as she worked, hoping to see him wave from across the room. Something serious must have delayed Rolando. Surely he'd arrive soon.

However, time never stood still, and she imagined he'd be proud of her if she were accepted to college. She was confident that if her acceptance didn't arrive today, it would arrive tomorrow, but each tomorrow came and went without the crucial letter. When the promised three weeks had elapsed and nothing arrived, Angelina became as confused as she was crestfallen. How could she have failed when she knew the answers? Since she'd told no one of her effort, not even Don Carlos Madrid, no one knew of her frustration. There had to be an explanation.

"It's our lunch break, Angelina. Forget what you brought to eat. Let's have a Cubano," said Carmen with her usual enthusiasm.

Angelina welcomed Carmen's zealous devotion to all

things Cuban. "My father told me everyone used to fall asleep after lunch, so the Cuban cigar factories started ordering proper Cuban sandwiches. He thinks the combination of pork, pickles, and mustard keeps people alert and awake."

Carmen's eyes widened. "Aha. No wonder everyone on our floor never stops talking."

"Let's split a sandwich in case it's too powerful," Angelina said.

Both girls giggled as they entered the deli and took a seat. The waiter came to their table, scribbled down their order, and yelled it to a man behind the counter. "*Oye,* Pablo, these señoritas want your best Cuban sandwich, cut in two."

"Makes you wonder why they bother to write anything down," Carmen said, shaking out a discarded newspaper and holding it up to read.

Angelina glimpsed at the date on the newspaper and tensed. How could Rolando not notice this much passage of time? What had gone wrong? Had he forgotten her?

"It's the Sunday paper. Let's see what we're missing since no one reads on our floor." Carmen skimmed the front page. "Hey, listen to this. 'Glacial temperatures and winds have left people dying in the streets of Manhattan. Others remain trapped in their homes without food. Even the sparrows who fall frozen from the sky are consumed by the desperate and hungry.'"

Snowstorms required imagination in Florida, and Angelina's thoughts focused on the plight of the frozen sparrows when Carmen read of an alligator that had killed a Miami man.

"What I don't understand is how a creature with such short legs can outrun a man," Angelina said.

Carmen lowered the newspaper. "Ha, let me tell you

something, señorita. The tiny mouse at my home outruns me every time."

"But alligator jaws?" Angelina rubbed her arms. "That poor man. I've heard people in shock feel no pain. When someone's about to die a horrible death, God numbs them."

"Let's hope that's true." Carmen kept her eyes on the paper. "Seems everyone in Europe is mad at everyone else. There's trouble there again, but did it ever stop? Spain's military is in the streets arresting and shooting people, and France and England want Germany to pay for that old Moroccan mess."

Angelina sighed. "There's even talk of a big war coming in Europe, and big wars have a way of becoming bigger."

"Yes, and watch Europe beg us to join their war. If they want to fight each other, I don't understand why we have to send our good-looking, single soldiers over there and leave our country with a shortage."

Angelina giggled. "Now, that's something that would never have occurred to me."

Carmen turned the page, and kept reading, "Uh-oh," she said.

"What is it?"

Carmen glanced up at Angelina with a beleaguered expression and hesitated before she spoke. "The owners of Williams Brothers Dry Goods were attacked Wednesday last, their inventory covered in horse manure. The assailants stabbed the victim's right hands and nailed them to the wooden counter with stiletto knives before fleeing. Although estimated damage to merchandise is in the hundreds, the victims could not name their attackers, and the matter remains under investigation by the Tampa Police Department. This attack came weeks after suspicion arose regarding the brothers brutal assault of a Sicilian immigrant. This crime remains unsolved."

Angelina froze.

Carmen leaned over. "Those men deserved it. That's all I have to say."

The memory of her father and his friends gathered outside the store returned. She'd never seen her father do anything violent or even strike a child, but he had a temper, like on the night Señor Garcia had died. Still, how could anyone be certain of what was in the mind of another?

"Angelina, you're as white as that snowstorm in New York. I know what you're thinking, but why should you care? They left your uncle for dead in the street. They sure didn't care if they'd killed him. Now they'll think twice."

"You eat my half of the sandwich, Carmen. I'm already more alert than I want to be."

~

By the time Angelina arrived home, made dinner, and helped stock the shelves after the store's closing, the evening seemed to trickle by in droplets. At last, everyone had gone to bed. She stood at the connecting doorway and watched her father make entries in the libretto.

"All the children are in bed, Papa."

"Good."

The moment had arrived. "Sunday's newspaper says the Williams brothers were attacked. Was that you and your friends?"

Domenico looked up from his record keeping. "Since when does a father have to answer to his daughter?"

He'll either get mad and lash out or hide his anger and remain calm, but I must ask. "I saw you that day—all of you—and two wagons carrying full burlap bags."

"And you've made a judgment."

"The newspaper said the brothers were stabbed through

the right hand and nailed to the wooden counters with a stiletto." She had one comfort: her father didn't own a stiletto and never would.

"The right hand, you say? Perhaps it's symbolic of something."

"Yes, something bad. Meanwhile, the police are investigating the attack on Zio Pasquale."

"And you've been on Earth for seventeen, eighteen years now and never been hurt, deprived, or hungry, and you know about men and the world?" Domenico got up and emptied a burlap sack of corn into a barrel. "Tell me, what have the police done to protect the Italian immigrants? The ravens must learn to outwit the fox," he said.

"You've changed the subject, Papa."

"Bisogna stare attenti." He pointed to his eye and tugged slightly at the skin beneath it. "Pay attention."

Angelina wanted a straight answer, not a fairy tale.

"There are natural laws." Her father went on. "A raven can't overpower a fox, but together, the ravens can outwit it. It only takes one raven to lure the fox and others to attack it from the back, sides, belly, head, and neck. The defeated fox learns an important lesson. Sicilians are like the ravens. History has recorded our invasions for centuries, even as far back as a thousand years before Christ. We never forget a kindness or an insult. We've stayed together to survive because no government has come to our rescue."

Domenico struck a match and puffed several times on his cigar. "Never forget—it isn't the raven who attacks first. It's always a fox." He stopped there, dipped his pen in the inkwell, and wrote in his ledger.

Her father had always been difficult to understand. He'd suffered more than being tied and whipped, and he'd known injustices graver than the scars on his back. Still, she had to know. "Each raven does his part. What was your part, Papa?"

He glanced up and met his daughter's gaze. A tense moment passed between them. "It was a story of ravens, a children's tale. Go to bed."

She'd go to bed, but nothing he'd said would help her sleep.

CHAPTER 22

"I'm not giving you money to buy a dress. Your dresses are fine." Domenico's voice shot across the room and quivered like a dowser's stick locating water.

"I have nothing nice to wear to Rosa Caprici's wedding."

"It's impractical. You'll wear the dress for a few hours, and then it collects dust. With that same money, I can buy a barrel of beans and make a profit. Wear what you have."

"Papa, it doesn't have to cost a lot of money. Mama would have made sure you gave me the money. I receive my pay envelope and deliver it to you sealed, and you give me a little for myself, but it's not enough to buy a new dress."

"Angelina, did you or did you not give me the money and tell me to send it to Sicily to help our family over there?"

"Well, yes," said Angelina with a bit of hesitation.

"So, I sent it."

"I see how hard you work, Papa, and I want to help the family, but now I want to buy a dress." She should have altered her plan and opened the envelope first.

"People don't attend weddings to show off clothes, Angelina. They go to congratulate the bride and groom."

"That's right. And their guests arrive in their best clothes as a sign of respect." She'd have a new dress if her mother had a say. "Last month, you bought Sal two pairs of pants, extra shirts, and new shoes. Why can't you buy me one dress?"

Her father already looked disinterested in the conversation. "Whatever I buy Salvatore goes down to Vincenzo, Filippo, and Giuseppe, so I'm buying for all four sons. That's practical."

"Well then, buy me a dress, and I'll pass it down to Lily."

"Lily is six. We will store the dress for years. Impractical."

"I can wear it for years to come. And what will people think if I show up in an old dress they see me in all the time?"

"They'll praise you for being sensible." Domenico pulled a cigar from his breast pocket, slipped off the band, and lit it.

Angelina glanced at the discarded cigar band and then back at her father. "You see how plain and unattractive your cigar looks now? Factories dress up the cigars with colorful bands, then take wooden boxes and stamp them inside and out with company crests, attractive drawings of their factory, the owner, or a pretty lady. They write their names and a message in fancy lettering. They even give cigars impressive names, like Perfectos, Royals, and Los Presidentes. They are so attractive. People collect the boxes and the bands."

Domenico took a puff of his cigar and met his daughter's eyes. "I've never doubted that you're clever, Angelina. You argue well."

"Papa, I don't want to waste money, and I need nothing fancy, but—"

"I promise you a new dress for the wedding—"

Angelina gasped. She raised her arms in the air to throw them around her father in gratitude, but she froze when he completed his sentence.

"*Your* wedding," he finished. "I'm not buying a new dress

every time someone gets married. Ridiculous. In Sicily, we did the best we could and wore the best we had."

"And this is America. I work, Papa. I should have some money."

"You have some money."

"Not enough to buy a new dress."

"Next month, I will give you more."

"Now is better."

"Next month is best."

AFTER TWO DAYS of arguing with her father, Angelina stood on her neighbor's porch with an old blue dress over her arm.

"Aha, there you are." Signora Bertelli swung open the door with her usual burst of energy. "Come in, come in. I was just saying to myself, 'What happened to that girl, Angelina? How can she walk right past my house and not stop by to say hello?'"

A flush warmed Angelina's cheeks as she stepped inside. "I'm sorry, signora, but I'm working all day, and when I come home, I still have to help my family. And now I'm embarrassed. I need your help."

"And if I refuse you, may my feet be plagued with bunions."

"It's my father. We don't agree."

"And you think this is news? He's a father. You're his daughter. The two never agree. Even the neighborhood goats know this."

"Did you hear us arguing?" asked Angelina.

"Imagine, after all these years, I still have my hearing," Signora Bertelli said with a wink.

"My friend is getting married, and this is all I have to wear." She held up the dress. "My father doesn't think Rosa's wedding is reason enough to buy me anything new. My mother altered this dress for me before she died, but it's been so long it doesn't fit well."

The middle-aged woman reached for the garment, rubbed the fabric between her fingers, held it at a distance, and then brought it up close. She turned it inside out, then right side out again. Nothing slipped her notice. "Your mother, may she rest in peace, was smart. She cut nothing, just took it in, as if she knew what we'd be up to."

"I work, I give my father my earnings for the family, and I keep only a little for myself. Now he refuses to buy me a new dress for my friend's wedding. Is that fair?"

Signora Bertelli threw the dress over her shoulder. "The only thing that's fair, Angelina, is that life is equally unfair to all of us."

Angelina could well accept that philosophy.

"It's no secret your father is a disciplined man and true to his Sicilian beliefs. If he is keeping your wages, it's because he has a plan for the money."

"Like what? Buy more salami?"

Signora Bertelli's eyes sparkled. "He's saving it for your dowry."

"Dowry? Who packed up that idea and loaded it on the boat to America?"

Signora pushed her glasses up the bridge of her nose and gazed at Angelina. "It's not such a terrible thing. Your father wants his daughter to have a decent dowry to attract a man worthy of her."

Angelina pursed her lips. "There are laws against selling your children, you know."

"It's tradition. Your father's proud of you and believes it's his duty. These are very old ways and laws."

"So these men stop by, leave their name, and my father picks one out of a hat?" Angelina cringed. "There are also laws against raffling off your children." She had no intention of walking around town like the prize in a neighborhood lottery.

Signora Bertelli placed the dress next to her sewing machine and matched threads to the color of the fabric. "Never argue with an alligator thrashing about in water until after you've crossed the river. *After* your friend's wedding, tell your father what you think."

"He's always talking about hardship and hunger while he owns a store full of food."

"Sicilians are proud that they were once miserable." Signora Bertelli nodded as though this was a good thing. "They say, 'Better a full stomach than a new skirt.' But why go hungry while you're waiting for a chicken to lay an egg? I say sew a new skirt and have both."

The similarity between her uncle and neighbor did not escape Angelina. Whatever the tragedy, they both extracted a pearl. "If my mother hadn't died, she'd insist I have a new dress."

"If your mother hadn't died, you'd have two new dresses, vegetables would grow larger, birds would sing sweeter. Meanwhile, we'll please her by doing our best, sitting down at the table, and examining our possibilities."

Angelina reached for the scissors. "I'll help you sew it, signora."

"Not this time. There's more to sewing than cutting fabric and pushing and pulling a needle. It takes time. My sisters and I had to sew, or we had nothing to wear." The lines in Signora Bertelli's her face had deepened, and Angelina worried she was asking too much of her.

"Perhaps this is not a good time for you to do so much."

"Nonsense, I can do this with one eye closed." She winked. "My mother had sixteen children."

"What? That's amazing."

"Or maybe it was seventeen. By the time I was born, several had left home. After that, I'm not sure anyone ever counted. So my mother did her mothering the way she said the Our Father and Hail Mary. After the first few hundred times, her mind wandered, and she'd say them while thinking of something else. Now and then, my mother would give me one of those looks, like she was trying to remember if I was hers or if I belonged to a neighbor."

Angelina chuckled. "I think you're making that up."

Signora Bertelli laughed too. "Well, I was never quite sure. Next week, you'll come to see me. I'll make you a skilled seamstress or a great wind will blow down my house. When I'm through with your dress, the bride will wish she'd worn it."

"Since my mother died, I feel closer to you than my mother's sisters." It felt good to voice her affection to the woman who had meant so much to her mother.

"May your sainted mother rest in peace."

Angelina looked over the dress one last time. "Rosa is so happy. I wish you could meet her. She says the passing days mean nothing at all, not until the day she marries Luca."

"Don't believe it. There is no such thing as a day that means nothing. Every day someone is born, and every day someone dies. Every day someone's heart breaks, and every day it thrills someone else to be alive. Not since that first day, at the moment of creation, when God separated the light from the darkness and declared it was good has there ever been a day that means nothing."

"I guess I never thought of it that way." Angelina recalled the day her mother died and how it still echoed in her memory. "There are some days that I wish had never happened."

CHAPTER 23

Despite the sun gleaming brightly on Rosa Caprici's wedding day, Domenico had cast a shadow of gloom. Angelina suspected he'd added chores to delay her departure.

"You will not leave this house without a chaperone," he told her.

Angelina accepted the demand. She was convinced her father had given the job of chaperone to her Zio Pasquale. However, to her uncle's delight, Cuesta had just hired him as a cigar maker. Wanting to impress his employer, Pasquale spent all his spare time with Belarmino learning new techniques. And to Angelina's great disappointment, Salvatore received the order to accompany her to the wedding. What could her father be thinking? Who sent a foolish sixteen-year-old to escort a responsible almost eighteen-year-old?

With a glance at the clock, Angelina excitedly slipped on her blue dress, attached her gold pendant watch, and glanced in the mirror. Her face lit up. Signora Bertelli had performed magic. She'd removed the cumbersome sleeves, let the seams out where needed, added fabric that complemented the dress, and replaced the bow with lace.

If only Rolando could see her in this dress. Angelina took his medal from the back of her drawer and clung to it as if it possessed a magical power to bring him back. Two weeks had come and gone, two months had come and gone, and then they'd come and gone once again. Her heart burst for some news from him. Why didn't he send a message? She'd casually questioned a few who worked with him as a matter of curiosity and even asked her zio, but once again, no one knew anything.

Angelina stepped into the parlor. "Come on, Sal, or we'll be late." She hurried out the door, giving her brother ample opportunity to run the opposite direction.

"I'm right behind you," Salvatore said.

Angelina raised an eyebrow. "Is it the thought of the wedding cake that inspires you to keep up with me?"

"Of course!"

"Of course." The answer was an obvious one. Angelina rolled her eyes and led the way to the church.

She took pride in her gift for the happy couple. Rosa Caprici's wedding present had taken a lot of thought. For Angelina to have extracted a sufficient amount of money from her pay envelope, she related her gift to family honor.

It will look dreadful, Papa, terrible, if Rosa Caprici does not receive a generous wedding gift from the Pirrello family, who own a grocery store popular among Sicilians. Everyone will talk. We'll be disgraced. Angelina enjoyed reliving the thought of how she'd shamed her father into opening the cash register. Her mother must have discovered the same method of dealing with him. She'd never lacked for anything. It seemed so many things still reminded Angelina of her mother. *Grieving is a strange mixture of holding on and letting go,* she thought.

Along with the money, Angelina penned a letter of

congratulations to Rosa and her new husband, Luca Cabuto. Although Angelina had earned the money for the gift, she signed her family's name with pride.

"Hey, Angie, look who's coming toward us," said Salvatore.

Angelina hadn't seen her Aunt Violetta since her father threw her out of the house, but then again, Violetta lived in the more elegant part of town, and it was unlikely they'd run into each other.

"Zia Violetta, it's so good to see you." Both she and her brother kissed their mother's sister as tradition dictated.

"Salvatore, I'm surprised to see how much you've grown, and you look lovely, Angelina. I remember your mother once had a dress that same shade of blue."

Angelina saw no reason to share that the dress was the same one, now wondrously transformed by Signora Bertelli, not when her aunt ordered her clothes from New York dressmakers and tired of them as quickly.

"So, how are you managing with that father of yours?" Violetta said with her usual contempt.

"Terrific," Salvatore said.

No matter what she or her brother answered, their words would be exaggerated and passed around the Cacciatore family to inflame the already-lit torch of discontent. "We've never been better, thank you."

"We're on our way to my friend Rosa Caprici's wedding," Angelina offered.

"I don't remember her as one of your school friends," said Violetta.

Angelina could not imagine why her aunt thought she should know every friend she had. Angelina looked longingly down the street and knew just how to shorten the conversation. "I don't go to school anymore. We work together."

"You work?" Violetta's cheeks sunk into caverns.

Angelina remembered the woman's aversion to making beds and washing dishes.

"What kind of work?" Her aunt's eyes widened.

"At a cigar factory." *No sense in mentioning my position, or she'll scream,* thought Angelina.

Violetta made the sign of the cross. "Oh, dear God, at least your mother worked in the home, where no one could witness it." She took hold of Angelina's arm and spewed her perception of women who worked. "It's unseemly. Be proud your blood is half Cacciatore and marry no one from a cigar factory—unless he owns the enterprise. Your mother should have listened. Don't make the same mistake, Angelina." Violetta flipped open her fan and waved it furiously, as if the air had become polluted by a sudden vulgar draft of the working class. "I can't bear to think of it. It's deplorable. Quit, or you risk not being accepted into proper society."

The years had come and gone, but her aunt remained fossilized in her thinking. *Not unlike my father,* thought Angelina, though she doubted either of them would appreciate the comparison. However, today, a happy day, belonged to Rosa.

"It's so good to see you, Zia." Angelina quickly kissed her mother's sister goodbye. "I love you, but if we don't hurry, we'll miss the ceremony." They dashed away before her aunt could uncover something else from her bag of revulsion.

"Hey, Angie, what's the matter with her, anyway? Didn't you tell her money is the root of all evil?"

"The *love* of money is the root of all evil."

Salvatore had his usual wide, teasing grin. "Same thing. I think you should tell her."

Angelina giggled at the thought.

They entered the church through the large double doors, dipped their fingers in the small font of holy water, and blessed themselves. Saint Teresa of Avila said nothing made the devil take flight like holy water. Angelina considered this, and since they'd run into her Aunt Violetta, Angelina dipped her hand in the holy water and blessed herself a second time. What could it hurt?

Arrays of fresh flowers lined the aisles and enticed the guests to their seats while soft organ music floated on the air. Rosa looked radiant in her mother's wedding dress. In contrast, Signor Caprici's suit was too long for his arms, too wide for his shoulders, and his mustache was too large for his face, but when he smiled at his daughter, his awkwardness became endearing.

The ceremony gained momentum, and Angelina tried to imagine her father as proud of his daughter, but the scene evaded her. She listened to the priest's recitation meant to join Rosa and Luca's hearts, and a wave of sadness washed over her. She'd have to marry without a mother's love and support. Still, if her mother and Signora Bertelli believed in spirits, then her mother's presence might appear on her wedding day.

The young priest stood tall and spoke in a commanding voice. "For three weeks, we have announced the banns of marriage between Luca Cabuto and Rosa Caprici. No one has come forward to say why this couple should not marry. If anyone has an objection, please speak now."

Angelina grimaced. It didn't matter that they had been engaged for months and everyone knew it or that the banns of marriage were announced every Sunday for three weeks before the wedding. Now, at their wedding, the priest kept looking for trouble. Rosa loved Luca. He loved her. That was that.

With the vows spoken, Angelina imagined trumpets sounding in heaven.

"Hey," Salvatore whispered. "Stop daydreaming. No one will marry you."

Angelina stepped on his shoe and ignored his exaggerated agony.

Good wishes and grains of rice showered the bride and groom all the way from the church to their open carriage while the parade of well-wishers followed them for the two blocks to Anselmo's Restaurant.

Angelina and Salvatore stepped through the doorway into a lavish world filled with the finest cuisine's aroma. White linen tablecloths, bentwood chairs, and floral-print wallpaper created an air of elegance. Above their heads, decorative tin tiles adorned the ceiling. Beneath their feet, ceramic tiles of black and white patterned the floor. The mahogany bar ran the length of the room, with carved Roman warriors in chariots displayed at the base. Venetian murals hung everywhere. For the first time in her life, Angelina stood amid opulence, and it overwhelmed her.

Rosa's father poured a glass of wine. "A toast to the bride and groom. May they know love forever," he said.

"And," added Rosa's mother, "may that same love give us lots of grandchildren."

"Mama!" shouted Rosa.

Everyone laughed. Luca's face reddened, and toasts of "*Salute*!" cascaded around the room.

With glasses raised, guests cheering, and mandolins playing, Anselmo's Restaurant gushed with celebration. Seducing both the eye and the appetite, an abundance of delectable cuisines and wondrous aromas lay in silver trays and crystal bowls. Rosa Caprici's wedding rivaled a Biblical feast.

Angelina wasted no time in congratulating the bride and groom with a hug and kiss. She placed her gift in Rosa's hand. "I wish you both every blessing and the greatest happiness!" she said.

"You are so kind, Angelina," answered Rosa. Luca nodded in agreement. They all hugged again, and a line to congratulate the newlyweds began to form.

"Where's your dish of food?" Rosa's mother handed Angelina a plate. "If you don't eat, you'll insult my cousin."

Angelina accepted the dish of gleaming china, catching her reflection in it. She admired the abundance and variety at the long banquet table, but her eyes narrowed when she saw her brother at the far end, helping himself to a growing mound of food. "I'm sorry, signora. It appears my brother is eating for both of us."

"What else can we expect from a growing boy? Come, let me introduce you to the master chef." The woman turned toward an older man who appeared to have enjoyed much of his cuisine. "This is my *cugino* Sam Anselmo."

Angelina shook his hand. "You're a cousin? It must be wonderful having you in the family. I've never seen so many exceptional dishes all at once."

He glanced at the food. "I'll tell you a secret. When my fear of hunger disappeared, abundance appeared, but please excuse me for the moment. I must check on the kitchen."

"Try his gnocchi. It's like eating little clouds," whispered Rosa's mother.

Angelina gazed at the trays and their symmetrical arrangement of graduating sizes and categories. The table, like all works of art, displayed a canvas of colors and textures. Perhaps others did not notice, but Angelina intended to memorize it all.

When the restaurant's owner returned, Angelina spoke up. "Signor Anselmo, it's so clever the way you present the food."

"Nothing good happens without a little thought and effort. You selected a lovely dress to wear, and I offered a feast."

Angelina beamed at the mention of her dress.

"It's all a matter of technique. Would you like to know mine?" he said.

She leaned closer.

"If you put good things into the pot, good things come out."

Angelina smiled. "I'll remember that when I'm cooking."

"And when you're not cooking. Good returns good—in everything." The chef tapped his forehead the way Italians did when something wise was noted. He seemed a wise businessman and reminded her of Don Carlos Madrid. Angelina decided she liked Rosa's cousin for his wisdom, cooking, and the artistic way he displayed his food.

"Angelina. *Ven aca.* Over here." Bertha Perez waved Angelina over from the opposite end of the banquet table. Angelina didn't know her well, but well enough to know they had nothing in common with which to seal a friendship. Bertha was a bit too aggressive, worked across the large room at the factory, and they rarely spoke. That worked out satisfactorily for Angelina.

"Come, try this," said Bertha as she pointed to a tray of antipasto. "It's so good." She held a morsel on her fork, took a bite, and closed her eyes, savoring it.

Signor Anselmo looked pleased. "Go to your friend, Angelina. We'll talk again."

Angelina combed the crowded restaurant for Carmen, then glanced at the entrance, hoping to spot her coming inside. Instead, a young man entered through the hand-carved double doors as though he'd walked out of the pages of a novel. He wore a white shirt with a wingtip collar, a gray vest, a single-breasted jacket, and pinstriped pants. For a moment, she couldn't take her eyes off his dark good looks.

Perhaps it was because he'd arrived so well-dressed, or perhaps because he'd appeared at the wrong time of day or the wrong day of the week. It was the brown cap that triggered her memory. He was the same young man she'd bumped into when rushing to work. The one who was cordial but didn't smile. She remembered pointing to the cigar factory where she worked and he right away switched from speaking English to Spanish.

This time he removed the brown cap he'd worn when she first saw him. He revealed a mop of black hair, which gave him a bit of an unruly, independent look, as if he didn't take life too seriously. The combination of his dapper dress and wild hair somehow seemed a contradiction. He appeared to be searching for someone when his eyes met Angelina's. He nodded as if greeting her. Embarrassed, she turned away.

"Oh, I almost forgot," Bertha said. "Carmen told me to tell you she'd be a little late. She's taking care of her grandmother until her mother arrives." Bertha gazed around the room with widened eyes, surveying the guests. "And what about you, Angelina, did you come here alone?" The woman dabbed her mouth with a napkin.

"No, my brother Sal is with me."

Bertha perked up and craned her neck. "Oh, where is he? I don't believe I've had the pleasure."

Angelina found this woman annoyingly predictable. "I have four brothers," Angelina said.

"Four brothers?" Bertha pressed a hand to her heart. "I had no idea. Are they cigar makers?"

"They all work at our family's grocery store."

Bertha held up a meatball she'd speared with her fork. "Your family owns an entire grocery store? Well, I'm ashamed I haven't gotten to know you better."

Angelina couldn't decide if the abundance of brothers or food had caused Bertha's gleeful reaction.

Salvatore rushed over. "Hey, Angie, you gotta taste the cake. It's as good as Rizzo's Bakery."

"That's because Rizzo baked it," said Angelina.

Bertha raised a suspicious eyebrow. "Who is this, Angelina?"

"Salvatore, this is Bertha Perez."

Bertha narrowed her eyes. "You must be Angelina's youngest brother."

"What's she been telling you? I'm the oldest brother. I'm also the tallest, the best-looking, and the smartest." He spoke with cake clinging to his lips.

"You forgot to mention the humblest," Angelina added.

"Think of me as perfect, Bertha." He wiped his mouth on his sleeve. "Angie, did you know they have two kinds of cake?" He dashed back to the banquet table.

Bertha tugged at Angelina's arm. "Why didn't you tell me his age?"

"Was it important?" said Angelina, concealing a grin.

Bertha stomped her foot. "Yes, it's important."

"Hello, Bertha," said the young man with the brown cap in his hand.

"Fabian. You showed up!" Bertha gave him a quick hug.

It seemed highly unlikely to Angelina that the dark-haired young man she'd shamefully watched as he entered the reception knew Bertha and now stood before her.

"Missed the wedding, but I'm here to toast the happy couple."

Angelina excused herself, but Bertha hooked her arm and pulled her back. "This is Angelina. We work together at Cuesta Rey, but she sits so far away from me, we never get a chance to talk." Bertha wrinkled her nose. "Angelina, this is Fabian Dominguez. Isn't he handsome? And what bad luck—he's my cousin."

Angelina nodded at Fabian, avoiding eye contact.

"I believe we've met before, Angelina."

Bertha seemed oblivious to the remark. "Have you tried the food?"

"Not yet." The dark-haired young man raised his glass. "But the wine is excellent."

"I'll be back," Bertha said. "I want Angelina to explain something to me."

Fabian said nothing. Angelina turned and caught him gazing at her. The moment felt awkward, and she looked away.

Bertha lost no time. She moved closer to the bride and groom and lugged Angelina with her. "Look. What are Luca and Rosa giving out in those small bags?"

Angelina glanced in their direction. "They're filled with sugar-coated almonds. It's a little gift given to guests, thanking them for coming. We call them *bomboniere*."

"Really?" said Bertha, wide-eyed. "And why is everyone yelling *bacio, bacio*?"

"They want them to kiss."

Bertha puckered her lips. "So *bacio* is *beso.* One day I'll have a big wedding—bigger than this one, with twice as much food, and I'll give out large bags of candied walnuts, not those little ones."

"They're almonds."

The woman looked dreamy-eyed. "I like walnuts."

"Are you planning on marrying an Italian?" Angelina said with some irritation at the thought.

"No."

"Good, have walnuts."

Bertha pointed toward the banquet table. "Look, girls from work. Let's go see them."

Angelina looked to where six young men stood near two women. Without waiting for Angelina's reply, Bertha glided across the restaurant as if drawn by a magnetic pull. Angelina had no interest in following. She turned around and faced Fabian Dominguez, who was still standing near her.

"Your cousin Bertha will be right back," she told him.

He glanced at his cousin, who leaned over another banquet table with a selection of food and men. "I don't think so." He turned back to Angelina. "Can I get you something to drink?"

"No, thank you."

Angelina contemplated wandering away.

"It's you, isn't it? You're the girl who bumped into me on your way to work."

Angelina swallowed. "Yes, that was clumsy of me." She rubbed her hands together and looked around the room, searching for a way to change the subject.

"I knew you worked at Cuesta Rey. I saw you walk into the building that morning, and I knew my cousin Bertha worked there."

Was it possible Bertha and Fabian had discussed her? Was this why Bertha, whom she hardly knew, was trying to keep her attention at the reception? Angelina made light of it. "Yes, I suppose that's critical information."

So far, Fabian had not smiled. *He's so serious or brooding. Is something wrong?*

He gazed around at the guests enjoying the feast. "So, Angelina, which one of these men has the honor of accompanying such a beautiful girl?"

His reference to her as beautiful thrilled her more than she wanted to admit. It had to be her newly redesigned dress.

Fabian calmly awaited an answer. However, Angelina had no intention of drawing attention to her escort. To avoid this cold splash of reality, she pointed in the general direction of her brother and several other men.

Bertha rescued the moment by waving from across the restaurant. "Angelina, come quick. Rosa's throwing the bouquet, and she won't start without you. Hurry. Don't you ever want to find a husband?"

Fabian shook his head, glanced at her, and in a most serious voice, said, "I rather doubt that'll be your problem, Angelina."

Before she could react, Bertha appeared, hooked her arm through Angelina's, and led her toward the bride. "All right, Rosa, we're all here now. You can start."

Rosa glanced at her friends. "I hope you'll all be as happy as I am today." She turned around, yelled "*Buona fortuna*!" and flung the elegant bouquet high into the air. All single women moved in unison toward the prize—except Angelina.

The bouquet came down. Three women lunged, crashed into each other, and knocked the flowers off course—right at Angelina's feet. She reached down, but as her fingertips brushed against the stems, Bertha plowed into her, pushed her to the floor, grabbed the bouquet, and landed on top of her.

A collective gasp resounded from the spectators.

Bertha jumped up, waving her prize, while Angelina remained facedown, just inches from the floor. Worse, she wasn't sure if her dress had risen. She caught her breath and checked her dress.

Angelina could not imagine a more humiliating scene, and at a formal celebration amid well-dressed guests, many of which knew her, and in such elegant surroundings.

Rosa hurried over, helped her to her feet, and whispered in her ear. "The flowers should have been yours. It will take more than a bouquet to help that one. Are you hurt?"

"I'm not hurt, Rosa, but so far this is the most embarrassing moment of my life."

"Bertha's the one who should be embarrassed," said Rosa.

Bertha waved the bouquet over her head as if she had won the right to claim a man.

Carmen suddenly appeared, rushed to Angelina, and helped her dust off her dress. "I walk in the door and find you flat on your face. Tell me you're nearsighted and looking for something on the floor."

"Yes, my pride. Do you see it anywhere?" Angelina glanced at the door, but it would only compound her shame to run out.

"Even a horse with four legs can fall down," Carmen said. "Besides, I've heard that falling on your face at a wedding is good luck."

"You're making that up."

Carmen winked. "Or is it good luck if it rains on your wedding day?"

Angelina rubbed her the tension pressing the back of her neck. "Another lie. What else can they say to the poor bride when her hair is dripping wet, her gown is ruined, and her guests are running for cover?"

"Well, you'll have time to practice staying on your feet. I can see into the future. You'll be attending more weddings."

"If you can see the future, you should've told Angelina to stay clear of Bertha when I threw the bouquet," said Rosa.

"Sometimes even the stars in the heavens collide," replied Carmen.

Rosa hugged Angelina and rejoined her new husband. A few musicians were playing the traditional tarantella. The younger guests danced, and the older ones clapped their hands and sang. Across the room, Angelina glanced at Fabian as he leaned against the wall, looking in her direction. If he'd been watching her, he must have seen her fall. Her stomach churned.

Three women approached him. As they talked to him, he glanced back at Angelina and raised his goblet to her. How could she be foolish enough to look his way—again? Mortified, she turned her attention to the bride and groom. Their love for each other seemed to engulf the room. For a moment, she closed her eyes and thought of Rolando. At least he hadn't seen her fall.

Angelina searched for her chaperone among the growing crowd of dancers. He'd vanished. She made her way through the gathering, past the banquet table that still held a captive crowd, and past several women who flipped open their fans. They seemed quite charmed as they spoke to Fabian.

Angelina slipped outside and heard her brother's staccato laughter coming from around the building. There, she found him with two other boys, each drinking a glass of wine and exhaling cigar smoke.

"Salvatore! What are you doing?"

"Angie . . . uh, care for a cigar? You can have mine. I feel dizzy."

Angelina reached for his glass. "You aren't speaking clearly. How much did you drink?" She poured out the wine, yanked the cigar from his mouth, and tossed it away. "So you know, it's not customary to drag your chaperone home."

Fabian walked up behind her, picked up the cigar she'd tossed away, and examined it. "He has good taste," he said in a deep voice of authority.

"That's comforting to know. Goodbye." She marched away, holding on to her brother.

"You're not leaving?" he called out.

She could not imagine a more embarrassing afternoon. "I'm not staying." She didn't look back.

By the time she reached home, Angelina had pushed the embarrassing fall from her mind and thought only of the beautiful wedding. She went straight to the deli's display case, rearranged the dishes according to size, and added some green olives and roasted red peppers for color and appeal. The day had filled her imagination and lingered into the night.

In her room, she took Rolando's gold medal from her pocket and closed her hand around it. Every chance she had, she glanced out the window at the passengers stepping off the train, hoping to see Rolando among them. The bustle of people had ceased. A single streetlamp grappled against the moonlight. Only the occasional sound of a horse-drawn wagon breached the silence. Homes sat in shadows with oil lamps trickling bits of light through their windows, as though each home concealed a secret behind its curtains.

Angelina had a secret as well—her memories of Rolando. In bed that night, she slipped the medal under her pillow and prayed for Rolando's protection and safe return. A tear rolled down her cheek. If only she knew what had become of him. She tossed about, thinking of him until she fell into a dream that swirled about her. In it, she saw herself alone, seated on a train, and gazing out the window. Rolando entered the car, gave his ticket to the porter, and then Rolando came to her in that mystical way people move about in dreams.

"It looks like this seat hasn't been taken," he said. She awoke with a start. It felt as if the words were a prophecy of something to come.

CHAPTER 24

Angelina sat reading on the porch swing when Domenico walked out of the house and approached her.

"Set the table for four more on Sunday. Signore Paolo, his wife, Carmela, Cristina, and their only son, Rico, will be our guests."

"But, Papa, the Braccios are customers. You never invite customers to eat. Why are they coming?"

"Use your mother's good tablecloth and china. I want you to make lasagna and a cake like the one you made the day my brother arrived from Sicily."

"Papa, Zio Pasquale surprised us when he arrived. Why is it you can't remember anything about my birthday?" Angelina grew suspicious. Why should her mother's special dishes and linens grace the table? "Are we trying to impress the Braccios?"

Domenico took a last puff from his cigar, blew a ring of smoke, and watched it fade away before answering. "The Braccios are a decent family, and your cooking's improved." He dropped his spent cigar on the porch and crushed it with his foot. "You'll find me in the garden trying to get the pomegranates to grow."

"You know, Papa, if we use Mama's very best, the table will look especially nice. Aren't you afraid the Braccios will think we're impractical instead of sensible?"

He turned his back and walked away.

At last, she'd said something he didn't have an answer for. It was a minor triumph, but a triumph. Angelina delighted in the rare moment.

BY MIDAFTERNOON, Angelina had made her way toward a row of stores. She trying to decipher the enigmatic request Signora Bertelli had given her. After her grand success in transforming her mother's dress, Angelina wanted to repay her friend by running errands or in whatever way she could.

"Buy me blue fabric—the color of the Mediterranean Sea," Signora Bertelli had instructed. Angelina had never seen the Mediterranean Sea, but that seemed beside the point.

Gray clouds were bathing the sky when she reached the fabric and notions store. With no logical way to explain what she needed, Angelina searched for the mysterious color. If wrong, perhaps Signora Bertelli would blame the discrepancy on her own memory or eyesight.

Angelina grabbed a bolt. "I'll take six yards," she said to the clerk holding a measuring stick in one hand and a pair of large shears in the other. The clerk cut, folded, and wrapped it in paper and tied it with string.

"Here you go, miss."

With the purchase completed, Angelina had just stepped outside when the dark clouds ripped open. She scurried along the walkway and slipped, but was able to regain her footing. She took shelter beneath the nearest store awning.

As she looked out at the rain pelting the street, she saw Fabian Dominguez rushing toward the same large awning where she stood. Surprised at first, she reasoned it would not be uncommon for two people to run into each other. Ybor City consisted of a mere forty acres with a few principal streets.

Fabian hurried for cover and joined her underneath the awning.

"Hello, Angelina. We meet again."

"Hello. Yes, we seem to run into each other in the strangest places." She raised her voice over the increasing downpour.

Fabian stood next to her and whistled a little tune she didn't recognize.

"The streets are treacherous right now. I'm glad you kept yourself from falling this time," he said.

This time? Her face grew warm. He'd seen her slip. What kind of man reminded a person of her most embarrassing moment unless he was trying to get her to hate him? She wanted to strike back and looked disinterested. "I'm sorry. I've forgotten your name."

"Fabian Dominguez." He smiled. Angelina wondered if that meant he didn't believe her. Once again, his classic good looks were hard to miss. She imagined warriors during the rise of the Roman Empire looked like Fabian, but this was 1908 AD, not the days of Augustus Caesar. Besides, he wasn't as tall as Rolando, and his voice wasn't as soothing. She looked away.

"When I left home, the dark clouds must have been hiding behind the fluffy, white ones. Now they're throwing a temper tantrum," Angelina said.

"See all those people out in the street? Some will say the rain makes them feel alive. It smells fresh, rejuvenates the earth, and washes away the dirt. Other people will complain they get wet. Which group do you belong to, Angelina?"

Angelina looked out at the rain. "So have you come to sell bags of sunshine to people who complain about getting wet, Señor Dominguez?"

Angelina saw the corners of his mouth quiver, as if he were trying to control a smile.

"Actually, I belong to the first group. I love the rain, especially when it beats against my window and lulls me to sleep," she said.

Fabian nodded. "Still, it's interesting God chose rain to destroy the earth."

"It's more interesting you would think of that. Anyway, better rain than fire." Angelina pushed aside a lock of her wet hair. "It's slowing down. I should go."

Fabian quickly pulled off his cap and offered it to her. "In case it gets worse before you get home."

She held up a hand to refuse. "Thank you, but I won't shrink if I get wet. Give Bertha my regards. Goodbye, Señor Dominguez." Ignoring his offer to accompany her, Angelina dashed away without looking back.

She hurried through the drizzle and puddles, enjoying how refreshing the rain felt. Fabian hadn't been unpleasant either. She was certain women threw themselves at him and marveled at everything he said. *Some women are so silly.*

At last, Angelina arrived at Signora Bertelli's. Her neighbor's enthusiastic greeting made her grateful she could help her older friend in light of her countless kindnesses.

"Come in, come in," said Signora Bertelli. "Such weather! Here's a towel to dry off."

Angelina accepted the towel, handed over the package, and held her breath as her neighbor uncovered the fabric.

"And to think you got caught up in all this downpour to bring this to me. The saints are making notes of your good deeds. If I'm lying, may this cloth fall to pieces in its first wash." Signora Bertelli held up the fabric and squinted. "This will make beautiful bedroom curtains and remind me of the Mediterranean Sea as I close my eyes and dream of Italy. I knew you would bring me the right color."

The remark seemed curious. "I hoped I was right, but I wasn't sure."

"You were sure. You have an imagination, or you could never become a writer. Some people have so little imagination, they can't even conjure up a dream when they go to sleep." Signora Bertelli took a deep breath. "I can almost smell the sea."

CHAPTER 25

The breaking rays of daylight darted across the sky in long streaks of coral and amber and dissolved all traces of the night. Angelina left her bed, pulled aside her curtains, and listened to the fragile chorus of sparrows. It had not escaped her notice how the Lord had given these tiny creatures only one note to sing and they sang it over and over, charming all who listened.

The new day's range of possibilities entangled with Angelina's memories of Rolando, which never seemed far from her thoughts. Like always, she watched from her window as the early-morning trains pulled in. Perhaps today he'd surprise her. She wanted nothing more than to reverse time and make him promise not to leave her, but time didn't care. It never stood still and never amended the past. The DiLeto's dog ran past her window, barking and chasing a cat. Torn from her thoughts, she readied for the day.

Angelina's father had ordered her to give up her only morning to sleep in to prepare a meal for the Braccios. Even more annoying, she had to cook the sauce early and let it simmer for several hours to release its full flavor. Worse, to fulfill her Sunday obligation and have the meal ready in time, she'd have to attend 6:00 a.m. Mass—a Mass mainly attended by the elderly.

She left the house and walked toward Sacred Heart Church while she considered the curious fact that so many older people got up at dawn to go to church when they had nothing to do all day and could attend anytime.

When she arrived, Angelina blessed herself with holy water, made the sign of the cross, walked down the center aisle, and genuflected before taking her seat. The elderly moved more slowly and nodded when they looked her way. As the young priest appeared and enraptured the church with the miracle of the Mass, Angelina continued to reflect on the mystery of early-morning attendance.

She listened to the first gospel reading and joined in the response. However, after the second reading and before the homily, a kind of logic took shape. It *was* wiser for the aged to attend Mass as early as possible rather than risk sudden death later in the day without the benefit of Holy Communion. However, she also found it curious how this advantage had not occurred to Father Cavalli, the oldest priest, who left rising early to the youngest to serve.

Angelina also considered the sacrament of communion. Those who'd eradicated their sins in the confessional left their pew, walked to the front of the church, and, before everyone, knelt at the altar to receive the body of Christ in the form of a host. Those who didn't leave their seats gave credence they remained sullied with sin. If she were in charge, she'd plan something more discreet for the sinners and less exhibitionist for the saintly.

When Mass ended, Angelina headed toward the door and stopped before the statue of the Blessed Mother. She stared up at her and then lit a candle. "Oh, most gracious Virgin Mary, protect Rolando wherever he is, keep him safe, and bring him home soon. I miss him so very much." Angelina paused, made the sign of the cross, and stared at the statue for a moment. "Oh, please hear my prayer." Angelina sighed, walked home, and entered the kitchen with Rolando still on her mind.

She reached for pots and pans, an array of condiments, and simmered the sauce, meatballs, and sausages. When finished, she intended to bake the cake her father had requested. He surprised her when he entered the kitchen, paced a moment, crossed his arms, and then uncrossed them. He wasn't a person who hesitated in saying what was on his mind, so his behavior was suspicious.

"Your lector at the factory doesn't read all the local news." Domenico held up the Italian newspaper and pointed to the headline, *"Ignazio Lupo del* Mano Nera *cutturato."*

Angelina glanced at the large print stating the police had caught a man named Ignazio Lupo of the Black Hand.

"I've never heard of him." She glanced back at her father, unsure where he was going with this.

Domenico's face flushed red. "They said the man strangled sixty men, then burned them to conceal their identities. We call them all the Black Hand, but there's no such organization. They use the name to scare people. Nico Trezza has men who join him in his crimes, while others operate alone."

"I read about what the Black Hand did to Enrico Caruso," said Angelina, unsure what had brought on this line of conversation.

Domenico appeared deep in thought as he picked up a cigar and spun its colorful band around. "A famous operatic tenor is big news, but when these things happen to ordinary people, everyone is afraid to report it. Gangsters burn down homes and kidnap the children of those they threaten." Domenico set down his cigar and passed his hand over his face as if he were shutting his eyes to something he saw in his mind. "Caruso paid the first demand of $2,000 and kept it quiet, but when he received a second demand of $15,000, he went to the police."

"And they caught the two men, right?"

"Yes, but who were they, Angelina? Ordinary men, the most unlikely. Two successful businessmen picked up the money. They saw an opportunity to enrich themselves even more. Now they're in jail."

"Has something happened in Ybor City or Tampa, Papa?"

"Something happens every day in Ybor City and Tampa, and not everything is in the newspapers. You're safe working in a large building with hundreds of adults. Not everyone's daughter is as lucky." Domenico poured a cup of coffee and left the kitchen. Angelina glanced at the clock. The Braccios would arrive soon, and she had no time to solve her father's riddles.

Like all Sundays, everyone fasted until they received Holy Communion, and noon Mass would be over at 1:00 p.m. She visualized Father Cavalli slowly giving his closing prayer accompanied by the sound of grumbling stomachs. It seemed curious her that father expected everyone to attend Mass, though he only made appearances at weddings, baptisms, funerals, and an occasional Holy Day of Obligation. He was a man of many curious habits.

As expected, Pasquale and the children arrived famished. If the Braccios intended to impress her family as much as her father intended to impress them, they'd better arrive on time.

One knock and Domenico opened the door to receive his guests. "Welcome. Come in, come in." He shook hands with the men and greeted them all warmly.

Angelina eyed her father with suspicion. However, always gracious, she also shook hands with the father and the 'only son,' as her father put it, but Rico's handshake was loose and flimsy, which Angelina found annoying. Rico was taller than his father, with a crown of thick, wavy hair. He had a narrow face and was reasonably attractive. He just appeared unhappy to be there, which was fair. Angelina wasn't happy he was there either. Nothing about Rico struck up a memory, and she never forgot a face. He'd either transformed or she'd never met him. It didn't matter which.

Carmela and her daughter, Cristina, embraced and kissed Angelina. Cristina had been her classmate, and her visit delighted Angelina.

"We miss you, Angelina. Mrs. Mixell always talks about her best student," Cristina said.

"I wish I could have stayed." Angelina narrowed her gaze at her father for signs of guilt but saw none.

"Ah, something smells wonderful. *Ho fame*," said Signore Braccio. The man tapped his midsection with the back of his thumb, the gesture for hunger.

"Angelina's been working hard. Please, have a seat. The food she prepared is ready." Her father gestured to the dining table.

Loud chatter and the slam of the front door announced the arrival of Pasquale and the children.

"Hello to everybody. And the food, she smell so good." As always, her uncle seasoned everything with excitement, and Angelina felt a release of tension.

"You're in time, Zio. How was *afternoon* Mass?" Angelina gave her father an icy stare to remind him of her early-morning sacrifice.

"Church is good. Father Cavalli, he say we have to pray, and if nothing happen, we pray more. I think I gonna pray 'more' first, so it no take so long."

"Good idea, Zio." Angelina waited while everyone gathered around the two tables pushed together and adorned in prized linens.

Domenico surveyed his children. "Whose turn is it to say grace?"

Ten-year-old Filippo raised his hand. "It's mine."

Angelina glanced at her brother, certain his quick response had sprung from hunger, not devotion. Filippo took in a deep breath. "Bless this food, O Lord, and these Thy gifts, which we are about to receive from Thy bounty through Christ our Lord, amen." Filippo's words of gratitude to the Almighty collided like derailing trains in his apparent rush to end the prayer as quickly as possible. Her brother's voice had grown higher in pitch from loss of air until his final gasp of "amen." He made the sign of the cross with his right hand and stabbed his fork into a meatball with his left. The ambidextrous maneuver impressed Angelina.

Domenico eyed his son. "Were you speaking in tongues, Filippo? I hardly understood you. If you eat as fast as you pray, we may not be able to revive you."

"Filippo is smart boy, Domenico. He no want the food to get cold." Pasquale patted the child on his back.

Domenico returned his focus to his guests. "Have some wine. It's from an old recipe of my grandfather."

Paolo Braccio held his glass up and examined the color, then sipped. "Mmm. My compliments. What this country needs is a magnificent Sicilian wine." Paolo Braccio nodded toward his son.

"Rico will pass. He never drinks," said Paolo.

"A Sicilian who doesn't sip a little wine?" said Domenico, surprised.

Rico met his father's eyes. "No, I never drink."

Angelina could not help feeling awkward around Rico. He appeared uncomfortable, his attitude was questionable, and his social skills were lacking.

Carmela Braccio broke her silence. "Angelina, you're a wonderful cook."

"Thank you, signora. I'm so glad you approve. I learned from my mother, and our friend Signora Bertelli has taught me so much as well."

"Angelina is the very best cook in all Ybor City," said Pasquale. "She can make anybody fat like a pig if she wanna to."

Domenico cleared his throat and squinted at his brother.

"Ah, but she no wanna."

Both Cristina and Angelina giggled.

"Well, I suppose that's a big compliment." Paolo chuckled. "Rico, what do you think of Angelina's meal?"

"It's good," he blurted out, looking down as if talking to the plate.

Angelina had no interest in his opinion but felt compelled to respond. "I'm glad you like it, Rico." In case her father didn't think she could be gracious, she'd show him he was mistaken. "So, Rico, doesn't your grandfather own the company that makes the cigar boxes for Cuesta Rey?" she asked.

Rico raised his head but seemed to look past her as he tossed a thin reply. "Yes."

He could have said much more. Angelina tapped her foot under the table and tried again. "The crests are so detailed. Who stamps them on the boxes?"

He paused. She was sure something whirled around in his mind, but it wasn't an answer, so she reduced her question to multiple choice. "Is it your company or Cuesta Rey who stamps the boxes?"

Rico met her eyes. "Our company."

Angelina's chitchat with Rico died of lethargy.

Signore Braccio resuscitated it. "My father bought the company from a German. They invented lithography, you know, and our workers are exceptional at stamping crests."

Angelina glimpsed in her father's direction. He couldn't

say she hadn't been hospitable even though she suspected Rico concealed a secret and was pleased she didn't know it.

"You *nanno* give you work, Rico. That's good." Pasquale took over the burden of the conversation, freeing Angelina to relax and take a bite. She savored her mouthful and admitted she had outdone herself.

Rico nodded. "My grandfather's a good man and good to all the workers. I've been working there since I turned fourteen. He works as hard as everyone else. I've learned every phase of the business, even the bookkeeping. We're expecting a large shipment of wood tomorrow. If you want to stop by, I'll show you how we make the boxes," Rico said.

Her uncle had a gift for stirring conversation. Or perhaps Rico didn't like her. She preferred the latter.

Angelina slipped into the kitchen to escape and overheard the men discussing importing olive oil and balsamic vinegar. From the tone of the conversation, the dinner had been more of a business meeting. Her father imported food from Italy, and Paolo Braccio had family connections there. She picked up the cake platter and set it on the table to speed up the afternoon meal.

"Look at the cake!" Lily shouted.

Angelina served their guests first. "I'll take Vinny's piece," Salvatore said. "He doesn't want his."

"That's a miracle," said Angelina.

"Yeah, don't count on miracles, Sal. They don't happen on Nineteenth Street," said Vincenzo, spearing his cake with his fork.

Angelina reached in her pocket to feel Rolando's medal. Vincenzo was never right about anything, and she counted on him being wrong again. Every day, she prayed for a miracle on Nineteenth Street.

"Since we talk about the miracles, why I no tell you about Santo Antonio Abbate?" Pasquale moved to the sofa. The children gathered around, balancing dishes of dessert. Then Pasquale began his story.

"This miracle, it happen one time only. And then it happen every time since the first time."

"What happened?" Lily asked, her eyes shining in wonder.

"Tomorrow is Santo Antonio Abbate's name day. Tonight, if children hang a statue or picture of Santo Antonio Abbate where the goats and pigs gonna sleep, you no believe what happen."

"What, Zio Pasquale?" asked Giuseppe.

"At midnight, you gonna hear all the goats and pigs talk."

All the children's eyes opened wide.

"Are you sure, Zio? I didn't know goats and pigs could talk," said Lily. Then she turned to Angelina. "How come you never told us, Angie?"

"I'm surprised too." Angelina joined in. The children's excitement was contagious.

Pasquale shook his head. "Maybe in l'America, the goats and pigs, they don't know Italian so good."

Giuseppe rushed to his father. "Papa, can we sleep outside tonight so we can hear the animals talk? Please, Papa?"

"But we don't have a statue or a picture," said Filippo with a frown.

"Is no problem. Santo Antonio Abbate, he no so fussy."

Domenico nodded at his children. "It's a shame to miss a miracle when it's right in your backyard."

The children cheered.

Paolo Braccio laughed. "As a boy, I tried to stay up for the miracle." He sounded somewhat sad and overcome with nostalgia. "Sometimes I miss the old country. A piece of my heart is always there."

"Yes, I know." Domenico took another sip of wine. "Sometimes I sit alone and think of the people I knew in my village. What could I have done differently? Life was too hard, unbearable, and the government taxed us for everything. People said they wanted to take our eyes so we couldn't cry. As long as I live, I will never go back." Domenico put down his wineglass and gazed into the goblet as though it held a portal to the past. "Life is hard here, but not hopeless."

"Who could forget the land we had to feed our families? It was rocky and so small we called it a handkerchief." Paolo sipped his wine. "The north has always been indifferent to the people of the south, so we left by donkey cart or by whatever means to reach a ship and escape." Paolo sighed. "Such a picturesque island scarred with tragedy."

Domenico nodded. "In Sicily, beauty and brutality hold hands."

"*Salute.* To full bellies," said Paolo as he tapped Domenico's glass.

The conversation grew long and spirited. In the end, the two men patted each other on the back. The family thanked Angelina for the meal, Domenico for his excellent wine, and Pasquale for his memories of miracles.

As soon as the Braccios left, the children's excitement filled the air as they followed their uncle outside to stare with renewed enthusiasm at the two goats and a pig.

As Angelina finished the dishes, she was surprised when her father returned to the kitchen. He usually retreated to his overstuffed chair to read the Italian newspaper.

"Did you like the dinner, Papa?" she asked.

"I'm certain you made your mother proud." A rare compliment. Angelina delighted in it.

"What did you think of the Braccio family?" he asked.

"They're all right, I guess. Cristina and I talked about our friends at school, but her brother I didn't like."

"Why not?"

A familiar pit began growing in Angelina's stomach.

"You're the one who tells me to be more observant. Didn't you see it? He was uncomfortable, and he made me uncomfortable. It's like he's hiding something."

"The Braccios are decent people. For years they've been our customers, and we've reached a business agreement."

Her father never discussed customers this way, he never asked her opinion, and he never discussed his business agreements. Feeling uneasy, she changed the subject. "Papa, did you hear Connie Peterson had twins yesterday? Everyone is talking about it. The boy came first. Ten minutes later, she gave another scream and a girl was born—a tremendous surprise for the entire family."

"Her name is Constanza." Domenico huffed.

"She goes by Connie now. It's easier for her husband, Harry Peterson, to say."

"You see what happens when people marry outside their own kind? People forget who they are."

Convinced that even though the world spun on its axis and changed positions, her father never budged. "Don't worry, Papa. No one will ever forget we're Sicilian."

"That's because we hold on to our traditions and are proud of who we are."

What is he up to? He'd been a perfect host, complimenting her food, allowing the children to spend the night with the animals, and bringing out his best wine. Now she sensed a shift.

"Paolo Braccio came to me and has asked for your hand in marriage to his son, Rico. I have agreed."

Angelina dropped the plate she'd just washed. The statement had not been loud or harsh, but the words froze her heart and crushed her dreams. Only by fierce determination did she muster her protest. "I won't do it!"

"Rico is Braccio's only son. He will inherit everything from both his father and grandfather. I've done well for you,

Angelina. Priests don't marry people during Lent, so we'll wait out the forty days until after Easter. You'll learn to love him and have a good life."

Angelina gripped the back of a kitchen chair with both hands, lifted it a few inches, and slammed it down in disbelief. "You can't do this."

"He comes from a fine Italian family. You'll never have to worry about anything. It'll be a good life, Angelina. Next year you'll thank me."

"Thank you? Never. Good life? I can't even have a good conversation with that man."

"I understand, but in time, you'll learn to love and respect him."

Did her father think she had no feelings? No mind? No aspirations? "I don't even like him. It's outrageous. How could you agree without talking to me? You and Mama loved each other so much. Have you forgotten you married for love?"

"That's rare, like being struck by lightning."

Angelina pushed her hand into her pocket, closed her eyes, and made a desperate plea with Rolando's medal in her hand. *Everyone who has ever lived is entitled to at least one miracle in a lifetime. Can I please have mine now?*

"I know what's best." Her father's words rang with finality, but Angelina had no intention of backing down.

"No, you don't. I want to live my life, not your life for me."

Domenico raised his voice an octave. "The world can be a dangerous place, like the story in today's newspaper. You have security, and when your children come, you'll both be happy."

"Children? Throughout the meal, I heard you discussing business, but it never occurred to me that my life was what you were negotiating."

"Think well, Angelina. In Ybor City, poor immigrants arrive daily. I see in their eyes why I left my home. Few men of means are Sicilian and unmarried, and fewer walk into my grocery store. It's a blessing Rico's interested in you and can give you a good life with a proper home and not a little *casita,* like a factory worker. And you won't work at all. You should be happy. I've chosen well for you."

"No, Papa. The choice is mine."

"I'm protecting you," Domenico said.

"I don't want protection." Her longing to see Rolando grew unbearable. "I want to fall in love the way you and Mama did, the way Rosa and Luca did."

"And who will you fall in love with? You bring me a dozen cigars from a stranger named Rolando Aguirre. He's 'nice,' you say. If only I could meet him, you say."

It stunned her when her father brought up Rolando and even remembered his full name, as though he could read her mind.

"Next, you go to your friend's wedding, and Salvatore tells me of another 'nice' man you met. These men are not Italian. If they come to me for your hand, I will refuse them. A father protects his daughter all her life and must choose a good man for her."

Angelina fumed at the thought her father had interrogated Salvatore for information or, worse, sent him along to spy on her. "What about *my* feelings?" she asked.

"Why can't you see, Angelina? It's honor and protection I'm offering."

"Protection from what? Finding happiness? Is this why you brought up the Black Hand? You think my getting married and staying home all day will protect me?"

"Paolo Braccio came to me. He said his family noticed what a hard worker you are and how pleasant with the customers. They welcome you into their family."

"I'm a hard worker and pleasant. That's all they want to know? What if I suffer fits, or am a thief, a liar, or have strange, irritating habits?" She trembled now.

"They know you come from a respectable, hardworking family. That's enough."

"That's nothing. Don't they want to know if I even like their son? Doesn't anybody want to know how *I* feel?" Tears burned Angelina's eyes and spilled down her cheeks. "I'm not a slab of meat that you can wrap up and hand over!"

Her father lowered his voice. "You're my daughter, and I'm doing this for you. One day you'll thank me. When you get to know Rico, you'll see I'm right." He spoke calmly but forged his words in iron. "No woman in our family has had this kind of wonderful opportunity."

The lump in Angelina's throat prevented her from talking. Her father got up, poured himself a cup of coffee, and walked out. Angelina continued to shake. She'd spent hours imagining Rolando's return, but she had to face the truth. It had been far too long. Even flowers withered without sunlight and nurturing.

OVER THE NEXT TWO WEEKS, Angelina enraged her father twice. The first time, she overcooked Sunday dinner for the Braccios and served it anyway. The next, she refused Signora Braccio's invitation to learn how to embroider pillowcases. Yet, despite Angelina's attempts at dissolving her nuptials, they remained intact.

Rico knocked on the door. Her father greeted him with an outstretched hand and a pat on the back. Although Rico spoke more often now, he still said nothing of interest. The burden of dissolving this engagement fell on Angelina alone. When Domenico stepped away to meet with a vendor in the grocery store, Angelina seized the moment and got straight to the point.

"Tell me why you want to marry me, Rico."

"It's a suitable match, and my family likes you."

"Why should that matter? Your parents are not the ones getting married here. What do you think of me?" said Angelina with a firm determination to hear his answer.

"Even though your last dinner wasn't as good as your first, I know you can cook. You're good-natured and healthy." Angelina resented the remark. It sounded like things to consider when purchasing a cow.

"That's not a reason to marry anyone," Angelina said with obvious irritation.

"I'm ready for marriage. Arranged marriages have always worked in my family. Our families come from the same region of Italy, we speak the same language, and we have the same customs."

He was more annoying than she thought. Every one of those reasons was foolish, and it annoyed her that he had no objection to marrying her. She eyed him with suspicion. "You don't love me, and I don't love you. That should scare you!"

"My parents and grandparents learned to love each other, and so will we." He looked away. She might have believed him if he'd met her eyes.

"And you're willing to take such a chance? We could also learn to despise—even hate—each other." Like so many others, he accepted the unreasonable as reasonable.

"It's already agreed, Angelina. We'll marry."

Angelina was just as determined no such thing was going to happen, but it would be better if it were his idea.

Her father insisted she be chaperoned around Rico. This might be her only chance alone with him. "There's something I haven't told you, Rico." Angelina fidgeted in her seat, wrinkled her brow, and rubbed her hands together. "I think it's only right you should know."

He raised an eyebrow. "What is it?" This time he met her eyes.

She let the tension linger. "It's hard for me to talk about." She avoided his stare. "I can never have children."

"Wh-what?" His stutter pleased her. "That can't be true. Your mother had so many."

"I was shocked too. I went to the doctor, but the subject is delicate. I'm sorry I can't repeat the details."

At first, Rico's forehead wrinkled and he appeared crest-fallen, then he raised his left eyebrow and looked suspicious. "Why has your father said nothing?"

"He doesn't know." Angelina hugged her stomach protectively. It seemed logical that such a condition should trigger a cramp.

"Why doesn't your father know?"

She had his attention now. "My mother thought it best not to upset him."

"When did Dottore Martino tell you this?" He lowered his voice.

Angelina lowered her voice. "It wasn't him."

"Then who?"

"I don't remember. Before my mother died, she took me to someone in West Tampa." Angelina made sure her facial expression matched the gravity of her alleged affliction.

"You were so young."

"Yes, and it was already too late."

"Why haven't you told your father?"

"And break his heart? I hope I'm not upsetting you. Am I?" Rico had no one to blame but himself for mentioning her good health.

"Are you sure? I mean, absolutely sure?" His look of concern pleased her.

"Yes."

"What if the doctor's wrong?"

Angelina refrained from groaning. Rico asked too many questions instead of making his escape. "Maybe you're right . . . maybe it's all a mistake. Let's wait ten years and see if he's wrong. Would you mind if we don't have children? Ever?" Rico rubbed his hands as if lathering away dirt with a bar of soap while Angelina kept up the momentum. "All alone, every day, we'll have lots of time to learn to love each other—don't you think?"

Rico stared at her as though trying to envision this sculpture of hopelessness she'd carved for him. If she looked away, he might not think her sincere, so she locked her gaze onto his. With rounded shoulders, Rico redirected his gaze to the rendering of the Tower of Pisa on the wall and then stared at the floor. Unwilling to interrupt his visible moment of deflation, Angelina sat in what she considered the personification of splendid silence.

Rico took out his pocket watch, switched it from one hand to the other, and without even glancing at it, said, "I have to go, Angelina. I'm late. I have something to do."

"I understand."

He moved gradually in the direction of the door as if expecting her to retract her words. Angelina harnessed her tongue with her teeth to prevent it from moving. Rico stood at the doorway. Angelina accepted this as the official dissolution of their engagement.

"Please tell your father goodbye for me," said Rico.

Angelina nodded and continued to hold her tongue incarcerated between her teeth. She had no intention of telling her father anything. Rico slipped out, and Angelina hurried and turned the latch on the door. Arranged marriages should have been denounced for what they were—a crime, no different from selling a daughter, like a prized cow.

CHAPTER 26

"Angelina!"

Angelina had grown accustomed to her father's angry roar, but this one soared above the rest. She stepped into the doorway of the parlor.

"Did you want to talk to me, Papa?"

"My God. What on earth have you done?" His furrowed brow, piercing eyes, and flushed face made her certain the name Braccio was about to ignite a fire. "Not one but three women came into the store today to give me their sympathy because my poor Angelina can't have children and telling me I can find comfort in that I still have five more to give me grandchildren."

"Oh, that." She should have asked Signora Bertelli to cast a spell to dilute her father's rage.

Domenico slammed his fists against the kitchen table, glared at her, and shouted something mysterious in Sicilian. "In the middle of our lunch rush, with people standing in line —I received an angry visit from Paolo Braccio. He called off the wedding. He wants grandchildren. And he wanted to know why I tried to hide your condition."

Angelina inhaled. "Papa, I . . ."

"Answer me." His voice quaked with fury. "Do you take me for a fool, Angelina?"

She had prepared excuses, gone over them, and selected the best one, but suddenly the truth floated to the top. "Every time I imagined myself married to Rico, the thought made me sick. You didn't want to hear my opinion. Rico didn't seem to care. So I rescued myself."

Her father grabbed her by the shoulders. "Not only have you shamed the entire family with your nonsense, but this could affect your entire life. The Braccios have told everyone in Ybor City what you said." He pushed her away angrily.

"I can't imagine why Rico repeated it. It was personal."

"It was a lie." Again he banged the table, and the flower vase she'd put there tipped over.

Angelina set it straight, using the moment to avoid her father's eyes. "Any man who passes on rumors about his fiancée doesn't deserve a wife," she said.

"*You* handed Rico the match. He lit it, and his family has used the flame to set the town ablaze with the news. For someone so smart, how is it you don't think ahead? No one wants a young wife who cannot have children, and the warning has spread to every home in the city." He looked into Angelina's eyes with an outrage she'd never seen. "Once you've scrambled an egg, you can't unscramble it. No Italian family will want you to marry their son now, and you've brought this upon yourself."

Angelina did not altogether consider this bad news and offered her opinion. "If I'm not eligible for marriage, then I'd better get educated right away so I can take care of myself." It seemed like an opportune time to ask about her entrance exam. "Has a letter arrived for me?"

Domenico cursed and threw up his hands. "You're strong

because a part of me exists inside you, but you're not my equal."

He walked out, slamming the door, but his words remained. It didn't matter if she was his equal. What mattered was that she could think for herself.

THE NEXT SUNDAY morning marked the third anniversary of her mother's death. Everyone sat around the table, sharing memories and shedding tears. Melancholy salted the air. Though her father rarely attended church, today he accompanied his family to Mass. The moment Angelina entered Sacred Heart, all eyes fell upon her. It was clear the close-knit, Sicilian-Catholic community had heard of her inability to conceive. Showers of sympathetic glances shot in her direction, and Angelina's face grew hot. Her father was right.

She'd have to find a means to reverse her infertility. She avoided the humiliation of compassionate glances by following her family to a pew, kneeling, bowing her head, and closing her eyes. She committed a sincere prayer to the Blessed Mother. Who better to understand a female's plight?

OUR DEAR, sweet Blessed Mother, please don't abandon me.
I need your wisdom and help—very, very quickly.
Amen

SIGNORA BERTELLI SAT RIGHT behind her, nudged her shoulder, and whispered, "Leave everything to me. Once, I helped a young wife with your problem. Now she has nine children. This time I won't use so much garlic. Consider yourself cured, or may a palm tree fall on my head."

Angelina fidgeted in her seat. "Thank you, but I'm cured."

"You see? It's working already."

Strains from the organ began, and Angelina pushed away all thoughts of sterility. If only her mother were alive. She'd know how to handle this.

Father Cavalli entered the pulpit in his usual regalia. Everyone rose. "God be with you," he said.

"And also with you," came the response from the pews.

To Angelina's relief, parishioners stopped glancing at her and turned their focus to the priest behind the podium.

"Please be seated," said Father Cavalli.

He began with church business and then prayers said for the sick and the soul of an old woman who'd died during the week. Father Cavalli called out the names of the altar boys serving at next week's Mass and announced meetings for the Knights of Columbus and the Altar Society—all in his monotone. To Angelina's surprise and those already comfortably seated, the priest's voice gathered an uncommon burst of energy. "It's my pleasure to announce the banns of holy matrimony for Rico Braccio and Magdalena Pizzolato." Father Cavalli looked frustratingly pleased.

A collective gasp escaped the parishioners. Again, all eyes landed on Angelina. She slid down in the wooden pew as if coated in olive oil. Was it necessary for Father Cavalli to say, 'It's my *pleasure* to announce?' When did he acquire such joy, and why announce the banns of marriage between Rico Braccio and Magdalena What's-Her-Name on this day? He knew full well that her father only attended Mass on her mother's death date, Easter, Christmas, and a sporadic holy day. This was no coincidence.

The air hung heavily about her, like meat spoiling in the deli counter. With no other option, she turned her gaze to the ceiling to avoid a second round of compassionate glances. She considered God's omnipotence. Perhaps He'd consider an appearance or a sudden hurricane. Like testing hot soup so as not to get burned, Angelina slowly turned her head in her father's direction. His eyes met hers with his familiar look of anger.

When the service ended, Angelina rushed out and dashed across the street to wait for her father. He didn't come out as quickly as she'd hoped. She moved farther down the block to avoid the parishioners and waited there. Then she moved down a little farther to the next block. In the end, she went home.

The moment her father stepped through the door, she braced herself and spoke before he did. "It looks like Rico Braccio's getting married."

"Rico Braccio was always getting married, but not to Magdalena Pizzolato."

"If he wanted to marry me, it shouldn't have made any difference about my condition."

"You don't have a condition."

"That's not the point." Unsure why, Angelina found it insulting that the Braccios had replaced her so quickly. "It doesn't seem to matter to any of them who he marries. They should be ashamed of themselves for spreading rumors about me. Next time, I'll pick my husband."

"And who'd that be, some lazy fool with no way to put food on the table?"

Lily ran up and slipped her hand into Angelina's. One day it would be Lily standing here.

"There's lots of ways to kill myself, and one is to marry a man I don't like." The pause between them lasted longer than expected, but Angelina held on to her courage and her sister's hand. The weight of her two souls—one Sicilian wrapped in old-world traditions and one American shedding them—lingered inside her.

Her father narrowed his eyes as though he had to strain to see her and waved Lily away. "I approached no one to marry you. Never. The Braccio family came to me, and I saw it as a blessing."

"It wasn't a blessing. Mama would have told you so. Do you remember her telling me about a wolf who refused to enter the lion's den? The wolf saw many footprints leading into the lion's den but only the lion's coming out. Marriage to Rico Braccio is that lion's den, and I refuse to enter."

"I did what was best for you, Angelina."

She glanced at her father's stern expression.

"No, Papa. *I* did what was best for *me.*"

CHAPTER 27

Angelina took a cleansing breath as she checked her reflection. Even her physical appearance had changed. Her cheekbones had become more pronounced, her drive was more focused, and she'd become more protective of her heart. It had been a long time since she'd worn Rolando's gold medal around her neck or carried it in her pocket. Now it resided in her drawer, beneath folded clothes, fading memories, and the residue of a broken heart.

The cigar makers hired Don Carlos Madrid at Cuesta Rey, and seeing him every day inspired Angelina—he with his wisdom and Angelina with her eagerness for knowledge.

"Señor, what made you become a reader?" The question had been on her mind for a long time.

El lector paused a moment, glimpsed at the newspaper on the bench across from them, and picked it up. "All memories have a purpose. They sober us up to the fact we've lived. The hope is that we've learned something and that, through it all, our hearts have remained intact."

He gazed down at the newspaper again. "When I was a young boy, every evening my father came home from work with the newspaper under his arm. Even though I didn't understand a lot of what he read, he made my brother and me listen. 'It's important to keep informed and share your knowledge so people will think of you as someone to respect.' His words meant a lot, but back then, they meant little to me."

"I understand that. My father reads the Italian newspaper every day. He keeps up with the old country and gets upset when the news is not good," said Angelina.

"Then he's a man who knows the importance of staying informed. At our home, we ate dinner, and while we were still sitting at the table, our father opened the paper and read to us." The tone of Don Carlos's voice grew softer. He appeared pensive, as if he'd drifted back to that dinner table. "Every story he ever shared had a lesson, a moment of revelation. It wasn't until much later that I discovered my father could not read."

Angelina widened her eyes. "Why did he do that? I mean, *how* did he do it?"

"He wanted us to know the world was much bigger than our village and that we needed to stretch our imaginations beyond the horizon. Knowledge empowers and liberates."

"But if he couldn't read—"

"Every day, before he went home, he stopped at the newspaper office, bought a paper, and spoke to the employees about what they'd printed. They liked him, discussed the news with him, and shared their opinions." Don Carlos offered a weak smile. "My father died when I was twelve. All the men from the newspaper came to his funeral to offer their condolences. That's when my brother and I learned our father couldn't read. Our mother never revealed his secret."

"He must have loved you both so much to do that every day," said Angelina.

"We learned to read, and he insisted we read books and

report the stories to him every Sunday. Out of respect for our father's memory, we both read countless books, along with the daily news. I can think of no better vocation than to read to those who can't, those who don't have books, or those who have never imagined such an immense world. Throughout all the centuries, nothing has changed. We all experience love, joy, anger, regret, birth, and death."

Angelina already thought highly of Don Carlos Madrid for his skill in captivating the workers as he read, but now she appreciated what had driven him to develop his talent.

El lector cleared his throat. "I have something rather curious in my possession today."

"Something curious?" Angelina wondered what a cultured, well-traveled man considered curious.

"On the day of the fire, a favorite leather book of mine singed, and the water used to put out the flames wrinkled the pages. Like all great literature, it endured. I've replaced the book. Yet, I could never quite bring myself to discard the original. To whom do I give it when so many can't read?"

"Because I know Italian, Spanish wasn't hard to learn. I can read in all three languages—Italian, English, and Spanish," Angelina offered quickly.

"You realize our Southern vernacular is a different suit of clothes from the king's English." Don Carlos reached in his bag and pulled out a large book. "The pages are thin, and the book is heavy, but every page is still intact. It's now yours."

Even with its blackened face, scars, and wrinkled pages, the volume emerged as a treasure.

"Oh, my. Thank you! I'm so thrilled. You're so kind." Angelina couldn't contain her excitement. A real prize lay between its covers. She passed her hand over the title etched in gold letters and read aloud the words on the cover in a tone heard more often in churches. "*The Complete Works of William Shakespeare*. It's a treasure I never expected to own."

"Every time someone opens a book, the writer lives again," said el lector.

"Shakespeare will never die." Angelina held the large book close. "Once, when I was passing your floor, you read Shakespeare's *Twelfth Night*. 'Some men are born great, some men achieve greatness, and others must have greatness thrust upon them.' I memorized it."

"Words thunder and roar or whisper and whimper. Saying them, we can either repel melancholy and joy or instill them. Now, let's turn to *Hamlet*."

Angelina eagerly opened her new book to find the play.

El lector recited Hamlet's words, and Angelina absorbed the ebb and flow of them as if they were lyrics from a song.

"I wonder, señor, if there's an answer in this book for me?"

"That depends on the question." Don Carlos Madrid leaned forward.

"My father doesn't understand how I feel. He suffered such hardship in Europe, and because of that, he wanted me to marry someone who understands our ways—a Sicilian he selected who could offer me security. I don't want his help."

"It's been that way throughout history, from peasants to kings," el lector said to Angelina's great agitation. "It's hard to appreciate what you've never seen. Security is a prize. Your father knows life can become showered in tragedies. It breaks the backs of those trying to make a living from brittle earth, and they enter this country still wrapped in the sounds of their screams. These are hard lessons to forget. Some never release the experience. Arranged marriages are often the answer to protect a daughter."

Angelina had imagined that a man privy to the greatest loves and heartbreaks in literature would applaud her desire to chart her course. "Then you agree with my father?" she asked.

"I didn't say that." Señor Madrid adjusted his collar. "It's only natural for your father to find someone to protect you. He believes it his duty."

"He thinks I can learn to love my husband."

"That's true for many, or you could at least learn to admire and respect him."

"Or I could learn to hate the loss of my freedom and despise him," said Angelina, growing irritated. "Why take such a chance?"

"It would be a great tragedy if such a delightful young woman never knew love."

Angelina considered all the tragedies she'd known. "To have no control over my life, for the rest of my life—that's beyond a tragedy." She'd already had this argument with her father, and she'd grown weary of not winning. "I know our time's up. Thank you again for this wonderful book."

"I hope you're not upset."

"No, not at all." She had no idea men thought alike. Didn't her father use the exact words? Protect her from what? Who'd told men women were helpless? And what kind of man deliberately married a woman he didn't love? Angelina glanced at some children chasing each other at play and then out to the street, where she nearly gasped at the sight of her father driving his horse and cart and looking straight at her.

"Is something wrong?" Don Carlos said.

"No. I mean, I remembered something I must do. May we continue next week?"

"Yes, of course." Don Carlos rose from the bench.

It always surprised Angelina that he wasn't taller. When he read to the cigar makers, he appeared a towering presence.

"We'll meet next week, Angelina."

Perhaps they'd meet and perhaps not. A cataclysmic event could happen in a week. "I look forward to next week," she replied.

The man hesitated a moment. "Do you know the story of Icarus from Greek mythology?"

Angelina shook her head. "I guess not."

"The father loved his son," said Don Carlos. "He made Icarus wax wings but warned him not to fly near the sun. Icarus didn't listen, the wings melted, and Icarus fell into the sea and drowned. Sometimes, fathers are trying to do what they consider their best, and we can't see it."

"Maybe, but I can't live my life strapped to wings of wax." Angelina saw no point in continuing the conversation. "We'll talk again very soon, but I must go now." She shook his hand, stepped out, and headed toward her house.

If I don't sprout my wings, my father is going to strap his onto me. This thought haunted her. Zio Pasquale was the answer. He had been teaching her the art of rolling cigars, and these lessons became a necessity to financing her independence and following her dreams.

~

ANGELINA STOOD in the doorway connecting the house and the store when a vendor placed her father's order on the counter.

"Where's your father, Angelina?"

"He should be back any minute," she said.

The vendor glanced up at the clock. "Well, here's the receipt for his deliveries. Please give it to your father."

"I'll put it inside his desk for safekeeping."

The man left as quickly as he arrived. As Angelina opened the desk drawer, reached in the back, and pulled out the receipts box, an envelope somewhat different from the rest got caught beneath it. She pulled it out and gasped when she saw her name in elaborate script and the return address. The man at the testing site had said she would hear from them only if they accepted her. The seal had been broken, and her hand trembled as she slipped the letter from its envelope.

Dear Miss Angelina Pirrello,

It is with great pleasure that we inform you that you have passed our academic exam. We welcome you to Florida State College for Women. Please respond to us by the first of July as we have limited enrollment and will need your confirmation to secure your spot for our fall program.

Respectfully,

Dean Watson

"No! No! No!" Angelina cried. She gripped the edge of the counter with an almost uncontrollable urge to break something. Again and again, she read the words: "We welcome you." The deadline to respond had long since passed.

Angelina crushed the letter meant to spare her from stripping leaves, household chores, caring for children, and endless loads of laundry. Worst of all, its message served as evidence of her father's intent to misdirect her life and block her potential.

He would never get away with hiding this from her. How could he be so heartless? Once again, he had gone too far. A raging fire burned inside her. Did he think she would not notice, or care, or try again? She vowed to never stop trying to complete her education. If her father thought this was the end, he'd underestimated her.

That night, Angelina kept her eye on her father. She wanted his full attention when she confronted him, with no one around and nothing to distract him. As soon as he locked up the store and flipped the sign to closed, she pressed her crumpled letter against her heart to smooth it out and handed it to him. "How could you do this to me, Papa?"

Domenico raised an eyebrow. The element of surprise was not something he often encountered. "Where did you get that?" he asked.

"Where you left it—hidden under a box at the back of your drawer. Papa, I do everything you want, and you know how much I wanted this. How could you do this? Have you no feelings?" Angelina's voice quivered as she attempted to harness her anger.

"I intended to tell you, but it slipped my mind. You were about to marry. I had already made certain you had an even more secure and stable life."

Angelina didn't want to hear his excuses. "It slipped your mind," she said sarcastically. "You came to America because it gave *you* freedom. I was born here, yet you deny me the same freedom offered to the millions who land here."

"I never threw out the letter. I put it away. I wanted to discuss it with you."

Angelina squeezed her hands into fists until she could feel the prick of her nails. "Then why didn't you?"

"I run a store, I make orders, I take orders, I cook for customers, and I care for my house and my children. I work no less than fourteen hours a day. I put away the letter, and I forgot it."

This was something so vital to her life. She could hardly endure her anger or believe this was a simple oversight.

"You forgot it?" Heat flushed through Angelina's body, its flame growing harder to control. "What you did was cruel."

Domenico's stiff posture did not change; his expression remained the same. He didn't look uncomfortable or contrite. "I do the best I can. I am sorry I forgot the letter, but I didn't think it was that important. Women don't need an education."

A tempest of exasperating thoughts filled her mind. She wanted to scream, denounce her father, run away, and vanish for good. How could she believe him? Still, if he didn't want her to see it, why not throw it away? It was also possible he meant to conceal it from her and forgot to throw it away. Distrust had a vulgar taste.

"Only you know what you really did and why, Papa, but this meant so much to me, and it will never happen again. I will make sure of it." She would take the test again, and this time have the results sent to Carmen's house.

ANGELINA'S NEED TO become self-reliant grew stronger. She walked straighter now and scrutinized every word her father said to her. If she didn't like the comment, she said so. Not like before, not like she had no direction in mind, or purpose, or backbone. Belarmino had taught her uncle, and now they could both teach her how to roll cigars. Her hands were nimble. She studied and learned quickly. Something vital had changed inside her with the loss of Rolando and her dream sabotaged.

As she and Carmen returned from their break, they climbed the stairs and paused at the doorway of the second floor to listen to Don Carlos. He always read accounts of the same events from four newspapers, like the four accounts of the gospel in the New Testament. Of late, world news told of a bubbling, hot cauldron across the sea. There were unrestrained reactions from the workers.

"England and Germany are in constant disagreement," someone said.

"Damn the English!" yelled the German workers.

"Italy has taken over Turkish ports," bellowed el lector, and the Italians cheered, "*Evviva l'Italia*!"

The paper also reported local grievances and strikes among factory workers all over the country. Angelina walked with Carmen back up the stairs to their workstation. "Have you noticed, Carmen, how cigar makers pay the lectors to deliver news that ultimately incites anarchy against their employers?"

Carmen whispered as they continued their climb. "Yes, and I think there'll soon be a strike. Remember Montoya's murder? There's something brewing. I think they know which cigar company paid to have the job done, but proving it is another thing. Look around you, chica. The mojadores stand in two to three inches of water all day, bending over, humidifying tobacco leaves. We should force factory owners to put a member of their own family on that job. Do they ever think of us as they get fat with profits? Those no-good *desgraciados.* When we strike, we'll give them cigar smoke, not cigars."

Angelina hated to admit it, but her father had long ago warned her of strikes devastating households. "My uncle was a mojador. Now he rolls cigars."

"You can't believe the ruthless things coming down the rumor mill—even kidnappings. Keep paying your union dues."

"I always do."

"Too bad Rolando isn't here. He refused to stop until he found out what was going on. The union hated him, and there's no one like him. My cousin says he's our most valuable troublemaker." Carmen's expression grew somber. "But he's in Spain."

"What?" Angelina's legs weakened at the revelation, and she tightened her hold on the railing, but she couldn't control the astonishment in her voice. "How do you know this?"

Carmen glanced at her with a knowing look. "You miss him, don't you?"

Unsure she'd convince anyone if she denied it, Angelina avoided answering. "Well, he kept us informed about the union negotiations."

"Is that all you miss about him?" Carmen spoke in a low tone.

Angelina grew impatient and didn't want to delay what she needed Carmen to tell her. "How do you know he's in Spain? Why would he be there? And how long have you known this?"

Carmen raised her eyebrows. "If I know, then you know, and I found out last night. There's been a kidnapping of one of the big union officials. It happened some time ago. Shall we say they *escorted* this man to Spain?"

"Who are *they*?"

"*They* are the gunmen the big cigar barons hire and pay well to clean things up. They're probably the same ones who killed Montoya. It's the way the rich keep control and eliminate the not-so-rich and the never-gonna-get-rich. They have tricks. I've heard they kidnap families and drop them in another state, where our union leaders have no idea how to find them."

"Seasons have come and gone, Carmen. Rolando told me he was going to Key West. Why hasn't he returned?"

"That's where the story gets lost in the Everglades. The union has a few tricks of their own. They tell you to pack your bags and turn right in case someone overhears, and then they whisper to go left. There's a rumor they sent Rolando to Spain. With so much secrecy, I'm sure he didn't know where he was going. Anyway, that's where they traced the kidnapped union leader's whereabouts, but something else must have happened or Rolando would have returned by now."

Angelina was suddenly frightened. "There's a rebellion in Spain. It's so dangerous there."

"Since he's from Spain, perhaps he stayed with his family to fight in the revolution." Carmen theorized.

"Why hasn't he sent a letter or told Belarmino or anyone? If he were coming back, why hasn't he said so by now?"

"I hate to say anything upsetting, but with all the violence . . ." Carmen trailed off.

Unwilling to reveal the moisture clouding her eyes, Angelina looked down as she worked.

CHAPTER 28

On her way home from work, Angelina hurried past the rows of identical casitas built initially by the factory owners for their workers. As it said in the Bible, "Ye shall know them by their fruits." Cubans planted mangoes and guavas. Italians planted figs and prickly pears. At every home sat porch dwellers, fanning themselves and waiting for the early-evening parade of weary cigar workers.

Angelina heard someone behind her singing a Cuban song she'd heard before and turned to see who it was.

"Fabian Dominguez." Without thinking, she'd blurted out his name.

"Then you haven't forgotten me," he said.

"It's nice to see you, Señor Dominguez, but I have no time to talk right now. Say hello to Bertha for me. Goodbye." Angelina turned away.

Fabian stepped in front of her. "Don't call me señor. Call me Fabian."

Amid the rows of casitas and passing trolleys, the risk of being seen with Fabian conjured up a vision of the pulsating vein in her father's neck.

"I enjoy walking alone, Fabian." Each time he appeared, she had trouble ignoring his good looks. Still, she had better sense than to allow anything so superficial to sway her.

"It's only polite I walk with you on the side closest to the curb."

"And why is that?"

"People might throw garbage from their two- and three-story windows, and that way it has a better chance of landing on my head instead of yours. Not only that—"

"There's more?"

"Also, by walking on the outside, I can shield you from carriages and wagons splashing mud on your clothes."

"Well, since casitas are only one story and the streets are paved with bricks, not dirt, I feel safe to walk alone."

"I'd better accompany you just in case."

Angelina stopped. "Fabian, you're confusing. Why are you walking with me?"

"I'd like to take you to the dance next week at El Círculo Cubano, our Cuban social club. Your brother can chaperone."

Angelina suppressed a smile. "I doubt either of us would survive meeting my father."

Fabian pulled a coin from his pocket. He tossed it in the air, caught it, and began weaving it over his knuckles, each finger moving in sequence, like a piano student practicing scales. "Let's take a chance."

"Why battle a hopeless situation? My father is a definite no."

"Then we'll meet at El Círculo Cubano, and we'll go into the dance together. Afterward, I'll walk you home." Fabian seemed to enjoy the conflict of wills.

"I'll be too busy at my father's store."

"I'll stop by the store and help you finish sooner. And

when your father sees how helpful I am, he'll give his permission."

Angelina stopped walking. "Maybe I'm not making myself clear. My father is strong-willed, traditional, set in his ways, and usually angry. Only the Divine hand of the Almighty can change his mind."

Fabian looked unconcerned, and she had no desire to make her life more complicated.

"It was nice seeing you. Good night, Señor Dominguez. A thousand times good night." Angelina stiffened. Embarrassed by her reference to Shakespeare, she waited for Fabian's laughter, but he didn't appear to have noticed. Perhaps he wasn't familiar with the classics.

"I'd like to tell you about something that happened to me. One day, on my way to work, I spotted a beautiful girl walking with an older man, and she passed by at the same time every morning. She never glanced in my direction, but for months I looked forward to seeing her. She had dark, flowing hair and was always distracted by her conversation with the older man. If only I would get the chance to meet her."

The revelation that he'd noticed her months ago amazed her.

"Then, on a day I thought I'd missed her, she rushed around the corner and bumped right into me. It stunned me. It couldn't be just chance. Three weeks later, I arrived at my friend Lucas's wedding reception. Now, who do you suppose was there? That same girl, and her name is Angelina Pirrello. This can't be a coincidence. It's fate."

A warm feeling sprung up inside Angelina.

He reached for her hand. "I want to see you again."

Angelina gently pulled her hand from his. "I'm flattered, but why me, Fabian? You walk into a room and all the women turn their heads. You should seek out one of them."

"And tempt fate? This powerful feeling between us has been going on for months without your awareness. However, after today, you can't pretend you didn't know about us and your deep affection for me."

Angelina burst into laughter. Fabian's resistance to smiling made him even more amusing.

"I can't be responsible for the other ladies you mentioned. However, it's interesting that whatever power or spell I have over them has skipped right over you."

"Imagine that. This must be a shock for you."

"Yes, but I know how to correct the blunder. We'll start out as casual friends. Then, after a time, we'll become the closest of friends. After that, you'll think of me often, preferably several times a day. And then . . ." He reached for Angelina's hand once again. "Think of it as holding hands and never letting go."

Angelina's thoughts of Rolando had now become conflicted. Although desperate for his return, how much time was too much time to wait without word? He'd told her not to fall in love with anyone else. Was it a premonition? "I must go, Fabian." She started for home.

"Again, Fabian stepped in front of her and walked backward when she didn't stop. Then go to the dance without me, Angelina. I'll see you there, and we'll dance all evening."

She met his gaze for a moment. "Goodbye, Fabian."

When she walked away, he called out to her. "Parting is such sweet sorrow."

Angelina laughed at herself. How foolish. Fabian knew Shakespeare. Every lector read it. Every cigar maker heard it more than once. For someone who had forgotten how to smile, he had quite a sense of humor.

As soon as she arrived home, Angelina slipped on her apron and started dinner. She envisioned herself arriving on Saturday night. She'd appear at the dance in a beautiful dress she didn't own, escorted by Fabian Dominguez, whom she'd be forbidden to see, and dance all evening at El Círculo Cubano, a place she'd been warned never to enter. How ridiculous that her father thought her mature enough to marry but not responsible enough to attend a dance.

She liked Fabian and began dancing around the kitchen, thinking of what she'd miss. Would she still feel the same about Rolando after so many prayers for his return and still not a word?

Pasquale popped into the room with his usual enthusiasm. "Angelina, you never gonna believe," he exclaimed.

"What?"

He took a seat, and so did she.

"Luigi's cow get lost today, and he want Belarmino and me to help him find it."

"You were out looking for a cow?" Angelina giggled.

"Luigi say somebody open the fence, and when the people see a cow walking down the street, they get mad and call the police. The police get mad, too, and call Gustav, but Gustav get more mad. He say he no gonna catch no cow."

"Who's Gustav?"

"You remember, Gustav is the dog catcher who have the wooden leg. The police say he have to catch the cow because Ybor City no have no cow catcher."

Angelina could almost visualize the scene. "Strange. I wonder how the town overlooked such a need."

"Poor Luigi, he so worried Gustav gonna find his cow first. So Belarmino and me, we help him. Then you no believe what happen."

"I can't wait to hear."

"Gustav find the cow first, and he say the cow, she's too big for the dog cage, so he gonna take her to jail.

Luigi face get so red, and he say, 'If you put my cow in the jail, I gonna come back with a big saw, and I gonna cut off your wooden leg.'"

It wasn't easy for Angelina to stifle her laughter. "That's terrible."

"Gustav, he say to Luigi, 'If you cut off my leg, how I gonna catch the dogs?' Then Luigi, he say to Gustav, 'If you put my cow in the jail, how I gonna get the milk?'"

Angelina burst into laughter. "What happened then?"

Pasquale blotted his forehead with his handkerchief. "They make the deal. Gustav, he no put Luigi's cow in the jail, and Luigi, he no cut off Gustav's leg. Everybody happy. And Luigi, he so happy he give to me and to Belarmino—and even Gustav—the milk and the butter." Pasquale held up his gifts and then hand them to Angelina. "That's a nice, no?"

"Yes, that's really nice." Angelina smiled as she accepted the milk and butter. She would never forget this story. Pasquale reached for a loaf of bread, sliced and buttered it. He handed a slice to his niece and held his up as if making a toast.

"Only in l'America, Angelina, you always get the bread *with* the butter."

CHAPTER 29

"Angelina!" The foreman's gruff voice shot across the large room. "Señor Cuesta wants to see you in his office."

Carmen narrowed her eyes. "Uh-oh. Be careful what you say. Remember—to a quick question, give a slow answer."

Angelina's body tensed. A sudden flashback of her uncomfortable visits with Claudio Garcia returned. What could Cuesta want? He couldn't have fallen in love with her mother too.

Rosa leaned in closer. "He's probably mad about something. The rich are always mad."

Carmen picked up a tobacco leaf and fanned herself. "That's because rich people haven't found a way to get poor people to die for them."

Armed with her friends' advice, Angelina hurried out, down the stairs, and to the front desk, where a man with more hair on his face than on his head sat. She cleared her voice to summon a bit of attention. "Señor Cuesta has sent for me."

Several winged insects flew in through an open window,

buzzed around, and clung to the walls and ceiling. Undisturbed and hardly looking up, the man pointed to the owner's office. "Well then, go see him."

Angelina walked into the paneled office and faced the owner of the factory.

"Angelina Pirrello?"

"Yes, Señor Cuesta."

He put down his cigar and shuffled through several papers on his oversized mahogany desk. Angelina stepped forward onto a luxurious rug. Business must be good because the office didn't have a rug when she'd started six months ago. In her entire life, she'd never stood on anything so opulently cloudlike, and she surreptitiously rocked a bit to feel its softness beneath her feet.

"Sit down, Angelina."

Angelina hadn't planned on moving to the chair so quickly as she was still enjoying the softness of the rug.

He looked up. "I said, sit down, Angelina. Please."

"Thank you." She quickly took a seat.

Angelina knew very little about this man, except he was wealthy and owned several cigar factories. Unsure if it was rude to look the rich in the eye, she focused on his large mustache and wondered if it itched in such heat.

"We have a few openings for cigar makers. Your uncle has assured me you can roll cigars as well as anyone under this roof. Is that right?"

In her mind, Angelina jumped from her seat, screamed with joy, and danced about the room, but on the outside, she sat composed, except for one foot that tapped furiously over the thick carpet. She wanted to say the right thing, not seeming boastful yet not downplaying her ability.

"I can roll cigars according to Cuesta Rey's high standards," she said.

The older man grinned. "You'll start tomorrow making

the *cheruto* cigar, and your wages will depend on you. But if you can't keep up, you'll go back to where you are now."

She'd waited a long time for this moment. "I won't disappoint you, Señor Cuesta."

"We expect our cigar makers to produce between 1,100 and 1,300 cigars a week. You'll earn eight dollars per thousand. If your skill develops and we have an opening, you'll roll our finest, the Perfectos. Then you'll earn twenty-eight dollars per thousand. So far, no woman has rolled them at my factory, so your skill had better be exceptional."

With this raise in pay and the possibility of raising her production to an even higher level, Angelina imagined paying her way to university and receiving a diploma. She reached out a hand. "Then I'll be the first."

Señor Cuesta gave a hearty laugh. "Well then, welcome, Angelina Pirrello. You start tomorrow."

Delighted, Angelina shook the man's hand with both of hers and ventured one last comment. "Carmen Velasquez is a wonderful cigar maker too. She's been practicing for years."

"Send her up next," he said. "And I'm also ready to hire Rosa Capric—I mean Cabuto. She married recently. Her husband has been teaching her how to roll cigars. Do you know her?"

"Oh yes. I'm sure she's talented." Angelina stood one last time and felt the opulence of the rug beneath her feet. "Thank you again, señor." She left the office elated. Her future looked glorious with a new job, more money, and soon—an education.

HUMMING ALL THE WAY HOME, Angelina had within her grasp the means to establish an independent life. The thought flowed through her like warm liquid and soothed her soul. It filled her imagination with an enormity of possibilities.

She burst into her house with great excitement. "Papa, I have wonderful news. I'm going to roll cigars at Cuesta Rey. It's a big raise in wages, and I'll make more when I learn to go faster."

"That won't be necessary, Angelina. I also have good news. I had a visit from Umberto Rizzo. He's asked my permission for your hand in marriage, and I've agreed."

Instantly, the air in her lungs vanished. "The baker? He's at least twenty years older than I am and puts shoe polish in his hair to look younger."

"Yes, and because he's a widower with four children, he's willing to accept your 'unfortunate condition.' He's a decent man, prosperous, and he'll treat you well. You'll have everything you need for the rest of your life."

A scream erupted inside Angelina. She clenched her teeth to keep it from escaping. After one long revolting moment, she found her voice. "Except for the most important thing in my life—happiness." Incensed, she took in a deep breath. "It's cruel and unreasonable to expect me to become the mother of four children not that much younger than I am. It's—it's ridiculous!"

"He already pays someone to help with the children. He wants to build you a home. He said he's willing to do anything to make you happy."

"Then tell him to marry someone else. That would make me happy." Angelina looked around in desperation. She needed to hold on to something to ground herself—the furniture, the pictures on the wall, anything familiar. She refused to release control and let it all slip away.

"Is he not a kind man? A generous man? Is he not a man well established with a successful business? I want the best for you."

Angelina considered her friend Sophia and even Signor Braccio's daughter Cristina. As far as she could tell, no one was making plans for their arranged marriages. Angelina grabbed the chair with both hands. "Yes, but that doesn't matter to me. It only matters to you. No sensible person gets on a horse and starts galloping without reins to control where they're going."

"Of course not, but I'm your father."

"And I'm your daughter. I won't go through life without tightly holding the reins that control my direction." Angelina turned and stormed out.

CHAPTER 30

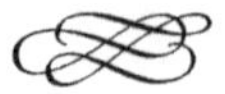

It had been three days since their quarrel, and although Angelina had made her refusal clear, her father remained entombed in a fortress of the past. She suspected he believed his daughter would obey him and marry the baker regardless of her protests. If taking control of her life meant a continuous battle, she'd gird up her loins, as the Bible put it. Perhaps she should seek advice from someone with a spell for everything.

She knocked on Signora Bertelli's door. While she waited for her neighbor to answer, she admired the woman's flowerbed—something her father considered frivolous.

The front door flew open.

"Your flowers look lovely, signora."

"Ah yes. April does the work, and May takes all the credit." Signora Bertelli raised her eyebrows. "I thought your father had planted flowers with that wispy greenery in his yard until he pulled one up and handed me a carrot. 'We plant food, not flowers,' he said."

One thing above all—no one could accuse her father of being impractical. "Yes, I know. He's down-to-earth."

"Come in, come in, Angelina, and tell Signora Bertelli all that's happened."

It amused Angelina that the woman referred to herself in the third person. Perhaps it gave her the illusion that she didn't live alone? "Do you ever get lonely, signora?" Angelina asked.

"Ha! Loneliness is exhausting. You must feel sorry for yourself day and night. It's too much work. I want no part of it." She pulled out a chair. "Sit down. You're in time to have some fresh espresso, and I've been making pastries all morning."

"The pastries smell wonderful, but the espresso is too strong for me. I take mine with milk."

"Aha, like the Cubans. *Café con leche*."

Signora Bertelli set down a cup of her strong coffee for Angelina. "Fill it to the top with milk if you like." She sighed. "My Frank used to love it." She patted the ornate bronze centerpiece. "Didn't you, Frank?"

"Are you speaking to the vase?" Angelina poured milk into her cup, took a sip, and waited for Signora Bertelli to laugh.

"It's not a vase. It's an urn."

Angelina choked on her coffee, and Signora Bertelli patted her on the back. "You look rather pale, *bella*. I think you work too hard." She offered a sympathetic look and then continued. "When my Frank died . . . well, I couldn't bear to come home without him after the funeral. So I brought him back and set him right here on the kitchen table, where he always enjoyed a good meal."

Angelina wasted no time reviewing the funeral in her mind. She distinctly remembered the coffin lowered into the grave. "But, you buried your husband."

Signora Bertelli winked with noticeable satisfaction. "That's what everyone thinks, but I couldn't endure it. So I paid the Graziano Brothers Mortuary a pretty penny to close the empty casket and close their mouths." Her neighbor leaned back in her chair, appearing pleased with herself. "I took my Frank back home with me. Now, I ask you, how can that be bad?"

Angelina pushed aside her shock. "Does your husband's family know about this?"

"Ave Maria. No!" Signora Bertelli quickly made the sign of the cross. "And neither does Father Cavalli. You know what the Church thinks about cremation. I say what's the difference if he's in the ground or on the kitchen table?"

Angelina took a sip of coffee and avoided giving an answer.

"Every April fourth, our anniversary, I go with Frank's sisters to the cemetery, and I put flowers on his grave so they don't get suspicious. When I arrive home, I set a plate of rigatoni in front of him. I ask you, what's better, lilies or pasta sauce with garlic?"

Another unanswerable question, another sip of coffee. "Signora, your husband died when I was ten or eleven. Are you saying that all this time, he's been on the kitchen table?"

"Right here in plain sight. No one cremates, so everyone thinks it's a decoration."

"Who else knows about this?"

"Only you and me and the Graziano brothers." With a sudden rush of vitality, Signora Bertelli threw up her arms. "And may I fall and break both legs if I ever tell anyone else."

"Why tell me at all?" Angelina pictured the look of wrath on Father Cavalli's face—the one she knew so well.

"Frank adored you. You always came to visit, always helping your mother—such a wonderful girl. If something should happen to me, I know Frank would want you to care for him."

"Care for him?" She drew a blank stare.

"Keep him safe."

"Keep him safe?" Angelina envisioned shoving Frank Bertelli's remains under her bed to keep him away from her brothers. If she set him outside, the DiLeto's dog might find him. "It's an enormous honor, Signora Bertelli, but I'm not worthy. You should pick someone in your family."

"Nonsense. How can I ask my family to take care of Frank's ashes if they think he's under six feet of dirt? I will hear no more of it." She patted the urn with one hand and Angelina's hand with the other. "One day you'll understand because you'll have the love of a good man, like my Frank. I miss him so much. Sometimes I want to die to be with him, but like life, death has its limitations." Signora Bertelli sighed.

Angelina narrowed her eyes and looked more closely at the urn's etching of paradise—the lion and the lamb.

Her neighbor watched her. "It's nice, isn't it? The Bible says the lion and the lamb will lie down together, but a smart lamb sleeps with an eye open." She gave a knowing wink.

Frank Bertelli had been a rather sizable man, and Angelina stared in amazement at the little urn. The Graziano brothers must have an exceptional talent to have reduced their customer to his present powdery size.

Her neighbor set down a plate of delicacies. "I have *cannolis, napoleons,* and some *boconnottos*—I can't imagine why they call them cream puffs in America."

It seemed inconvenient that Frank Bertelli's final resting place lay right next to a tasty cannoli.

"Don't be shy. Have one and, after that, have another one, or you'll insult me." Her neighbor pointed to the tray.

Angelina pushed Frank Bertelli's conspicuous presence from her mind and grabbed the pastry closest to the edge. "I'd almost forgotten why I came over. I want your advice."

"I should find myself without a roof over my head in the

middle of a hurricane if you can't count on me. How can I help?"

"You know my father's a practical man. He thinks I should marry the baker because he's Sicilian and a generous man who offers security. I've refused, but it's the second time he's tried to marry me to someone."

"Italian fathers rule the family. My own arranged my marriage. He never knew Frank, and I had already agreed to it. Ha." Signora Bertelli looked pleased and winked at the urn. "Remember, Frank?"

Angelina didn't want to ask opinions from those in the hereafter and risk receiving an answer. "Maybe we shouldn't bother him."

"You're right. What do men know about women, anyway?"

"I told him I won't marry a man I don't love, but he keeps insisting I should be grateful to him."

"Your father thinks he's made a good bargain for you. You insult and embarrass him by not accepting it. Everywhere you go, Angelina, you'll find arranged marriages that work, but sometimes, one tries to kill the other." Signora Bertelli closed her eyes as though she needed a moment to extract an incident from her memory. "Do you remember Isabella? Perhaps you were too young when her father arranged her marriage to a man she disliked. Isabella put rat poison in her new husband's pasta. After that, she went straight to Sunday Mass to receive communion without first confessing or offering penance. I never could decide which was the greater sin. What do you think?"

Angelina poured another cup of espresso. This time, she didn't dilute it.

CHAPTER 31

As Señor Cuesta walked into la galería, a hush of silence blanketed the room. The only sound was the groan of the wooden-planked floor as he moved toward the podium. He usually kept himself cloistered in his office, and only on rare occasions did he step onto the second floor's grand room to address the cigar makers.

Angelina wanted to impress Cuesta with her production. She was eager to gain speed but also eager to hear what he had to say. She glanced back at Pasquale across the room. He raised his eyebrows as if to say a visit from the boss was something worth paying attention to.

Señor Cuesta cleared his throat. "El lector has taken ill and cannot join you for his usual afternoon's session. So there will be no reader today." An audible groan washed over the room, and Carmen threw down her *chaveta* knife.

"I can't believe it. I was so eager to hear what happened next in the story."

Rosa fanned herself with a tobacco leaf. "Such a sad life for Anna Karenina, married to that cold, miserable count."

Carmen spoke up. "Señor Cuesta, do you know if Don Carlos Madrid will return tomorrow?"

"If he shows up, then he's here."

Another wave of disappointment washed over the room.

Cuesta picked up a book and held it high. "If anyone here feels they can fill Madrid's shoes, the book's in my hand."

The room reverted to whispering, but no one spoke up.

Angelina slowly got to her feet, and all eyes turned in her direction.

"Señor Cuesta, if you like, I've read Anna Karenina several times and discussed the story with el lector, Don Carlos Madrid. I know the book well and can translate it into Spanish as I read."

Señor Cuesta's look of surprise did not escape Angelina, nor did his hesitation in answering her. "You're young, Angelina Pirrello, and have no experience. I can tell you that reading to cigar workers is difficult and translating as you read is nearly impossible. Few readers can do it. I can't do it." He turned away from Angelina and once again looked over the workers. "Is there anyone else willing to read?" He paused. "Anyone?" No one responded.

Angelina read literature nearly every day. She spoke up again. "I can do it. If I read, everyone will enjoy the story. If I don't read, it will be a long, sultry afternoon."

Cuesta regarded Angelina with a raised eyebrow. Angelina regarded this as an opportunity to satisfy her curiosity. No one hired women lectors, but the world was changing. She wanted to be ready. Lectors earned far more than cigar makers.

"Why don't you stay and listen? If you don't like how I read and want me to stop, I will. You have nothing to lose."

Once again, Señor Cuesta addressed the room. "You cigar makers pay the readers, not me. The book is here. Do you want me to give it to Angelina to read?"

Angelina looked around the quiet room. "I respect everyone here. If you don't want me to read, say no. The word *no* is the same in English, Spanish, and Italian. There's no way to confuse it with any other word."

The cigar makers looked at each other and then slowly replicated applause by tapping their *chaveta* knives against their worktables until the entire room resounded with approval. Angelina beamed, made her way to the podium, and with a wide grin, picked up the book and opened it to the page with the bookmark.

In her strongest voice, she read a paragraph in English, then translated that paragraph into Spanish. She used all the mannerisms she'd seen el lector use and changed the pitch of her voice to differentiate between characters.

"'I think . . . if it is true there are as many minds as there are heads, then there are as many kinds of love as there are hearts.'" Angelina read for two hours without fumbling and without a break or a lengthy pause, but when her time had ended, her voice had a hoarseness she'd never experienced. Instead of the usual applause of the *chaveta* knives, the cigar makers rose to their feet and applauded. Thrilled by their acceptance, Pasquale stood up, shouting, "You the very best, Angelina!" He waved his approval and threw her a kiss. Angelina beamed, offered a quick bow, and took her seat between her friends.

"Oh, Angelina, that was magnificent," Rosa said. "Just magnificent."

"Thank you. I enjoyed it, but now I have a much greater appreciation for los lectores. It takes a man's powerful voice to do that every day."

Carmen nodded. "What a performance. Everyone's impressed with our little señorita."

"You read perfectly, and you kept the suspense going," said Rosa.

Carmen set aside a cigar she'd just rolled. "So, here's the big thing. How do you translate as you read? I mean, you must read fast to stay a few steps ahead of the story you're translating. I always thought you were smart, but as you read, it seemed like a magic trick."

"Next time, I'll show you how I pull a rabbit out of a hat," Angelina said.

Carmen smiled. "Ahh, if only you had a hat."

"If only she had a rabbit," said Rosa.

They laughed, and Angelina kept a sobering thought to herself. The Suffragettes had taught her not to accept the present limitations of women. Female readers were not hired as lectors, not so far, and not for a lengthy list of other jobs men thought they were fit to do. They'd arrived at the 20th century, and she was certain nothing would remain the same.

CHAPTER 32

The factory whistle blew. The workday ended, and those around Angelina went home. Still, today she had permission to stay a little longer and practice new techniques to pick up her speed rolling cigars.

Alone in the grand galería, with its high ceiling and rows of large windows, Angelina imagined she was in the majestic hall of a European castle.

Life is real, life is earnest, and the grave is not its goal.

Dust thou art and to dust returneth was not spoken of the soul.

Amid so much poetry read within these walls, Angelina recited Longfellow. There was something soothing in poetry. It evened out the rough edges of life.

At the sound of footsteps, Angelina dropped her half-rolled tobacco leaf and looked behind her.

"Fabian! You startled me. What are you doing here?"

"I came to see you."

"But how did you know I was here?"

"I have a long train of spies who said you were staying late."

Angelina glanced at the entrance door. "How did you get inside the building? The doors are locked, and there's a guard."

"As fate would have it, Pedro's the guard and an old friend." Fabian reached for the tobacco leaf on Angelina's worktable, held it up, and examined both sides. "You see this? It's nothing but an ordinary leaf. As cigar makers, it's our job to find the perfect match for it.

Angelina's memory of Rolando weighed on her. She didn't know how to handle the emotional anxiety of his total absence, and each encounter with Fabian had left her less certain and more bewildered.

"I've been wanting to tell you, Angelina, that I like you. I like your face, your smile, the sound of your voice, and the way that lock of hair keeps falling across your face. I even like how I can still see you when I close my eyes."

Angelina ran her hands through her hair to try and secure it. She turned away, leaving him staring at the back of her head. Fabian walked around, stepped in front of her, and grabbed her hand.

"What are you doing?"

"You're making this very difficult," he said.

"I don't think so. I'm not the one rushing around me. Fabian, it's not that I don't like you because I do. It's not that I don't appreciate and enjoy your company and conversations because I do, and like every girl in Ybor City, I find you very attractive, although I don't know why you're following me when I've done nothing to encourage it."

"Then what is it?"

Angelina lowered her head. Without looking up, she said, "There's something you should know about me."

"You rob banks, have twelve toes, you practice Voodoo? I accept this."

"If only that were the case." She gazed up at Fabian and

swallowed hard. "Fabian, you should look for another girl. I think it's only fair you forget me." Although they were alone, she lowered her voice. "I gave my heart away already, and I don't know how to get it back."

Fabian said nothing, and the moment lingered far too long, as if time had to sail across the sea and they had to wait for its return. All the while, Fabian kept his gaze on her. The stillness in the room grew intense and for the longest time, he said nothing and gave no indication of his thoughts. Finally, he tore through the haze of silence, "Why isn't he with you?" He spoke without urgency, as if the answer had little consequence, as if blowing on a spoon of hot soup and cautious not to get burned.

Worse, Angelina had no answer. "I don't know why. He went away for two weeks but hasn't returned." The truth was hard to admit.

"And how long has he been gone?"

The question hurt. She didn't answer.

"How long, Angelina?" His voice was even and soft but insistent.

She inhaled deeply and squeezed her eyes shut to prevent unwanted tears. "Months. Maybe a year . . . probably longer."

"And what does he say is his reason for staying away so long?"

Angelina stumbled on her answer once more. "I don't know. He's never sent a letter or a message. He just vanished."

"Is this true?"

Angelina had kept this to herself for so long, and now that she'd released it from its place bottled up inside her, it sounded ridiculous. Rolando was probably never returning. It hurt more than she realized. She'd been distracting herself by studying and reading to avoid the obvious. Love was strange. Though no one could see or touch it, it was real and powerful. Did Rolando feel it as strongly as she did? "I shouldn't be here."

"You are exactly where you're supposed to be, and I'm here because wherever you are, that's where I'm supposed to be." He moved closer. "You can't scare me off that easily, Angelina Pirrello. If he hasn't come back and never sent word, then what is he saying? Finding love is one thing; keeping love is the challenge.

Angelina blinked away her tears. "I'm not sure I believe in love anymore, and I don't want to be hurt like this again. You have so many girls to choose from. It's better you forget me.

Fabian once again reached down for Angelina's half-rolled cigar. "When we find that matching leaf, we wrap them tightly around one another. We take another leaf to seal them together, then another, and another to bind them into a smooth, perfect union. This is how what was once ordinary becomes extraordinary. Angelina Pirrello, I am certain you and I can become something extraordinary."

Fabian eased Angelina off her chair and into his arms. "We have something in common. I also have suffered a great loss of love and couldn't handle the pain. I began to drink to forget. My drinking became a habit until it was ruining my life. I forced myself to quit and went back."

His embrace comforted and reassured her.

"It's a strange thing about the heart, Angelina. It can break, and yet it still keeps beating—until one day it discovers what it never knew."

"What do you mean?"

"That the heart can love again." It was gradual, subtle, and unexpected, but for the first time since Angelina had known Fabian, he offered his warmth in a smile. "Sometimes it takes a moment for the mind to tell the heart what it already knows."

For a time, they stood in silence, as if their thoughts had entwined and there was no need to speak.

Still holding her, Fabian pressed his lips to hers. The pleasure of his kiss surprised her. It was warm and gentle and showered her with a menagerie of feelings, lifting her spirit. For the second time in her life, her heart opened, but Angelina fought the feeling. In this moment of newly found happiness, traces of fear remained, and she braced herself for the impending assault on her heart that would surely follow.

Fabian did not release her. Instead, he pulled her closer, until the heat of his breath caressed her cheek. She knew then that her feelings for him were far stronger than she wanted to let herself believe. The moment seemed both fleeting and prolonged. Neither said anything, and she sensed they had drifted into a wondrous place where words didn't exist.

"The best cure for heartbreak is to take a chance and love again," said Fabian. "When I first saw you walking down the street, I was drawn to you. Every day, I looked for you. If I can't get you off my mind, it means you belong there."

Angelina willed this special moment with Fabian to drown the memories of the past, but she couldn't fully rid herself of them. "I'm not so sure love is worth the hurt," she said.

"Hearts aren't practical. They wander off where they don't belong. Still, everyone searches for love wherever they can." He cupped her face, then kissed her again. His touch filled her with a sense of sweetness and the promise of something wonderful, and his words were like balm on her wound. "I think you have a great capacity to love, and when you're ready, I believe you'll love like you've never been hurt," he said.

Angelina did not consider herself a frivolous person, then why did these emotions feel so real? How was it was possible to be in love twice and so close together in one lifetime? "I should leave."

Fabian passed his hand over the softness of her cheek. "You have strength in so many things, but not the strength to face the obvious." He stroked her cheek. "I dream about you every night," he said with a gleam in his eye.

She smiled. "Do you expect me to believe that?"

"Well, sometimes you come into my dreams disguised as other people, but I always recognize you."

Angelina laughed.

"I have something else to tell you, and it's important."

"What's that?"

"You owe me a dance. You didn't show up at El Circulo Cubano. I waited for you."

"Well, I'm not sure why. My father might have shot me if I left. If only I'd remembered he didn't own a gun."

Fabian took her by the hand, wrapped his arm around her waist, and began to serenade her with Spanish love songs as he led her in a waltz around the factory floor. Angelina believed it magical and closed her eyes. Once again, she imagined the grand galería as a reception hall in a majestic European castle.

It occurred to her that love was never the same. Each love was unique. It happened slowly, steadily, and quietly, like awakening from a dream with no way to stop its force.

CHAPTER 33

The next day at lunch, Rosa approached Angelina. "I've been wanting to talk to you and Carmen, but since she's not here today, do you mind if we talk alone?"

Angelina looked up from where she sat. "I'm always glad of your company."

Rosa smoothed her skirt. "I have so many things on my mind but, most of all, Luca and I are having a child."

Angelina jumped to her feet and hugged her friend. "That's wonderful! Congratulations. I'm so happy for you."

"So are we. Luca cried when I told him. Can you imagine?"

"He loves you so much, Rosa."

Rosa nodded, but then her expression sobered as they both took a seat at the table. "Did you know Luca was married before?"

The remark caught Angelina by surprise. "No. I didn't know. What happened to his wife?"

"They murdered her."

Angelina's hand flew to her chest. "Oh, my God, Rosa. Who would commit such a terrible evil?"

Rosa leaned closer and whispered, "La Mano Nera. Who else? Even their name causes terror to run through the veins of all Italians." Rosa rubbed the back of her neck as though the subject had stiffened her muscles.

"It was Luca's first anniversary, and his wife was with child. He stopped to buy her some flowers before meeting her at Galco's Restaurant. As he came around the corner, he could see her seated by the restaurant's window and waved. At that same moment, a man ran by, brushed against him, and threw a bomb through the window. It blew up and killed her right before Luca's eyes."

"What a horrible thing to witness."

"Luca went crazy. He still thinks he could have stopped it, but it happened so fast and without warning. How could he know what was on that man's mind? He still has nightmares and wakes up screaming. It was all because Vito Galco refused to pay their demands for protection money and they delivered a black wreath to his restaurant."

Angelina held Rosa's hand as she spoke.

"Within the hour," Rosa went on, "Vito Galco was dead. The bomb killed so many innocent people. Luca ran inside, but his wife's condition was . . . he can't even describe it. The whole city cried together at so many funerals, one after another. Luca was inconsolable. He couldn't even identify the man because he had only seen the back of his head. I think that was a blessing. There's no telling what that man would have done to Luca or what Luca might have tried to do to him."

"I remember that," said Angelina. "It was five years ago, right? I read about it in the newspaper. My father says a new country doesn't mean a fresh start. The Black Hand lands here too. These men act quickly and think later or don't think at all and bleed people with no more blood to give."

"The priest said Luca's reward will be greater in the next

life for such suffering in this one." Rosa held a handkerchief and nervously twisted it back and forth. "Our child will come in late spring, but he is so worried the same thing will happen to me. These men are everywhere. They rule the streets."

"The bomb was never meant for Luca's wife. Why not start over somewhere else? Maybe go to New York? Talk to your cousin Sam Anselmo, where you had your reception. He's from New York and can give you advice."

Rosa patted her stomach as if trying to reassure her unborn child. "Do you think so?"

"I've thought of New York myself. If my life becomes impossible, that's where I will go—lots of people, cigar factories, and colleges. It's the perfect place." Angelina took Rosa's hand. "Soon you'll have a baby, and then another. Their faces will steal your heart, and your sad memories will fade." It was the way Signora Bertelli spoke of such things, and Angelina always found her words comforting.

The factory whistle blew.

"I tell you this, Angelina. Warn your father. He has a store. These men don't fear God or the devil. They'd kill the Pope."

Rosa's story relit Angelina's memories of seeing the man named Blessed dead in the street. "I know all about them, Rosa. They wash their hands and faces with their victims' blood."

ANGELINA LIKED to walk along the beach and sink her feet into the sand. The ocean served as a refuge whenever she found a free hour or two, and when Fabian discovered her habit, he joined her. The last few weeks with him had been pleasing as they shared stories.

"To hear the melodious ebb and flow of the ocean waves

is worth the trolley ride here, even if I don't stay long," said Angelina.

Fabian looked out to sea and nodded. "The ocean has a language all its own. It's been here for millions of years and knows all of Earth's secrets."

"There's a tranquility about the sea, like nowhere else in the world," said Angelina.

"It's serene," said Fabian.

"It's captivating," said Angelina.

"Mesmerizing," said Fabian.

It was Angelina's turn. "Fearless."

"Mysterious, powerful, and peaceful."

They looked at each other and laughed.

Together they watched the seagulls circling the sky. "They take me back to memories of my childhood in Cuba."

Fabian's seriousness washed over his face again. These memories didn't seem like happy ones to Angelina, so they walked for a while in silence.

"It's funny how our spirits are so fragile when we're children. As adults, we're stronger and more able to defend ourselves against difficulties. Still, each time I think of something that happened in the past, I once again become that fragile child, and the pain remains as I left it so long ago." Fabian's voice sounded cautious, as though treading on broken seashells.

Angelina studied his expression. "Is there something you'd like to talk about?" she asked.

He met her eyes for a brief moment. "No."

There was stillness in his answer. She'd not seen this reflective mood.

"Fabian, something's troubling you. Why not tell me? Maybe I can help."

He reached for her hand and lightly squeezed it. "Everyone in Ybor City knows Vincente Martin Ybor left

Spain and went to Cuba. My father and uncle joined him in the revolution for Cuban's independence."

"War's terrible. Even winners lose."

The seagulls flapped their wings, swooped down, and then flew high above the seaside. "Seagulls fly inland, you know. They don't go far out over the sea as some birds do. They also sense the change in air pressure and tell us when a storm is coming." Fabian pushed a strand of Angelina's hair behind her ear.

He watched them for a moment. "Ybor was sentenced to death but escaped to Florida. My father remained in Cuba, but that was long ago. Later something much worse happened, and he wasn't strong enough to endure it." Fabian glanced up at the seagulls. "It belongs to the past."

It was obvious he didn't want to say more, and the moment lingered. Finally, Angelina spoke. "My friend Rosa told me a terrible story about what her husband suffered. It seems we've all suffered tragedy."

"When I'm with you, I feel a sense of peace." He turned to her. "Not all of my memories are dark. Sometimes they just overshadow the rest."

"We all have sad memories. When my mother died, the doctor said there was nothing he could have done to save her. I thought about his words for a long time. I was angry with him. Why didn't he try harder?"

Angelina glanced at the sky as if looking up prevented tears from falling. "It still hurts. And I was angry with God, but maybe through heartbreak we evolve into who we're meant to be. We learn little when so little goes wrong. Shakespeare said, 'He is the most wretched of men who has never felt adversity.'"

"Do you believe everything Shakespeare says?"

Angelina would not allow him to challenge her on her hero. "I believe *he* believes what he says, and he's no fool."

Fabian wrinkled his brow. "Many people think Sir Francis Bacon wrote Shakespeare's plays."

What? That can't be true, she thought. "Who would say such a thing? The entire idea seems absurd."

Fabian rubbed his palms together as if in deep thought. "Well, maybe it isn't, but then maybe it is. Not only was he knighted, Sir Francis Bacon was a philosopher, inventor, scientist, politician, and led the literary society. So it makes sense, don't you think?" said Fabian with his usual serious expression.

Angelina threw her hands in the air. She refused to allow anyone to rob Shakespeare of his glory. "If Sir Bacon was all those things, when would he find time to write forty plays and over 150 sonnets, and why would he let Shakespeare take credit for his work?" Her voice sounded like a chair dragged across a bumpy floor.

Fabian raised Angelina's hand to his lips and kissed her. "A brilliant argument. Let's leave the dead peacefully in their graves."

Angelina wasn't sure if the conversation had distracted Fabian from something he wanted to share, so she asked him the question she had asked before. "Is there something you'd like to talk about?"

He offered a humble smile, one he must have saved for an emergency. "One day, Angelina, but not today."

CHAPTER 34

Angelina had made a cloth bag to hold Shakespeare's works, hoping no one would notice the book's poor condition. Best of all, she knew where to read without interruption. She approached Sixteenth Street, where every Friday the aroma of freshly baked bread filled her senses.

"Wait, Angelina!" Angelina turned and saw her mother's friend from the days of baking bread in brick ovens. Signora Fortuna's hair was tied in its customary bun to prevent it from falling into the dough. Yet it all seemed so long ago now someone's husband offer to make the sign of the cross on the bottom of a loaf, kiss the knife, and give the first slice of bread to the eldest grandfather out of respect. *Salute, Nanno, you're as good as bread.* Angelina vividly recalled the saying. 'As good as gold' was the American expression. 'You can't eat gold when you're hungry,' her father would say.

"Signora Fortuna, I was thinking of when my mother and I baked bread with you."

"Thinking of me isn't good enough. You must stop and visit. On Friday, everyone's at the brick oven in my backyard, and you walk right past my house without stopping. How is this possible? And what if I didn't see you between all the shrubs and hedges?" Her frown was familiar, like someone whose lifetime of complaints had forced the corners of her mouth to turn downward.

Still, those days at the brick oven with her mother were happy ones, but attending alone where women arrived with their daughters would be heartbreaking.

"My father always needs my help at the store, so I go straight home after work."

"Today your father can call on his other five children to help him. Now, tell me about your job at the cigar factory."

"Work is fine, signora. Time goes by quickly with el lector. Even girls working short hours will sit outside on a blanket near an open window to hear the rest of a story. The books are wonderful."

"I ask you about work, and you tell me about books. You've always been a smart girl." The woman handed Angelina two loaves of bread. "Tell your father my niece Regina Sardanno made these especially for your family with her regards."

If Regina ever makes bread, then God made a miracle. The words spoken long ago by Carolina still rang true. *No one is as lazy as Regina Sardanno,* she'd said, but Angelina kept that memory to herself.

"How kind of your niece to think of our family."

"Don't forget to stop by next Friday. Every week has a Friday, so no excuses." The woman sighed, crossed her arms over her large midsection, leaned forward, and raised one eyebrow. "Tell your father Regina sends her regards."

Angelina understood the message—another Italian trying to marry off a relative. It amused her to think of her hard-working father married to lazy Regina Sardanno. She hugged the older woman and kissed her cheek. "I promise to tell him."

Angelina left her mother's old friend and walked down the avenue until she found a bench away from the rush of people. The days were longer now, and she had enough daylight to enjoy a little time alone. She pulled out her book, ready to consume its richness. Nearly lost in her reading, she glanced at her pendant watch. It seemed impossible, but her golden hour had passed so quickly. She put her book in the cloth bag and turned toward home.

"Where are you going?" Angelina recognized Fabian's voice, and her heart leaped, but her excitement quickly sobered at the thought of being seen by those passing by.

"I missed you today." He took her hand. "Come, let's talk. I've heard all your excuses about your father. It's time we had a serious discussion."

"About what?"

"Our fate. Sometimes people meet because they're supposed to meet. It's their destiny."

Angelina stared into his dark eyes for a moment. "I'm not sure I believe in fate. If you work hard, you earn money. If you don't work, your pockets are empty. If you cook, you have something to eat, and if you plant, something grows. That's not fate. It's reason."

"What about winning the *bolita* lottery? Is that luck or fate?"

"Far more people lose than win."

"And maybe that's their fate. Nothing changes fate, but don't forget what happened to Benito Baltazar."

The name didn't sound familiar. "I don't think I've met him."

"And now it's too late." Fabian shook his head. "It wasn't so long ago that fate struck Baltazar like a bolt of lightning in a village outside Havana." A smirk grew at the corners of Fabian's mouth. Angelina had her suspicions that the story might lack truth—perhaps one of those fishermen's tales?

"Baltazar had a small rash on his thumb, hardly noticeable, until it spread over the poor man's arms, across his belly, down his legs, and up his back. He scratched night and day, applied ointments and creams, crushed mint, basil leaves, and poured potato flour all over himself, with no relief. He had no choice but to consult an expert."

"A doctor?" said Angelina.

"A *curandera*," said Fabian. "Much more practical. She not only cures but, for absolutely no extra charge, will tell you your fortune. So Baltazar searched for a poster and found one nailed to a tree. He followed the arrows to the curtain of good-luck beads held by a rope tied to a pair of palm trees. He entered the no-walls, one-table, two-chair establishment. The curandera took his money, slipped it down her blouse, spread her tarot cards before him, and then gasped."

Fabian paused, leaned back on the bench, and stretched out his legs.

"Well, what did she see? Tell me," Angelina probed.

He shook his head. "A terrible thing. The rash was Baltazar's body's way of saying *"Adios, amigo."* He'd soon die and from a most unusual circumstance that would have people talking about it for years."

"How could anyone know that?"

"The power of a curandera is incontestable. They see and know everything. Baltazar was, for good reason, distressed. He immediately asked if the woman might have misread the cards. He could provide her with a list of others named Baltazar—it must be one of them."

"Oh yes. There are hundreds with that name," Angelina teased.

"Exactly what Baltazar said. 'You must be mistaken,' he told her. 'Mistaken?' said the curandera. 'You insult me. You ask this question of an established professional.' Her skills were incomparable, her predictions as accurate as the solar system. No one dared dispute that. If she said Baltazar was going to die, she expected him to comply as a simple matter of decent courtesy."

"Comply?" Angelina said, holding back her laughter.

"Comply, cooperate, conform. In her fury, the curandera jumped to her feet, slid open the curtain of good-luck beads, and ordered poor Baltazar to leave."

"Oh no," Angelina said with widened eyes.

"Baltazar opened his trembling mouth and in sheer panic begged, 'Please, please forgive me.'"

"And did she change her mind?" Angelina suspected Fabian had altered the story to amuse her.

"Not at first, but it was only logical to consider his limited life span. 'Let me have another chance,' said Baltazar, wringing his hands together."

"La curandera paused. 'Well,' she said at last. 'I'll grant you your dying wish.' She then busied herself consulting her notes, the ones she kept in a metal box shoved in the hollow of a tree and tied up with rope. They proved invaluable for the more troublesome cases. Sparing nothing, she laid before Baltazar the most powerful tools of her trade. She tapped a teacup with a chicken bone and waved a handful of feathers from the same chicken over Baltazar's head. After several incantations, her original prognosis became irrefutable. This time, something else had also crystallized. 'You will die at the feet of an alligator.'"

"An alligator?" Angelina feigned terror. "What a terrible death. The poor man."

Fabian remained serious. "Teacups and chicken feathers never lie, Angelina."

"Is this going to be a really sad story?"

"I can offer you a handkerchief in case of tears," Fabian said, reaching into his pocket.

Angelina shook her head. "I'll control myself."

"Good, because things get more dismal." Fabian paused as if to recapture the passion of the story. "Baltazar coughed and nearly choked to death on his fear. He went home to worry without interruption. When he slept, he dreamed of powerful alligator jaws tearing flesh and bone. To no one's surprise, by the end of the week, his hair had turned white."

"This happened in one week?"

"It was a longer than most seven days, which only allowed one thing left for Baltazar to do. He packed his bags for New York City, where no one had ever seen an alligator. But on the day Baltazar was to leave, there was a most unusual occurrence."

Angelina caught on to Fabian's silent signals. He raised his eyebrows when he wanted her to act surprised or scared. He narrowed them and made his jaw quiver when he wanted her to react with worry.

"Gomez, the grocer, ran through the streets and shouted warnings that a huge alligator had eaten a goat, a chicken, and two watermelons. No one could catch the slippery reptile. Baltazar trembled and dropped his travel bag and sightseeing brochure. In a panic, he hurried down the street and then, confused, went up the street again, back and forth, up and down, until he ran into Pedro, the barber. Pedro tried to calm him, but Baltazar placed his hands on his heart and fell to the ground, dead at Pedro's feet."

Angelina raised an eyebrow. "So then none of what the fortune-teller said was true."

"We are talking about fate here, a serious topic. Baltazar died with his eyes wide open, staring straight at Pedro's new alligator shoes."

Angelina burst into laughter. She had to admire the serious look on Fabian's face, which never wavered as he told the story.

"In Dante's *Inferno,* fortune-tellers have to go through hell wearing their heads backward as their punishment for predicting the future," said Angelina.

"This isn't fortune-telling. It's fate. Tell your father it's time to meet me."

Angelina's expression sobered. Her father controlled her life, not fate. "I can't bring you into my argument with my father without making matters worse—much worse. I'm strong enough to face him alone. Besides, this is an old fight between us. Today is when people come to the store, open their pay envelopes, and buy more than usual. He'll be in a good mood tonight."

"And do you think Friday is so different from the rest of the week?" Fabian removed the two loaves of bread and the book that separated them.

"Fabian, if you try to kiss me here in the street, someone I know might see us. I don't want to complicate things more than they already are. Please, let me handle this my way."

"I've told you before that I don't think you should do it alone. I should be there with you."

"No," she countered. "You don't know him."

Fabian reached for Angelina's hand, and his eyes drew her to him until she sensed the pulse of his heart. "I watched you for months from afar, even before I knew your name, and these last few months, I've thought only of you. You're my jewel. Tell me you'll become my wife because we love each other, not because we're victims of an arranged marriage." He tightened his hold. "Say you will, *mi vida*."

"I have to go forward, make a new life for myself, and release my hold on the past, but I'm also afraid." She looked into Fabian's eyes as if searching for answers. "Everything I do now will change the way I live. I've made mistakes, and I can't make another." Her voice was light yet determined. She had believed that love's immense emotion came only once in a lifetime. She now believed life had the power to heal a broken heart. Fabian had a sensitive side, made her laugh, and wanted to be with her always. The decision now fell on her alone and on her free will.

"I love you, Fabian." The words did not come easily, but they were the right words. They were both young, in love, and eager to make a life together—all things lacking in her father's business-like marriage arrangements for her.

Fabian kissed her with tenderness, and then more intensely. It didn't matter who saw them together. Nothing mattered. At that moment, Angelina believed that love could withstand anything. She ran her hand over his hair, reassuring herself that he was really there.

He reached for her hand, bringing it to his lips. "One day I'll buy you a mansion where you'll ring a bell and servants will come." Fabian kissed her again and then looked into her eyes. "I'll be over at my cousin Bertha's. I won't leave until I've heard from you. You've made me happy, Angelina. Beyond any happiness I've ever known."

Angelina didn't want to leave, but the day had darkened. She grabbed the bread and book and headed for what she knew would be a war of wills.

"Angelina," Fabian called out after her. "I'll even buy you a nicer book."

She waved back and hurried home. When she reached her front door, she released a nervous breath. She entered the kitchen, where Filippo sat at the table doing schoolwork. She placed the bread on the counter, still wondering how to best approach her father.

"Angie, you've got to help me. The teacher says I'd better know how to spell these words by Monday morning. Do you know any tricks?"

"I do. Study them."

Filippo threw down his chalk and slate. "What's so

important, anyway? Half the people around here can't read or write."

"Yes, but you belong to the other half, little brother. Never forget that."

The door swung open, and Domenico walked in with Salvatore and Vincenzo. Angelina had waited all day to speak to her father, and now he wasn't alone. She reassured herself she deserved a life with love. She pointed to the bread. "Papa, Regina Sardanno made these two loaves for our family and sent her regards."

"That woman can't even slice bread, let alone bake it," her father grumbled. He rarely missed anything.

The door rattled open. Pasquale entered more radiant than usual and had with him a tattered-looking Asian boy wearing a grin as big as Pasquale's.

Domenico didn't wait for introductions. "Pasquale, who is this?"

"I want you should meet my son, Wei Chen."

"Your son? What are you talking about?" Though her father's voice sounded calm, Angelina did not believe this tranquil moment would last.

"Wei Chen, he work in the street to shine the shoes. He no have no mama and no papa. I have no son. Can you believe? Such a good luck we find each other." With obvious pride, Pasquale said to the child, "Wei Chen, this is you zio Domenico."

Angelina smiled at the little boy. His face and hands held a mixture of dirt and shoe polish. He'd outgrown his shirt, and his pants needed mending. Both articles of clothing needed washing, and for a shoeshine boy, his own shoes remained scuffed, scarred, and lacked shoelaces. The world had not been kind to the child.

"Domenico, this is you *nipote,* Wei Chen."

"This is nonsense." Domenico shook his head in obvious

frustration. "Do you see how hard I work to support my children? Children mean sacrifices." He pointed to his temple to indicate that his brother wasn't thinking of the seriousness and responsibility.

Pasquale grinned at his brother, then at the child. "I gonna work hard too."

"You already work hard."

"Now, I gonna work harder."

The little boy kept fidgeting as he watched the exchange, wide-eyed. Afraid her father had frightened him, Angelina took his hand, smiled, and winked at him.

"You can't do this. Wei Chen isn't even Italian!" Domenico shouted.

Pasquale hit his forehead with the palm of his hand. "Maybe because we call him Wei Chen. I gonna change his name." Pasquale turned to the boy and reached for his other hand. "Is no problem with you, Wei Chen? I'm gonna change you name so everybody know you Italiano."

All the children remained motionless as Pasquale looked to the ceiling for inspiration.

"We gonna call you . . . ah . . . Pasqualino." He put his hand on the boy's head as he spoke. "Pasqualino—you like you name?" The boy beamed at his new father and nodded. "You see, nobody have to worry no more. Pasqualino is Italiano."

Once again, Angelina saw the tenderness of Pasquale's heart. In his uncomplicated way, he faced her father's objections with a wide grin. While she appreciated her uncle's simple approach, she'd now develop her own.

"Take the boy back where you found him. Someone will look for him."

"I look for him, Domenico, and I find him. He was in the street shining shoes. Everybody say he have nobody. Maybe he get hurt. Everybody need somebody. Belarmino, he want I should go tomorrow to Key West for the work. He say maybe we gonna make more money, so me and Pasqualino, we think we gonna go, and maybe we buy a little casita for *la mia famiglia.*"

"Your family is right here."

"Si, Domenico. Now, I make a new famiglia too. Every family start with one person." He pointed to himself. "Then two people." He pointed to Pasqualino. "And then maybe we get more." A light shone in her uncle's eyes that Angelina had never seen before. Her father seemed to miss it altogether.

The news of her uncle's plan to move distressed her. "Pasquale, you're moving to Key West?" She'd miss his stories and his love if he lived so far away. "What about work?"

"There's work in Key West."

"Pasquale, how do you expect to find a good Sicilian wife who wants to start her marriage raising a son, half grown, Chinese, not Catholic, and *not yours?*"

Pasquale answered the question with his usual logic. "You right, Domenico. We no have nobody like Pasqualino in *la mia famiglia*. We have such a bad luck." He shook his head, and his face lit up. "Now I find Pasqualino, and everything is good."

Pasquale walked past his brother and headed toward the front door. "Pasqualino, we go now and buy you some nice clothes." He then turned back to his brother. "You remember, Domenico, when I try to buy shirts and nobody like me because they say I dago? From now on, Pasqualino and I no make the mistakes, so we no worry no more, and you no worry too. Non ti preoccupare."

It amazed Angelina the ease with which her uncle had kept his new son and won his point without surrendering his smile or raising his voice.

Still, she knew something critical was about to happen that would change her life forever.

CHAPTER 35

With the floor swept, the windows cleaned, the shelves stocked, and the displays replenished with a variety of foods, it was now Angelina's turn to face her father. She glanced at the clock. The moment was quickly approaching when she'd announce her intention to take control of her life.

Domenico stepped into the kitchen, and Angelina took a deep breath.

"Did you have a good day, Papa?"

"*Cosi, cosi.* It could have been better. It could have been worse. Those who didn't buy this week will need more next week."

"Is there anything I can do to help you?"

"Tomorrow night when the store is closed, if customers buy, restock the shelves. If they don't buy, dust them." Dark circles had appeared under his eyes. Perhaps he hadn't slept well, and this wasn't the best time to make her declaration. Then again, if not now, when?

"I'm good with numbers. I can help you keep your libretto in order, inventory the stock, bargain with the salesmen—"

"And what do I do?"

"Whatever you want to do. Rest. You work so hard. I know how to run the store. I can do it all alone." Angelina pointed to a few items. "Papa, if we put what sells the most at the back of the store, customers will see other products along the way and buy more. If the sweets sat on the counter next to the cash register, customers might think to buy them. If you gave them a small sample, they'd buy a full bag, and you'd do more business."

Domenico didn't seem to be listening. He looked more preoccupied than usual as he moved three cans of tomato paste from the kitchen's second shelf to the first. A moment later, he moved them back again. "Enough talk. Deliver this pot of sweet sausages and rigatoni to the church." He waved her off.

Perhaps her father was still worried about her being in the store alone. She could do the books in the house, and if she helped him rearrange the store, she could do it when the store was closed and the shades drawn. If she bargained with the salesmen, she wouldn't be alone. It seemed to Angelina her father always grew more troubled. If only he had confidence in her.

"Take the food before it gets too cold."

Angelina had the habit of recording her thoughts in her notebook. Now, facing such a critical crossroads and with so much to write, she was delivering a meal of sweet sausages and rigatoni to Father Cavalli. She had brothers perfectly capable of doing the job.

All the way to church, she occupied her mind with the best way to phrase her sentences when the crucial moment arrived to face her father. Nothing would remain the same. When the large cross came into view, Angelina went around the building and straight to the rectory door, where she knocked, and then knocked again. Priests never seemed to hurry. Must be those long gowns they wore.

At last, Father Cavalli answered. "Hello, Angelina, what have we here?"

"My father sent some food for your dinner. He made the sausages himself. They are wonderful. Everyone says so." It struck her as odd that her father would send a meal for the parish priests. He'd never been especially religious or associated with the clergy—at least not to her knowledge.

"Well, please give your father our heartfelt thank-you. It's generous of him, and, Angelina, allow me to offer my congratulations. I will begin announcing the banns of your marriage at church a week from next Sunday."

Angelina froze. "Banns? What banns? I'm not getting married."

"Well, unless this other Angelina has the same father as you do and she's also to marry Umberto Rizzo, then perhaps I'm wrong."

Had her father and the baker made this disgraceful arrangement without her? How dare they plan her wedding? It was beyond unbelievable.

"Don't announce the banns because I won't be attending the funeral."

"You mean wedding."

"I mean funeral because if I'm forced to marry Umberto Rizzo, I will kill myself."

Fueled by anger, Angelina raced home. Life *was* stranger than fiction, and hers had become a nightmare. She dashed into her house and went straight to her father. "Why on earth did you and Rizzo go to Father Cavalli and tell him I'm marrying the baker?"

"You will have every protection from a man who admires you."

"Admires me?"

Angelina fought hard to calm herself. It had become a war of wills, and every word she wanted to say blazed with rage.

"The baker is kind and generous. He'll find someone good to marry him—but not me."

Domenico waited a moment before he responded. "Is that all?"

"It's all that matters."

He opened his libretto and spun it around so it faced Angelina. "Look." He pointed to recent entries. "I give food to those who come in and have no money with only their mark in my libretto that they will pay, but I can't do it for everyone or I can't feed my family. I'm practical. I work hard, and all I ask for is your trust."

"Mama said I was like you in spirit. I never understood what she meant, but now I see it. I'm practical too. If I make mistakes, I blame no one but myself."

"This is more than a mistake, Angelina. This is throwing away the fruit to eat the bitter seed. Fortune has smiled on Umberto Rizzo, and he wants *you* for his wife—a huge blessing—but I have the only Sicilian daughter in all of Ybor City who defies her father."

"Umberto Rizzo can find someone else. He still looks young—except for his hair."

"While you were playing with dolls, he worked hard to establish himself. Now, he's ready to offer you a wonderful life. You'll learn to love a man who treats you well and protects you. Remember, Umberto wants to build a fine new home for you. He could close his store tomorrow and never have to open it again. You'll have everything." Domenico's jaw was set. "I refuse to see you penniless and living in a small casita, so I gave excuses to others who asked for you until Rico Braccio came in with his father, and after him came Umberto. I selected the best. You should be honored."

"Just because someone knocks at the door doesn't mean

you have to open it." Angelina's stomach tightened. "It shouldn't matter who wants to marry me but who I want to marry. Papa, do you love me?"

"Why do you think I made this arrangement? Some people live in the streets, like I once did. Factories can close their doors. Then what?" Domenico shook his head. "So many live from payday to payday."

In a desperate move, Angelina clasped her hands together as though in prayer. "Papa, if I married Umberto Rizzo, I'd despise him for bringing such sadness into my life."

Domenico held up the libretto. "Sadness? I'm preventing that. Perhaps I've gone hungry too many times and seen too much heartbreak. Dying of thirst is not the time to dig the well. Umberto Rizzo dug his well long ago. If I should die, he's told me he'll take care of all of you—your brothers and Lily too. *Stessa faccia, stessa razza*."

"Same face, same race? What's that supposed to mean?" She threw her hands in the air in frustration.

"It means we belong with our own. It's our protection. Maybe it's time you understood you're the daughter of a penniless immigrant. I see the same look I had back then on other men's faces."

Her father's voice trembled with frustration, while Angelina trembled with anger.

"Once, I was dizzy from hunger while cooking sausages for other people, but I refused to eat until I sold enough to change my life. Many good men marry and have children, then something goes wrong and they lose everything. Their clothes become rags, their children must live with others, and it shatters families.

I want to sleep knowing my daughter is safe. Maybe you have an egg in your pocket now, but Umberto Rizzo has the hen."

Angelina had no intension of submitting to this. "You always return to the past. I live in the present."

"There'd be no fruit in the present if we hadn't planted seeds in the past. The past is rich with lessons and warnings."

Angelina saw her father as a good, hardworking man, but they had backed each other into lonely corners. "Papa, I know you have no interest in marrying Regina Sardanno. Still, she owns a lovely home and has inherited enough money from her grandparents to take care of you. Would you marry her for that reason?"

"I refuse to talk about fools. Rizzo's a smart businessman. You even admit he's a kind man. Why is this so hard to understand? You'll have a wonderful husband and children to bring you joy."

Angelina studied her father's expression. "Do I bring you joy, Papa? Do I?"

Domenico didn't answer.

"You know nothing about life." Her father spoke more quickly and sharply now.

"I know enough. I'm the one who has to live my life, not you."

"Appreciate what I'm doing for you," Domenico grumbled.

"I'll die of a broken heart."

"No one dies of a broken heart, Angelina, or I'd be buried next to your mother." Her father's voice resonated with the chords of anguished memories. Why didn't he want her to have a love like his, one that transcended time?

She and her father had crossed a line. All their months of arguing had collected into this one moment. Angelina's heart pounded. Her blood raced. The distress and frustration she'd held inside suddenly erupted. "I won't marry the baker. I won't. Ever. You're trying to kill me like you killed Mama!" The words came out like hot bile and shattered the room into fragments. Angelina had never thought such a thing of her father, but somewhere in a dark alcove of her mind, she had stored her Aunt Violetta's accusation. And now, when reason failed, Angelina reached inside and withdrew it like a weapon.

Rage flushed Domenico's face red, and as quick as lightning, he grabbed his daughter by the hair and swung his hand hard across her face in rage. Angelina cried out and fell to the floor. His entire handprint left stung and numbed her face. Blood dripped over her tongue and from the corner of her mouth. The shock of his violence hurt more than the heat of the physical blow. Her throat tightened. She couldn't speak or hold back her tears. Part of it was shock. Her father had never touched her or his other children.

Domenico reached down, pulled his daughter to her feet, and held her chin in his hand. She tried to pull away but couldn't escape. He wiped the blood from her mouth with his hand and held it up to her face. "You see this, my child? This is my blood." His voice became calm. "You are *sangue del mio sangue* or you are nothing to me. I mean everything I say."

An ominous moment of stillness passed before her father released her with such force she fell backward. He stared at her with an almost tangible anger, one that could shatter the room and one she'd never forget. In that dangerous silence, he turned his back and walked away.

CHAPTER 36

The words between Angelina and her father had piled up like bricks and formed a wall. She paced back and forth. Nothing would be the same. It had taken a physical blow to startle and awaken her to the fact that all she'd hoped for had dissolved. *I have only myself to rely on,* she thought.

Angelina went to bed that night, tossing about without a moment's peace as she formed a plan. The next day, she stayed out of her father's way and waited for him to leave. His usual run to pick up supplies took a little over an hour. As soon as his wagon pulled away, Angelina hurried to catch the trolley and rode to her grandmother's house, where she knocked frantically on the door.

Her tension increased when Zia Violetta opened the door instead of her grandmother. Violetta lived in the more affluent section of town. Angelina hadn't expected to see her, and she couldn't think of a worse time to face her.

"Well, I'm surprised to see you, Angelina."

Angelina kissed her aunt as her hope for a sympathetic

visit with her grandmother deflated. "Hello, zia. Is nonna here?"

"No, she went out with your Zia Gina. Why has it taken you so long to visit?"

"Our father has forbidden us."

"And you listen to that foolish man?"

Angelina didn't see any reason to narrate the past. "Zia, I need help."

"What has happened?" Violetta lifted her chin as if whatever the answer, it would fracture her sensibilities.

"It's my father—"

"What has that man done now?"

"He wants me to marry the baker."

Violetta widened her eyes in apparent surprise. "You mean Umberto Rizzo, the baker?"

"Yes. We had a terrible fight. I may need to leave home to protect myself from such a marriage."

"I don't understand. Why would you fight about this?"

Violetta's remark stunned Angelina, and it took a moment for her to realize what her aunt implied. "How can you ask that? He's almost my father's age."

Zia Violetta wrinkled her brow. "It sickens me to think your father and I agree on anything, but the baker is a wonderful match to rescue you."

Angelina's stomach quivered. "Rescue me from what? He has four children the ages of my brothers and Lily. Not only that, but we have nothing in common. It would be a horrible match—beyond horrible. I don't love him."

"Love? What on earth does love have to do with marriage?"

"Everything."

"Nothing." Violetta narrowed her eyes. "Now and then, even a madman like your father has a rational thought. Stay with us if you wish, but I will insist you marry Rizzo, and I know him well."

An unwelcome heat surged through Angelina. "Oh, please don't say that."

"It's perfect. Umberto Rizzo is a rich man. Everyone goes to his bakery, and not too many people know he has a second successful bakery in Tampa. He owns an impressive house and several homes he rents out—all paid for."

When had her aunt learned such personal information about the baker? Her father had been right about Violetta. She had never known a love like the one he'd shared with her sister. "Umberto Rizzo's money makes no difference to me."

Violetta rolled her eyes in obvious disgust. "I have protected you and kept your embarrassing secrets about working in a cigar factory and being the daughter of a simple man who owns a small grocery store. It's hardly the social standing that attracts a proper suitor."

Angelina had many issues with her father, but he'd never been a 'simple man.' It occurred to Angelina that her aunt didn't dislike her father as much as she objected to his social standing and lack of wealth.

"Marriage to such a successful man as the baker is wonderful news. He'll give you everything, and you'll be able to travel to Europe and shop at the finest stores. I'd be the first to share your incredible news with everyone. It's foolish to risk losing him."

"I've already lost because I don't love the baker, and he doesn't love me." Her hope began to fade. How could so many people reduce marriage to a business transaction, like selling your child to the highest bidder?

"Love is not a requirement in marriage. I don't love my husband, and I never have, but I love the prestige it affords me as the wife of a successful banker, and that's what matters."

How can Zia Violetta even admit such a thing? thought Angelina of her aunt's outrageous opinion.

"I can't believe you, Angelina. Surely you must see this as an exceptional opportunity to have everything you ever dreamed of."

"That's not my dream. My dream is to have the freedom to live my life my way, attend college, and have my own family who loves each other, not money or possessions."

"Don't be foolish, child. Your mother married for love and look what happened to her. She had no servants, no lovely gowns. She even had to do her own laundry. There were no trips to Italy and all those children to care for." She cleared her throat. "Naturally, I love all of you, but the whole thing was unnecessary and revolting for my sister and her children."

Even if her mother's wealth had equaled her aunt's, they'd still have nothing in common. "Zia, what would you do if the banking system collapsed and your husband lost his job, money, and everything else?"

"That's a ridiculous question. The stock market is strong, and it's paying us large dividends, but at your age, you don't understand finance. Not to mention they've just instituted the Federal Reserve Bank. Banks will never fail."

"I'm happy for your good fortune, but what if something goes wrong? What if people go to the bank to get their money and the bank closes its doors?" Angelina tapped her foot anxiously. She could not believe they were actually related.

"That's impossible. I'd expect my husband to correct it immediately. I come from a family with money, I married a man with money, and I refuse to be reduced to a pauper. It's obscene."

Angelina glanced at her pendant watch. She had to hurry back home. She kissed her aunt, reached for the door handle, and spoke with finality, something her aunt probably didn't realize. "Goodbye, Zia Violetta."

"Remember, I expect to see that wedding invitation. You'll be glad you took my advice."

Angelina turned away. There was only one path left to her. She went over every detail in her mind as she hurried down the street and vital that nothing went wrong. As she made her way around the corner, she passed a large Suffragette poster plastered on the side of a building. Its commanding message read that no one person or government could stop a woman's will. Angelina paused a moment, struck by the powerful words. It intertwined the Suffragettes' fight with her own. They were both fighting for their rights. Angelina put her hand on the poster as if drawing from its strength.

With no time to waste and the trolley nowhere in sight, she ran the rest of the way home, arriving almost out of breath. The little bell rang as she stepped inside the grocery store and froze at the sight of Fabian.

"What are you doing here?" Angelina asked in disbelief, then looked both ways for her father.

"I think it's time I met your father and told him of my feelings for you,"

"Oh, no. No, no, no! You can't do that." Angelina's voice trembled. She had seen her father angry, but this would engender new heights of rage.

"Why not? I work hard, and I love you," Fabian voice was calm in contrast to Angelina's rising pitch of alarm.

Angelina glanced out the window, caught sight of her father coming toward the store, and blurted out her intentions. "I will never accept what he plans, but my father has arranged for me to marry Rizzo, the baker, because he wants me to have a secure life."

"I can give you a secure life," said Fabian, unfazed by Angelina's panic.

Angelina pushed him toward the exit. "He believes a father must find his daughter a husband. Leave now, and he'll think you're a train passenger who stopped in."

"Maybe if you were ugly or simple. Beautiful, intelligent women don't need help. Besides, it appears I've arrived in time to save you."

"It's complicated. My father believes Italians should marry Italians. It's set in stone, and the stone is in his mind, so he carries it everywhere."

Fabian reached for Angelina's hand. "Maybe you aren't using the right approach?"

The door opened. Domenico stepped inside, his look hardening when he saw them. Angelina quickly pulled her hand from Fabian's grasp.

"Angelina, who is this man?" Domenico's voice was unmistakably coarse, threatening, and unreceptive.

"Papa, I . . ."

Fabian offered to shake hands with Domenico. "It's good to meet you, Señor Pirrello."

Domenico looked at him and tightened both hands into fists. "Who are you?" he snarled.

Fabian did not appear to lose his composure. "My name is Fabian Dominguez. I'm a friend of Angelina's."

"A friend?"

Fabian took a moment before answering. "I'm a very good friend—a friend who would like your permission to marry her. I have a good job, I can provide for her, and I will treat her well."

Angelina gasped, certain the store might quiver and the windows break from the mere sound of Fabian's proposal. She could think of nothing worse he could have said to her father.

Domenico's eyes grew large and intense, and his face flushed red. "Angelina is already engaged, so you can leave and forget about her."

"That would be impossible." Fabian looked at Angelina, whose eyes had widened and lips had pursed. With all that had already taken place, there was no telling the outcome of this confrontation.

"You'll never marry her. Get out of my store."

"She loves me too."

This was the last time Angelina would accept this, but she wasn't foolish either. She remembered the strange conversation she had with her father over the attack on the brothers who had beaten Pasquale so severely. Unsure if this situation could spark violence, Angelina feared finding out. More certain than ever about what she had to do to free herself from her father, she pulled Fabian by the sleeve toward the door.

"Get out!" Domenico roared in a thundering voice as he raised his fist in Fabian's direction.

"Sir, I have the utmost respect for you, but don't you want your daughter's happiness?" Fabian looked from Angelina to her father.

Nothing good had ever come from her father's outbursts, and this would be the worst. "Fabian, please, just go." Angelina felt her heart racing and made up her mind.

Domenico narrowed his eyes at Fabian and shouted, "Get out of my sight!"

Angelina gave Fabian a pleading look. "Please."

Fabian met Angelina's terrified expression. "For you, Angelina." He turned, walked out, and quietly closed the door.

Domenico's chest heaved. "You defy me? Are you trying to destroy your life?"

"He's a good person, Papa."

"I forbid it!" Domenico slammed his fist on the counter. "You are never to see him again. Never. Do you understand? *Hai capito?*"

Angelina doubled her hands into fists. "Yes, I understand, but this is my life, Papa. It's time I made my own decisions and my own mistakes."

"You will do as I say, and that's the end."

Not this time, not anymore, she thought. Her father expected to have total control of her life. Splintered by the finality in his demand, it became clear she no longer had a choice about what to do. At the first opportunity, Angelina left in search of Fabian. When she found his friends, they directed her to his aunt's home. She stood visibly shaking when he opened the door. He led her to sit in the parlor, where a sea of pent-up defeat gave way to a downpour of tears.

"I hate that it's come to this. Nothing good has happened since my mother died." Angelina remained trapped in her father's past. It was like a song replaying the same chords, and she couldn't stop the threadbare melody.

"What do you want, Angelina?" Fabian's voice was low, sympathetic, and filled with concern.

"This world isn't ready to give women a chance, but I have to try. The mold has to break sometime." Angelina met the seriousness reflected in his gaze.

"What are you saying?"

"I hardly slept last night. I kept reliving my father's angry reaction. Something should have occurred to me long ago. My father married for love. It was a beautiful, passionate love that grew even stronger. When my mother died, my father's heartbreak left him stricken with a wound that festered. He stopped laughing, lost patience, and the void grew deep. I've learned our hearts don't fully awaken until we fall in love, but what becomes of us when love is gone? My father was never the same after he lost my mother. Perhaps he believes he's protecting me from that pain if I marry for practical reasons and without emotion?"

Fabian pulled her into his arms and caressed her hair. "I'm not perfect, Angelina, and I make mistakes. I've been hurt too, and I've hurt others, but adding darkness doesn't rid the darkness that's already there. You've become my light. With you, I can learn to breathe again. Marry me. It's not me rescuing you from a controlling father. It's you rescuing me from an empty life."

Angelina listened with the intensity that had been stirring inside her for so long. She wasn't so foolish to believe Fabian's good looks was a reason to spend her life with someone. Looks faded. Love, hard work, determination, and devotion changed lives and built the strongest armor. What more could she expect?

"There's nothing I'd deny you if it made you happy." He kissed her forehead, then lifted her chin and kissed her lips. His tenderness gave her a fleeting sense that all was right in her life. "I think we should marry, but I want you to know I'm doing this purely as a community service. How else can I protect the other men who might run into you and your pushcart of troubles?"

Angelina saw no fault in Fabian, but she was cautious, something she'd learned from Rolando's disappearance. No one jumped into the fire twice. "I don't want to bring you into my problems. I can work, learn to write, and support myself. I'll be independent. If we leave together, I'll love and be good to you, but we are equals. I will never again allow another man to rule my life." Angelina choked on her words.

Fabian held her tight. "We'll be equals." He paused. "Does this mean I take your name, or you take mine, or we trade names?

Angelina grinned through her tears.

"It's happening the way it's supposed to happen, Angelina. It's our fate to have found each other. You've never gone farther than a trolley ride. Together we'll go beyond the horizon." His words anointed the air with dreamlike visions of their life together.

E'finita. "It's finished," as her father would say. He would not allow her back, and she was not returning.

Fabian kissed her and whispered, "Your dreams are my dreams. No one can stop us. I'll wait for you tonight. We'll marry in the morning." Fabian kissed her forehead. "In case you need help to remember, tonight comes right after today."

"'It must follow, as night follows day,'" quoted Angelina.

"That's right. From now on, it's only you, and me, and Shakespeare."

Angelina couldn't find the strength to smile "I can't make any more mistakes, Fabian. The world is a harsh place for a woman and even worse for one alone, but I can do it. I know I can. If I go with you, I need to know you won't become demanding or I'll leave. I will."

Fabian took her hand and squeezed it reassuringly.

"There's something else important you need to know, Fabian. Carmen gave me my college acceptance letter. I had it mailed to her home, and I left it with her for safekeeping. I will start in the fall with a small scholarship, and nothing will stop me from going."

"Then you must follow your hero, Shakespeare's, advice. 'To thine own self be true.' I won't stop you."

She wiped away her last tear, but her voice still held the remains of her anxiety. "I never thought it'd happen like this. In my father's world, it's a disgrace for a daughter to leave home. He's a proud man. He may never forgive me."

"You don't need his forgiveness. He had yesterday. We'll have each other and all the tomorrows to come." Fabian kissed her and held her until she knew she had to leave.

"I'll miss you," she said.

"I missed you long before I met you."

Angelina smiled and went home, warmed by Fabian's words of love. When she arrived, she stepped into the kitchen, prepared a large dinner for her family, helped her brothers with their chores, and made sure they did their schoolwork. When night fell, after the house had been still for hours, Angelina lay awake with her face turned into her pillow to muffle her sobs. Fabian had come into her life at the right time. He was someone who truly loved her, someone she loved in return. He must be right. It *was* fate.

The day had long ago relinquished its light, and the endless night seemed darker than usual. Angelina slid out of bed, lit a candle, and packed her valise. Beneath the last article in her drawer, she uncovered Rolando's medal of Saint Jude, the saint of miracles. She enclosed it in her hand and thought of how she'd once relished their moments together. Rolando had now become a phantom of the past. Her love for him had been swift and intense, like a comet or shooting star burning a path across the night sky. He had filled her mind and heart but was never again seen or heard from.

Falling in love with Fabian was not the same. It came slowly, like drops of water steadily filling a glass, like the way one drifted off and falls into a dream. Angelina had resisted at first, tried to safeguard her heart, but life wasn't a straight course. It had many bends in the road. She returned Saint Jude to the drawer and closed it.

The framed picture of her family taken a short time before her mother's death sat on the shelf. Each brother held a toy, Lily a basket, and Angelina a delicate fan—each vibrant color transformed into intricate sepia tones. Her mother was with child, yet nothing in the picture gave warning of the tragedy soon to come. The photograph captured a single heartbeat frozen in time. Nothing could bring back that moment. She slipped the picture into her bag along with Claudio Garcia's picture of her mother. William Shakespeare went in next, and Zio Pasquale's brick went into a smaller bag, which was then placed with the rest. She needed his brick to make her shattered heart strong again.

Angelina pinned on her pendant watch and closed her eyes to absorb the essence of the room she'd lived in all her life. Lily slept, sweetly embraced by the dreams of children, and seeing her almost crumbled Angelina's resolve. She scribbled a brief note to her siblings. *I love you, and I will love you forever, but for now, we'll see each other in our dreams.* To her uncle, she wrote, *Don't worry about me. Non ti preoccupare. You are the best, the very best. I will always keep the brick, and no matter what happens to me, I will be strong.*

She wrote to her father and then, frustrated, tore it up. The words that had passed between them spilled onto the page, already exhausted. Still, he'd cared for her all her life. After several failed attempts, she pressed her fountain pen to the paper and wrote the painful truth. *We've broken each other's hearts, Papa, but always know I love you.* She folded the page with a slight tremble and placed this note with the others, kissed her sister, and turned to leave.

When she reached the doorway, a powerful impulse overcame her, and she returned to the bureau. She pulled open the drawer, retrieved the medal, and read the writing etched on it. "Pray for us." The medal appeared to gleam in the darkness. It struck Angelina once again that every human being in the world deserved at least one miracle, and she hadn't used hers. She needed her miracle now. Perhaps Rolando had never meant to return to her, and perhaps Fabian was meant to be the one. Unwilling to defy destiny, she slipped the medal and its gold chain around her neck. The house had its own unique tranquility, a soothing quality, like leaves falling from their branches without making a sound.

Angelina entered the parlor and paused for an instant, captured by the ticking of the pendulum clock. She'd heard it all her life, but for a curious moment, the sound reminded her of loss, like it had the day her mother died. She felt compelled to make the sign of the cross before slipping out the door.

Though the night air remained mild, it inexplicably chilled her. She pulled her shawl around her and crossed the street with the caution of someone avoiding broken glass. She glanced over her shoulder at how the streetlamp showered its light on her father's sign, Domenico's Fine Italian Food. A knot caught in her throat. Still, Angelina's resolve remained.

The DiLeto's dog barked from behind a fence. It always had sporadic fits of barking, and no one bothered to push aside a curtain to look outside. In two hours, the sun would rise, and everyone would awaken to just another day. Yet, it wouldn't be just another day, not for Angelina, or Fabian, or her family. In the distance, Fabian stood below a streetlamp. He wore the same brown cap and the same smile he had on that first morning she'd bumped into him.

His face lit up, and he hurried toward her. The bag she carried slipped from her hand when he reached her, pulled her into his arms, kissed her, and whispered, "On the darkest night shine the brightest stars."

Still, there was something more. An overpowering, bittersweet sensation washed over her. She glanced back at her home and saw the tapestry of her childhood fading. Overcome with emotion, she had the strangest impression that time had shifted.

The present had just become the past.

EPILOGUE

Rolando carved yet another mark on his cell wall, one for each day he'd spent in Barcelona's infamous prison. It had been months with hardly a change of clothes and without sufficient food. Most unbearable, he had no way to get word to Angelina or anyone else. Neither she nor his family knew of his plight.

The guard rattled the door's bars with his gun. "*Oye,* you, *Americano.* Come and get your steak dinner and fine wine before I drop it on the floor." The man's laugh caused his large paunch to shake.

"What's wrong with you, *tío*? Don't they teach you to say *gracias* in that America of yours?"

Rolando said nothing. He had already said he was not a rebel, not an anarchist, and not interested in overthrowing Spain's government or their policies, but he'd arrived at the wrong time and found himself in the midst of revolutionaries.

After the guard walked away, Rolando ate the Spartan meal, dropped down on the narrow cot, and gazed up at the ceiling. He knew every crack in the plaster and every discoloration of its faded paint. His mind drifted back to that last day he'd held Angelina in his arms and felt her heartbeat next to his. He thought of her beauty, the love in her eyes when she looked at him, the softness of her lips.

He had lost so much in the dark confines of this cell. But one thing remained as strong as it was clear and bright—his memory of Angelina. Whether awake or asleep, he found she was his constant companion, like a dream that lingered even if he had no way to reach or get word to her. She became his anchor as he endured the misery of his existence.

If only you could hear my thoughts, Angelina. Wait for me. I promised I'd return to you, and when I do, nothing will ever separate us again.

Nothing.

SPECIAL ACKNOWLEDGEMENTS

My best friend Debbie Edwards, who has always had great faith in this novel.

My exceptional daughter Lisa, who helped edit all the chapters more times than I can count.

My longtime husband Gennaro who never wavered in his belief in me.

My sons Gennaro and Joseph and daughters Cristina and Ann-Marie whose encouragement, love, and support have meant everything to me.

ABOUT THE AUTHOR

Sandra Montanino lived in three different countries by the age of eight. These rich exposures gave her a wealth of appreciation for her own multicultural heritage. Inspired by the life of her Sicilian grandmother, Sandra has penned The Weight of Salt from the richness of family stories instrumental in igniting her imagination of a time that once was.

Encouraged by the publication of her article in Ancestry Magazine, Sandra has won numerous literary awards from the League of Utah Writers and is the recipient of the Southern California Outstanding Fiction Award. *The Weight of Salt* is her debut novel and the first in her series.

Originally from Southern California and the mother of five, she now lives in Utah between the lake and the mountains with her husband Gennaro of many years, a cat who loves to sleep, and a big dog who thinks he's a puppy.

CPSIA information can be obtained
at www.ICGtesting.com
Printed in the USA
LVHW090444190321
681907LV00019B/257/J